Convert

Clive Hallam

Copyright © 2013 Clive Hallam

This edition 2016

Clive Hallam reserves the right to be identified as the author of this work, under the Copyright, Design and Patents Act 1988

Okay, so The Convert is a work of complete fiction. I have set the action in areas that will be known by you, but that's all. The individuals, situations and action are all things that I have made up. I wanted to write something that is entertaining but which is realistic as well. Hopefully I've achieved that and if anything appears to relate to individuals, living or dead, or actual events that is purely coincidental.

This book is dedicated to my family, who always support my endeavours, regardless of the sense of them. Thank you for your love and support

My thanks to Laura Sharpe who helped me make this novel what it is, who showed me where I had made mistakes, where my grammar wasn't quite what it should be. Thanks also for supporting my enthusiasm and idealism which might have made this novel less than it is.

Thanks also to Gary Rogerson for working his magic on the cover. Truly a magnificent effort. Rome might not have been made in a day, but a great cover certainly was.

No man is an island, entire of itself, everyman is a part of the continent, a part of the main ... Any man's death diminishes me, because I am involved in mankind, and therefore never send to know for whom the bell tolls.

It tolls for thee.

John Donne

If you know the enemy and know yourself, you need not fear the results of a hundred battles.

Sun Tzu

Prologue

Trafalgar Square, London: Saturday Midday, July; 2 years previously

He watches her progress intently, every fibre tingling with anticipation. The woman in the black burqa is a little way off. She pauses: does she stare directly at him? His trigger finger flexes as her eyes narrow. Is it fear or hatred that makes her hesitate before advancing once more? Slowly, deliberately, he settles the stock of his Heckler & Koch MP7 to his shoulder; his finger slips easily over the trigger (years of training) and feels the tension in the slender metal bar.

Breathe in: one ... two ... three ... four. Out: one ... two ... three ... four.

He hears his voice call out to her, as if it is somebody else. 'Halt, armed police!' A bead of sweat runs ice-cold down his back but he remains still. He has her in the circle of the sight – searching the eyes which seem to stare back: prisoners encased in black. Her voice calls out from behind the niqab but, at this distance, the voice is indistinct. It sounds like "leave".

'I say again: Halt! Armed police!'

In slow motion her right hand reaches out to him. There's something in the fist her fingers make: a small black object – what is it?

Time is at a premium; choice a luxury in the cordoned-off area between Admiralty Arch and Trafalgar Square. He and his colleague have been there only minutes, responding to the emergency radio call identifying two suspected female suicide bombers. One body already lies in the road, a maroon pool still expanding across the dirty tarmac. The other continues to walk towards him.

Again. He reaches out his left hand momentarily to indicate she should stop, aware he is unbalanced. 'Stop: armed police.'

The figure raises her hand further and it opens. Everything becomes a blur. A voice behind him screams the word "Grenade!" as the black object she is holding falls. He is puzzled in the fractions of a second he uses to processes the information, before he squeezes the trigger and a three second burst of bullets cuts into the woman's body. Another burst, as the pumping adrenaline squeezes his finger again.

She lurches backwards, screaming with the pain before the last bullet silences her and her body crashes into the tarmac.

Weapon at the ready, he steps forward warily, eyeing her and the object she discarded in the road. As he passes it he recognises the purse and he fights back the vomit which stings in his throat.

Fuck. Fuck!

He kneels by the body and his fingers seem to struggle to part the atmosphere as he reaches for the edge of her niqab. The face is well known and, from behind, a ragged scream tears a hole in the lunch time air.

*

Present Day

Steve Logan sat bolt upright and shivered involuntarily. The sheets were drenched and freezing,

2

as they were most nights. He couldn't get her face out of his mind, couldn't believe he hadn't recognised her voice as she called his name. Couldn't admit he had killed Raifah, sister of his firearms colleague and friend Sayed Assiz.

He walked from the bedroom into his kitchen and went to the third wall cabinet from the kitchen door. The bottle of Laphroaig rested reassuringly in his hand; the liquid washing from the glass burned his throat, drying the tears of remorse and self-loathing, and drawing a veil once more over Raifah's accusing face.

However much he drank though, it never wiped out the anger, the venom of his partner, her brother. When he gazed down on the shattered form of his sister, Sayed Assiz's words rang through the nights, through the tears and the alcohol tremors – "What have you done? What have you done to my Raifah, Steven Logan?"

One

Somewhere along the border of Afghanistan and Waziristan

The air was cold and clear, not yet reacting to the early sun touching the peaks above the waking valley. Rough-hewn houses clung to the sides of the mountains like block caricatures of the goats which foraged across the rocky terrain. From the room of his small house overlooking the tiny hamlet, Imam Mohammed al-Siddiqi considered the wells and peaks of grey light that threw the scene into bas-relief and smiled. Contentment filled him, reflected in the weathered features of his bearded face. Even as he contemplated, he knew the first chapter of a great jihad was opening. Somewhere, beyond the mountains, in a different country, Westerners would perish at the hands of their own evil, turned against them by his glorious soldiers; aided by the implacable man from the east. In that place his men had secured vital supplies of food: coffee, maize, lentils among other staples that would feed them all for some considerable time. Food unwittingly donated by the UN in a magnanimous gesture to those they kept under the heel of their craven boot.

A sound focussed him though he didn't turn. He felt the presence of the other: calm; composed and ready. It was comforting in this moment of apprehension and excitement.

'Teacher.'

'Pupil. Are you ready?'

'Yes. All my preparations are made. Travel is arranged. I will give my final prayers before I return to the infidel's world.' Sayed Assiz came to stand next to his instructor and regarded the slowly awakening mountains, reaching up to clear the slumber from the dark places below, drawing the sun in. Soon it would be his turn to draw in the sun, but his desire was destruction not life and, inwardly, he cared not what the greater cause was or whether Allah was indeed on his side. Only one thing mattered and that was to avenge a death; a life raped, a family dishonoured by an infidel who had received its hospitality.

'Allah be praised for your commitment my brother.'

'Thank you, teacher. It was not a difficult decision and I do what I do to send a clear message to those who would besmirch Allah's name and defile his holy places.'

'Noble indeed; but do not forget the purpose for which you have trained and prayed. Killing the serpent of Satan comes second to removing the head of the Beast himself.'

'I shall not forget.'

The imam regarded his pupil. He saw hatred and desire swirling, barely controlled, in the dark gaze of Sayed Assiz and knew his teaching had been good.

Soon the West would know of his wrath.

Sayed Assiz turned back to see the sun cascading off the grey cold rocks. Soon, very soon he would avenge his sister.

*

The British Pakistani stared confidently at the camcorder on the tripod before him. Dressed in traditional Pashtu costume Sayed Assiz was far from

5

his previous existence as a member of CO19, the elite Metropolitan Police firearms squad. Handsome by any standards, his hooded brown eyes, strong straight nose and high cheekbones had seen him the target of many an infidel whore back in the home of the devil. At the time he had succumbed to their wayward charms.

Now he had seen the light and embraced the way: such weaknesses were behind him. It had been an act of wicked betrayal that had caused him to renounce his homeland and embrace the country that had given his family shelter from the Taliban back in the early part of the century. Misleading information from Satan's children had caused his forebears to turn their back on their homeland.

The shooting of his sister had finally opened his eyes. That he had befriended the man, a seconded MI6 officer; let him into his home, made the betrayal all the worse. She had been an innocent bystander caught up in a moment because of the traditional costume worn in deference to her religion and status – that's what he told himself. They had assumed she was on the "wrong side". Even when they'd seen it was his sister, he could see they were unrepentant: just another dead Muslim. What was it they'd said? "The only good Muslim was a dead one."

Imam al-Siddiqi had shown him the light. More importantly he had unwittingly given Assiz the opportunity to follow his own personal jihad against the one who had spat on his hospitality and friendship. Yes, they had joked and laughed about so many things that had seemed funny at the time but which, he now saw, were rank and cancerous to "The Truth". The West wanted to change the Muslim, make him more like them: hadn't Logan spoken often of faith in condescending tones, as a parent might to a child's constant questioning? They thought they could change the believers of the one true faith. They would soon see this was not the case and that Allah would visit upon them a mighty wrath from which they would never recover. At the last, the mighty Satan and his servants would be scratched from the surface of the planet.

Yet he had one last personal message to send to his one-time friend. For him the true jihad would then begin. Assiz took in the spartan room one last time. It showed little of the man who had occupied it for the last 12 months, learning the way of the Koran; of the teachers and of the martyr. A thin mattress on the bare concrete floor, a prayer mat and a small table at which to eat meagre meals, were sufficient for his needs.

And now those needs were done with: a journey waited on the other side of the bare wooden door. For a while he would have to embrace the decadence of the West but not for long. He showed no emotion for what he was about to do. It was the way. He had a political message to deliver but he also had a far more personal one that mattered to him.

Assiz checked his passport and tickets. All were in order for Farouq Hamadi to fly on the 14:32 flight from Islamabad to London on Friday 21st July where the jihad would begin. A day's journey by pickup would take him to the airport and his personal war would begin.

*

Dressed in an olive combat jacket with a shemagh covering head and face, the figure was menacing

7

enough. The sword, reflecting the stage lights, merely served to reinforce in the mind of the viewer the terror which was visible in the shaking, hooded, form. The figure held the blade against the neck of the quaking captive and addressed the video steadfastly recording the vista.

'Look at this America.' He moved the glinting edge against the cloth of the hood. 'Look and be afraid for the coming wind of justice will bear down upon you and take the Head from the Body of the Beast. You will know the pain of retribution for your sins as you have visited pain upon all those who dared to stand against your hypocrisy. Just as this, your emissary will know the pain of Allah's judgement for the deceptions he has wrought in your name.'

Muffled groans emanated from beneath the cloth. The masked swordsman continued to stare at the camera. 'Are you ready to see your pain, America? Are you ready to witness the justice coming before you from Allah?'

The camera zoomed out to include others who held the captive's arms outstretched, hands flat to the heavy wooden table, straps, maybe tourniquets, tied round each wrist. With a smooth, flashing motion the blade arced away from the neck and descended fast and true. The force of the strike made the captive buck, the arm spraying blood as it jerked in the air, the hand remaining on the stained wood. A stifled scream, ululating in pain, accompanied the blow, deepening and strengthening in feeling as the sword came down across the other wrist. Blood spread slowly, evenly across the table from the two stumps, the mutilated figure groaning with shock.

The swordsman approached the camera. 'This is your misery America, soon to be visited upon you:

watch your servant suffer before the end.' He pointed at the mutilated figure. 'This is your emissary, an agent of the CIA. Now he knows the pain of his sin. Now it is the time for his execution. We will deliver him to you beheaded ...'

A scream of denial leaked from the moaning captive.

'... as you, America will be beheaded. Then you will writhe in the agony of your descent into hell. Allahu Akbar!!'

The sword rose in the air. Its sharp, bloodied blade reflecting in the lights. Beneath it, the head of the prisoner was held to the desk. There was a moment as the figure struggled feebly to resist but a blow to the side of his head ended the weak fight. Two guards held the head gingerly, clearly anxious that their hands would not become accidental victims in this barbaric act. Another loosened the collar of the captive's jacket and pulled the hood out of the way so that ...

... the blade flashed downwards and scythed into the bare flesh. The blow was too little and it took another two cuts before the head fell away from the torso. Glistening blood spilled across the table top.

The executioner stared into the camera, sword held up for the camera to see, blood sliding across its shining surface. 'We will deliver the body to his friend, in London.

'America, it is time to prepare.'

Two

"Breaking News: Aden, Yemen; 05:00 local time. Insurgents overrun UN Food Station Bravo. Elements of the 27th Marine Recon Unit from the US aircraft carrier, John C Stennis were dispatched to remove the enemy fighters and re-establish control."

'Good Morning America, this is Casey Edwards with your current affairs bulletin from CNN. Top of the news this hour: Marines go into action in the Arab state of Yemen. After months of posturing between Chinese backed insurgents and the US Carrier Strike Group, John C Stennis, matters finally took a turn for the worse when fighters overran a UN humanitarian station on the outskirts of the coastal town of Aden. Invoking emergency powers under UN Resolution 2351, US Marines were ordered in to restore order by Secretary General Rikyu Oshikuro, in spite of Chinese abstention and verbal protest.

'Shortly before dawn Marines rappelled into the area of the station from Blackhawk helicopters and immediately encountered heavy fire. Reports, unconfirmed at this time, indicate at least one Marine fatality. We'll keep you posted on developments during the day.

'In other news ...'

*

'Sierra Two-Zero, Sierra Two-Zero. This is Baker Five-Nine. Do you copy?' A longer than usual pause then ...

'Baker Five-Nine: Sierra Two-Zero we copy.'

'Baker Five-Nine is TIC and taking heavy fire

10

from multiple hostiles.'

'Roger that Baker Five-Nine. Troops in Contact. Sitrep?'

Sitrep? Thirty Marines caught in a total cluster fuck over coffee and maize in the ass-end of beyond. What was to report, wondered the sweating Marine Corps J-TAC. The successive "crump" of mortar rounds landing around him told the story. 'One-fifty plus hostiles with heavy mortars at grid reference Five-Five-Eight-Seven. Keypads One, Two and Three are pinning' – another pause – 'us down with shells and a variety of automatic and small arms fire. We are unable to respond. We have one marine scratched and two neutralised. Request immediate close air support.'

'Roger that Baker Five-Nine. Confirm your coordinates by laser designating your front-line.'

'Painting it now.'

'We have your location. Stand by.'

*

'Skyhawk Four-One, this is Sierra Two-Zero on Tac Five.' The command coordinator on board the C130 Spectre gunship called his air support.

'Sierra Two-Zero: Skyhawk Four-One.'

'We have trade for you. Multiple hostiles engaging Marine battalion, call sign Baker Five-Nine. Assets pinned down by heavy mortar rounds and unable to return fire.'

'Roger that. Transmit coordinates.'

'Copy. Transmitting now.'

'Target location received and locked in. Advise ground assets we are inbound, weapons hot.'

'Roger that Skyhawk Four-One. Transferring to Baker Five-Nine control. Good hunting.'

*

Captain Sean Fellowes, Twenty-Seventh Marine Recon Unit, raised his helmet and wiped a large, gloved, hand across his dark, sweating brow. He hated the Yemeni heat and its energy sapping intensity (made worse with all their equipment and body armour) with a vengeance. What's more, this was not in the Marine Corps script. Being pinned down by a bunch of fundamentalists was not his idea of glory. Never mind: they were about to find out what happened when you pissed off the US Marines.

A nudge in the ribs started him. Fellowes regarded the source of the intrusion. His signals op was holding the phone to him. 'Sierra Two-Zero,' he observed by way of explanation.

'Thanks Gutierrez.' Fellowes took the handset. 'Baker Five-Nine responding.'

'Advise you have fast-air inbound your position; six minutes out. Transferring control to your comms. Designate your targets and keep your heads down. We will engage when fast-air departs. Await our "all clear".'

'Roger that Sierra Two-Zero.' Fellowes looked round at his troops and called up the battalion comms grid on his helmet computer. 'Heads down everybody, the cavalry is inbound on our position. Gutierrez: designate the kill box for our fly boys.'

*

'Baker Five-Nine, Baker Five-Nine. This is Skyhawk

Four-One. We are four minutes out. Confirm target painted?'

'Transmitting coordinates now. What are you guys carrying?'

'Two five hundred pounders, ground burst; two five hundred pounders, air burst; two Mavericks.'

'Air one deliver ground bursts. Air two go air bursts.'

'We have your target ident on grid and locked, Coordinates confirmed. Advise you are danger close.'

'Understood. You are cleared weapons hot.'

'Enjoy the fireworks guys. We are two minutes out.'

*

The two F-35 Lightning IIs hurtled over the rugged desert towards the food transit station. Twelve hours previously heavily armed raiders, claiming to be al-Qaeda backed had stormed the place, killing or driving out the workforce. A supply helicopter had almost been shot down over the site; its pilot hastily retreating and filing a report.

By the time the Marines had arrived, the raiders were embedded and they found themselves pinned down in the rapidly abandoned village outside the food station. Notice of al-Qaeda's intent and determination in Yemen appeared duly served. Unfortunately for them, US Marines were not known to take such situations lying down and the hostiles were about to be served eviction papers.

In the lead Lightning, Navy Captain Bev Avery checked her panels one last time as she dropped the lithe aircraft down on the deck, flashing past burnt out wrecks at just two hundred feet. Her head-up display flashed red as the designated targets in the "kill box" came in range. A tactical screen showed the laser designated target clearly. She checked the cluster of small buildings where heat sources crouched behind walls – they were armed and hostile alright.

Flicking the master arm on the five hundred pounders in the now open bomb bay she called her wingman one last time. 'Weapons hot, engaging now.'

'Roger that. No anti-air showing. I'm right behind you.'

The two aircraft streaked across the site as if displaying at an air show. A walk in the park.

*

Fellowes watched the final run in. The angle looked wrong. He looked round for his comms. 'Gutierrez. Call in our coords.'

The Marine looked round frantically. 'No contact! No contact! Guardian has been breached! Firestorm! Firestorm!'

The words dreaded by any fighting man: "Firestorm" meant enemy forces had compromised all battlefield e-systems. Fellowes checked his comms. The picture seemed right but the fact nothing moved in his helmet display meant Gutierrez was right, the Guardian, battlefield protection software had been compromised. Shit and fuck. How??

Plan B.

He drew flares from his belt, lit and held them aloft. At the same time he screamed over the comm-grid, as loudly as possible: 'Fire in the hole!'

*

Shapes tumbled from Avery's aircraft, towards the abandoned village. The crump of the explosions showered concrete and disintegrated brick on the Marine positions. Fellowes felt himself lifted and hurled brutally into a high wall. He slumped.

*

Roberts, levelling out for his run, thumbed the weapons toggle. A colour, flaring in the corner of his vision, caught his attention. A flare: red for danger. Figures falling because of the bombs: camos; helmets: Marines! Even as he registered the fact, his pressure increased on the toggle. Avery's voice crashed in his ears, increasing his distress.

'Friendlies! Abort, Abort!'

Too late!

Thinking instinctively, he dipped the left wing, changing the trajectory of the bombs – God willing...

*

The air was rocked by further explosions that threw shrapnel over the compound. Screams could be heard over the blast wave's final echoes.

'Baker Five-Nine, this is Sierra Two-Zero. Stand by for phase two.'

'Negative! Negative! Sierra Two-Zero lay off! You are contacting wrong coords.' Fellowes's voice was weak and unheard.

The earth shattering explosion originating from a 105mm howitzer shell fired from 10,000 feet shook the ground around them. Seconds later the vicious rip of the gunship's multi-barrel 20mm rotary cannon rent the air over Fellowes like a buzz-saw.

*

The unnatural quiet seemed eternal in the aftermath. Fellowes checked himself. His face felt raw and he realised shrapnel had burned his left cheek. As the ringing in his head subsided he began to experience other sensations. Chief among them was a light-headedness and intense lower back pain. Strangely he could feel nothing below his knees – bad.

He tried to raise himself but nothing happened – there was no strength in his arms or his upper body. All around, he could hear the sound of Marines moaning in agony. Blue-on-blue. The worst possible battlefield outcome.

'Captain!' The voice sounded far away but, squinting, he could make out a dishevelled Gutierrez looking tattered, with blood streaming down the sides of his face.

'How bad is it?' Fellowes meant his squad but now he could make out Gutierrez's face he could tell it didn't look good for him.

'We need to get you out of here, but we're still under firestorm.'

'Keep trying.' He felt the weakness increasing, his extremities becoming colder.

'Okay, I'll ...' The Marine buckled and fell forwards, a toppling stone landing on the incapacitated Fellowes. The captain tasted the blood from the man's head wound just before the lights went out.

*

For the second time that morning al-Siddiqi

acknowledged the presence of another in his room. The sun had finally broken the wall of the valley and its warming rays bathed the opposite hillside with gold. It was a good omen.

Al-Siddiqi turned and greeted the other. 'Brother.'

'Teacher.'

Al-Siddiqi nodded, the glow of self-satisfaction bathing his heart with colour that challenged the best efforts of the sun. This one was his glory, for whom Allah had prepared him. In this one the infidel would be smote from the Earth. And again he asked the question of his acolyte.

'Are you ready?'

'I am.'

'Then go: with the speed of Allah and the power of his mighty sword in your hand. Do his bidding my pupil.'

*

Sand tumbled in the dry wind as the gathered men covered their faces against its scouring touch. Lines of canvassed shapes stood cowed by wind and grit, mechanical hulks alluding to a deadly nature lurking beneath. Hulking sentries, faces trapped in shemaghs, and with aviator sunglasses hiding eyes, stood guard. G36 rifles were cradled at the ready: men prepared to repel any of the huddled purchasers who might chance their luck. One man stood alone, upright, thoughtful. Farouq Jamal considered his options – it was an inauspicious start to the sale. It did commerce no good for prospective purchasers not to be able to see the goods.

A figure detached itself from the huddle and advanced. Jamal recognised the swarthy Eastern

European arms and drugs dealer – a frequent visitor but a reluctant buyer. The man, average in height with jet black hair, approached with a swaggering gait that spoke of confidence and surety. His dark hooded eyes regarded the Egyptian.

'Rado. What brings you here? Are you ready to part with some money this time?'

The eyes were set, the chin resolute. 'I buy when I'm ready and I have a market, Jamal; not because you desire to offload low grade shit from a destitute Chechen Army.'

Jamal chuckled, a gravelly noise that rumbled up from his belly unchallenged. 'You hurt me, my Kosovan friend. Everything here is first grade, guaranteed to work and at a bargain price.'

Rado Kiric regarded the Egyptian. 'Well general, what we can agree on is that there is much here. I'll reserve judgement on the remainder of your statement when we've had chance to inspect it. What hides beneath these canvases?'

'T90s, BMP2s,' Jamal replied ignoring the implied slight in Kiric's words. 'But the piece you will want to see is Lot 14.'

Rado Kiric raised an eyebrow.

'It is a Kamov.'

'Which one?'

'A Scorpion. The one the West calls Hoodoo.' Jamal noted the lights brighten in Kiric's eyes and realised he had a potential buyer. 'It is fully armed, has been checked out by a type-rated pilot and is ready to ship today.'

Kiric smiled – the man really had no clue. 'You expect to sell this machine? Genuinely?'

'Of course,' replied the Egyptian feigning a hurt expression. 'You doubt the goods?'

'Not at all, Jamal. I doubt anybody's ability to be able to support such a thing. Who would want to buy such a specialist piece of equipment? The infrastructure required to maintain it would be more than the majority of terrorist groups could provide together. It's a nice prospect, but a white elephant in reality.'

The Egyptian's face darkened. 'You don't realise what is sitting in front of your eyes.'

Kiric grinned. 'On the contrary my friend I realise only too well.'

Gunfire ripped the disturbed air, scything sentries and customers alike to the ground with clinical precision. Malik had little time to react as the bullet from Kiric's Sig Sauer sliced through his forehead blowing out the back of his head. His body was dead before it hit the sand.

Rado dialled a number on his satellite phone. 'We have the goods.'

There was a pause as he listened. 'Very good. Do you have my consignment? Excellent. It would seem we have a deal.'

Cutting the call, he turned to his men. 'Let's get these machines ready to move. We have a transaction to conclude.'

Three

River Thames, London, early morning

Change, the man decided, as he descending the steps from London Bridge to the shingle below, was in the air. The early morning July sun was already heating the air, but here, beneath the bridge was a cold like winter. He shuddered involuntarily: the next few minutes wouldn't be pleasant despite the noncommittal call from the Police. Change was happening but it didn't seem good.

Steve Logan yawned, ruffled his thick black hair then thrust his hands deep in his coat pockets as his feet crunched and slipped on the glassy pebbles. He insinuated himself into the dark group inspecting a shape on the ground. The poor unfortunate he looked upon had no such issues with the cold down here. A lack of head and hands meant he would never experience, or feel, the weather again. What remained advertised a person of some standing and wealth. A cashmere overcoat covered a Savile Row suit and shirt which topped handmade shoes. All that wealth hadn't protected the guy though.

Logan spoke to one of those next to him. 'So?'

The figure turned, an ascetic looking woman, almost anorexic in her thinness with lank, blonde hair. She looked as if a good meal wouldn't go amiss. Her voice, when she replied, conjured the brittle sound of dry snapping twigs. 'The body was found laid in this position by local officers. We can confirm he's Caucasian, possibly mid-forties.'

'And wealthy.'

The woman nodded, disdainfully it seemed to

Steve.

'Were any possessions found on the body?' Logan looked round at the officers.

One of them handed a plastic evidence bag over. There was little in it save a leather wallet, a set of keys and a spectacle case. 'Wallet was empty, except for some receipts and a coffee shop loyalty card. Guess he'll not be having free coffees anymore.'

Logan ignored the tasteless remark – too much death did that to officers – and knelt next to the body, wrinkling his nose at the metallic odour of death and decay rising from it. As he inspected the corpse his eyes were drawn to its tie, a striking paisley design – he felt his heart lurch and he put a hand on the shingle to steady his quivering body.

The body had been there a little while, but not too long, he guessed. After a moment he turned again to the woman.

'Doctor, how long would you say this man has been dead?'

The pathologist regarded the body from afar, as if she wished not to be contaminated by its death. 'I'd say between twenty-four and thirty-six hours.'

'It's been here for over a day?'

'No,' she sniffed, 'I mean he's been dead for that time. I would say the body was placed here last night, possibly the early hours.'

Logan raised himself, an easy supple move. He looked at the spectators of this macabre tableau. 'When was the call received?'

The detective constable consulted his idev. 'A call was made to us at 5:32 this morning from an undisclosed number. We sent a uniformed team to investigate. Then we called you.'

Logan noted the officer didn't say MI6 or SIS;

21

specifically addressing him. He guessed the answer though he had to ask. 'Why?'

The DC looked at him squarely. 'Because the caller said you'd know him.'

Logan glanced at the officer before once more taking in the body of his friend. What a shitty end to a life. Who was capable of this sort of brutality and knew of their relationship? He stared at the form which looked less and less human at each viewing and his vision misted over. Whoever it was would have to pay a heavy price.

*

Ten o'clock showed on the clock in the situation room at Vauxhall Cross as Team One took their chairs in anticipation. Much chatter filled the ether, a dawn chorus of opinions, as everyone deliberated on the reason for such a hastily called meeting. At the end of the table Steve Logan sat alone with his thoughts.

The large oak door opened and in strode Station Chief Amanda Galbraith looking professional as ever: pinstripe suit and open-necked white shirt. The rest of Logan's team were occupying various states of readiness around the glass-topped table. She sat at its head and waited for the noise to subside.

'Good morning ladies and gentlemen. Thank you all for attending at short notice. I can tell you're all eager to find out what might be the reason for this and so I'll allow Steve to fill you in with the details, such as they are. Steve.' She looked to her senior officer; all followed her gaze.

Steve stood, his piercing blue eyes regarding the team. Confident and at ease with himself, Steve

Logan had been a career soldier who had applied for, and been accepted in, the Special Air Service. The gruelling training had brought his tenacity to the fore. He hadn't come first in many tests, but he'd always finished top three despite injury and that had impressed the commanders more.

Serving two tours with the regiment in Yemen and Afghanistan, Logan had fought with distinction against al-Qaeda and the Taliban, receiving the Military Cross for gallantry in the face of overwhelming odds. He had also received the Order pour le Merite from the French government for masterminding the non-lethal rescue of French nationals from the Kabul Embassy after local insurgents laid siege to the place.

His conduct had drawn the attention of the Secret Intelligence Service. An asset with such understated commitment was always in demand. Steve's conversion had been easy and succinct. Two contacts from a handler, whom Steve had known briefly in Afghanistan, and he'd been brought in.

It had been a move that suited both; Steve settling quickly into frontline covert operations. He had completed operations in some of the worst flashpoints in the modern world: back to Afghanistan; Pakistan; Georgia and others the British government preferred not to discuss openly.

Recently he'd worked as a controller at Vauxhall Cross managing a number of agents across the world. It wasn't his forte though and he itched to get back in the field. What he was about to discuss might present the best opportunity in a while.

Steve nodded to Amanda. 'Thanks Boss.' He glanced round the table. 'Early this morning I was called by the Met to attend a scene of crime at

London Bridge. This,' he flicked a photo from his idev to the LCD screen on the wall, 'is what confronted me.'

He directed his audience's attention to the image. It showed the decapitated, handless corpse lying forlornly on the shingle under the bridge.

'The individual was found in this mutilated state. There were few identifying effects found.' He went through what had been shown to him by the detective constable. 'Nothing, at least, that could formally identify the body.'

'Do we have any clues as to who it could be?' Galbraith asked, unable to wrench her gaze from the mutilated cadaver.

'Yes, one.'

'Which is?'

'His tie.'

'His tie?' This interruption came from senior analyst Des Farrow. Farrow was a geek: lopsided glasses, scruffy pullover and crumpled slacks: appearance was not his thing.

Logan nodded and smiled at Farrow's confusion. 'It was a tie I bought for him in Florence while on holiday a couple of years ago.'

Galbraith raised an eyebrow. 'So; somebody you knew quite well.'

Logan nodded. 'Yes, and whoever killed him did it to attract our attention; if not me specifically.'

'Don't keep us in suspense any longer then. Who is this?' Galbraith indicated the disturbing image.

'Drew Faulkner.'

A stifled cry made everyone jump. Debbie Turner, the operations manager, held a hand over her mouth, visibly drained at the news. It took a lot to shock Turner, acknowledged as a difficult and demanding officer. Steve, though, knew that she and Drew had been active jointly on the Westminster Tourist plot of two years previous. Working closely together they had uncovered a plan to hijack a bus of American tourists and crash it into Jubilee Tube Station before detonating a bomb. Had it succeeded, the carnage in such a busy part of London would have been horrific. It had quickly been identified that the talent behind the threat had been home grown, though training had taken place in Afghanistan's northern borderlands with Pakistan. Faulkner had been instrumental in helping SIS negate the threat before it returned to British shores. In turn Debbie had assisted on the planning and execution of an operation which had seen fifteen al-Qaeda operatives neutralised and two training camps wiped out. Pyrrhic victories, but vital nonetheless.

Logan had been point man between the joint operation and Secret Service action on the Mainland so his involvement had been minimal, but he and Drew went back nearly ten years. They had become close friends and Steve felt this loss keenly though he didn't show it. And what of Carla, Drew's ex-wife: how would she cope when she was told?

This was a personal message to him. Did the killers want to make contact? If so: why? Had they got a deal they wanted to present? What was their motive? Unclear: he maintained his counsel.

Debbie had removed herself from the room and through the frosted glass wall he could make out her form slumped against the opposite wall, her chest rising and falling in a quiver of released emotion. Obviously there was more to her relationship with Drew than he'd appreciated.

'Did he have his chip, do you know?' Eddie

Powell, the signals and communications expert had been quiet till now. A young guy educated at Cambridge, he was ambitious but not at the expense of his first love. There wasn't a communications system he couldn't crack and raid for everything it had.

Logan looked up sharply. Of course! Why hadn't he thought of that? 'Good call Eddie. I'll follow through on that.'

Galbraith was speaking. 'I'm intrigued that they called for you specifically, Steve. Do we know what the CIA's current focus in Europe is, what Faulkner was working on? And was the organisation involved in anything that wasn't run by me first?'

Farrow chipped in. 'We've monitored some traffic that indicates CIA and NSA are keeping tabs on some ex-Kosovan smugglers who major in drugs and arms. But not people. Their leader is a heavy-handed Muslim called Rado Kiric. Mr. Kiric has been linked with a recent arms deal in Northern Iraq. I say deal; Kiric had the organiser, his staff and several other potential purchasers gunned down and he made off with the whole stash.'

'Do we know why he did that?'

Farrow shrugged. 'He's got everything on the move to various dispersal points but none which immediately stands out as anything other than a transit point so it must be for a purchaser elsewhere; and one who is very well hidden.'

'Do we have any involvement?'

Farrow shook his head. 'Not on this matter. There is an SAS detachment in the Yemen, working long range reconnaissance for the US, but they report directly to the local Marines commander. The CIA are keeping our people out of the loop – "national security".' The analyst grimaced.

'Which brings us back to the question "why you"?' Galbraith considered her top agent.

Logan shrugged. 'We were friends, but I'd had no contact with him for nearly two years.' He refrained from saying it was about the same time as the Trafalgar Square shooting. 'It has to be something bigger than arms smuggling. A killing like this is symbolic. Until they get in touch with more information anything we speculate is just that. They hold the cards.' He paused. 'I think I'll go down to the morgue and follow up Eddie's idea.'

Galbraith nodded. 'Okay. Meanwhile we'll set up an incident room and pull a team together. We'd better start getting an intelligence report together: the chair of the JIC will want to know of this soonest. I don't think it will be long before whoever it is, gets in touch.'

As the team filed out of the office Logan worked through his memories of that morning. Just what the fuck was going on? Why had al-Qaeda decapitated Faulkner, why was Faulkner important? Perhaps there would be answers at the morgue.

Four

Beverley Hilton Hotel, Los Angeles

The woman stretched her body against the cold silk sheets and murmured as the fabric whispered over her skin. Grasping the pillow in both hands she nuzzled its coolness and smiled a little to herself. Business was good and so was pleasure, she told herself sleepily as arms pulled her close and she felt his erection nestle between her buttocks. A little sigh of contentment broke from her full lips, staining her chin.

'You okay?'

She reached behind and pulled her lover's head close. His lips brushed her neck slowly and she felt his tongue flick, oh so delicately, across the skin, sending shivers through her whole being. 'Very,' she replied placing a hand longingly on her breast.

Her lover chuckled then abruptly rolled energetically away. 'Well, my darling, I have to get going – busy day ahead. And you have a plane to catch back home don't you?'

Penelope Hortez propped herself up in bed and nodded, pouting as Senator Harry Johnson stood proudly looking down at her. 'Not till much later, Harry. Won't you come back to bed? Just for a while?' Penelope fluttered her eyelashes, thinking *"What am I like?"* as she witnessed the amused look on his face.

'Think of your boys. They haven't seen you for weeks because of your fashion road show. Which is very good, by the way,' Johnson added hastily in case he caused offence.

'I know,' Penelope replied smiling, 'And you have a Presidential campaign to run.'

'Not today my darling.'

'Oh and what does Senator Harry Johnson have to do today that could be more important than running for President of the United States of America?'

'I have an appointment with the Senate oversight committee on food smuggling operations in Latin America.' He walked to the bathroom, speaking over his shoulder. 'We're getting updates on the continuing operations by US Marines and local Special Forces on the Colombia – Venezuela border. A big operation is just concluding. If successful it could spell the end of one of the biggest cartels Colombia has ever seen.'

Penelope looked up. 'Which one is that?'

'The Cucuta Cartel.' Johnson turned at the bathroom door. 'Say, are you okay?'

Penelope nodded. 'Yes ... and ... you're right, I must get home.'

*

Somewhere on the Colombia – Venezuela border 10.52 Zulu

The movement was infinitesimal and could easily have been mistaken for the slightly shifting breeze that gently wafted the tall green grass atop the hill. That it wasn't, but no-one knew, was testament to the skills of the two men lying in the warm dirt, surveying the complex of buildings below them.

Staff Sergeant Leroy Durant kept his eye to the scope of his Barrett M82A1M sniper rifle. His fingers made slight adjustments and he grunted quietly, confidently.

'Two guards; west corner, transiting left to right towards the main building.'

Durant nodded as the words of his spotter crept softly into his ear. He'd seen them already but the time wasn't right yet. He laid his finger on the trigger guard. Easy now - it'd kick off real soon. He'd learned over the course of forty-five missions as a sniper to be patient. Patience was the sniper's best friend.

The two guards stopped at the corner of the large barn-like structure and looked all ways. One stared up the hill directly at Durant. To the uninitiated it could have been unnerving. As Sniper One, Durant knew there was nothing for the man to see. He was just doing his job, waiting for a good old-fashioned frontal assault.

Shit. The guy was in for a real shock if he survived the first bullet – which was doubtful: Marine snipers tended not to miss. Durant, his spotter and his Sniper Two buddies on the hill to their north-west had spent the last week bedding down and preparing for what would transpire in the next hour or so. They had comprehensively studied the layout of the compound during that time; watched the schedule, and the routes of the guards; shift changes; calculating when maximum damage could be inflicted on the enemy.

In the valley just south of Durant's position, hidden by the jungle undergrowth, a platoon of Marines waited, tooled up and ready to go. As soon as he gave the signal they would begin their assault. Further south a MH-60 Blackhawk and Apache gunship sat on friendly territory, rotors turning; ready to give hot support to the attack.

Durant mentally shook his head. This was another

Colombian food smuggling operation taking advantage of Venezuelan animosity to the United States that was in for a real surprise.

He glanced briefly at his watch: any moment now.

Right on cue figures walked out of the main building and made their way towards the corner of the barn, the changeover point for this side of the operation. Durant knew that over the other side, watched by Sniper Two, a similar exchange transpired.

Inhale, exhale. Slow and easy: control your breathing.

The figures waved at each other and a moment of bonhomie ensued.

'Tomahawk. Say again: tomahawk.' Whispered into his mike it was the signal to engage.

The two groups began to part. Durant tensed, eased off, sighted his target and squeezed the trigger. The first new guard crumpled as the bullet seared through his skull, just behind his left ear. Durant often wondered at his own dispassionate ability to despatch people with a single bullet. Perhaps it was because he painted a cruel face on the visage of each target. A face that ensured he pulled the trigger without hesitation each time; to pay for the hurt.

And so another domino fell.

And another.

Four bodies lay in the dust of the yard as, from the south, the platoon cut through the chain link surrounding the cartel's operation and began to engage the alerted dealers. Overhead, the Apache loomed large and menacing, dominating the compound with its presence, its chain gun sweeping the area clear of the enemy. As it circled to the west of the compound, the Marines took the fight to the house.

Durant, watching from his vantage point, concluded it was all pretty one-sided. The only issue came at the house when the Colombians tried to hole up on the second floor and direct fire down on the troops, pinning them in the yard.

A quick call and the Apache raked the second floor of the building, shredding it. Nothing survived.

As they mopped up the last of the resistance the Marines called in the Blackhawk and began the job of collecting intel.

*

Durant walked slowly, easily, up the steps into the parlour of the large house. It now resembled a much abused training block back at Lejeune. He walked through the rooms where Marine colleagues were going through drawers and desks, filing cabinets and boxes, checking for any information that would increase the efficacy of future clashes.

'Hey, sergeant, come here.'

Durant turned. Stood in the doorway to the house's lounge stood the platoon lieutenant, Tony Bridges, a tall rangy and hard-bitten individual. It was always difficult to be sure whether his tone was one of congratulation or censure. Durant took off his helmet and ran a gloved hand over his sweat coated baldness.

He stopped before the lieutenant. 'Sir?'

'Good shooting up there.'

'Thank you sir.'

'Keep up the good work.'

The sergeant looked round the ravaged room. Good work? In one corner three bodies were stacked unceremoniously. It was a moment before he processed the fact that two of them had to be children. 'Who are the bodies?' Durant asked, trying to cover his sudden nausea.

Bridges glanced up briefly. 'It's Suarez; the kids we presume are his. That's the Cucuta Cartel fucked,' he concluded laconically.

Durant hesitated. It was rarely that easy he figured. He looked around at the ransacked boxes. 'Found anything?'

The lieutenant nodded. 'Hell, yeah. Seems these guys were diverting considerable consignments of maize and coffee to Afghanistan and Iran in return for training in insurgency techniques, including the use of IEDs and remote explosive deployment. The coffee was due to be shipped to Asia and the Middle East. They're contravening UN resolution twenty-one oh five which strictly prohibits the redirection of foodstuffs against agreed quotas. This is a major scoop.'

'Hope we've put a dent in their op from this end.' *Fuck*, he thought, *we're fighting over coffee.* 'But coffee? We used to be taking them down because of drugs.'

'There are drugs here. Plenty of coke powder and crack,' the lieutenant advised the shooter sternly. 'Don't think this wasn't a major operation, Durant. The level of al-Qaeda and Taliban involvement these guys have suggests a significant trade arrangement for both sides,' confirmed Bridges. 'Thanks to our intervention our Colombian compatriots should see a down turn in insurgent attacks.'

'Sure hope so, lieutenant. I'd appreciate the option of seeing home sometime soon.'

'As would we all, Sergeant. For now, take these boxes out to the 'copter. They'll want to analyse this

33

down at brigade.' Bridges indicated a Dell laptop lying in the wreckage of coffee table. 'I'm gonna take a look at this; see if there's anything on it worth salvaging.'

Durant hefted the three boxes and made his way back out of the building. He ambled down the veranda steps and then found himself flying through a vacuum of sound and jagged rainbows of light. As he hit the dirt, the sound of the explosion slammed into his body, rippling under his skin as if to flay him.

After what seemed an eternity he raised himself gingerly. Flames licked from the windows of the wrecked building; smoke curled up to the sky. Durant heard the moans and cries of wounded marines; others had gone past the point of caring any more.

One of those was Lieutenant Bridges whose armless body hung from what remained of the ground floor where the blast from the laptop (it had to be the laptop, didn't it? A trigger?) had thrown him. How could such a small bomb have caused such mass destruction? It must have been a master arm for the whole building, triggered if the lid was lifted or something. The dealers knew they weren't going to get out alive.

Five

Chinese Embassy, Bogota, Colombia

Leong Chaozheng leaned back in the Louis XVI armchair and considered his young compatriot. Yuan was pretentious and something of a loose cannon. Undeniably strong-willed, forthright and capable he had a propensity for hot-headedness which was neither attractive nor to be condoned.

For his part, Yuan Zhiming looked upon his mentor with mixed feelings. Leong was – not exactly long in the tooth – more of a different era. He came from a line of Politburo grandees who had power bestowed on them through connections. Yuan knew his power came by right of lineage. Still, there was use in the relationship and he was astute enough to foster it for as long as it served him.

Leong sipped his black tea and placed the cup back on its saucer. Every movement was deliberate; functional and precise. It was part of his upbringing, part of his psyche and it had made him respected and feared by his men.

'What news do you have Zhi?'

Yuan coughed. 'I think we can count the test as a complete success.'

'Do they suspect?'

Yuan regarded the words. Suspect? 'Not yet but it will not take long. After all there are few with the capability or capacity to achieve an operation of that complexity quite so easily, not even they yet.'

'Good. You have done well but there is more yet to accomplish.'

'I understand.'

Do you? Leong picked up his idev and scanned the latest report on the screen. With a flick he dropped a document on the table screen. An article from the Herald Tribune, it talked of US Marines taking out Colombian drug dealers in a surprise attack. 'We should have been ready for Venezuela. That has set us back somewhat but it cannot be helped.'

Yuan nodded. 'We are in a better place now, to exploit our contacts and our options.'

'Agreed; do you know what to do next?'

'Yes. My contact has advised me that he has the goods in transit. They will be in place when we are ready.'

'Very good. Do you have the protocols in place?'

'Give me a few days.'

'Can you coordinate it with Yemen?'

Yuan stiffened. Don't react; it was a soldier's question. 'Of course.' He couldn't help the thinly veiled sneer. If Leong picked up on it, he didn't show it.

'That is good. We must maintain progress but ensure that the CIA and the NSA in particular do not become too interested in these activities. Always be sure of your cover.'

Yuan merely stared at his mentor.

'Always,' Leong reiterated emphatically. He pointed at the photo on the table screen. 'This is our next target. She has to be brought on side with our other local asset or neutralised. Currently she is involved in a series of shows that next take her to Berlin. She's unknown to the Americans but could be key to our success. Ensure we make contact when she is in Germany.'

Yuan knew the right person. 'There is such an asset. They have mutual interests.'

'Good! See that it happens.'

*

CIA Headquarters, Langley, West Virginia

The BMW coupe accelerated off the interstate, following the signs to and eventually slowing for the security gate at CIA Headquarters, Langley. The driver dropped the window and handed her pass to the guard. She thought she recognised him, certain he knew her and she flashed a smile at him; a reflex action.

The guard scanned her retina and nodded as his idev flashed green. 'Good morning Miss Richter.'

'Good morning,' she checked the badge, 'Harry. How's things?'

Her attempt at politeness turned up a blank. 'Fine, miss.' He indicated the raised barrier precluding further discussion. 'Enjoy your day.'

Suit yourself, Charlie Richter told the ungrateful guard silently as she shifted into drive and powered under the rising barrier. Stung by his rebuttal she drove faster than allowed along the tree lined thread of blacktop and into the car parking area.

Her normal spot was taken and she cursed the ignorant individual who'd committed such a heinous crime. Finally, she slotted the coupe into a free space some two hundred yards further away from the office. By now she was in a foul mood and vowed to wreak revenge on anyone who stood in her way this July morning.

Her office was cool and the coffee machine in the corner was soon pumping out the vapours of her favourite French filter blend.

She poured a mug, savouring the dark, thick liquid as she gathered her thoughts, staring at the view from her third floor window. Slowly the anger subsided and her thoughts turned to work. As a senior analyst in the Crime and Narcotics Centre she wasn't expecting anything majorly exciting this morning. Drug running was still steady business with Colombia hitting back at Peru and Mexico whose rivalry with the old school country had caused such damage to their trade.

What had become an increasingly more important battle was that against food smuggling operations. In a world where cultivatable land was becoming a premium and crops were at the vagaries of increasingly mercurial weather patterns, the shipment of foodstuffs to disaster areas was big business. Smugglers and rogue states thought nothing of hijacking ships or diverting consignments to the highest bidder, or to those whose politics matched their own. The result? Further misery for those countries which couldn't afford the premiums.

Charlie tapped her desk-screen on, sipping more coffee as it powered up. As she stroked the edge of the screen, it snapped to an angle of forty-five degrees, her preferred viewing angle. The graphene frame booted her in-tray, which held two i-notes. She dropped the oldest one onto her active space. It was a leaving do for Dee Williams, a director over at the WINPACC for whom she'd been an intern in her first two years here. She'd look forward to that, a chance to let her hair down and say good bye to one of the good guys, even one whom she knew very little of. For now, there was business to attend to – orders and demands from above that needed her undivided attention.

Sliding it into her pending tray Charlie then drew the second forward. The ident of her current director, Sarah Markham, flashed and she anchored it on the action frame, preparing for the task that would be uncovered. Sarah was good but hard. She hated anybody who might look as if they were there for the ride: which meant not putting in her level of effort. Most of her underlings remarked that she was part-Langley. She was always the first in, and last to leave. Nobody knew her background, whether she had family; a partner: she was effectively a closed book. One wise guy had openly contemplated the idea that she was a clone, specifically designed to work twenty-four/seven for the government and "ride the backs of her minions like bitches". That guy had suddenly found himself redirected to a forgotten field outpost, never to be spoken of again.

Charlie swiped her finger across the message icon with some trepidation. What would she find? The contents pointed her to the secure mail in her box. Pulling up her retina cue and logging into the system, she waited impatiently as the obligatory stream of messages spread their communicable disease to her mailbox; soldier ants carrying interference, designed to block and confuse and all originating from her own side: a kind of cyber friendly fire.

The second from last new message was the one she wanted. An MP4 file was attached to the body of the mail which she opened immediately. It was video footage recorded by US Marines on a clear-up op somewhere hot and humid. The vid showed bales of cocaine powder being torched; large stocks of foodstuffs being counted in a large shed; marines moving laptops, computers and boxes of paperwork to a Blackhawk helicopter. Signs of battle lay all around. Bodies littered the ground and the top floor of the house they were searching showed signs of intense ravaging, perhaps from the Apache helicopter, the clip occasionally picked up, circling in the background.

A marine lieutenant provided a running commentary to the investigation. The border operation had been taken down as it was about to move what, on the surface, appeared to be a huge shipment of maize and coffee from Maracaibo, to a destination in Western Asia, under a UN mandate to impoverished areas of the world. The manifests found had been altered from their Bangladeshi destination and it seemed that the foodstuffs were being used as cover for transportation of cocaine. That could only have an insurgency use; both Taliban and al-Qaeda fighters were well known to score prior to going into battle – encouraging and embedding the euphoria of suicide.

It appeared that Ferdinand Suarez, head of the cartel, had been caught in the crossfire and was confirmed dead. That was both good and bad news – the vacuum would be filled all too quickly after the ensuing bloody feud. As she read, Charlie noted that part of the report had been redacted. What was so sensitive?

This could be serious for Colombia. For some time, the government, with American help had controlled the activity of the cartels. The US government had pumped billions of dollars into the country, aimed at encouraging coffee growing and reforestation at the behest of the country's President but also providing state-of-the-art technology and armaments in the fight against the cartels. Some successes had been achieved and narcotic operations had been hit through a combination of targeted military action and governmental inducement.

That hadn't been the cartel's only problem. Competition from the hated Peruvians and a terror campaign by Mexican traffickers had added to their woes. So when Venezuela had offered a lifeline and new committed partners, the cartels had joined forces with their violently anti-American neighbours. Meeting secretly with Suarez, head of the Cucuta Cartel, President Ernesto Ortega had provided secure bases across Colombia's northern borders where they could run operations with impunity, covertly supported by Venezuelan Special Forces. Subsequently, it had been easy to move over the border, whenever the Colombian authorities had raided the Cucuta area, or when Mexicans attempted to take out shipments, returning when everything died back down. And Venezuela brought new friends with new tricks to take on the diverse enemies ranged against the beleaguered. Al-Qaeda and the Taliban had become strong allies.

Now the cartels were hitting back: through intimidation; incentives and bribery and robbery. Food was the new currency: farmers who had grown coffee and maize under government schemes found it was much safer to trade it with the cartels when families were threatened with death. The cartels were relearning old ways and discovering new ones from their Taliban advisors: regimentation, discipline, focus, the use of cells. Savagery increased, confrontation descending into eighties style wars between the opposing sides. It was difficult to fathom who was winning at the moment.

In this respect the report detailed nothing new. The Cucuta cartel had launched a new insurgency-style campaign against the Colombian government using naïve, malleable youths or enforced family members to deliver IEDs against high-profile targets; this merely confirmed the CIA's activity reports. What would the loss of Suarez do to their campaign?

It would be difficult to maintain operations over the border into Venezuela at the current level of intensity, but it might be necessary to try. This was a heads up and Charlie knew she must analyse the intel as quickly as possible.

She figured it was time to talk with her colleagues, down the corridor, in Remote Sensing and GIS, to see if they were able to identify key movements over the last few months. Then, she would have to task Operational Support to collate field intelligence from Colombia, Venezuela and Afghanistan. It was clear from the director's note that Markham wanted answers yesterday.

There was a lot to do if the CIA were to stay one step ahead of the cartel: her boss would expect no less.

*

Steve Logan opened the door to the morgue. The temperature sent an involuntary shiver through his muscular frame. It had been a twenty-minute tube journey to Guy's Hospital near London Bridge where they were holding Faulkner's body prior to releasing it back to the US authorities. The hospital was busy on the surface but, as he headed deeper, people had become fewer and far between.

A mortuary technician appeared, as if by magic, from behind a door.

'Can I help you?' She was a willow of a woman

who looked as if the cold of the room would stream right through her. Logan showed her his id which she glanced at perfunctorily.

'I'm here to see the body brought in this morning.'

'Which body?' Boredom hung heavily on her words.

'The ... decapitated one.'

'Oh yes! Weird, huh?' She seemed visibly excited at the thought of Faulkner's mutilated body, almost vampirical Logan figured as he caught the sudden brightness in her eyes. 'When they brought him down I thought he must have been –'

'He was a friend,' Logan interjected before the conversation got messy. 'Where is he?'

Flushing, she led Logan past banks of old steel square doors: filing for bodies no longer required. She stopped and pulled on a handle. The drawer rolled open. Under the clinical shroud, Logan admitted the body did look incongruous without a head.

Taking clinical gloves from a box and pulling them on, Logan hesitated as he lifted the hem of the shroud. Even though he'd seen Drew's body first thing that morning he felt unprepared for the finality of this setting.

The cadaver had the look of old parchment, an affliction of the dead, giving it the appearance of an old manuscript, roughly used, and with many stories to tell. If only someone dared turn the pages. Logan started at the top, the neck, where the frayed skin reminded him of decayed autumn leaves, and continued his investigation across the chest, in the armpits and down the torso.

Nothing.

'What are you looking for?'

Logan ignored the technician's question and instead indicated they should roll the corpse over.

The woman shrugged and together they pushed and pulled the body onto its stomach. Logan continued his search. What he was looking for he found at the second attempt. At the nape of Faulkner's neck was a large mole. He ran a finger over the irregularly shaped blemish.

Yes, that was it. Quickly he reached into a pocket, retrieved a Gerber multitool and began to make an incision with its blade.

The girl was alarmed. 'Hey! What do you think you're doing?'

'Don't worry. It won't hurt him.'

'You can't … can't do that.'

Logan peeled back the skin and smiled. Just under the surface lay a chip the size of a small shirt button. He levered it gingerly with his knife and slipped the little device into a small plastic bag. He turned to the technician. 'Where are his clothes and personal effects?'

'Why?'

'Just show me where they are.'

The girl pouted but led Logan to an office at the other end of the morgue. Banks of steel cabinets lent a gym-like air to the room –an odd image for a morgue.

'Which one?' Logan felt frustration rising like bile – it was like pulling hen's teeth.

Silently the girl walked to one and paused.

'Open it.'

'I shouldn't be doing this,' she told him flatly.

'Just do it.'

Retrieving a key from a chain on her belt she unlocked and opened the drawer. Depositing everything on a bench Logan quickly, methodically, went through all the clothes there pausing briefly as he touched the hand painted silk tie.

Wallet next, pen: all the things which had been in the evidence bag. Then the small leather case that looked like a reading spectacle case – except Drew didn't wear glasses. Logan opened it: nothing. His fingers picked at a lifted corner of the lining and found something which he dropped in the palm of his other hand: a small electronic reading device. He smiled and pocketed it.

'You'll have to explain to the coroner what you've just done. I'm going to file a report about this.' The defiance in her voice was shaky, as if she didn't quite believe herself.

'No you won't.'

'Yes –'

Logan turned on her. 'No! You didn't see or hear anything; nothing. Do you understand? Do you?'

She nodded mutely.

'Good. In which case, I'm done here. Thanks for your help. Good day.'

And with that he was gone.

Six

A cemetery, Cucuta, Colombia

Black suited her: after today she would always wear something black. The large brimmed hat and veil protected her from the strong afternoon sun beating down on the cemetery and hid her from prying eyes. She stood away from the funeral party, a figure seemingly out of place, no-one acknowledging her. All attention concentrated on three graves: one large and two smaller ones either side, a daddy and his two children, going to their final home. She felt the saltiness of her tears which ran over her lips and fell from her chin. It was as if her blood was draining from her.

Three hearses halted by the mouths formed from the dirt. Shining coffins were pulled from the rear of each, the bearers solemnly carrying them to their resting places. The mourners parted to let them by: a black sea of sorrow suddenly repelled by the appearance of death. Beyond the gathering, men overtly carrying guns kept watch for any unwanted interruption. This was a difficult time for the cartel once led by Ferdinand Suarez. Police and Army might be tempted to make arrests, while competitors were always looking for takeover opportunities.

The internment lasted only a short while though, for the woman in black, it seemed an eternity before people began to disperse and the gravediggers began the laborious task of closing the chapter in the lives of the departed. As she waited for the mourners to move on her thoughts turned to one Harry Johnson. Had he known this would happen? Absolutely not. Was it his responsibility? Absolutely. Would the Senator be made to pay? Undoubtedly but, for now, Johnson must not know who she really was. And Penelope Hortez had to control her emotion. She walked past the three graves without looking – *goodbye my darlings, revenge will be mine.*

*

Senator Harry Johnson was pleased with himself. The Venezuelan operation had been a complete success and was, he was sure, just the start of the final push in the war against the smugglers. That would be fantastic for his Presidential campaign. Coffee and maize worth $100 million on the black market had been seized; paperwork, showing a clear link between the government of Venezuela and the Taliban in Afghanistan and al-Qaeda, had been passed to the CIA.

Into that mix, the killing of a major cartel leader meant a violent turf war as the other gangs sought to fill the vacuum, giving the US the upper hand and a firm base from which to launch operations into Peru. Add to that the significant military aid his committee had appropriated for Colombia's "Coffee War", as it was now dubbed, which would aid his good friend Eduardo Sanchez, hoping for election as their next President, and it was a good day.

He started at the chiming in his head. Would he ever get used to the goddamned chip that every Senator was now virtually expected to have implanted? There was no privacy anymore. He could be interrupted anywhere, at any time. Progress, he thought cynically. The caller ident flickered over his retina, more irritation: his aide, Bob.

'Answer,' There was a click in his head. 'Hello?'

'Senator. It's Bob.'

'I know. What's the matter?' There was a tone to his aide's voice that immediately rang alarm bells.

'It's Venezuela.'

'Well?'

'There's something you need to see that the Marines reported, which was redacted.'

'What?'

Silence. 'I'd rather you come and see for yourself Senator. It's delicate.'

'Fuck, Bob, enough already with the cloak and dagger. What gives?'

More quiet, deeper and with it a meaning that suddenly dawned on the politician.

'I must insist you come to the office to see this. You'll want to make a decision.'

'Why wasn't I told last week, straight way after it happened?' Harry Johnson huffed into the silence. 'Very well. I'll be down just as soon as. Is that it?'

'Not really sir.'

'What now?'

'There was collateral.'

'That's unfortunate, but this is a war Bob.'

'It's Suarez's children.'

Johnson drew an intake of breath: that changed everything. 'Dammit, Bob, this was supposed to be a smooth, clean operation with only the bad guys taken out.'

The pause seemed to echo in the Senator's head. 'Well?'

'Our intel told us it would be a clean strike sir. We'd no idea Suarez's children were with him.'

'Oh well, that's good, just peachy. Shit Bob, where's Suarez's wife?'

Another pause. 'We don't know sir. She's not a well-known figure, even to the Colombians. No females were found at ground zero.'

'That's not good.'

'Quite.'

The quiet was uncomfortable. 'You have to find her Bob. These people are known for their vendettas. You have to find her and silence her. Now.'

*

Penelope Hortez stood on the veranda of her villa looking out over Cucuta. It was difficult to control the tears, even after the burials; when the dirt had covered her babies. She guessed it may never be that she was able to comfort the ache in the centre of her heart. There was a way, however, to salve the pain.

Her cell chimed. A chill clutched at her as she saw the name on the screen. Drawing a breath, she accepted the call. 'Harry, how are you?'

'Hi honey, how was the Lima show?'

'Oh, you know: the usual hassle with models, designers, stylists. Fortunately, there were no deaths!' Penelope laughed easily but the words sliced her open easier than a knife.

'But otherwise everything –'

'Was a complete success!' She managed a smile, though her heart was cold. 'And how is my Senator today? How is Mrs. Johnson?' A cheap shot. She marvelled at her control.

Senator Johnson didn't bite, too self-absorbed as usual. 'I'm very well, thank you. Did you see what our Marines achieved in Venezuela? That was me.'

Time stopped at the words – *"Venezuela", "that was me"*. Did she ask? Did she confirm her worst

49

fears? He would tell her surely and then she would know for definite. 'I saw something of it … yes. Was that …?'

'You bet!' he enthused, 'And we got the head, one Ferdinand Suarez! Enough to say there are fewer smugglers to profit from the misery of the world's poor because of our Marine Corps. How are the boys?'

Penelope sat, fell, in to a chair, as her legs stopped supporting her. Bastard! She wanted to cry wanted to vomit; needed to hit something. 'I'm sorry; I'm going to have to go.' *Cover the tremor in your voice.*

'Hey, honey. What's wrong?'

If you only knew. 'It's just the show – it wiped me out. I'll be okay by. Will you be at the New York event?' *Please say you won't.*

'I wouldn't miss it for the world. And after, we can do dinner and perhaps ...'

'Yes, perhaps ...' Penelope hoped that her tone held the right amount of expectation and desire. Could people hear vengeance?

It was time to plan.

Seven

'What is it you want to show me Bob?'

Johnson leaned back in his studded leather armchair and regarded his aide with a look of smugness on his face.

Bob Vega dropped an image from his idev onto the desk screen. It showed a slim, older Chinese man with obvious military bearing. Johnson stretched the image and scrutinised the face. 'Who's this?'

'Leong Chaozheng, a general in the PLA. He's tipped to be the next Chairman of the Party ...'

'And?'

'And he's currently in Bogota.'

Johnson looked up sharply. 'Bogota? What's he doing there?'

'That's what we're trying to establish. The Company is only now starting to track this guy.'

'What's our interest?'

Vega dropped a document from his idev onto the screen. 'Leong has increasingly been seen in Central and Southern America. One view is he's interested in bankrolling the Latin America Pact. Certainly he has been visiting all the major players down there,' pause, 'including our Mr Sanchez.'

Johnson looked at the face again. Just how did the Chinese manage that inscrutable look? 'What do Sanchez's aides have to say about that?'

'They've made no effort to hide the contact. Officially? Mr Sanchez is open to discussions but is happy with the current arrangement with the US and yourself.'

Johnson grunted. 'And when he can stick us in the ass he will, is how that reads over.' Vega smiled thinly. 'Ok Bob, keep tabs on the whole thing. Let me know if Mr Sanchez has any more visits from our Chinese friend here.' He flipped through the document Bob had supplied.

'Senator, you should be aware that this could be a serious threat to your relationship with Sanchez, and your candidacy.'

Harry Johnson looked up. 'No shit? Well, Bob, you'd best keep on top of Mr Leong, and find out what the fuck he wants with our ally. And find out just how far over Eduardo is prepared to bend.'

'Sure thing. Now, can we talk about the upcoming debate?'

'Okay. Should be a walk in the park, shouldn't it Bob?'

Bob Vega raised an eyebrow. While he admired his boss's confidence most of the time, sometimes the guy's easy arrogance irritated even him. 'Don't take anything for granted sir. While you have a healthy lead over Appleton, she's a wily customer and an astute debater. She will attack your anti-drugs record.'

'What has she done about drugs, particularly on her own turf? This debate at Harvard is in her backyard and Boston has one of the worst records on fighting drugs in the whole country. She'll lose.'

'You need to treat her with more care Senator,' Vega cautioned. 'Appleton is going to challenge you over your support of Sanchez and the Venezuelan operation. She will say that killing Suarez has potentially stirred up a hornet's nest that the country could have done without. Christine Appleton is your closest challenger for the ticket, and a serious

Democrat candidate. The Harvard debate is pivotal. You screw it up: you lose.'

Harry Johnson regarded his aide. He respected Bob Vega, knowing he often disagreed with his boss's decisions and always said it how it was. That was why he trusted him so much. 'Ok Bob, tell me what I have to do.'

*

It was a backwater house in a southern suburb of the city of Cucuta, close to the border with Venezuela. The single track road that ran between the closely packed houses, many of them squats, was dusty and littered with the detritus of human existence. Penelope Hortez had been careful where she stepped as she climbed from the RV. She told her driver, a young off duty cop with a wife, two infants and plenty of debt, to keep the motor running and his eyes on the surroundings. She wasn't so naïve as to believe she was safe because she was a woman. Indeed, an unknown woman in these parts was a trouble magnet, no matter how disguised.

The house she was visiting was one of her husband's labs. It was an ordinary building, indistinguishable from all the others in the street. She knocked on the door.

It opened a crack and a small head peered from the darkness. The one visible eye looked her up and down furtively for a second, before recognition brought a smile to the part exposed lips.

'Senora Suarez!'

Penelope pressed a finger to her lips. 'Hector. You must call me "Hortez".' She smiled, ignoring the quizzical smile. 'Can I come in?'

53

'Of course, of course.' The door opened minimally it seemed and Penelope slid through the gap. The interior of the house was, it was fair to say, disgusting, but she wasn't there for the decor. The smell of chemicals, smoke and drugs was overpowering, but Penelope Hortez was made of stern stuff. She also had a job to direct.

'Would you like a drink, a cup of coffee perhaps?' Hector smiled ingratiatingly.

Penelope looked at Hector and then the contents of the kitchen. Though she smiled in return, her stomach turned at the thought of consuming anything in this place. 'No Hector, I cannot be here long because of other commitments.'

Hector sulked, and then shrugged it off. 'What can I do for you Senora?'

'You were my husband's most trusted lieutenant; the person to whom he turned when he wanted the special jobs done, when he wanted to understand the dynamics of a particular subject.'

Hector looked visibly upset. 'Senora, allow me to express my sincere condolences at your losses. Your husband and I went back a very long way, back to school in Medellin. Senor Suarez helped me very much in those days. I would do anything for ... him.'

Warmth seeped briefly into her smile. 'Thank you Hector, I know you would. Tell me; when the Americans hit the ranch last week; what was the impact on his operations?'

It looked as though the little man might break down at any moment and for a second Penelope couldn't think why her husband had thought so much of the man. Then ... never judge a book by its cover.

The little man took up his own offer of a drink, warmed water and made a coffee. He picked up the mug and drew in the vapours of the dark liquid, before thrusting the grimy receptacle under Penelope's nose.

'What do you smell?'

'Coffee?' Her voice tinkled with nervousness at the comical situation.

'Money, senora. You smell money.' He sipped the dark pungent liquid, savouring for a moment its harsh descent of his throat. 'This is a modified coffee, self-pollinating and designed to withstand extreme conditions. It is grown quite easily high in the mountains by farmers who are subsidised by the government. It brings in cash from the UN fund for developing and emerging economies. They also receive financial support from the US for donating fifty per cent of the crops to third world markets. The same goes for maize and lentils.'

'My husband grows ... grew these crops?'

'NO!' Hector almost laughed at her. 'His farmers do, and they ... pay ... paid ... part of their subsidies to Senor Suarez.'

Penelope Hortez considered the brown liquid in Hector's cup, moved to the countertop and picked up the jar of coffee. Twisting off the lid she smelled the contents – it wasn't a smell that she enjoyed. 'I don't get it Hector.'

'It is simple Senora Su- Hortez. All the farmers in the region pay a rent – paid a rent – to your husband. The government brings the beans; farmers plant them and harvest the crop. Senor Suarez would provide the transportation into Cucuta, levying ten per cent from the agreed profit. He stored it over the border at Barranca and arranged transport to Maracaibo.

'From there it would be shipped, with the help of the Venezuelan authorities, as per the reworked manifest; usually somewhere in Asia. Senor Suarez ran an online auction run by a front company with a legitimate UN licence for trading in food stuffs, but which was in actual fact one of his portfolio organisations. The money from the transactions was laundered through this company to his Grand Cayman account.'

Penelope nodded, deep in thought. 'What else was he doing, Hector?'

Hector looked away.

'Well?' Pause. 'Hector: what else was he doing with the foodstuffs? I need to know.'

'It wasn't my idea.' Genuine fear constricted the man's voice and Penelope registered the emotion in his eyes. So the little lieutenant's saviour was also his biggest bully. Different tack.

'I understand that, Hector, but I need to know if I am to continue my husband's business. I need to know everything he was doing.'

'He said you would be angry with him … because of the boys.' Hector's gaze dropped as he saw the loss in Penelope's face.

She had known the pain would be great whenever anyone mentioned her beautiful boys: she hadn't realised how much. Gently, because she didn't wish to hurt the trembling man she responded. 'Hector, there are many things my husband and I were unable to agree on – the children were not one such matter. And my boys would be angry if I were not to do all in my power to right this wrong, which was committed against them. Anything my husband was doing that will enable this I will follow through.' She let the tears run unchecked down her cheeks to reinforce the passion she felt. Hector visibly lifted himself, handing a handkerchief, impeccably, and incongruously, clean to Penelope.

'Of course, Senora.' He drew a breath, conscious of the effect of what he might say. 'Your husband was reinvigorating his cocaine business through the food trade.'

Penelope bristled, experienced a flush of righteous anger before dousing the flame – it would do no good now. Manuel and Eduardo were dead and buried. No amount of railing against her equally dead husband would bring them back. 'How?' she couldn't help the curt edge to her tone.

'We had devised an emulsion that could be sprayed over the coffee, or lentils, or maize, or infused into the material through any preparatory process. It was designed as a means by which to regenerate the drugs trade which isn't what it was.'

'And the process works?'

'Oh yes, though dependency is built up over a longer period and there is the new problem of people not really understanding what is happening to them.'

'How do you mean?'

Hector paused. 'The individual who drinks the coffee experiences a high, a change in their emotive state but obviously doesn't understand the coffee is infused with a narcotic.'

Penelope considered this. 'I presume Ferdinand was working on a means to ensure their cravings were clarified for them.'

'Definitely. He asked me to devise a new distribution network that would target certain groups and neighbourhoods which had been recipients of the doctored foods. However other groups also requested the modifications to be carried out.'

'Such as?'

'Al-Qaeda wanted to use it with their newer

57

recruits in Yemen, who were perhaps less inclined to use drugs to enhance performance or who needed "encouragement" to fight. In return we were able to try the technique out with heroin which we then offered to move into the US on their behalf. It was one of a number of successful trades your husband concluded with the Yemenis and Afghans.'

She digested that last statement. Though she had heard of his contacts with the Taliban, they'd seemed to make strange bedfellows, with only a hatred of the US as a common bond. Penelope was surprised it had lasted as long as it had.

'What else did they give him?'

'We were trained in the production of IEDs and they helped us organise into cells when the last purge came two years ago.'

'And they received what in return?'

'Cocaine; either as a powder, or rocks. The reason they attacked the UN food station in Aden the other week is that part of Mr Suarez's consignment of coca infused coffee had inadvertently been diverted there. Rescuing it gave them the opportunity to test out ... other ... technologies.'

'Good for them,' Penelope retorted laconically. She remembered the austere Afghans she had briefly encountered at her husband's ranch. Al-Qaeda was probably no better but ... perhaps there were opportunities. 'Tell me, how effective is this coca-fuelled food?'

The little man's eyes lit up and a grin split his face. 'Very, senora. We have been conducting experiments.'

'What sort?'

'Senor Suarez had us conduct live tests on animals.'

There was much she didn't know about her animal loving husband, Penelope decided. 'What did he use?'

'Principally rats. They exhibited heightened sexual activity and animated conditional behaviour: that was down to addiction. Do you want to see the evidence?'

'Thank you, no.' She had no desire to see rats fucking, or fighting. Time to change the emphasis.

'Hector. Tell me how my husband hoped to make this a viable prospect. How was he going to infect the US with these products?'

'We have … had a strategy. The first part was to ensure the product flooded the streets and was being consumed. We went to all our old markets, not just in US cities, but also Europe, getting people using again, just when the authorities believed it had all been defeated. The individuals in these areas will then be susceptible to the second part of the strategy which is to launch a volume marketing strategy running "self-medication" to control the effects of the foods – heroin.'

'I thought you said heroin was being infused into the foods.'

'No, Senora, it doesn't seem to work as well as cocaine in binding with the foods. However, it's a good downer from the effects of cocaine. By the time we've sold people enough, they'll want full grade coke to bring them up again. The market is open once more. With our partners we have the means to bring the West to its knees.'

Simple and effective – that was one thing Penelope admired her dead husband for: just the one though. 'The Taliban are not so powerful that they could do the logistics for this?'

'No, but they worked with partners who were; and

Senor Suarez hoped to court them, to help him move these goods.'

Penelope waited expectantly and, as the silence grew uncomfortable, she prompted Hector for the information. His reply surprised her.

'The Chinese?' Penelope was stunned and intrigued all at once. 'And how successful were the talks?'

'Very Senora, they are very interested.'

'Are they? What were they going to provide?'

'That I cannot tell you Senora, I think the negotiations were very young.'

'Do you have a contact?'

Again Hector shook his head. 'No, senora, your husband would not let me know. He said he was ... protecting me.'

Penelope looked at the man whom Ferdinand had thought so highly of. 'Do not worry, I will find out.' Ferdinand had had his reasons. 'Do we have any materials ready to move?'

'Much was destroyed when ...' Was Hector going to cry? He drew a breath. 'But, we have maintained some production despite having to disperse.'

Penelope nodded thoughtfully. 'Hector, I have to go now, but I will be in contact with you next week for moving out the next shipments. I need as much as can you have ready by then. What do you think?'

Her scientist considered the question. 'It would be possible to get two tonne made up from our current outlets.'

'Then what?'

'It goes to our food processing plant, here in Cucuta and then on for shipping.'

'Does it all goes in one direction?'

Hector chuckled. 'Yes. We have to ship through

Venezuela, whether it goes to Boston or Karachi. Shipping is from Maracaibo on the Gulf.'

'There are no other routes?'

'None that can yet take the volume we want to move; or with the security afforded by the Venezuelan military.'

Penelope perused Hector's words. 'Okay, sort out the cargo and I will arrange logistics. We will do things differently from now on.'

'If you ... insist Senora.' It was the scientist's first hesitation at her words.

'You doubt me?'

Hector flinched, as if he'd been physically slapped and Penelope found she liked the control. She realised why her husband had fed off his power over others.

'No ... not at all!' affirmed the frightened little man.

'Good. Somebody has destroyed my family. Do not think I won't be as resolute as my dead husband would have been, in making them pay.'

*

'Federico how do I get a large consignment of drugs out of this country, without using the Venezuela route? I think it will be watched from now on.'

Her driver glanced across at her. 'There are many people in the pay of the Americans watching seaports, airports and our overland routes. Senor Suarez had established a good route through Venezuela.'

Penelope nodded. 'I know. They have made all our traditional routes very difficult. Will they be expecting a change in tactics following Ferdinand's death or...?'

'If I may Senora, they expect nothing. They

believe they have defeated the cartel. They are waiting for the battle of succession. Anything you do now will catch them off guard.'

Penelope Suarez smiled. 'Thank you Federico, that is most gratifying to know. I think I have the perfect cover to move the drugs out of Colombia.'

'Yes?'

'What do you know of the Chinese?'

Federico gave her a look which made the answer clear: nothing. 'What I read. Why?'

'Very well, it is enough for you to drive for the moment, Federico. When you go to work, I need to know what ...'

Federico seemed to divine the concern in his mistress. 'Do not doubt me Senora Suarez ...'

'Hortez,' she corrected.

'Si, si, Senora Hortez.' Do not doubt me. You have brought me security and safety. I will not let you down. I will provide you with the information you require on the American surveillance.'

Penelope Hortez nodded. Partly she wanted to pacify the eager, but anxious young Federico, all the while aware that his timidity would be the very thing that he betrayed her by.

When his time was done...

Eight

Charlie tucked a stray strand of hair behind her ear, scratching absent-mindedly at the itch which inhabited the spot on her face where the hair had been. She slavishly attended the screen before her, reading the report from the Yemen field agent on AQAP politics and strategies. Fresh partnerships were being developed and embedded in the battle against the West, and the structures, politics, made for riveting reading. The cells, which made this all work, were in a constant state of flux, countering years of successful Coalition and NATO attacks on the heads of the organisation. New internet technology, in the shape of the emerging Mesh, encouraged instant communication between people, even a world apart. The networks had morphed into interconnected cyber identities: electronic virtual cells, hell bent on global warfare. Real groups formed only as and when hard action was required. That way it was much harder for the hated Westerners to track and eliminate them. This was definitely a serious threat emerging from the dust and hills of Yemen. NSA and Britain's GCHQ would have their hands full for years.

The agent painted a picture of sleepers and cells that had reached into many legal and not-so-legal organisations, delivering systematic and orchestrated attacks, real and cyber, on the West and its allies. It made what had taken place in the aftermath of 9/11 look like a tea party. Links within the Saudi ruling party were being exploited as never before and the threat to oil supplies had begun to wreak havoc on

Western commerce and politico-military force projection. Afghanistan had been witness to over-border incursions by active militants, exploiting centuries of Pashtun unrest to make a complete American withdrawal impossible to achieve. An unofficial Taliban government of Afghanistan had established in the border regions south and north east of Kabul (which became a West-sponsored enclave of sorts), intent on the destruction of Western society through the deployment of cheap narcotics, and selling guerrilla tactics to anybody, with even a whiff of money.

Their reach was amazing, given the avowed public stance of non contact. They were believed to be in alliance with Venezuela's government, Somali pirates and al-Qaeda in Yemen. First identified two years ago it had been dismissed as unsustainable; a mere sideshow to exploit market forces. This now burgeoning market was a significant threat to global stability. So much for that enlightened assessment, Charlie observed wryly. Using Venezuelan tankers as a vehicle to move unopposed globally, Taliban advisers were understood to be working with Colombian drug cartels; trading expertise for routing heroin into the US. In return they took cocaine for their own, and Yemeni, fighters and Somali pirates, as well as offering a new route into Europe and Russia. Yemen often provided a port of convenience for Somali pirates in their struggle to dodge the massive international anti-piracy operation in the Indian Ocean.

In addition, was a report on Colombia and Venezuela. It detailed the growing power struggle raging between the ineffectual, pro-American government of Miguel Cordoba and the Anti-

American, hard line Venezuelan government of Ernesto Ortega. A more lopsided quarrel was hard to imagine.

Cordoba was under threat from all sides. The US, despite its own reservations over the Colombian President's ability to win a second term in the upcoming elections, continued to bolster his failing regime. His poor response to food smuggling, and the high tech, low volume, cocaine production of the cartels, had caused much fulminating within the White House Administration of Jonah Lincoln. His half-hearted actions had seen some limited initial successes, quickly reversed by a series of cartel bombings aimed at the usual targets: government and police officials and buildings.

This time it was the deployment which differed: suicide bombers, young idealists or naïve individuals, duped into delivering a message of defiance to those in government; IEDs buried beside roads and taking out officials on their way to work, sometimes in full view of families. Resignations became epidemic-like, after all nobody had signed up for this. In a period of ten months, fifteen bureaucrats and many more civilians had been killed or maimed in orchestrated attacks that were difficult to track back to any defined sources. An insurgency ensued, the end of which was currently nowhere in sight. Eduardo Sanchez, hopeful of taking over from Cordoba, was leading the opposition diatribe against the Chilean President. Sanchez's own food logistics business was being heavily hit by the actions of the cartels and he took every opportunity to rail against his President's lassitude.

Publicly the US Administration had provided arms, expertise and money to try and counter the cartels; they'd smiled and shaken hands with the man looking towards enforced retirement. In private both the current administration and Presidential hopeful, Senator Johnson, courted Sanchez with increasing vigour. Knowing that Cordoba couldn't argue, the US had planned a concerted response, directed by excellent intelligence from Eduardo Sanchez's contacts, against known cartel bases over the border using similar tactics employed successfully in Afghanistan and Pakistan.

Charlie stretched and reached for her coffee, grimacing as she sipped the cold, bitter liquid – had time really flown by so quickly? Her blueberry muffin was in a similar state of abandon; dry crumbs scattered haphazardly across papers – another trail leading nowhere. She placed the sorry remains in the bin and sighed. Checking her watch, she saw she'd been engrossed for an hour and a half. It was time for a break and to stretch her legs.

Strong knuckles rapped on the door to Charlie's small office and, before she could invite the owner in, it swung open aggressively. Sarah Markham, Director of Crime and Narcotics, was a determined and dominating woman; striking rather than pretty; bothered exclusively with delivery and results. Any discussion would be focussed, presenting Charlie with a series of tasks to be completed quickly and to exacting standards.

Markham took the chair on the other side of the desk, placed a folder and envelope on it, and stared squarely at her senior analyst. 'Well?' Her tone was as clipped as her manner and Charlie thought fast, knowing she had to be aware of Markham's focus.

'It's real interesting, like analysing an octopus. There are so many – tentacles – so many different strands to their activities; it's hard to trace them all. Just when you think you're sorted and heading in one direction, some report sends you off at a tangent.'

'What have you found out so far?'

Charlie proceeded to provide her director with the lowdown as she'd analysed it. Markham sat perfectly still, listening intently, making no interruption as her senior analyst continued in animated style, outlining her theories. Eventually Charlie ran out of breath and sank back in her chair waiting. Markham remained silent and Charlie wondered if she had been too enthusiastic over her description of the pirating, terrorist and rogue government connections.

Eventually Markham broke the silence. 'So, is Ortega behind this?'

Charlie shook her head. 'I'd like to say it's clear one way or the other, but it isn't. He's hiding behind rhetoric; claiming he knows nothing. No clear links exist ...' she shrugged.

Sarah Markham arched an eyebrow. 'But he provides a safe haven for the cartels and his government controls the Venezuelan oil industry.'

Charlie flushed at the barely concealed slur on her skills. 'My dad loves football. He moved from Miami to Washington but he doesn't support the Redskins. If Venezuelan armed forces are working with the cartels, we have no conclusive proof that would stand in court. We can't presume Ortega is behind this.'

Sarah smiled: a cold; calculated thing. 'Point taken, but I believe you're being generous to the man.'

'I guess, and you're right there is something else, a pulse that runs beneath the surface; but I can't put my finger on it.'

'Go on,' Markham recovered.

'The upcoming elections for one,' Charlie answered. 'Eduardo Sanchez worries me. For sure he speaks about friendship and strengthening commercial ties with the US, but his past is a closed book. No one really knows his background or where he's from.'

'Are you … My God! You're saying that Sanchez is involved?? But he's a personal friend of Presidential candidate Johnson.'

'I'm not suggesting anything. I'm saying I don't know. There's a lot more that I have to work on before I can be clear about this.'

Markham looked alarmed. 'Make sure you keep on top of this Charlie. While you're at it here's something else for your portfolio, that might be connected.' She slipped a manila folder across the cluttered desk.

'What is it?'

'A body was found by the Thames in London, just over a week ago under London Bridge. An unidentified caller to the Metropolitan Police asked for a specific MI6 operative. The body had been decapitated, its hands removed. The agent said nothing to the Met but he filed a report to his superiors, putting a name to the corpse. This is a transcript.'

'Who was it?'

'The CIA station chief for London.'

Charlie's hand flew involuntarily to her mouth.

Markham extended a hand with a small white envelope held between finger and thumb. 'Look at the contents. It seems this assassination was a signal.'

'For?'

'That we're less clear about. I want you to do some digging. It may require a visit to London. If it does, come to me and we'll clear you some equipment and papers.'

'Okay,' Charlie replied carefully.

'If there's nothing else, I'm gone.' Markham raised an eyebrow in question and Charlie wisely shook her head. 'Very well, let me know how you get on.'

Markham exited the office, already on her next mission, leaving Charlie with her thoughts. London? Her only time out of the States was her graduation trip to Paris (*how predictable?*). Now she was being asked to play secret agent in a foreign country. This project was attaining a standing way beyond an analyst's remit.

She picked up a letter opener and sliced the top of the envelope, tipping the contents on to her desk. One object was a slip of paper with a cell phone number on it.

The other was way more interesting. It was a CIA standard issue chip, inserted into all field agents from 2013. This would hold a complete record of what had happened to the agent up to the moment of death.

She was surprised that whoever had taken him hadn't thought to remove it. Perhaps it was one of the CIA's better kept secrets, though obviously the Brits had found it. Charlie felt a frisson of excitement as she handled the tiny device. Hold it, she told herself. Savour this little bit of information. Have that break then come back and find out what secret the chip holds.

Nine

Sarah Markham stared from her window at the gently swaying trees, vibrant and clean, unlike the world she inhabited. Richter was talking a game changer. A sigh dropped from her lips as she considered the politics of the situation. A peacock for a Presidential candidate; an unknown and dangerous Colombian businessman, and insurgents from across the globe: Johnson's delicate position in all that was a worry.

But, what to do about it?

Nothing: much more intelligence was required yet. From where first? Ortega? Taliban? Both high risk ... so who? Al-Qaeda in the Arab Peninsula? The vociferous cohort in Yemen? What about their links with Somalia? The Somali piracy problem had been a persistent one since the turn of the century and, apart from a couple of short, quiet periods, had not abated. If Richter was correct it meant the Somalis had changed their economy, as had Colombia and the Taliban. Taking advantage of AQAP to provide overland routes, using the guise of international piracy, they were making the most of the situation.

Perhaps a strike was order of the day.

Nodding to herself, Markham tapped the comms icon on her desk. The table lit with her contacts. She scrolled through and highlighted one, then waited for the call to connect.

'Hello? Thomas here.'

'Dan, it's Sarah Markham; I have a job for you.'

*

The UAV had shadowed the Venezuelan tanker *La*

Conchega for twenty-four hours. It was heading steadily north-east along the Somali coast. Intel suggested that if local pirates were aiding the Taliban and Colombians they could board the ship anytime in the next thirty-six hours, and certainly before the ship was in the crowded mouth of the Strait of Hormuz. For now though, everything appeared normal.

The operator back in Nevada kept the vessel firmly in the sight of the Hawkeye UAV. How normal did a situation have to appear? She'd been on this particular watch for over five hours and as much had happened in those five as in the previous five and all the ones before that. But hope sprang eternal as the saying went.

She panned the main camera, ensuring the SLAR and thermal imaging cameras still recorded the vessel. The ocean was empty ... no, wait! Adrenaline hit her stomach: was this it? Something – north-north-east of the tanker - was moving fast towards the Venezuelan vessel. A typical pirate ship: low silhouette; fast, ten to fifteen men on deck.

As she watched, the vessel altered course, skirting the stern of the tanker. Grapples were quic kly and expertly deployed, allowing men to swarm quickly to the deck in a rehearsed and expert fashion. The UAV operator smiled ironically. Knowing what to look for she could see the intel was spot on. There were no guards; no rails or anti grapple panels. No anti-boarding paint to stop the expert clamber to the deck. It couldn't be more staged. The technique was in the speed of the operation: an untrained or unsuspecting observer would not recognise it as fake.

The pirates would soon be well on the way to port, Venezuela would pay the ransom, make a song and dance about it before the tanker carried on its way.

Not today. Unbeknownst to the players, enacting their seaborne drama, the US cruiser *Anzio* had tailed the tanker since passing Jo'burg. On board, helos waited, rotors turning, to speed Marines to the "rescue" of the hostage Venezuelans.

The operator brushed a thumb over the comms icon on her desk screen which blinked live. Dragging the cruiser's comms tag onto the icon she opened a secure channel with the vessel.

'Captain Hayland.'

'Captain; Operative 951672. You are cleared for action.'

'Roger that.' The line went dead and the operator turned her attention back to the pirates and the tanker. They were about to get one hell of a surprise.

*

Rappelling rapidly to the deck, Marines dropped the first two guards they met, before moving to the superstructure. Though well-armed the pirates were no match for the Americans, who advanced resolutely on the bridge. The action was over quickly with no further loss of life. If ever there was a more obvious clue as to the relationship between the Somalis and Venezuelans that was it. The captain of *La Conchega* was less than effusive in his thanks.

Back on the *Anzio*, the Marines quickly and expertly searched the pirates. Lieutenant Bennett, in charge of the boarding party, logged each item meticulously, even down to the bundles of khat discovered on their boat. It was time to interrogate.

The ringleader was led to a spartan room, deep in the ship's bowels. A metal table and two chairs occupied the centre lit by a bare light bulb. There was just room for Bennett, the pirate and two Marines guards. The lieutenant sat across the table from his captive, the chair creaking beneath his weight. He clicked on the recording equipment. Leaning back Bennett placed his hands on the edge of the table and regarded the stoical African.

'Sir,' he began, 'you and your crew have been detained, as part of the ongoing Operation Ocean Shield II, tasked with eliminating piracy on the high seas. Your detention and interrogation will be conducted following the rules laid out, under the Geneva Convention.'

The Somali merely stared back, dark eyes displaying no emotion.

'We want to talk about your relationship with the Venezuelans.'

Was that a twitch?

'You seem to have a very healthy interest in their vessels.'

Nothing.

'We've been keeping tabs on your activities in relation to Venezuelan ships transiting the Horn of Africa. What's interesting is how quickly you resolve things with the Venezuelan government.'

The Somali remained silent, but a small bead of sweat ran down the ebony skin.

'Isn't it strange you can hijack a tanker, take it to port and within twenty-four hours it's ready to move on again? And isn't it odd that you always manage to get one close enough to the coast that it doesn't cost too much for you to 'jack?'

The Somali fixed his gaze on Bennett, unmoving.

'To a casual observer, say me for instance, it would look like a deal was being made.' Bennett leant forward suddenly; his prisoner remained stoically silent but another rivulet of sweat traced a crooked path on his face. 'You seem quite hot,' Bennett glanced at the guards. 'You hot, Noriega? How about you Huckler?' Both men smiled ironically and shook their heads. 'Strange that, my buddies and me are ok. But you seem real hot. Or … you're hiding something.

'So, which is it?'

The Somali smiled suddenly. 'You think you can intimidate weaker people with your attitude and fancy weapons, and your vaunted democracy. We know we cannot fight you the way you fight – we do not aim to. There is a revolution coming that will change the world. Weak people will rise and then you will worry.'

'How's that?'

The Somali chuckled. 'We say in my country a man throws stones not words. I have nothing to say to you. If you kill me, you make us stronger; if you let me go you make us stronger and if you imprison me you make us stronger. You have no idea what is going to happen.'

Bennett settled back in his chair and smiled. 'Well it seems you have the bases covered. What do they call you?'

'Mekonen.'

'Okay, Mekonen. It seems we're at an impasse. Your people might get stronger because of what we do, or don't do, to you, but right now I have to hold you all until we get to a port where you can be transferred to the authorities. My immediate concern is not any wider aspiration you may entertain. So, Mekonen, you are my guest until we dock. We'll keep you and your men comfortable.

'Take him back to the brig.'

*

The report dropped into Charlie's in-tray. With a slender index finger, she slid the document to her desk screen. It was only a short piece of work with succinct wording, taking little more than four pages. Twelve pirates had been taken off a Venezuelan tanker while four tonnes of cocaine, unimaginatively stacked in barrels in the crew hold, had been confiscated. No Afghanis or Yemenis were found on board.

Charlie found that interesting. If not on the tanker, how did they get back? Had they been taken out in the raid? She hadn't picked up report of any aliens; she'd have to go back through the evidence. Had there even been any this time? For now, the Yemeni connection took all her attention. Starting with previous shipping logs, Charlie checked on the dates of pirate attacks. Taking that info, she began tracking unusual activity through Somalia, listening to the trade between agents and contacts. This was going to be a long day.

Time seemed to stand still as Charlie remained fixed to her desk. The coffee machine worked overtime, keeping her fed with caffeine, whilst her store of Hershey bars diminished by the hour. The light possessed that afternoon glow when she finally paused. Stretching, Charlie walked to the coffee machine and picked up the pot, shuddered and replaced it. No more! It was making her head spin.

The information she had was comprehensive: the system very simple. It relied on minimal structure and contact, just like the Taliban used. That way no-one knew who was in command; nobody could be shopped – the perfect system. Now it had been exposed it might be easier to dismantle. Though, they'd only find another route. Where would that be? Surveillance of all activity into and out of Colombia and Venezuela would have to be stepped up. The Cucuta Cartel appeared dead now, but somebody would be taking up the reins. There was any number of others who could step up to the plate. Forero, out of Medellin, and Burgos from Cali, were both home grown talent. Neither was imaginative with their capabilities, but who knew what might happen?

Whatever, there wouldn't be a vacuum for long and the CIA would have to be ready to respond. A change was about to happen and it wouldn't be for the best.

Ten

New York was an unqualified success – people loved Hortez's designs, flocking to see her interpretation of South American culture. Maintaining a business face had been hard, the losses still bit deep, but revenge was best served by her keeping working, keeping the lid on that part of her life. Johnson hadn't attended in the end (business, he'd said) but had called to find out how things had gone. "Well," she'd replied, "I understand," all the time her skin crawling. Her show was moving to Europe now and there would be no Harry Johnson for a while; perhaps, by the time she returned to the Americas...

German fashion and perfumery company, Hint, had approached her out of the blue, to display at their Berlin show – a withdrawal, could she? They fostered many connections with Eastern Europe and Near Asia where business scruples were ... different; ambition prevalent and life a commodity to be traded like anything else. Anything could be sold if you knew the right people.

The ICC Berlin had been taken over by Hint, intent on showcasing fashion and style that wasn't White European. Penelope's range of Andean-inspired clothing was proving a storm. Many beyond Colombia had initially dismissed it as a mix of ethnic Peruvian hats and ponchos. Los Angeles had changed that: A-listers flocked to her show and formed a disorderly queue to purchase, what was quickly badged prosaically "the new avant-garde". Paris and Madrid followed but the big player, Milan had proved more haughty, aloof and ultimately resistant. That had been a blow.

This year she'd turned them down. Berlin would be smaller but give her a chance to stage her range as part of a fashion revolution. Hint was delighted, leading on her styles while showcasing Indo-Chinese, Eastern European and South American fashion houses. Milan fulminated vocally and Penelope knew she was in charge. In attendance were celebrities galore: politicians and business leaders; film and music stars and then those with money but who preferred to stay in the background. Her people had been doing some digging and had unearthed a potentially lucrative contact that could develop her other business, who was attending.

As she circulated at the pre-show buffet she searched for the man whose face she had memorised.

Where was Rado Kiric?

*

Ben Carpenter felt awkward, drawing a hand through his lank blonde hair, cursing the short straw he'd drawn for this assignment. He cursed himself for making so much of being a photographer. To be honest he felt a twat, at a fashion show, with a camera slung round his neck, attempting to pass as a freelance photographer. It had definitely been the unwanted task at the Embassy; surely one for a female operative, though none argued too vehemently for the gig.

Unquestionably The Hint Fashion Event wasn't what he believed a field operative of his calibre should be doing. The station chief had been very insistent. It was an ideal opportunity to observe someone known to be running guns; smuggling drugs and humans and involved in any number of other transnational crimes. Rado Kiric had an impressive portfolio of activities that Interpol and other European and international security agencies would love to know more about. MI6 were interested in his marketing of high value weaponry, and his movement of drugs from Afghanistan to Western Europe was also of value.

Ah well.

Carpenter made a decision and pushed himself from the wall and began circulating through the glitterati, snapping with the camera in what he hoped was an approximation of a professional at work.

He weaved in and out of the slow moving throng for close on an hour before his quarry appeared. The scant profile MI6 had on the man portrayed an individual proud of his Kosovar roots; a man who would butcher another for the fun of it. A focussed individual, he was orphaned in the Srebrenica massacre of 1995. That had given him all the justification needed to kill Christians when, where and how he could. When he couldn't do that, smuggling heroin into Europe and the US, arming insurgent groups in Iraq, Yemen and Afghanistan, provided scope for collateral damage. Not necessarily intelligent but cunning and brutal for sure.

That man now walked assuredly to the nearest waiter and took a drink from the tray – so not a completely devout Muslim then, observed Carpenter. The agent clicked away at the people between him and Kiric, making small talk with his subjects and flashing the smile he was famous for in the Embassy. All the while he was aware of Kiric's movements.

The woman who approached the Kosovar was stunning and for a moment Carpenter was distracted.

'Well? Do you want this photo or not!?'

Carpenter turned to the portly, glistening and over-valued person he had approached for a photo and looked him up and down.

'Well?' demanded the star, 'I can't stand here all fucking day waiting for you.'

'No? Maybe you should sit down and take some weight off your brains or before you have a heart attack.'

'What? You shit! You can't talk to me like that!'

Carpenter checked over the person's shoulder on Kiric and his mysterious blonde. They were still there. He looked the celebrity in the eye and nodded knowingly. 'Yeah, I can. I just did.' Before the star could react Carpenter was wending his way through the crowd towards his target.

On his way he snapped a few others, always contriving to get Kiric and his companion in the frame. Then he was stood before them. Well, why not?

'Excuse me, do you mind?' He waved his camera at the pair. The blonde started, a rabbit in the headlights. Kiric regarded Carpenter with a hooded gaze, his dark brown eyes dissecting Carpenter to lay bare his true identity – or so it seemed.

'No.' It was an order not an answer. The upraised hand reinforced the command.

'Just one. How about you?' Carpenter asked the woman who didn't look European: he couldn't place her nationality. Her piercing blue eyes had the look of a cornered animal. She merely shook her head, though the panic was not from a fear of the paparazzi, Carpenter surmised. Something else.

'If you don't leave us alone, now, I will take your camera and club you with it here and now until you do leave. Is that clear?'

Carpenter raised his hands in mock surrender. 'Okay, okay I only asked. I'm sorry.' He moved away and circled once more. Kiric and the woman talked a little and then withdrew mobiles and seemed to exchange information. Carpenter pulled his from his pocket ensuring his Sabretooth app was on. This passively interrogated every device in the room, collecting and collating recent activity. He time checked the log so he could pick those of most interest.

Kiric was moving; the woman also, but in the opposite direction. There was little else he could do here. Taking a few more snaps for the sake of appearances Ben Carpenter left the show and headed back to his apartment. There were better ways of spending an evening than photographing models and ingrates. Star Trek here I come!

*

'Rado Kiric. What's he doing at a fashion show in Berlin?'

Steve Logan was chairing a meeting at Vauxhall House, where he and his team were analysing the photos sent in from Berlin.

'That's what we were hoping to find out. Unfortunately, the agent attempting to find out basically walked straight up to him and asked him for a photo.'

Steve Logan grinned. 'I imagine that worked,' he remarked laconically, 'but ten out of ten for having the balls. Who's the woman?'

'Penelope Hortez. She's Colombian and owns a very well respected fashion house.'

'Do we have any background on her?'

Des Farrow harrumphed and shuffled in his seat. 'Nay. Young Penelope is a closed book.' When faced with a problem he couldn't solve he often dropped into his native Yorkshire.

'Well we can presume that she and Kiric aren't long lost pals, so there has to be something else going on there. What about Kiric, what is our favourite arms dealer doing these days?'

Farrow appeared visibly happier, back on safer ground. 'Ah, well, our friend there is rumoured to be moving some ex-Russian offensive air for Kurdish nationalists. He has a base in Azerbaijan where Iraqi forces can't touch them. The US has appealed to Russia, stating that it risks destabilising the region. Officially Russia has no knowledge and they've made some half-hearted representation to the Azerbaijan government. They don't want to complain too much in case they incur the wrath of local Islamist militants. Unofficially, they are offering support to the Kurds and to Kiric. That way they keep Muslims away from Russian soil. So they think.'

'What's the air?'

Farrow considered the list on his desk-screen, pinching the display to zoom in. 'Russian attack helicopters are inventoried here. He has two Kamov Hokums listed and three Mil Havocs; all with full complements of weaponry and support. But his big piece is a Kamov Scorpion.'

A whisper of surprise travelled across the table 'How did he get that?'

Farrow regarded Logan. 'He was at an arms market set up by an ex-Egyptian general, Farouq Jamal. Word is Kiric took out the whole shebang and disappeared with the goods.'

'Do we know if he's sold any of the items?'

Farrow chuckled. 'I think he may be having a bit more trouble with these than he expected. After all, maintaining an attack helicopter isn't easy without exposing yourself somewhere. And then there's finding a crew to fly them.'

'So what does he intend to do with them?' Puzzlement shrouded the diminutive Helen Reed's face. 'It doesn't make any sense. If nobody really wants them he's stuck with millions of dollars of redundant machinery.'

Logan shook his head. 'Kiric is very astute: he has them for a reason. We need to find out why and who's the lucky recipient: he only has them because somebody asked. What else does he have?'

'Er, a number of BMP-2s; a couple of T-90s and three T-72s at undisclosed locations across the New Islamic Triangle.'

'Good jump off for Afghanistan or Waziristan,' opined Turner.

Logan nodded. 'Maybe, but the action's more down in the Arabian Peninsula so the jury's out until we know more. Let's get back to our beautiful new friend for a moment. What would she want with a man like Kiric?'

'Not all ladies like a clean cut he-man like you Steve.'

'Thanks for the heads up Debbie though that wasn't really my thinking.'

Sure it wasn't: Turner kept her irony internal. 'Perhaps she was trying to sell merchandise to Kiric.'

Farrow looked puzzled. 'What on earth would Kiric want with Colombian fashion?'

'Nothing,' replied Logan, 'but there are a lot of other things that Colombia is renowned for. The government is fighting an uphill battle against food smugglers who are constantly diverting coffee and maize. Not only that, cocaine is fast becoming a popular export once more. Kiric sits between the Colombian and Taliban trade.'

'Still don't see it.'

'Well, try this.'

All heads turned on Helen Reed. Her hazel eyes were bright with ideas as she continued to the expectant gathering. 'Let's just presume that Ms Hortez has other business opportunities than fashion and that she has to maintain a lucrative market with Islamist outlets. We know from our friends at Langley that there's a two-way trade in coke, heroin and IEDs.'

'A big leap, but, for the sake of current discussions, okay.' Turner's sarcastic tone left the room in no doubt how she felt.

'A fashion show is the perfect cover for her other activities. She has a legitimate, high profile, reason for being there. Kiric has money to burn – fashion is as good a way to launder drugs or arms sales money, as any other. A pre-meet is what Ben Carpenter captured the other night. Another meeting will be scheduled soon.'

'I'm still not convinced.' Turner decided it was time to rebuff the ridiculous idea put together by her eager colleague. 'We have absolutely no evidence to suggest that Penelope Hortez is a major figure in the drug scene in Colombia, let alone a drug runner and marketeer. It's a ridiculous idea Steve.'

'Agreed, Debbie.' The operations chief smiled: victory. 'There is no evidence, however, we shouldn't preclude the possibility that our new friend,' he indicated the woman on the main screen, 'has connections of which we currently know nothing.

Whatever she was doing, she was with a known drug runner and arms dealer. And, they swapped contact details. I'm going to ask Galbraith to authorise covert surveillance of Ms Hortez. Let's find out what she's doing and why. There's something unusual about our fashionista and I'd like to know what it is.'

'Has everybody got work to do?' Logan took in the nodding heads and noted Debbie Turner's irritated air. 'We'll reconvene when I'm back from Washington. Ed,' he turned to the signals expert, 'While I work on Galbraith, I want you to team up with GCHQ, and track communication traffic out of the Berlin area. See if you can isolate anything from Hortez and Kiric.'

'Sure thing boss.'

'Okay, that's all. Let's get some intel on the table people.'

The team drifted from the room. As Debbie Turner reached the door, Logan called her.

'Debbie, can I have a word please.'

She turned and looked coolly at the senior agent. 'Yes?'

'Shut the door.'

Turner felt her cheeks burn but complied. 'What do you want?' Her tone was truculent.

'Sit. Now!' Logan ordered firmly as Turner vacillated. 'Debbie, you and I don't get on and that's fine, but you don't take out frustrations or foist your opinions on a fellow operative by being sarcastic and downright rude to them.'

'What the fuck, Steve? What are you doing here?'

'Laying down a marker. You don't like me, fine. But your attitude stays between us. What Helen said was worth investigating. As senior analyst you should have taken more note of what she said. Who knows what Penelope Hortez is doing? Shit, we have nothing on her; she's an unknown yet she was talking to Rado Kiric. You can't say she isn't running drugs.'

'Steve, if she was that involved the Yanks would know about it.'

'The Americans don't know everything, and neither do we. We leave no stone unturned.'

'I don't want to tell you how to do your job,' *I'm sure you do,* thought Logan, 'but, isn't our main task to find out what happened with Drew Faulkner?'

'Somehow, I think the two things are not so very far apart.'

Eleven

'Well?'

Eddie regarded Turner and sighed. 'I gave it him.'

Debbie Turner smiled. 'Should bring him down a peg or two.'

Eddie shrugged. 'Why do you hate him so much?'

'Because he's a fucking he-man, and we have no room for one of those.'

'He gets the job done.'

'Sewage workers get the job done, but we don't all invite them to dinner.'

Eddie stared at the operations chief. She was hard to figure; something had happened to sour the working relationship with Logan – but what? What could it be that made her want to see him trip and skewered? Had she made a pass and he'd rejected her? Perhaps she felt Logan had got her job? Ah well … 'Well, he's got the file. Are you telling Galbraith what is going on?'

'Galbraith doesn't need to know.'

'But –'

'Leave it!' Turner stared Eddie down and he shrugged his compliance. 'Find yourself something else to do now. Get those files about our cousins' work in Venezuela from Cheltenham and analyse them. Reference it for Taliban and insurgency. As far as anybody knows this didn't happen.'

*

Logan knocked the double shot of Lagavulin in one and gritted his teeth. Laphroaig was out at the bar so this was the next best thing. He stared at the bottles behind the long stained counter of the Royal Oak, not because he was interested in them, but because he wanted an image that blanked out the video he'd just seen.

'Hey, another please.'

The barman looked at him. 'You okay mate?'

'Good enough thanks. Just another double please.'

'Sounds like you've had a heavy morning.'

'Something like that.' Logan pushed the glass across the bar.

'Helps to talk.'

'No offence, fella, but if I want to talk I'll initiate thanks.'

The barman shrugged, poured the drink and took the money. Logan ignored his sneer and swirled the amber liquid, its viscous surface welling like freshly spilled blood.

Don't know how you can drink that stuff.

It's class my friend; I'd teach you but I know it'd be wasted on you with your Jack Daniels fixation.

Hey, Jack is pure quality buddy, pure quality.

Just try it – you'll taste the difference.

Hey buddy, I have, and I have no desire to down a glass of peat, smoky or otherwise.

There'd be no more comparing the merits, or otherwise, of Jack versus Laphroaig with Drew. They'd seen to that in the most gruesome way possible. He shuddered and not from the whiskey. Faulkner's tormentors had ensured that he suffered maximum pain and humiliation when they murdered him. The video of Drew's hooded figure, grunting as his nails were pulled; drugged with the pain he'd endured, was hard enough. When they'd started smashing his hands and feet with the hammer Logan had switched off. He already knew how it ended.

He sipped this time, sensing the flavours of the single malt, letting it torture the back of his throat as the knives of Drew's captors had inflicted horrendous pain and suffering. Logan saw the hands quiver and Drew's body arch as each was hacked from the wrist. The keening of his friend's agony at each strike and the spattering of the black red blood on the lens of the camera stained his memory as the amber liquid stained his gullet.

'Another.'

The barman looked up; opened his mouth to object. Thinking better of it he poured again. Logan regarded the golden surface, visualising in it the slice of the sword, which separated Drew's head from his body.

A gulp.

Then the face: accusing, demonic, uncaring. It was a face from the past and one he thought he might never see again. But to witness it in these circumstances: towering over a dead, mutilated friend a muted messenger, disturbed him. He knew what he must do.

*

'Dropping the assignment is out of the question.' Amanda Galbraith's features were set and Logan knew that he had, in reality, little chance of success. Still, he had to try.

'You don't understand …'

'I don't need to. Look, Steve, I like you when a lot of people here would rather see you trip and fall on your own sword. You get the job done and you don't take shit from anybody. I admire that in an operative and there're precious few round here willing to take that level of responsibility. But you have enemies who'd rather see a good man fail than understand the bigger picture. I need your focus; your commitment.'

'I appreciate what you say, and the support behind it, but you really don't understand.'

Galbraith sighed. Sometimes it was difficult to support people you knew were good but who had an overblown sense of their own importance – even when you liked them. 'Okay Steve, enlighten me. What don't I understand?'

*

Logan paused the playback. Amanda Galbraith was ashen faced.

'Steve ... what can I say? Is that Assiz.'

'It's him alright. We lost sight of him once he left the force – it was a traumatic time for him.'

'And there was no indication that he would become fundamentalist?' The question was rhetorical though Logan answered anyway.

'You could say we should have known.'

'Yes, I would have thought it was a possibility,' Galbraith replied laconically. 'You shot his sister when there might have been reasonable doubt as to her status. It's a damnable business when we're so bound up in fear and subterfuge.'

He shrugged. 'What's done is done. I wasn't proud of what happened.'

'Oh good.'

Logan bristled. 'Look. What's important is that Assiz represents a clear and present danger. What happened is a taster for the main show. It's symbolic – decapitating the Beast makes it directionless. Cutting off the hands means no retaliation. Our only issue is which comes first? This is election year in the States. Does he target the candidates; the President; Congress or Senate, or all of them? Senator Harry Johnson has to be a primary target, given his stance on drugs and terrorism, and his position in the ratings.'

'Well, we need to find out, and fast. We're after one man out of billions and he's ahead of us. You have to be up to the job, given the nature of the real and personal threat he's issued against you?'

'You've made it clear there isn't an option. Assiz has issued me with a direct challenge: "stop me". I guess if I don't try it will confirm his perception and he will see his martyrdom justified.' Logan pondered and sighed. 'You're right – I have to do this.'

She appraised her agent and felt a rising disquiet despite her earlier words. Did this cloud his judgement? Would the threat be neutralised by keeping him out of the equation, or would the attack go ahead anyway? She gave voice to her concern.

'I thought that if I kept out of the way that would make him more visible, more prone to mistakes as he tried to find me. But he's resourceful and he'll find a way to deal with both me and his primary mission.' Logan paused, deep in consideration. 'No, it's best I tackle this head on.'

Galbraith nodded as she digested Logan's words. A plan formulated in her head and she nodded her head again.

'Okay, start your planning. You must prevent Assiz from completing his assignment, but look out for yourself. Something tells me your presence is crucial to the best outcome of this.'

Logan rose. 'Thanks Amanda … for understanding.'

Galbraith looked squarely at her agent. 'Don't thank me until we've stopped Assiz.'

As he closed the door behind him Galbraith pressed the intercom button on her desk. 'Debbie, could you come up to see me please. Now.'

*

The hotel room was dark save for the glow from the idev's screen. Leaning against the headboard the viewer regarded the cryptic message from the imam. Faulkner's body had been left for the British authorities and the state of it could not have sent a clearer message to them and their American masters.

Assiz picked up the glass of whiskey. Allah would surely forgive him at this time as he prepared to blend himself with the accursed enemy. He watched the eddying currents in the liquid, while his mind processed the import of the message. Logan had counted Faulkner as a friend – if he had but known he would tremble at the thought of the coming storm.

Perhaps he did. Maybe Faulkner's British woman had delivered the message sent to MI6; that told Logan he was a hunted man.

Assiz downed the whiskey – Laphroaig, the only connection he now had with his one-time friend from London. Retribution would taste as good.

*

'You're booked on a British Airways flight to Washington D.C. You'll be landing at 16:20 Eastern Seaboard Time. A CIA agent will be waiting for you when you clear customs. Her name is Charlie Richter and she'll accompany you down to Camp Lejeune the following day. When you're there you'll meet the Marines who carried out the Yemeni and Venezuelan ops.'

The agent regarded the face staring back from the photo Galbraith had just pushed to his idev. Open expression, deep brown eyes staring from plain features, which were relieved only by good cheekbones. Nice, but in a crowd she'd be almost instantly forgotten – potential agent material. He noted she wore no makeup, meaning she was either very comfortable in her own skin, or just not bothered by outward expressions. He doubted there was a partner.

'What does she do?'

'She's a senior analyst with the Crime and Narcotics Centre.'

'Why her?'

'She's working on movements of drugs and personnel between Colombia, Yemen and Afghanistan. My CIA counterpart, Sarah Markham, and I believe the events are all related.'

'What do these Marines, that I'm going to see, know?'

'That's just it, they probably don't realise the importance of some of the things they've seen. It's your task to investigate and develop a response. They certainly won't link them to any attack on the Republican Presidential candidate. Don't forget, the Yanks will want to know the credibility of our intel so that they can plan their potential responses appropriately.'

'Is there an appropriate response to this threat?'

Galbraith remained silent as she regarded Logan. Then. 'A moot point but we need to ensure there is something, that it's the most favourable available and it protects those individuals who are threatened.'

Logan raised himself easily from his chair. 'In that case I shall get on with my public protection task. Is there an itinerary?'

'There.' Galbraith tapped her idev and pushed a file to Logan's.

'Thanks.'

'I'll expect a report tomorrow. We'll do a full debrief when you get back to London. Best of luck, Steve.'

'Thanks chief.'

Twelve

Logan settled into his business class seat aboard Speedbird 1378 bound for Washington D.C. A stewardess brought him drinks and nibbles which he grazed on as the Boeing Dreamliner fled the night pursuing them across the Atlantic. Logan checked through the files Galbraith had given him then, satisfied, dropped his idev into a pocket and shut his eyes – time to sleep before he got into the US capital.

*

'Change of plans.'

'How come?' Charlie considered her director who looked decidedly jittery today. That was unusual – and scary – she decided. It wasn't often Markham got spooked by events.

'Our friends in London have advised us of a credible threat, to the President and the Republican Presidential candidate, which is unfolding.'

'Harry Johnson?' It was a superfluous question, involuntarily exposed.

Sarah Markham raised an eyebrow. 'We believe so. Johnson's vocal and active support of counter-insurgency operations abroad has been a defining element of his campaign. He's a true believer in the "hit them first, so they can't hit us" philosophy. It seems to have favour in the home market and it's now having an effect abroad too.'

Charlie had to agree. It seemed highly likely Johnson would be the next President of the United States. Winning three in a row was all the Democrats had done, on the back of Republican disarray. Now the population were tired of broken social promises and ineffective foreign policies. They were eager to embrace the rhetoric of the current Republican candidate who promised "a return to the values that had once made America great".

Whatever those were.

Fine sentiments thought Charlie but, as a devout Democrat, she knew any advances were hard won and even harder to maintain. She knew the country would lurch from tired philosophy to the bankruptcy of social hierarchy and the old caste system. Losing Johnson might not be a bad idea.

Stop it! She reprimanded herself sharply. As a government servant she was not paid to think such things. A human being had a right to be protected, whatever their political persuasion. The bigger battle was for freedom of the individual and the state.

'Do we know where the threat is likely to land?'

'London couldn't or wouldn't give us any details. However, they're flying the agent you're to meet out today. They're interested to hear what you've uncovered about the situation in the Yemen and South America.'

Charlie nodded. 'Johnson is a big advocate of the Colombian opposition and has repeatedly vocalised his support of Sanchez who is seeking election as well. It can't be a coincidence that this threat ties in with the elections, both here and in Colombia.'

'Quite,' Markham replied. 'And Johnson's belief is that, if he gets into power, Sanchez will be able to destroy the drugs trade which epitomizes his country. Which is ironic,' Markham remarked thinking of Richter's earlier appraisal.

'Somebody needs to, because it's getting no better.' Charlie confided fervently, missing her boss's irony, 'but Sanchez?' We've beheaded the Cucuta Cartel and that vacuum will be filled quickly. Al-Qaeda will be looking for a contact quick and Venezuela will be happy to broker the deal with any new cartel owner. We have to support a pro-American Colombian government against that alliance. The one element of this we currently can't influence is the Asian one. We have less knowledge and we're mired in the Yemen after saying "no repeat of Afghanistan". The attacks against the coalition there are getting better organised, and there's every reason to suppose that another force is behind the Taliban and al-Qaeda, giving them technology to disrupt our operations. Look at what happened in the Aden debacle.'

'Fortunately it hasn't reached further yet. We need to be a step ahead in this game; against an enemy adept at hiding in the open.'

'So do we think the Brits have evidence we can use?'

'Who knows with them? It's probably jack shit but the guy's credentials are cast iron so we give him the benefit of the doubt.'

'When does he arrive?'

'He arrives early evening, on a BA flight from Heathrow.' Markham pushed a photograph from her idev to Charlie's. The picture on the screen showed a man with even features and cropped, black hair, whose face seemed to permanently border on a smile not mirrored in the searching green eyes. Charlie felt herself exposed and shivered.

'Why me? It's not my job, I'm not an operative.'

'No you're not. But you are the senior analyst on this project and I will put those resources where I consider they need to be.' Markham checked her watch, preventing argument. 'You've got about six hours before his flight lands. Check him in at the Hilton; then you gotta to pick him up early in the morning.'

Charlie felt a sinking feeling hit the bottom of her stomach. 'Why?'

'You're down to Camp Lejeune for lunch time, where you'll interview Marines from the Twenty-Seventh and Forty-First Marine Recon Units.'

'I won't even ask.'

'Good. Report back day after tomorrow, at seventeen hundred hours,' were Markham's final words before she disappeared leaving Charlie with her jumbled thoughts.

*

Charlie's eyes flicked from the photo to the lines of people heading out of customs and back, attempting to identify the Englishman she'd been tasked to rendezvous with. Being short was frustrating as it disabled her in situations such as these. The sea of humanity rolled towards her, all types, shapes and sizes. Where was he?

'Hello.'

She started; turned and there, stood next to her, was the man she'd been looking for. Immediately she could see the eyes weren't as unfathomable as the photo had suggested. In fact, they held a pool of humour, which complemented the smiling face just right.

'Are you –?'

'Charlie …'

He smiled again and she felt herself go slightly weak inside. 'Sorry. You go first.'

Charlie mentally pulled herself together. 'Steve Logan?' He nodded. 'Charlie Richter, CIA,'

'Pleased to meet you.'

His handshake was easy, with just the right amount of pressure. His hand was large around hers. Stop it! 'And you.'

'You can let go of my hand now.'

'Sorry!' She withdrew her hand quickly and tried to stop the blush she felt rising. 'Do you have a case to collect?'

'Got everything I need in here,' Logan tapped the rucksack slung over a shoulder. 'I could do with a shower and something to eat though.'

'You travel light then?' The Brit's top lip twisted in ironic acknowledgement and Charlie coughed to cover her fluster. 'Well, let's get you to your hotel.'

'Sounds good, and where's the best place to eat?'

Good question Steve, Charlie thought, realising she knew nothing about the capital and, worse, hadn't researched anything before she came to pick up her ward. He'd think she was a complete idiot. 'How about I drop you off, and pick you up again about eight? That'll give you time to freshen up. Then I'll take you somewhere.'

'Pick me up at eight? Are you taking me out?' The sparkle in his eyes told her he'd be trouble. Hopefully!

'I might be; courtesy of Uncle Sam of course.'

'Of course.' Logan hoisted his bag comfortably onto his shoulder. 'You'd best get me to the hotel so I can make myself look presentable. Lead on.'

As Charlie led the Brit from airport arrivals a man regarded them silently. Charlie was oblivious but Logan knew he was there.

*

'Nice car.' Logan eased himself into the passenger seat of Charlie's Z5.

'Thanks: I bet it isn't as good as yours, is it?'

Logan laughed; an easy unaffected sound. 'You mean the Aston Martin issued to all MI6 officers?' Charlie flushed. 'Sorry to deflate your bubble but I don't have one. First, the government's budget doesn't run to it, second we're about blending in and, lastly, I'm not really a car man. I've got a Ford Mondeo,' he finished apologetically.

'Oh.'

'I see I've disappointed you already.'

'No, no, honestly. It just wasn't what I was … expecting … I guess.'

'Whoops. Quick let's get some dinner before British-American relations slip any further. Where are you taking me?'

'There's a steakhouse not far away. I thought we'd go there. It's reasonable,' *I hope!* 'And the portions are man-sized.'

'Interesting.'

*

The portions were indeed man-sized, Logan decided as the waiter took away their plates, if not cow-sized. He'd tried his best but he'd been unable to finish the damn thing off.

'Defeated,' he smiled at his hostess. 'So, while we sit here recovering, tell me more about yourself.'

'There isn't much to tell. I've led a pretty uneventful life. Never been out of the States save once; worked in government since leaving Stanford.'

'An exciting part of government though?'

'Well, yes, I guess. I've never thought about it before. Much of what I do is statistics and data analysis and interpreting what's fed into us. This is the closest I've got to a field operation.'

'Well I'd better make sure there's some excitement for you.'

'No thanks! My Z5's enough excitement for me.'

'Okay, how about coffee then? Thrilling enough?' Logan waived the waiter over.

Charlie smiled at his easy charm. 'I can just about manage that. And now, you have to tell me about yourself.'

'Where do you want me to start?'

'At the beginning.'

'Well, apparently, though I don't remember it much, it was quite messy.'

'Be serious,' she scolded him.

An hour later she knew more about him, he realised, than perhaps he'd told anybody in a long time. The coffees were drained as were the liqueurs they'd ordered and Logan felt unusually relaxed in her presence.

'So is there a Mrs Logan?'

Logan looked up sharply, cursing inwardly. He'd let his guard down, which wasn't good around strangers. Charlie showed no malice, no ulterior motive; just a sense of getting to know him better was all. Even so.

'There was. I think I was more married to the job than the woman – it didn't suit.'

'Oh, I'm sorry. How long ago?'

'Long enough not to need to remember it.'

Charlie coloured: she felt she'd overstepped the mark and sought another topic. 'How long have you

101

been with MI6?'

'I've been with SIS for about four years now.' He looked round for the waiter. 'Can I have the bill please,' he said as one moved towards the table.

'SIS?'

'Secret Intelligence Service. MI6 is the colloquial term for it like your CIA is known as "The Firm" or "The Company".'

'Oh right. What sort of things do you do?'

'Everything we do is beyond UK borders. Intelligence gathering; planning and operations.'

'Have you ever ...?'

'Ever what?' Logan stared at the young woman.

'Ever … killed anybody.' Her voice was low, a whisper, and ... embarrassed? It was, after all, a pretty ridiculous question. MI6 wasn't in the business of killing people. But when she took in the Brit she saw something she didn't expect – pain. Logan just stared at her: no words, nothing but a haunted look of torment.

An uncomfortable silence descended over them. They walked to the car, the distance between them breaking the earlier rapport which had seemed so easy to build. Charlie cursed herself for stepping on the man's toes. 'Look, I'm sorry,' she began.

'Don't be. You did nothing wrong, I'm just sensitive talking about my past. Anyway, it's beyond my bedtime and we have a busy day ahead, so, if you don't mind.'

'Mind what?'

Logan caught the tut just in time. 'Can I return to the hotel please?'

'Oh! Sorry, I didn't understand.'

'No problem.' Logan settled stoically into the passenger seat and waited.

As they pulled out of the parking lot an innocuous, dark coloured sedan followed them. Its lone occupant pursued them through the late evening Washington traffic.

Thirteen

Next morning Logan rose early, put in an hour on the weights and cardio at the hotel gym, and then headed for the restaurant. He took in the vast amounts of food being piled on the plates of huge Americans and shook his head privately, deciding to keep his options simple. A nation going to hell in a dietary handcart.

His mobile went off as he was eating. 'Hello?'

'Good morning.' It was Charlie Richter. 'I'm on my way to pick you up. I'll be about half an hour. We have to get to Andrews Air Force Base to catch a flight down to Lejeune.'

'Okay, I'm just finishing breakfast. Meet you in the lobby.'

'See you there.'

*

The MH-101 Merlin touched down at Camp Lejeune at eleven, oh-seven precisely, just as the Marine Captain pilot had said she would. Logan walked easily down the ramp, an exercise he'd completed many times in the past. Charlie managed it with a little less panache, cursing the skirt and heels she'd decided to wear.

Two striking individuals stood at the edge of the apron. Both wore battle fatigues with tall forage caps. One stood in a relaxed manner that belied a sense of suppressed energy. His features were deeply tanned as if he'd spent too much time in desert environs. The other, bolt upright with arms folded behind her, was the perfect specimen of a superbly controlled, combat-ready weapon. Her dark features were impassive and the skin had a healthy glow telling of a person in peak physical condition.

As Logan and Charlie stopped before them, the first extended his hand. 'Good morning miss; sir. I trust you had a comfortable flight from the capital?'

'Very much so, thanks,' Logan responded, 'and the pilot was spot on with her times.'

'Carla's our best, so that's no surprise. Well; welcome to Camp Lejeune, East Coast home of the Marine Corps. I'm the base commandant, Major Harry Shapiro – and no jokes,' he warned as he saw the look on Logan's face. It brought an easy air to the little gathering. 'This is Captain Baptista, my adjutant.' He looked at the Englishman. 'You must be Steve Logan?'

'That's right, Field Operations, Secret Intelligence Service and this,' he indicated his companion, 'is Charlie Richter from the CIA's Crime and Narcotics Centre.' After the obligatory handshakes they began to walk towards the main building. 'Do you know why we're here,' Logan asked Shapiro.

'I have a reasonable idea, but I'm willing to hear it from you. First, let's get over to the conference facility and meet the teams.' Shapiro set a brisk pace off the apron.

Logan continued talking. 'You have two separate narc wars on two different continents, which you may be aware are connected but not how, or the full extent.' When he caught the commandant's nod, Logan carried on. 'We had a situation back home last week when a body was found on the banks of the Thames.' Logan paused. 'It was the ex-station chief for the CIA in London; Drew Faulkner: a personal friend of mine too. Drew was investigating the movement of narcotics between Afghanistan and the

US. He was operating under the radar because of concerns over who he could trust. He'd been out of the picture for some time.'

'So how did you find out?'

'Long story.' The images still clung to his retina. 'Anyway, I've done some digging and it seems there are links between the poppy fields of Afghanistan and the cocaine plantations of Latin America. But there's something more.'

'Here we are.'

They were the first words spoken by Baptista, interrupting the discussion, as she held open a door for the party. They trooped in, Shapiro marching ahead, through double doors and then taking a right into a large, airy and cool conference room, inhabited by twenty or so Marines of various ranks. One stood out immediately: a big Afro-American Sergeant, with piercing eyes and a hooded appearance. Logan recognised a man with a clouded past, who wished for it to remain so. The door closed behind them and Shapiro addressed the assembled Marines.

'Ladies and gentlemen, I'd like you to meet Charlie Richter from the CIA and Steve Logan from the UK's Secret Intelligence Service, the people you probably know better as MI6.'

There were murmurs of greeting from the reclining Marines whose interest, Logan noted, was less than that of Shapiro and Baptista.

'So, what gives? Why you here?' This from the Marine Sergeant he'd first noticed when they'd entered.

'What's your name?'

'Durant.'

'Do you have a first name?'

'Durant'll do just fine.'

106

'Sergeant!' Shapiro began to admonish Durant but Logan laid a restraining hand on the major's shoulder.

'It's okay Major. Well, Durant, "what gives", is that we're at war on several fronts and why I'm here is to work with your people to piece it together.'

'And you'd be the man to do it?'

'Not necessarily. I'm just trying to help find some answers.'

''Cause a spook is what we need right now, ain't it?'

'Sergeant!'

'No, he has a point Major. You're right Durant, perhaps a spook isn't what we need right now, but it's what we have. You really want to know why I'm here? Okay, I lost a friend, a compatriot of yours. He was a good man, working for his country the way he knew best. For that … people … cut off his hands, then decapitated him, perhaps because it would hurt more that way, and humiliate him. So, it's personal for me too. It's a signal the West is threatened like never before; that al-Qaeda wants our head.

'More than that, the people who did this want us out of their country, so they can visit the unspeakable on their own people without sanction. How they're doing that is by flooding our countries with drugs: dividing our resources in ways that cannot be countered by conventional means.'

'Hey, buddy, what you trying to say about what we did out there? We took the fight to the enemy and wiped their shit from the earth.' Murmurs of approval followed Durant's words.

'You guys were in Venezuela, right? And you think that was the end of it, sergeant,' Logan regarded him squarely, 'you think these people are so easily defeated?'

'Hey, the sarge is right. We took those douche-bags down big time! They won't be back any time soon.' This from a suitably hard-core looking private, sitting next to Durant.

Logan smiled ironically and shook his head. 'I wish I shared your optimism. By the time your choppers were heading back with their stash, another five operations were plugging the gap. Drugs operations are like brambles. You can't take off the head and leave it at that, because the roots are so deep and complicated. You have to think differently.'

'And you're the man are you?' Durant shook his head. 'Man! You Brits always think you have the answers. We have to take the fight to them, on our terms and take no shit.'

A chorus of "hoo-ahs" rose from the assembly. Shapiro and Baptista let Logan fend for himself – he seemed capable; Charlie kept her head down too. Logan regarded the raucous Marines who believed they'd got him on the run.

'Okay, so you believe that you have those guys beaten, yeah?'

There were nods and affirmatives across the group.

'So why did Baltimore Police Department seize a fifteen-million-dollar shipment of heroin and twenty-three million dollars of cocaine off the streets at the weekend? Shipped via Maracaibo from an operation working just over the Colombian border in the town of Cucuta? The heroin was packed in bags with Pashtu writing on them – a clear sign that militants from Northern Pakistan were involved. This Monday the Colombian Minister for Justice, Carlos Estevez was murdered by a car bomb which showed all the hallmarks of a Taliban IED.'

Logan paced back and forth in the space in front of

the marines. 'This is an enemy who doesn't want to be seen, who can't be seen. It's an adversary who waits in full view, until he can see the whites of your eyes, before striking. You were lucky the other week, the intel was good, but it happens too rarely for you to make any real headway.'

'So what's your answer?'

'You fight their way – dirty.'

'You're a spook. What do you know?'

'I was a commander in Twenty-Two Regiment, and did a tour with Fourteen Company: one of only a select few Twenty-Two Regiment people ever to get through their training course.'

'What …?'

'Mr Logan is giving you the benefit of his history,' offered Shapiro sharply. 'He was a member of the SAS before becoming an Operator with a very secret and very select group of undercover paramilitary operatives in the British Army.'

'Thank you Major.' Logan saw the demeanour of the marines change. The SAS was held in deep respect by armed forces the world over. Fourteen Company was a shadow organisation known of by very few and Logan was impressed that Shapiro knew even as little as he did.

'So you're gonna tell us how to fight eh?' Durant still played hardass.

'If you like,' Logan riposted, 'though, right now, I'm more interested in what happened down south and how the Tally are reacting. Then we can decide how to take the fight to them. Agreed?'

Durant was silent for what seemed an eternity and all eyes gravitated on the big American. 'Okay, what do you want from us?'

'Just tell it how it was.'

The big sergeant shrugged, *"that's it?"* his expression said. 'Pretty much as the report says.'

'I read that,' returned Logan. 'Said, if it wasn't for your sniping the casualties would have been much higher.'

Durant made no comment.

'So talk me through what happened,' Logan encouraged. After a pause Durant obliged, speaking quietly and lucidly; ensuring he left out nothing important. He paused when he got to the point where the building had erupted in flame, killing his company commander.

Recovering, he finished reluctantly. 'You were right earlier. The Colombians are getting harder to beat. We were lucky and caught them off guard. It's not always like that anymore. They have help from some serious operators.'

Logan nodded. 'How's that?'

'They're organised in cells, like small military units. It used to be a business to them. Now they want to take over the country.'

'Strong opinions.'

'You asked.'

Logan turned to the adjutant. 'Captain Baptista, what's the Yemeni experience?'

'I wasn't there Mr Logan, however these guys have just returned in the last fortnight from their tour there.' She indicated the group of Marines who were sitting at the back of the room. There was deadness in the eyes, as if the memory of combat had drained love and emotion from them.

'Who was in charge?' Logan searched the etched faces.

A private answered. He looked old beyond his years, as if from some deep-seated weariness.

'Captain Fellowes was our commander. He took the hit for us.' The voice held that awe reserved for the memory of men prepared to sacrifice their lives for their comrades.

'What happened?'

'The guys we're encountering were wired. Sure, we've come across drug use for years but there was more commitment this time. And they were able to field better, more serious equipment. Some of your guys in the Royal Marine Commandos took a real bad hit too.'

'Who are you?'

'Gutierrez, I was comms.'

'What was the action?'

'We were responding to the takeover of the food station south of Aden. It was a trap. We were pinned down and when we called in fast air, they Firestormed it.'

Logan raised an eyebrow. A Firestorm was unusual in Yemen. 'And what happened with Fellowes?'

'When we couldn't abort the attack, the captain used flares to try and divert the planes. The first strike hit our position; the second landed in the dead zone between us and the enemy. If it hadn't been for him, we would all have been killed.'

'Is he …?'

Gutierrez's face darkened for a moment. 'He was flown home. He lost his legs and he's at Sinai now having new biomechanical ones fitted, lost a lung from the shrapnel.'

'I'm sorry to hear that.' Gutierrez and the others seemed grateful – they understood the sincerity implied in Logan's words. 'Firestorming is fairly unusual in that theatre isn't it? How …?'

111

'How'd they do it?' the Marine shrugged resignedly. 'It isn't the first time our comms have been subverted, but usually we maintain some function. This time was more sophisticated, better planned. Like they had newer kit; as if they were waiting for us.'

Logan turned to Richter. 'Charlie, what's your take on this?'

Charlie had been quite happy, forgotten at the side of the room. She coloured as she was drawn into the presence of so much testosterone. 'I agree with – umm – both observations. The Colombians are much better organised in terms of military style operations, and there has been movement back and forth of Taliban operatives. For the latter, they're able to get their opium to market faster, and thus make money, which funds the ability to buy better armaments for themselves and al-Qaeda, with whom they're strengthening their links. We can verify the Firestorm Gutierrez talked about. This is the first time we've seen it implemented so completely in the battlefield.'

'Meaning?'

'Meaning terrorist groups don't usually do that sort of thing without outside help.'

Logan perused the words. 'So the Colombians are better organised; the Taliban and the Arabs are better armed, better assisted and they're both getting their drugs onto American and European streets faster than ever. What's the score with Venezuela?'

'Well, before he died, Chavez took Ortega from the ranks of the military and into his inner circle. He confesses the same Anti-US sentiment as Escobar and so was a natural successor when Chavez was assassinated by US-backed insurgents back in 2015.'

'I remember that,' replied Logan. 'Weren't Covert

Nine responsible for providing support and clean up?'

Richter nodded. 'They were reputed to be the unit responsible though it was never confirmed.'

'And so relations deteriorated even faster and Venezuela became the unofficial broker for every nefarious activity imaginable against the US.'

'Exactly.'

'What about the current set up?' Baptista interrupted. 'Yemen was a big surprise for us. We figured Guardian was ahead of the game, but what they had ready for us took all of us by surprise. It was a Firestorm like nothing before it. Yet it was as if something was being tested, for a bigger gig.'

'The problem with the region is it's completely different to us in culture, religion, technological advancement, equality,' Logan responded after a moment's reflection. 'You name it, we couldn't be further apart. But it's always been like that with the Arabs; al-Qaeda is merely the militant aspect of that difference. No, what we should really be worried about is the level of support they now attract – that doesn't come from the likes of Ortega. Another, more powerful, nation must be behind this, whether it's the latest hardware making its way to the new frontline or IT which enables these guys to spike our software.'

Richter nodded in agreement. 'There is some evidence that the armaments are coming from surrounding "broken" Islamic states,' she commented. 'Kyrgyzstan and Turkmenistan both had volumes of artillery pieces and AFVs that were surplus to their requirements and on the market.'

'How complete is that evidence?' Shapiro responded for the first time in a while.

'It's compiled from ground Intel and overflights documenting movements and arms deals. We also received human intelligence on a recent deal which apparently went sour.'

Shapiro considered Richter. 'How current is the humint?'

'Very. Submitted to the Pentagon only last month. It was up to their oversight committee to decide how to employ it.'

'Good of them to tell our guys what was coming down the track,' Shapiro opined laconically. Logan smiled wryly. 'Is there anything else the CIA hasn't told the troops it might be useful knowing?'

Richter blushed and stammered. 'N-not as far as I'm aware.'

'Okay, well if you think of anything, be sure to let us know.'

The uncomfortable moment lengthened before Logan decided to break it. 'It's not Miss Richter who controls release, that's down to the Pentagon. Charlie, what do we know about the sales?'

Recovering herself, she reached in her holdall. 'I've got the information here on my idev. May I?' She indicated the big screen at the front of the room: Shapiro nodded. Minutes later Richter had her presentation running. Curiously, standing at the front, delivering to the group made her more relaxed, and she could hide the less confident Charlie behind a façade.

She clicked the button on the remote and a picture of a Middle Eastern man came up. Swarthy, thickset features were hidden behind a wiry jet-coloured beard. Dark hooded eyes pierced the observer inquiringly rather than malevolently, as if he needed to know just who you actually were.

'This is Farouq Jamal, Egyptian, forty-six years old and a relatively recent convert to Fundamentalist

Islam. He was a general in the Egyptian Army until 2013 when he resigned his commission to attend the University of Islamabad, taking religious studies and politics. He graduated in 2017 but quickly reverted to his old profession, using contacts old and new to become an arms dealer. During his time in Islamabad he set up contacts with the local Taliban networks and created his own quasi-political group called "The Light of Truth".'

'I've heard of them,' interrupted Logan. 'They weren't exactly a light in the darkness of political or religious reformation.'

'Quite. Anyway, Jamal used it as a front for working with some seriously loaded arms dealers across the frontiers. That way he was able to establish a market place for major military equipment at the crossroads of several Islamist cultures. Initially he kept it to materiel that could be moved easily so that excluded most aviation and anything naval. However, there is evidence that he recently took on a number of Army Aviation aircraft, including a Kamov Hoodoo assault 'copter.'

'Great, just what we need.' Baptista shook her head.

'I wouldn't worry too much about that in the immediate future,' declared Logan, 'We have the same intel and the SAS have it clearly in their sights and won't let it get anywhere near the frontline. But it does represent a clear escalation of the problem.'

'Sure does,' continued Charlie. 'However, the Taliban aren't moving from their tried and trusted formula of IEDs and suicide bombers. Jamal was seen last year at a maddrassah talking on several occasions to this man, Sayed –'

'Assiz,' Logan finished for the CIA analyst.

'Yes ...' Richter was intrigued. 'You know him?'

'You could say that.' *How much to tell?* 'He was an officer in CO19 when I first came across him. He went rogue after his sister was – shot – by mistake just for, as he saw it, wearing a burqa. We lost sight of him and wondered where he was.' Logan chose not to mention his hand in the shooting; the viral he'd seen of his ex-friend, or the message it bore – now wasn't the time.

'Well we're wondering now too. He was in Islamabad last Friday, then he boarded a plane bound for Heathrow. The trail goes cold there.'

'How credible a threat is this Assiz? And what does he have to do with what we're talking about today?' Shapiro looked enquiringly at Richter.

'We're not sure yet but he'd been identified at training sites across Northern Pakistan for several months following his resignation from CO19 and flight from the UK.

'He was also seen with this imam,' Richter flicked to another shot. 'Mohammad al-Siddiqi. He's a hardliner in the Taliban; came over from al-Qaeda and is wanted in several countries across the Middle East for fomenting unrest. He's also the chief suspect in the organisation and expediting of the Central Park atrocity last year.'

Memories of the massacre of thirty Jews at a wedding party, together with over a hundred bystanders injured and dying in the ensuing fire fight, loomed large in everyone's thoughts. It had been the single biggest shoot-out in New York's history with ten masked gunmen taking on New York Police Department's SWAT and the National Guard in a running battle that ran over two days.

They regarded the man in the photograph, now

viewed as Number 1 on the FBI's "Most Wanted" list. Richter continued. 'Al-Siddiqi was a low-grade lieutenant in bin Laden's network until the latter's termination by SEAL Team Six. In the aftermath he decided to establish his own operation, leading to the Central Park event as the first of many. He's now high on a CIA watch list.'

Shapiro nodded. 'What else?'

Richter hesitated then brought up the next picture. It was a charismatic looking man, whose clear features appeared a blank page, promoted by the politician's welcoming smile. The perfectly groomed hair, deep tan and expensive clothes, spoke of gained wealth, rather than breeding; of business, rather than inheritance.

'That's Eduardo Sanchez isn't it?' When Richter nodded Shapiro continued. 'He's the opposition politician in Colombia who's running in next year's election. Isn't he standing on an anti-drugs, anti-corruption platform?'

'That's right major.'

'He's also a personal friend of Harry Johnson, the Republican Presidential candidate.'

'Again, correct.'

'So where does he play into this?'

'That's what we'd like to know. Sanchez seems to have appeared from nowhere, inveigled himself into Johnson's inner circle and been accepted, even to the extent of being bankrolled for his own Presidential campaign. What does our man receive in return? Perhaps it's the kudos of being instrumental in the overturning of a known, corrupt system and defeating the drugs barons. We don't know yet.'

'And what does Sanchez get?'

'Political credibility; money; and the ability to

appear honest and fulsome for the American market.'

Baptista scrutinized the analyst. 'But you think there's something more to this?'

'The guy lives in shadows. I'd like to know what's in his past; to know what he does when the spotlight's not on him.'

Fourteen

The black suited bodyguards stood motionless beneath the blanket of early afternoon heat, aviator glasses reflecting back the copper sun. Beneath a pristine white awning sat a woman and two men, sipping long, cold drinks. The woman wore silk, a translucent affair hinting at the tanned, toned body beneath, mocking the heat of another Mexican summer's day. Her long dark hair framed features, perfect, save for a mole on her top lip; while her legs drew admiring glances from one of the men. Harry Johnson admitted her beauty, but knew there was more to this woman than mere eye-candy. He attempted to keep his attention on his business partner but it was difficult.

'Harry, the action in Venezuela last week was potentially detrimental to my aspirations in Latin America. It will serve only to strengthen popular feeling for Ortega and feed anti-American resentment.' The other man spoke the clear and precise language of learnt English. He was a lean, handsome man, who dressed easily but impeccably, his black hair cut and styled perfectly, his brown eyes clear and insightful.

'Eduardo, you know I have no power over the actions of the Administration. I –'

'You underestimate your power. Is that deliberate, or from naivety? You have shown yourself to be more than capable when it suits you: now I ask that you perform a miracle for me.'

Harry Johnson laughed uneasily and drew a hand through his thick, greying hair. He knew he didn't match up to the Colombian when it came to presence.

119

For sure he exercised hard and was careful with his diet, but ageing was a remorseless process which couldn't be halted, merely slowed for an indeterminate time. Sanchez was proof that younger men were always pushing at the door of power – Johnson just hoped he had a firm grip on the handle. 'Miracles don't come cheap and they're not like buses.'

'But doesn't the great USA like to please its friends?'

Johnson glanced briefly at his security detail, standing impassively a discreet distance away and seemingly oblivious to the conversation. He ran a finger inside his moist collar. 'We like to *help* our friends, and there's a big difference. My country has had its fingers burnt too many times in the past to go round pleasing people hey willy nilly.'

'You want Cordoba out of office and the Venezuelan problem resolved don't you?'

'Not at any price. The current US administration is conducting a foreign policy based on balanced power, and if I get in that's exactly the route I'll be following. Can you stomach that?'

'Power is never balanced Senor Johnson, that's the whole point of power. What we can hope for is that we gain enough to weaken our enemies and defeat them. You want Ortega out so that you can close down the coke and coffee trafficking.'

'Of course.'

'Well,' Sanchez opened his arms wide and smiled, 'we have the same goals.'

'But what of this connection between the cartels and al-Qaeda? How do we stop them working together? Either the cocaine ends up killing youngsters back home, or being used by al-Qaeda to fuel their fighters killing American service people in Yemen.'

'Do you think that is your biggest problem, Senator?'

The woman spoke up for the first time and Johnson looked her quizzically. 'How do you mean?'

She smiled at him; though her eyes hadn't joined in. Delaying her reply, she sipped on her drink, teasing the American with her silence. As he made to encourage her she spoke. 'You do not mention your role in the growing industry of artificially pollinated foodstuffs and the increasing cross border illicit trade in important foods: a trade that is beginning to rival drugs as the next great illegal activity.'

'Well,' Johnson blustered, 'the foodstuffs issues are a small part of the problem. Drugs remain the single most important criminal issue to be resolved.'

The woman smiled again. 'If you say so; others would disagree.'

'Victoria, please, you are embarrassing our guest.' Sanchez patted her leg, though the action patronised only the American. The Colombian turned to the Senator who looked distinctly uncomfortable.

'Apologies Senator but I believe you might find we are of some use to your endeavours.'

Johnson raised an eyebrow. 'How might that be?'

Sanchez smiled at Victoria. 'Please show our Senator-friend what we know.'

Victoria placed her idev on the glass-topped table between them. Pressing an icon on the device a slither of light spilled over the empty top of the table to construct a screen. She indicated it.

'If you will, Senator.'

Johnson watched at the pictures forming. A figure photographed from afar. A company logo and stock figure charts. All elements he knew. How was his poker face?

'And what is this?' He looked from Sanchez to the woman, trying to feign perplexity.

'Harry, please.' The plea was leavened with irony. 'Let us not have to explain this for you.'

'No, please. Explain it to me.' Keep a touch of righteous indignation in the voice.

A look of amusement passed between Sanchez and Victoria. The woman dipped her head in acknowledgement. Her heavy red lips beckoned him into the honeyed trap.

Victoria indicated the figure. 'Al Stern, head of BioGerm: a company you have a controlling interest in through your holding company, General Stocks. Mr Stern is an interesting person, Stanford educated and running his own gene modification company, two years out of university. He knows your wife who represents his company as chief commercial legal brief for Brightman, Chase and Parfitt. Five years on his company works hard to find a solution for the increasing issue of crop pollination and he believes they have solved the problem.'

Victoria paused …

'So, BioGerm – just how do they get so many UN contracts to provide seed stock to under-developed countries?'

Johnson bristled. 'That's no secret when a company has a set of products that can solve the world's problems. BioGerm is innovative and they provide people with the solutions they need. What's wrong with that? And what is wrong with buying into that dream?'

Victoria smiled. 'Nothing at all Senator, but tell me, what happened in Bangladesh with the rice crop?'

She knew her stuff: Johnson flushed. 'There was nothing to link the failure of those crops to BioGerm's research or techniques.'

'Or the Mozambique maize harvest which was decimated by an unknown blight that subsequently plagued Zimbabwean and South African crops?' She regarded the hardness in the American's face. 'Exactly what is BioGerm into Senator?'

Johnson couldn't help the colour rising in his cheeks. 'I'm sure I don't know what you mean ...'

Victoria's smile stayed - the smile of a crocodile. 'No? Aren't you the chair of the Agriculture and Foods Senate Committee?' No reply. 'The committee that put ninety million dollars in to research on self-germinating grains? Isn't it true the grains were mutations and of value only as genetic bombing material; that, the grains were susceptible to blights and rot, reducing yields? And that those eating the modified meal were exposed to all manner of disease and deformities of unborn children. Almost like some form of social engineering.'

Johnson maintained his silent, though inwardly he was seething.

'You see, Senator, it's easy to overlook the mundane, the everyday, in the search for the elixir of life. BioGerm seemed like a positive force, didn't it? But what it actually did was strip from people their only source of food with a promise that was as solid as the emperor's new clothes. What a weapon that could be: a foodstuff tailored to attack particular genetic types. Aren't you also on the Senate Defence Appropriation Committee?'

'Where is all this going?' Johnson glowered, while his words refused to leave his mouth willingly.

'You need to relax Harry,' Sanchez regarded his counterpart coolly. 'Your heart won't cope.'

'What do you want?' Johnson gradually realised he was being raped and he was helpless to save himself.

'Your anti-drugs stance.'

'What about it?'

'I want to renegotiate our current arrangement.'

'What the fuck?!' Johnson's lip curled in a snarl. A bodyguard turned, he calmed himself.

'It is important for our relationship, Harry, that we have a common understanding. I need to satisfy certain business commitments that join our two countries.'

'You can't –'

'Yes we can and we will. If you refuse, then the world and, more importantly, your peers will find out exactly how involved you are with the emerging scandal that is BioGerm. What will that do to your Presidential title bid?'

What could he do? What could he say? He needed time: to think; to devise his escape. But would they give him the time?

'Wh-what's your plan?'

'Patience Senator. All you need know now is we own you and when we are ready we will tell you what we want you to do for us.' A pause. 'I think the meeting is now over.'

Johnson's perplexity stood as a monument to US imperial decline as he gaped at his onetime protagonists, now turned potential enemies. Inwardly he was seething. How dare this Latino shit tell him what he was going to do, how he was going to run his presidency. But for now...

'I hear what you are saying Eduardo.' He rose

from his chair and stared down at his new persecutor with as much statesmanship as he could muster – precious little. 'Well I guess I need to think things over. Give me a couple of days and I'll be back to you.'

The Colombian gazed up at his new found puppet. 'Don't worry Harry, we'll let you know soon enough what to do.'

'Yeah sure,' Johnson riposted defiantly as he walked from the patio to his waiting SUV, accompanied by his stoic security detail.

Eduardo Sanchez watched the Senator's entourage disappear up the trail from his ranch. He felt rather than physically noticed another appear by his side. He was relieved to be finished with the American, though his new partner filled him with no more enthusiasm for any perceived equality of power: rather a dread of further abuse. Still … what they offered was significantly better.

'Well, Mr Sanchez. How does the new feel?'

Eduardo Sanchez turned at last to his new companion. A tall, athletic man with clear skin and lustrous black hair cut short, Leong Chaozheng leaned easily on the railing that delineated the patio and stared after the receding Americans, the pair joined by this moment of change.

'It feels – good.' Sanchez felt the hesitation though he tried his best to hide it. 'I'm looking forward to our new relationship.'

Leong took a long hard look at his latest acquisition. 'Excellent, Mr Sanchez, I think we will be good for each other. The Chinese government is anxious to help Colombia establish itself on the world stage as an equal partner, developing agriculture, environmental links. In particular, we would be honoured to help you establish your Central America Pact.'

I wonder why? Sanchez returned the stare. 'I am glad; my country will be glad, of the assistance your government is able to offer.'

'Of course and we will offer you that. First we need to set the ground rules of our little partnership.'

Eduardo Sanchez swallowed. 'What might those be?'

Leong smiled and it wasn't pleasant. 'Let us get a drink first, this may take a little while.'

*

Penelope Hortez leaned over and turned the clock. Shit! Ten past nine. She shouldn't be here! She glanced down at the body, hesitated; then ran a finger down the flank, which twitched before a grunt bounced across the pillow. Kiric lifted his head sleepily and wrapped an arm round her, dragging her close: she offered no resistance.

'How are you?'

She smiled. 'All the better for waking up next to you. And you?'

Kiric nuzzled her neck in reply. 'I believe it is going to be a good day.'

Penelope Hortez extricated herself, rose from the bed and made her way to the bathroom. She could smell his scent on her. Almost she regretted having to wash it off. He was powerful, assured and calm and there was a humour that sprinkled his voice with sherbet – fizzing and sweet – when he spoke or kissed her.

The water danced over her body which felt more alive than she could ever remember. Calm yourself woman, she admonished herself but found she couldn't. His lovemaking had been inspired and inspiring, taking her on a journey of discovery her body had never known before. At once commanding and appreciative he had pleasured her in a way that had shaken her to her core.

Don't forget business.

Her practical self asserted itself. It was right. Kiric was just another man – but – but nothing! Just another man. When business is completed dump him! She soaped over herself and the touch said other things to her but she kept herself sane, switched off the shower, stepped out and...

... jumped.

Kiric regarded her with that cool dark gaze, a slight smile playing on his lips. 'You should stay.' For a moment she was freaked out by his appearance.

'I can't. I have to ensure everything is in order for Moscow in two weeks' time. The shipping needs to be sorted today.'

'Others can do that. You have other, more important business.'

'Which is?' She arched an eyebrow then gasped as he took her and ran his tongue over a nipple. Shaking her head Penelope pulled away. 'You have to stop that! What is this business?'

'Drugs.' His tone was hushed as if he sensed he was touching on a taboo.

She pushed at his chest and searched his face: it was blank. *Is that your game? Is this just business?* 'Drugs?'

Kiric shrugged and pushed back at her without malice, exiting the bathroom – just business. Penelope watched him leave; wrapped a towel round and followed the Kosovan. He was on the balcony in just his underpants, pulling on a cigarette. Smoke drifted languorously from half open lips. God, he was, literally, "sex on a stick" she decided as she walked over to him and placed a hand on his shoulder. Quite different to Harry Johnson.

'So, drugs. What about them?'

The Kosovan took another drag on his cigarette letting the smoke curl away into the still Berlin morning air. 'My people have a shipment yours need. It was one that ... Ferdinand' – he glanced at her – 'ordered specifically. I have to move it soon and by different routes.'

'Why different routes?'

'The Americans are onto the Somali connection. It's more precarious taking drugs round the Horn of Africa now. But you take a different route.' Kiric suddenly pinned her with his gaze. 'You said, the other night, that it was there for the use. So, Ms Hortez, just how could you move five tonnes of heroin?'

The number was a problem though she didn't want to admit to her new partner. And that wasn't all. 'It isn't just the heroin is it? You don't know how to move Taliban friends – do you?'

Kiric didn't look, just smiled and inhaled on the cigarette. 'Don't forget lady, that my "Taliban friends" are crucial to the cartel's war against the government.' His voice was low, a curious blend of menace and pleading.

Yes, it was true: the experience the Taliban had brought to her dead husband's Cartel had been of almost untold quality, yet ... 'Nothing ever remains crucial for long Rado. We are coming to a moment when the energies that are being exerted against Colombian officials will be overcome by the political

128

process.'

'That process being?'

'Eduardo Sanchez is not celebrated in our country for the soft image he portrays internationally. He is ruthless, unforgiving in business and politics. It is well known, though no-one dares verify it, that a number of his business partners have met with grisly ends at his hand: either politically, or in real life – mostly real and very messy.'

'And he will ...?'

'He will win the next election for sure and when he does it is very likely he will upscale the attacks and scorched earth policy he has followed on the border with the help of the US. Then the cartels will feel the full fury of his anger and his brutality. No, Mr Sanchez is not a nice individual.'

'If you worry about how nice somebody is, already you have lost the battle.'

'I don't,' replied the fashionista coldly. 'I merely express an opinion borne of facts.' She felt the twin points of burning hatred light in her cheeks as she thought of the man who had helped her lover to kill her babies. 'And I can assure you Rado, Mr Sanchez will not profit from his election.'

There was something behind her eyes that checked Rado's response. He flicked the last embers of his cigarette over the balcony and nodded. 'I can see. Well, we have to make sure that Mr Sanchez is given some serious food for thought.'

Penelope Hortez looked deep into Kiric's eyes, but she couldn't see beyond the deep brown pits that reflected her silhouette. 'I'm going to get dressed,' she informed him. When he just nodded she turned and headed for the bedroom feeling empty, as if she had just been violated.

Kiric watched her go and, as she shut the bedroom door, he withdrew his idev from his pocket, lit it up and tapped a number on the graphene screen. No face appeared, but a distorted voice greeted him.

'Yes?'

'We're in. She will deliver the package. Just one thing you should know.'

'What?'

'She has a view on our mutual friend. It could be dangerous.'

'We have anticipated that. Continue with the plans. You know what you have to do.'

'I do.'

The screen died and he dropped the device on the table. For a moment he contemplated the other's words then, resolutely he walked to the bedroom.

Fifteen

Charlie cast a sideways glance at her driving companion. He was good-looking in a spare way. His profile was clean and sharp, nose neither too long nor too big; a brow that was lightly furrowed, with nicely tanned skin carrying that slightly weathered look of a thing regularly, but not overly, used. What was he like as a person, she wondered; as a lover? Was he gentle? Or uncaring; did violence lurk beneath that exterior of seemingly friendly indifference? There had been something last night, he was determined to keep hidden – a conundrum.

Logan continued to regard the screen of his idev, all the while aware of Charlie Richter's scrutiny. He was unsure whether he should be flattered or amused by the attention. Richter was an attractive woman but he was here on business and he –

'So, did you get what you wanted from our debrief back there?' *Get it back to business please Charlie,* the analyst admonished herself.

'It was something. Trouble is, they're at the sharp end, so their experience is valid only so far.'

'What did you expect?' Charlie allowed puzzlement to seep out in her tone.

'The info they picked up from the hit in Venezuela – that had to be a mother lode.' Distracting, she understood, as Logan changed tack.

'We're still sifting through it.'

'Who's "We"?'

'CIA, NSA, FBI, Homeland.'

'And?'

The question hung between them, like an inappropriate old uncle. After several moments of her concentrating on the road Charlie responded.

'And what?'

'What did you find?'

She sneaked a quick look at her passenger. 'I-I'm not sure I should be saying.' God! That sounded weak.

Logan cast a sidelong glance at her. 'That's a pity. I figured we had a special relationship.' Irony laced his words, irritating Charlie.

'"Special Relationship?"' Charlie allowed her anger to spill out. 'Well, you haven't been particularly open with your information either. You've given us just enough to keep us interested but not enough to make any difference.'

'Hmm. I guess you're better at the game than I gave you credit for in the first instance. Ok, I'll try to be more open, okay?'

Ignoring the Brit, Charlie staring fixedly at the tarmac stretching away in front of her. The early afternoon traffic around Andrews Air Force Base was quiet and the sky above was clear after the recent rains, just white puffs of cloud sitting in the ether. The silence wrapped them as tight as if cling film had been used.

'Okay. Do you fancy stopping for a coffee?' When he nodded, Charlie took the next interchange and headed to a nearby service area.

The service area coffee, when it came, was pretty good, which surprised both of them. They sat in a window seat looking out over the car park.

'So tell me what you know,' Logan encouraged as he sipped and regarded the cars pulling in and out for refuelling of motor and man. He watched her carefully, noting the pause, the reflection as she gathered together the words she would use.

132

'Well, the info we got from the hit on Ferdinand Suarez's outfit suggested he was experimenting with new methods of delivery. There's nothing definitive at this time, because the data we would need to confirm that just isn't there. There was also a large amount of foodstuffs: coffee, maize, lentils with the consignment numbers of other organisations.'

Logan considered the information for a moment. 'Do you think they're using the food to disguise their shipments?'

Charlie nodded after a moment. 'It's a thought.'

'What happened to the consignment at the depot?'

'Marines torched it as part of the final clean-up.'

'What do you think the effect will be?'

'That's anybody's guess.' Charlie sipped on the coffee and sighed before going on to elaborate on her own musings, about Colombia's changing cartel structures and the influence of Taliban. It was a dark picture that, Logan admitted, echoed some of the issues he'd uncovered in his time out there. Times were changing and their enemies were changing faster.

The Brit took a breath and swallowed more coffee. Beyond the window people laughed, smiled, argued; went about their daily business, without knowing what the hell was going on. Everyone he looked at he saw as an asset or a threat; direct or indirect. Truth was he knew nearly as little as they did. Nobody could know everything and every action was, inevitably, a reaction to something or someone.

'This is unusual isn't it?' Logan asked after listening attentively. 'Surely somebody would want to be seen as Suarez's natural successor. Isn't that how the cartels generally work?'

'Kind of,' Charlie concurred. 'They do like people

to know who is in charge so this does appear to be a different slant. We put it down to their close working ties with Taliban. Now you voiced the same concern maybe it's worth investigating.'

'Can you put some resource on that?'

Charlie nodded. 'I'll get a request to NSA for surveillance to be carried out; see what we can pick up.'

A silence descended on the table until eventually Logan made an apologetic cough. Charlie snapped from her reverie and waited what seemed a moment too long for the Englishman to say what was on his mind.

'Well?' she prompted when it was almost embarrassing.

Logan looked at her. 'Faulkner's chip.' There was that pause again. 'Did you … uh … find anything of use on it?'

'Oh you mean the CIA locator that you guys sent us. Nada,' she kept his gaze, 'It was damaged, we think by the neck trauma.'

Logan stared long and hard out the window and then checked his idev. 'I have a plane to catch. Can we?' He indicated the car.

Charlie regarded the MI6 agent. There was something he wasn't telling her, or some sense of business unfinished. 'Sure thing.'

The drive to National was quiet almost withdrawn. Charlie couldn't help the nagging feeling that Logan was holding back but felt too unsure of herself to call the shot. She watched him disappear into the departure lounge and then was left with her own thoughts.

*

'They don't know about Hortez.'

'Are you positive about that?' Galbraith's look switched repeatedly from the report on her idev to Logan's face.

'Absolutely. They know Suarez isn't defunct, so they can't understand why the cartel is still functioning without a visible head. They've put it down to imitating some of the Taliban's tricks around disseminated command and control.'

'I gather you haven't disabused them of this hypothesis.'

Logan smiled briefly. 'Not at all.' Why did he feel uncomfortable about that?

'Hmm. So besides that, what did you learn while you were over there?'

'Two things.'

'The first?'

'That they are very concerned about Eduardo Sanchez.'

'Wasn't he seen as an ally?'

Logan nodded. 'They thought so. It appears there are a number of things about Mr Sanchez the CIA are not sighted on. But he's a big friend of Harry Johnson and that worries them.'

'Should it worry us?'

He paused. 'Maybe. We should put a watch on him: look for patterns in his behaviour, unusual friends, that sort of thing.'

'Ok, I'll see to it. And the second?'

'They found nothing of use on Faulkner's chip we sent them. Their analyst said it had been too damaged, possibly when he was decapitated.'

Galbraith pursed her lips. 'Your friend Assiz has a lot to answer for.'

Logan shrugged the comment off. 'They're aware of Assiz; I thought it best to give them some insight.'

'Well, while you've been over there we haven't been twiddling our thumbs either. Take a look at these.' The station chief swiped a file from her idev to Logan's. He opened it and scanned the photos inside. Looking up he raised an eyebrow.

'The man you see with Mr Eduardo Sanchez is Leong Chaozheng.'

'He is?'

'Leong is a senior general in the PLA and a member of the Politburo. His public portfolio is overseas trade and mission. According to our people in Beijing, he has been widely tipped to be the next Chairman. General Leong has come up through the usual way in Chinese politics: nepotism – his father was a close aide of Deng Xiaoping in the late eighties. It was he who got Chaozheng a commission in the Army during the nineties. Leong was a junior officer in the PLA and responsible for some of the more ruthless quelling of anti-China riots in Tibet in 2008. He was believed to be the officer responsible for the killings in Lhasa during March of that year.'

'What's his connection with Sanchez? Where were these taken?'

'At Sanchez's ranch, outside Juarez, Mexico.'

He considered the photo of Sanchez in animated discussion with the Chinese general. 'Is it a coincidence, that Sanchez has a place in the hub of Mexican drug smuggling?'

Galbraith chuckled. 'Perhaps not. Staff in Mexico City see quite a bit of Mr Sanchez out there. Ostensibly he is garnering support from the government for his proposed Central America Pact. However, he's been seen at parties with some less diplomatic members of Mexican society. Only rarely and he always has a good excuse.'

Logan grunted. 'Don't they always? But what about our Chinese friend? Where does Leong fit into the equation?'

'We're unsure. The diplomatic angle is he's there promoting trade links with China and supporting the Central America Pact as a model of negotiation the regime is able to do business with.'

'Hmm.'

'Quite, and just moments before those photos were taken guess who else was at the ranch?'

Logan shook his head.

'US Presidential hopeful, Harry Johnson.'

Logan arched his eyebrows in surprise. 'Johnson was there? In the same place as Leong? I don't follow ... what about ...?'

'We don't think Johnson was aware of Leong's presence. He did seem to leave in a state though.'

'I'd like to know why.'

'As would we all. We need to know more about that relationship. Things on this side of the Pond are moving too. Our friend Rado Kiric had an interesting telephone conversation with someone yesterday.'

Logan leaned forward. 'Tell me more. Who?'

'Kiric was in bed with Ms Hortez in the Grand Hyatt in Berlin. Apparently they are cementing a working relationship,' Galbraith observed laconically. 'While she showered we recorded Mr Kiric on the phone to a certain Yuan Zhiming.'

'Who is?'

'Yuan is the twenty-nine-year-old son of Premier Yuan Xiping. He's precocious, not particularly talented, but he possesses plenty of ambition. As a princeling he is protected from scrutiny and therefore capable of far reaching changes and actions without any comeback. Here,' she flipped a photo to his device.

The young man looking back at him breathed arrogance, from his shaven head and brooding eyebrows, to his impeccable dress sense. An air of invincibility dwelt in his deep brown gaze.

'You think there's a connection to Leong and Sanchez?'

'Leong and Yuan certainly know of each other. We're unsure whether the relationship is more than acquaintance. It would be useful to confirm that, and whether Sanchez has a part in all this.'

Logan regarded Galbraith. She was the best boss he'd ever had – always ready to listen to her staff and adapt to circumstances. A confidante and taskmaster – a fair one – Galbraith expected the mission completing but not at any cost. How would she take his next words?

'I think I need to be back in the States.'

'To do what? Your sphere of influence is the Asian sub-continent.'

'Two reasons. First: Leong's presence, which puts this very much in my brief. If he and Yuan are working with Kiric then chances are they are involved in drugs and/or arms smuggling. If they are now working in Colombia also, that merely deepens my misgivings.'

'That's one.'

'Assiz. I could have sworn I saw him at Washington National. If he's already in the States, then I want to be able to pull him in before the Yanks ventilate his body for him.'

'Tread carefully with the Chinese – we need to know more. As for Assiz, you're right, we want him in one piece if we can. He's key to understanding what's happening in Afghanistan and Yemen. Be wary. If he intends what he said in the video, he won't be easy to take down.'

'I know only too well how hard he can be,' Logan affirmed. 'But the Yanks probably don't know what they're up against. I feel a bit like I left them in the lurch.'

Galbraith nodded. 'One thing, though.'

Logan looked up from his reverie.

'This is not personal.'

The agent shook his head. 'But it is. Assiz made it personal when he blamed me for the death of his sister.'

'That may be so, but don't let the personal cloud your professional judgement. A lot is happening and we need to stay on top.'

Logan considered the words: how easy would that be, he wondered. Best to be noncommittal. 'I'll head back in the morning. Right now I need a break.'

'Make the most of it, I fancy we won't have too much chance to rest for a while.'

Sixteen

Leong contemplated his compatriot's visage which filled the communication frame. Yuan Zhiming's arrogance would be his undoing, figured the older man, if a bullet didn't get him first. Constantly insinuating, interfering and making ill-judged decisions, he'd been lucky thus far. Today, the younger man's journey's found him in Eastern Europe. The call had been carefully routed to ensure it couldn't be traced and the latest brains in the PLA had put together an elaborate scrambler protocol which prevented prying ears from listening in.

'So, Zhi, how are matters progressing?'

'Satisfactorily. Kiric will soon own the Hortez woman. When that is completed we will be in a position to take control of her husband's drug business.'

'Do not show your hand too soon, Zhi. You forget Sanchez.'

Yuan barely concealed his resentment at Leong's rebuke. 'I do not intend to jeopardise the operation. I understand the stakes here.'

'Nevertheless, tread carefully and ensure all is in order before making your move. The planning of a thousand days can be overcome in a second's artlessness.'

'If you think –'

'Do not question me captain,' Leong invoked rank. 'This exercise is far more important than you. You will maintain progress as agreed.'

Yuan limited his reply. 'Yes, general.' Heaving with charged petulance the young man continued his report. Leong nodded, betraying no emotion in his open face. Everything was moving smoothly, without chaos or haste (what did the English say? More haste; less speed? How very true) and he was satisfied they would be in control of the whole of South America's drug trade within six months, maybe a little longer. Using Hortez's distribution network, and Sanchez's political muscle, an all-out assault on the US could be launched, disrupting its populace. This would be the diversion they needed for their own ambitions.

And it would be he, Leong, who had masterminded it. A suitable base from which to take control of the Politburo he decided. A new era of power politics, such as had not been seen in China for centuries, would be ushered in under his stewardship.

'This is very good Zhi. I am pleased with the work you have carried out. Tell me, though, how trustworthy is Kiric?'

'As much as any drug smuggler. He has an agenda and, for the moment, our paths cross.'

Leong nodded. 'When they diverge, you know what to do.'

Yuan nodded and Leong noted the quick smile that played across the younger man's face, underlining his own fears. He would need to be controlled, or put down – Leong couldn't afford any contest, especially from a countryman. Fortunately, Zhi knew little of the general's other operation, though he might have guessed at it. Leong had far greater trust in the ability of his al-Qaeda network to produce the goods than any drug smuggler and his whore partner. Still the drugs gambit would provide significant interference to the authorities when the time came and a healthy bankroll. At least he hoped it would. He needed maximum confusion for China to assume the rank of world superpower. And, all being well, he would be the first leader in that new era.

Time would tell.

*

He'd been in the country for a week, keeping a low profile and waiting to hear from his contact. It had been an anxious stay, aware of his mission and believing that somebody must divine it as each day passed. Thanks be to Allah, this had not happened.

Today, his contact would meet with him.

From that moment Allah's plan was alive … and he was but one step on the journey.

Sayed Assiz placed his flask, lunch and tablet carefully into his rucksack. He didn't need them, but it was important to look normal and to maintain a regular routine; to blend in. Now, to prepare. He shaved, slowly and meticulously, removing all facial hair. Allah forgive, but it was necessary to fit in. The beard would draw too much attention and common place was necessary for success.

And now was time for the first part of that process to begin. The meeting was at the Lincoln Memorial: plenty of people to hide among and look like tourists. He pulled on a Redskins tee-shirt and jeans; Nike trainers, before donning on a matching Redskins hoodie – a fully acclimatised Asian. Shouldering the bag, he checked his appointment once more time before leaving. Nothing out of place. He had a fifteen-minute walk to catch the bus at the corner of Michigan and Franklin.

Catching the Number Eighty he sat by the exit doors in the middle of the articulated bus. From there he could see everybody who entered the bus and would be able to exit quickly should he need to.

Today, there was no need to worry and the late morning ride was uneventful, save for the tired whining of the bus's air conditioning attempting, forlornly, to cope with another hot Washington day. At Farragut Square he alighted, labouring through the heat as he made his way to Farragut West metro station, where he took the line to Foggy Bottom. There he crossed metros and took the line south, finally disembarking for the Lincoln Memorial.

The usual melee of tourists mingled with government workers seeking respite from the rigours of work, by taking an early lunch in the shadow of their democratic hero. Inwardly Assiz scowled at the throngs of mindless individuals, each mired in petty, vacuous lives.

Not so he. His was a higher purpose that would bring this pretentious nation to its knees. These very people would be the vehicle, by which the purpose of Allah would become real, become known to every nation.

And that would only be the start.

'Salaam'

He turned. 'Brother, salaam.' Smiles played on the lips of the two strangers as they embraced under Lincoln's shadow. This was purely business, to be concluded as quickly as possible but, for the sake of any prying eyes, they had to appear long time buddies, or family.

'It is a beautiful day for the birds.'

'It is indeed a day fit for all of Allah's creatures.'

The other gestured to a bench. 'Let us sit, eat and take in the day.'

Assiz felt a strong urge to laugh at the incongruous yet necessary coded language, but curtailed himself. The urge to do Allah's bidding was far stronger. The two sat and, as if two office workers, drew lunch boxes from their rucksacks. Assiz poured green tea from his flask and reflected on the austere taste – it was good.

'Mother says to remind you of her birthday. She says how forgetful you have become now you have moved away.'

Assiz reached into his rucksack once more and withdrew a small box wrapped in birthday paper. 'Mother can rest easy, brother. Here is the present. Be sure to handle it carefully.'

The man placed it on the bench beside him. Carefully caressing the top, he nodded in satisfaction. 'And here is a little something for you. It was all we could afford. Do not be profligate with it; use it wisely.'

'I shall.' Assiz placed the package in his rucksack and zipped the top closed. Throwing his wrappers in a bin he rose and shouldered his pack. 'Well my brother, I have to get back to work now. Give my love to mother. It was good seeing you. Till we meet again.'

'Brother.'

With a quick embrace Assiz strode off in the direction of the Metro. If anyone was surveilling them they would have noted that Assiz's lunch box remained momentarily on the seat he had vacated. But the other nonchalantly picked it up and opened the lid as if it was his.

Inside was a slab of Semtex, innocuous and grey, a simple detonator attached to it awaiting a power supply. He nodded and, opening his backpack he placed it inside without the lid. He found and inserted the two ends of the detonation cords from the other four slabs linked in the bag. His fingers then searched for and found the master arm which he flicked on. There was a reassuring little gleam from the red "armed" light. Satisfied he pulled the top over and clicked the straps shut. Straightening, he shouldered the bag, picked up "mother's present" and felt the reassuring presence of the trigger mechanism as he ran his thumb over the wrapping. Faintly he could make out the rosy gleam of the trigger light. Push the button and the signal tripped the master arm.

He took a step.

'Excuse me.'

He froze and forced himself to turn. A smiling, unknowing, woman, with a small child, greeted him.

'You left this.'

For a moment he was confused. She had nothing of his and then he followed her eyes down. A small boy, her son, was holding the lid of the lunchbox.

'Give the gentleman his lid, Sammy.'

Sammy handed it solemnly to the man who took it.

He smiled. 'Thank you Sammy. May Allah favour you today. Thank you lady.' He pushed the lid quickly into a pocket, turned and left the bench, sighing inwardly at the relief. Purposefully he strode towards the steps of the memorial, lips moving silently, towards the throng of people gazing at the stone edifice of the Sixteenth President.

Placing himself at the rear of one particularly large group, who were being instructed on the President's Gettysburg Address, he mouthed the words *Allahu Akbar* and pressed the trigger.

Seventeen

The message was short and to the point: *Get back here now.*

Logan dropped the phone back in his pocket and looked at the girl he'd been drinking with. 'Sorry, work calls.'

'What, at six-thirty in the evening? What sort of work do you do?' She was clearly unimpressed.

'I sell carpet,' he replied as he slipped from the barstool and laid a twenty pound note on the counter. 'Barman, drinks for the lady please.' He noted she didn't say no. To be fair, it was a lucky escape – for both of them.

Taking a taxi, he arrived at Vauxhall House and made straight for the situation room. Galbraith was there, as was Turner and Eddie. The latter looked quite disgruntled, presumably because he'd been on a promise. Logan sensed and undercurrent in the room.

'What gives?'

'This.' Galbraith flicked the TV on. The BBC news channel was running a story on a bombing. The place looked familiar to Logan: he caught his breath and his heart sank as his eyes read the ticker tape, which confirmed his suspicions – Washington DC.

'Turn the sound up please boss.'

'... we know is that this appears to be the work of one man. Reports from the scene indicate a single man, of Asian or Arab extraction, was seen to walk towards the memorial moments before the detonation. Eye witnesses say he appeared deep in concentration, but purposeful. Moments before the explosion a woman and child had been seen handing the man something by a park bench. The woman is critically ill in hospital; the child lies dead, killed by flying debris from the blast. There is no indication at this time that the woman was involved with, what the authorities are increasingly terming, a terrorist attack.

'Early estimates put the death toll from this suicide bomb attack at one hundred, sixty-nine. At least a further three hundred are suffering from injuries, with the worst cases being dealt with by the Capitol's overstretched hospitals. National Guard troops now patrol the streets of the Capitol and a State of Emergency has been declared.'

'Assiz?' Eddie asked no-one in particular.

'Maybe, but I think it's somebody else. Assiz has another mission to complete. This is a precursor to the main event perhaps?'

Debbie Turner nodded. 'I think we have to believe there will be more. It was very well planned, quiet and executed without publicity, without histrionics: just a man in a crowd until the last minute. But nobody of substance was targeted.'

'What I don't understand is why? Presuming Assiz is in Washington, this has drawn attention to him. The city is in lock down and his movements will be severely curtailed. '

'Well, it should make the job of finding him a little easier,' considered Galbraith, 'This is high priority now. Assiz has to be caught before he can carry out his main mission. It's obvious he represents a clear and present danger and we have to let the Americans know the full extent of that threat. If he succeeds not only may we have the death of a President on our hands, it could also be the end of a beautiful relationship. And there is only one party who'll benefit from that.'

147

*

Assiz drove north on Interstate two-ninety-five. The car had been exactly where the contact had said it would be and he managed to vacate the city just before the barricades came down. By the time they realised it was a suicide bomber he would be well away.

*

The authorities would spend days sifting through the rubble but they had quickly identified the epicentre of the explosion and determined to work out from there. Investigators collected samples and searched for any fragments that could indicate how the bomb had been constructed; and detonated. A lucky break would come the morning after, as parts of the bomber's body began to be pieced together. Resting between Lincoln's feet a clenched hand, ripped from the body, was found. Scraps of paper and residues were discovered embedded in the skin. Inspection indicated it was wrapping paper which initially threw them off until the residue of explosive was found all over the surface of the hand. The samples were carefully packed for lab analysis.

For now, Special Agent Dale Camino, of the FBI's Joint Terrorism Task Force, surveyed the field of carnage as he mopped his brow with a crumpled kerchief. He was spitting feathers. Not only had a chickenshit terrorist attacked his beloved city and killed, or maimed, hundreds, he'd also screwed well laid plans for a nice gentle wind down to early retirement. And all he, Camino, could do was fulminate, and hope they'd all learn a lesson from this. Taking careful steps across the charred and strewn grass he got directions to the Capitol Police Officer in charge from a shell-shocked technician.

Captain Adam Fouré gazed down on the FBI agent, contempt filling his eyes. Unlike Camino, Fouré was immaculately turned out; a crisp white shirt perfectly enclosing his lean dark frame; a plain dark blue tie hung perfectly central, matching the dark blue of his suit. A sneer curled the lips and Camino took an instant, reciprocal, dislike.

'Captain.' Camino extended his hand which was encountered only briefly, coldly. 'What gives?'

Fouré paused and arched an eyebrow. 'It's under control,' was all he offered.

Camino chuckled wryly. 'Glad to hear it captain. It'll be so much easier to hand over to my team when they arrive.'

The police captain stared into the distance, beyond Camino's shoulder. 'That so, Special Agent? Well I don't see any "team" other than mine, working real hard to find out what happened.'

A sigh dropped from Camino's lips. 'See, captain, the thing is I don't give a shit what you see. This comes under the jurisdiction of the FBI as part of the latest NCTC protocol. You just need to police the area while we find out what really happened.'

Fouré's brow darkened and for a moment Camino felt intimidated – just a little. The police captain had a fierce reputation. Born of Haitian immigrants he had ambition, temper and strength in equal measure, and was ferociously devoted to his adopted country. Well he, Camino, was just as patriotic.

'Special Agent,' Fouré glared at the badge, 'Camino. This is a criminal investigation under the jurisdiction of the US Capitol Police. When the

149

National Counterterrorism Centre and your people get their shit together, I'll be more than happy to relinquish that authority over to you. Until then, let me get on with my job.' It was like staring into the jaws of a rock grinder.

Camino puffed his chest out, though defeat was writ large on his tired features. 'Just don't forget that and I expect any and all assistance to my team, to secure the site and ensure the investigation doesn't miss anything. Contamination can happen very quickly by people who aren't clear what they're looking for.'

Fouré's menacing look threatened to melt the FBI agent where he stood. 'Fuck you, Camino, you shit. My people are experts and they were here while you FBI guys were dicking around in the local office. In case you hadn't noticed, there's been a terrorist incident here.'

'Still my case,' blustered the agent. 'Don't forget that.'

'Fuck you very much. I need you telling me that!' The captain spat the words out contemptuously and strode off to the Memorial, leaving Camino shaking and shivering in the afternoon sun.

The special agent collected himself and looked at his watch – where was his team. Fuckers! Leaving him stranded like this! As his eyes scanned the Memorial field, which looked more like a battlefield than a place of reflection and homage, he could see the faces of some of the emergency service personnel. He registered the humour his embarrassment at the hands of the police captain generated. Shit, how had he handled it so badly? He needed Fouré on side so he would need a double portion of humble pie later – just not yet.

'Hey Dale, what gives?'

Thank fuck. Camino turned to see his partner, Jay Santos approaching; all smiles, hand outstretched.

'Where the fuck have you been?! I've had the local police captain crawling up my ass like a bastard over this situation.'

'Hey! The traffic is backed up like shit on the routes round here. All the Interstates are gridlocked. We had to get the National Guard to escort us through.' The guy looked hurt but Camino needed to feel better.

'Yeah well,' retorted Camino by way of acceptance and walked over to the steps of the Lincoln Memorial. The smell of charred flesh, rubble and explosives blanketed everything around, ruthlessly invading nose and mouth, and clinging to clothes. 'Let me introduce you to Captain Fouré.'

Fouré turned at the self-conscious cough and disdainfully noted Camino, before taking in the other. Play it cool, he told himself, after all not everyone from the FBI was a prick.

'This is Captain Fouré, Capitol Police. Captain this is Special Agent Santos. He's our explosives expert.'

'Good to have you here Special Agent Santos.' Fouré grasped the agent's hand and pumped it perhaps a little too enthusiastically, but it was worth it for the look on Camino's face. 'Do you want to see what our people have been doing?'

'Sure thing,' replied Santos, who raised an eyebrow at Camino as they followed in Fouré's trail and headed up the steps to what was evidently the epicentre of the blast.

A small team of people knelt in supplication to the event, working painstakingly to extract any and every piece of evidence that might exist in the place: from

151

traces of explosive, to skin and hair samples and fragments of clothing – nothing got overlooked.

'Guys!' The team looked up from their inspection. 'This is Special Agent Santos from the Joint Terrorist Task Force. He's here as part of the FBI team now responsible for this investigation. I want you to afford him every assistance.' Fouré pointedly ignored Camino.

Santos was greeted with nods and "hi's" from the officers. Pulling on latex gloves he knelt with them and looked round. 'So what gives?'

'A single detonation, by a lone suicide bomber. From the size of the crater we're thinking about six pounds of explosive.' The woman kept checking through the grit and rubble as she spoke. Santos looked round him: at bodies in various states of dismemberment; the cracked columns and the scars on the massive body of Lincoln. The scene was awful and, if not for appearances, he would have retched. He figured they were right, the blast radius had to be about a hundred metres.

'Do you have any ideas what explosive was used?'

One of the men looked up from his inspection of a piece of tattered cloth. 'Give us a break,' he said testily. 'We've just sent samples off for testing.'

Santos nodded. 'But you've already made a guess about blast radius, size of the bomb, you must have some thoughts.'

'No more than you should be able to guess for yourself.' Frustration was evident.

'Okay, so what? Semtex, C4?'

'When we figure, we'll be sure to give you a call.'

Santos stared at the heads, which remained resolutely turned from him, for a long minute before giving up and walking off to find Camino. This was

152

going to be a shit investigation … for so many reasons.

*

Assiz took his time on the drive to Baltimore: no need to draw unnecessary attention, he would be a target for "stop and search" without inviting it. There was nothing in the car that could incriminate him and his cover was watertight – being in the Police had taught him how to achieve that much. He had to reach his next objective in O'Donnell Heights quickly, but not at the risk of capture.

Forty minutes, or so, of steady driving brought him to the Fort McHenry toll tunnel under Baltimore Harbour. He'd taken this route for good reason. This toll was much larger than the Harbour Tunnel crossing. As a consequence, there would be a higher volume of traffic so, while security might be higher, they wouldn't want a bottleneck and the checks would, hopefully, be less attentive.

True to expectation the National Guard troop gave his papers only a cursory glance: his photo obviously didn't fit that on the soldier's idev. For that he briefly thanked his English mother. His looks were Anglicised enough to pass muster at a glance. Following the thumb, Assiz shifted into drive and pulled smoothly away. Allah was indeed on the side of the devout.

A half hour later he was driving down Dundalk Avenue, nearing his meet. Pulling over, Assiz took a cell phone from his rucksack, switched it on and dialled the first stored number. It rang twice.

'Hello.'

'I'm here,' he told the person on the other end.

153

'Be down in a minute.'

Short, familiar, unassuming. That is what they'd been told in training. Do not make references to Allah; don't use the word "brother" or anything else that might be picked up by NSA snoopers. Any conversation had to sound like you saw each other every day and this was just another coffee stop. Blend into the background.

Assiz didn't even know the identity of the man who slotted into the passenger seat of his hire car – he didn't need to, it was unnecessary information that could jeopardise plans were it to be extracted under interrogation. They shook hands in an American way, eschewing their traditional methods of greeting. Who knew who was watching?

Making the classic American right, right, right Assiz retraced his tracks – he wasn't being followed – and headed for a coffee shop. Dunkin Donuts made an ideal stop. Full of families and teenagers relaxing, talking and making noise, they would be just two more bodies in the throng.

Coffees in hand, and donuts for effect, they took a table in the middle of the café. They paid no attention to those around them – furtive glances all round were for the espionage movies, not real life.

'You okay?'

'Yeah, never better. New job starts today so I'm pumped. You got that address for me?'

Assiz reached for his wallet. 'Sure. The guy is good, won't hassle you too much so long as you do the right thing.'

'A quiet place? Need the sleep. It's shit where I am.'

'Nice and quiet. Here you go.' Assiz handed over a sealed envelope. 'Mention me when you see him.'

'Sure thing, appreciate this bro.'

'No sweat.' Assiz swigged the coffee: it was shit, as was the case with most coffee, but the after taste was slightly different to what he was used to. He took another mouthful. Though he preferred tea, that would have been out of place and he found he wanted a little more of the liquid before him. A bite of the donut for appearances, though it too was Western filth.

'Well, got to go. Good luck with the new job.'

The man waved his donut at Assiz who dumped his waste and the cell in the trash and headed for the door. He would have to get more of that coffee sometime. Perhaps he was getting too Western.

*

Sikandar watched Assiz exit the café and drive off in his car then casually followed suit, dumping his own coffee, half eaten donut and cell in the trash. Once outside he made for the nearest bus stop and took the next one headed downtown. There he walked into the heart of capitalism, found a small café, not far from the Transamerica Tower, and ordered espresso. Pulling a clean cell from his pocket he sent a text and waited.

A few minutes later the cell chimed and the envelope icon flashed on the screen. He opened the message, read it and nodded in satisfaction. He ordered another espresso and waited.

The man who walked into the café searched the clientele; his eyes sweeping over Sikandar without stopping, before he too ordered coffee and took a table next to the Pakistani. Chinese, the man was obviously waiting for somebody as he impatiently drank his coffee and regularly checked his watch. With a sudden heavy harrumph, the man took out his cell and checked the messages. Seeing nothing that improved his demeanour the man savagely dropped the phone on the table where it slithered and fell to the floor.

Swearing, he reached down to pick it up, apologising to Sikandar in the process for his bad manners. Sikandar said nothing, merely nodded in acknowledgement. The man gathered up his belongings and, with another curse, headed for the door.

'That guy just left something.'

Sikandar looked at the woman, then to where she was pointing. A USB stick lay on the ground.

'I'll get it.' He reached down and scooped it from under the woman's hand, rose and headed purposefully for the door. Aware he could be watched he searched for the angry Chinaman in the crowds then, as if he could make out the guy, he marched off in quick pursuit.

Time to attend the business of the moment.

*

The apartment was a stopover, rented in another's name, someone Sikandar didn't know. It was sparse – a table and one chair stood forlornly in the dining area; sparse decoration and plain curtains completed the feeling of transition – but that was as arranged. He opened his Macbook, powered it up, and inserted the USB pen in an interface. He scrutinized the file window and opened a program.

Eighteen

'Mr President, we have to evacuate you. Vice-President Carlisle is already on her way to Raven Rock. We have to get you away from the White House.'

President Jonah Lincoln knew his Secret Service detail was talking sense. The attack on his namesake's memorial was serious, not just for the casualties, but for its symbolic nature also. America revered its Sixteenth President and this attack would have shaken it to the core. Despite that he was loathe to move: he knew people might interpret evacuating as being scared. Hell, they'd be right: he was scared. What else was round the corner?

'Mr President?' Agent Cole continued to hold Lincoln's attention.

'Dean. If I run from Washington, what are the people going to think?'

'You won't have to worry that one if you're dead sir. The effect on the country, however, would be catastrophic. You need to be safe sir. Air Force One is waiting on the ramp at Andrews. You can make all the decisions you need once you're airborne. Down here ...'

A knock on the door of the Oval Office preceded the appearance of Secretary of State Siobhan Caplan. She was the only person who Lincoln allowed to enter without awaiting an invite. Their relationship was a close one: professionally and personally. Lincoln trusted his Secretary of State like nobody else.

157

'Dean's right, Jonah,' she opined, illustrating her usual, innate, ability to understand a situation with minimal knowledge. 'Staying here isn't an option. At least once you're airborne you can restore a measure of control over the situation. We don't know who, or what, else is active in DC.'

Lincoln regarded the diminutive Caplan and waved a hand in resignation. 'Ok, you got me. Let's get the "showboat" under way.' Like his predecessor he saw the Presidential aircraft as a luxury. He also understood, as leader of still the most powerful country in the world, it was a necessary evil.

Cole nodded and spoke into his wrist communicator. 'The First Customer is on his way, stand by.' Fortunately, he didn't see Lincoln's raised eyebrows at yet another display of the dreaded showboating. The agent stepped to the door of the Oval Office and waved both the President and the Secretary through.

Quickly Lincoln was ushered to his Marine helo and transported to Andrews Air Force Base. The ramp, on which Air Force One stood, engines spooling, was a hive of activity. Marines watched attentively, weapons ready, as black suited Secret Service agents closely escorted the President to his waiting transport. He shook hands with Colonel Everett, senior pilot and crew commander. Even as Lincoln was settling into his office, Everett was taxiing the VC-25 to the active runway for take-off.

Looking out the window of his office Lincoln's mind was not on the view. He wondered just what the next few hours and days would bring. It would probably be expedient to cancel the Presidential debate to be held in two days' time in Cambridge – that would piss off the opponents, especially Johnson, but it couldn't be helped. He pressed the intercom on his desk. 'Jane, will you join me please? I've got some diary changes to make.'

*

3.59 pm EST

Captain Wayne Poulter turned his plane on to the heading directed by Washington TRACON. He was looking forward to putting down and starting the three days' rest awaiting him. Not long now he thought and let a grin spread across his tired face.

'What's the big grin for?'

Poulter glanced across at Rick, his co-pilot. 'I'm imagining that ice cold beer and a hot little secretary from Baltimore who's on a promise this afternoon.'

'Does Sandy get home early from work on a Wednesday then?' Rick asked, referring to Wayne's wife.

Poulter laughed. 'She does when she knows she can get laid by her number one pilot!'

'Go you,' encouraged Rick. 'I don't say I blame you.'

'Well it's the best way to get a kid.'

Rick Rogers looked up from his instruments. 'No way!? Hey, congratulations man. It's about time you two stopped messing about and settled into the family groove. Damned thing!'

'What's up?'

'Can't disengage the autopilot.'

'Shit, I told maintenance about this bird only the other week, when we got back from Chicago. Let me have a look.'

'Sure.'

Poulter punched the autopilot button. The light remained stubbornly on. 'Okay, what options do we have Rick?'

*

4:07 pm EST

Sikandar worked quickly. Hacking into the aircraft systems and controlling the autopilot on Air Western Flight Two-Sixty-Two was the easy part. He had a window open on his Mac, monitoring what was happening on the flight deck. In a second window he was using another program on the Chinaman's USB stick to scan for VOR signals; in another he scouted for other aircraft and in the last he was patched into air traffic control frequencies. Yet another Mac was rigged for voice comms; he settled his headset.

He didn't have to worry about anybody tracking him: his activity was regularly being recycled across the Mesh, using a constantly cycling IP address. By the time the NSA had realised what he was doing and had narrowed their search field, he would have succeeded in his mission. There would be only one thing left to do.

Sikandar's fingers played the keyboard expertly and then he was locked into the VOR stations for Washington and Baltimore airports. Setting up the jamming took only seconds, but now he was in a race against time.

*

4:10 pm EST

Everett put Air Force One into a lazy left hand turn, establishing an orbit they would hold until the President decided there was somewhere more important to be. The full enormity of the attack on the Lincoln Memorial was only just sinking into those in authority. News was being carefully monitored but speculation couldn't be controlled. All the authorities could do was be sparing with the information they released. Controlling facts and hysteria was paramount at times like this. Everett didn't envy the President that task.

The big plane responded easily to his command. Flying Air Force One was the best gig in the Air Force and he was honoured to be flying the First Passenger.

'Who do you think is behind this attack?'

Everett looked across at his co-pilot, Scott Daikin; another career airman who wore his uniform with pride. The commander could see the genuine hurt in the guy's eyes. Who was it? Everett didn't often do second guessing. It could be al-Qaeda: they were getting harder to spot in a crowd. Or perhaps it had been home grown patriots, red necks tooled up for the overthrow of a government they felt was selling America down the river. 'I don't know Scott. What I do know is it ain't over. We'll hear from them again.'

The furrow of concern deepened on the younger man's brow. 'You think?'

'There was no warning, which kinda points to al-Qaeda. If that's the case they're already onto their next target.'

'Shit, this sucks man.'

'Tell me about it. At least we're in the best place to respond. Not much can get us up here.'

Everett checked the instrumentation by rote.

Nothing untoward showed up so he continued on the turn. This was nothing like what predecessor Tillman had seen on 9/11. Still, don't wish for action, he admonished himself silently; it was never certain whether you could handle it.

*

4:15 pm EST

Back on the ground in Baltimore, Sikandar hunched over his Mac. Things were going well. He had removed VOR from the equation, such that any traffic in the Washington – Baltimore area wouldn't be able to use the system if their GPS was knocked out. Tapping into Air Traffic Control gave him the ability to categorise all the types flying. Sikandar thanked Allah, and his chosen career, for being able to accomplish this work.

One blip stood out. There was no ident, no tag to signify the carrier, no course or other information to say who or what it was.

Except that was the biggest indication that he had found his target.

*

4:21 pm EST

An ATC operator at Washington International turned to her manager. 'Hey Bernie have you noticed anything about the VOR.'

'Nope Wendy, should I have?'

Wendy didn't like or respect Bernie. Overweight, lascivious and waiting for retirement, he ruled the tower with an offhand, overbearing manner, which fought with his belly in the size stakes. She'd be glad when he went.

'Yeah, you should've. Washington and Baltimore have gone down. I can't get a signal from either antenna.'

Bernie gave his barely perceptible shrug. 'Don't worry, nobody uses it these days and the weather is clear for a hundred miles.'

Wendy stared, thinking *Your funeral.* 'I'll log it', was what she said, and turned back to her console.

She noted the blip that had no call sign, cast a glance at Bernie, shrugged and left it.

Nineteen

4:23 pm EST

Sikandar felt a rising sense of righteous fulfilment: things were going to plan. He had control of Air Western Flight Two-Sixty-Two, knew where the target was and had remote possession of the local backup system. He could now take control of air traffic control. He allowed a smile. Allah be praised, this was easier than he thought it might be.

His fingers danced over the keyboard of his Mac. Everything was nearly ready. Adrenaline pumped a tiny sigh from his chest as he called up a command prompt window. Fingers working with purpose and intelligence, he had what he needed in seconds.

*

4:29 pm EST

Poulter punched the button one more time and shouted. 'Fuck!!'

Rick Rogers glanced across. This was becoming alarming. Despite their best efforts the autopilot remained stubbornly locked on. All procedures they would normally employ, save one, had been tried, repeatedly, until the two men were exhausted. He remained silent – stupid questions weren't needed right now.

Poulter ran a tired hand through his damp hair. The stress of the moment was causing him to sweat, making him feel cold and damp, unclean and out of ideas.

164

'Okay, we don't have an option anymore.' He looked at Rick, determined to root the required affirmation from his co-pilot. 'We're going to have to shut down and restart.'

Rick blanched: effectively switching off the ignition to reboot the aircraft's systems was not something you tried coming into a busy city landing pattern. 'There must be –'

'You know that we've tried everything.'

'But, we're over DC.' Rick didn't expand, he didn't need to.

'Hey, you got a better idea then it'd be great to hear right now.'

Rick shook his head slowly, dreading the next few minutes.

'Ok. Let's get on with this.' Poulter's determination underscored his tone and his set brow. He thumbed his intercom. 'Washington Control, this is Prairie Flight Two-Sixty-Two inbound to National, transmitting on one five niner decimal four.'

'Prairie Two-Sixty-Two, this is Washington Control. Reading you loud and clear.'

'Washington, advise we have a problem at this time.'

'Acknowledged, Two-Sixty-Two. What is the nature of your problem?'

Poulter glanced at Rick. 'Advise we cannot disengage our autopilot. All procedures have been followed and we are performing an engine-off reboot.'

'Negative, Two-Sixty-Two. We have Air Force One in your area. Do not attempt an engine off procedure at this time. We will attempt to feed in a course correction to take you out of the area. Wait our instructions.'

'Understood, Washington TRACON.' Poulter looked across at his co-pilot and shrugged. 'New one on me. They said they can feed in a course correction to the autopilot.'

Rogers frowned. 'Me either. Still he seemed to know what he was talking about.'

Poulter chuckled. 'Sure wouldn't do to crash into Air Force One.'

'Definitely a career stopper,' concurred Rogers.

'Prairie Two-Sixty-Two; Washington Control.'

'Washington Control, Prairie.'

'Prairie: can you access your command MFD?'

Poulter reached forward and rotated a switch top right of the display. To his surprise the multi-function display scrolled. 'Er, yeah, Control, affirmative.'

'Access your UHF screen and retune to one eight eight decimal six.'

'One eight eight decimal six. Affirmative.'

Suddenly the plane started to bank away from its original course.

'Looks like we're starting to do something.'

Rick nodded but his attention was caught by a glint of sunlight off an aircraft in the distance. They seemed to be turning towards it. Perhaps that was his imagination.

Twenty

Wendy looked at the plot, which had started to turn from its original track. Why had it done that? She highlighted the icon and pulled up the details: it was an Air Western commuter from New Jersey that should be landing at Washington before going on to Houston.

Things were wrong. It was too high, and climbing. Out of place, its trajectory was taking it north-west of the city. She watched as it steadied onto a course and then she plotted that forward.

It made no sense. The new course took it over the middle of the Appalachians. Nothing for miles around.

'Bernie, something you should see.'

What the fuck now?? These new controllers they were sending out were – 'Yeah Wendy, what gives?'

'I've got a flight – Prairie Two-Sixty-Two. It's just made a course deviation heading west-north-west.'

'And...?'

Wendy turned and faced Bernie direct, commanding his attention. 'The flight plan has them landing here at National but they're turning away. I've got no contact with them and none with Washington TRACON.'

Bernie noted the position of the airliner. It was a little unusual that Washington Terminal Radar Approach Control had not advised Wendy, as the local controller, of Two-Sixty-Two's approach. It was a lot more worrying that it was moving on a trajectory away from the airport.

'Can you contact them?'

'I've tried.'

'Try again.'

Wendy turned back to her panel and thumbed her intercom. 'Prairie Two-Sixty-Two this is Washington Tower. Please respond.'

Nothing.

'Prairie Two-Sixty-Two from Washington Tower. Do you copy, over?'

The silence, despite the chatter of other controllers, was deafening. Bernie moved to Wendy's terminal, concerned now. He jabbed a finger at the screen, at a green unidentified blip. 'What's that?'

She shrugged. 'It appeared a few minutes ago.'

'Direction?'

'From the south east.'

'Shit!'

'What?'

'Air Force One,' was all he said. 'Are you sure you can't raise Prairie?'

'You heard.' Wendy scowled.

'Okay.' Bernie perused the plots and the trajectories.

'Well?' Wendy pressed.

'We've got a problem.'

With a speed that belied his bulk Bernie got back to his position and picked up his phone. 'Get me North Virginia.'

*

4:37 pm EST

At the Air Traffic Control System Command Centre, Northern Virginia, Annette Symonds sat back

168

and considered what she was hearing from Bernie Tranter. He probably didn't fully realise what he was saying, but the enormity sank into Annette's mind with the heaviness of lead.

'You need to get all traffic down right now and stop all take offs.'

'You think it's that serious.'

'Yes, I do. Now, excuse me, I need to make a call.'

*

4:41 pm EST

Lieutenant Colonel Dick Fletcher was watching the late afternoon news when the call from the Command Centre came in. He listened intently as Symonds gave him the low down. Though the director pressed him Fletcher neither confirmed nor denied the presence of Air Force One in the skies above DC.

All he said was 'What is the ident of the commercial flight?'

There was a pause. 'Prairie Two-Sixty-Two.'

Fletcher was business like. 'Thank you Director. What steps have you taken to secure the airspace over DC?'

'I've instructed Washington to get everybody on the ground immediately. Trouble is they have no contact with Prairie.'

'Understood.'

'What are you going to do?'

Fletcher resisted sarcasm. 'Scramble the fighters.' With that he cut the line.

*

4:43 pm EST

Captain Jesse James, call sign "Cowboy", was sat in the QRA shelter next to his F15 Eagle. A commercial airline pilot, he was proud to serve his country through his Air National Guard service. With over ten years in the seat he was also proud of his captain's bars and worked hard to maintain them. He approached his task as part of the Air Sovereignty Detachment with twice the commitment of his airline job. He'd been a pilot in Gulf War Two, flying combat air patrols in Eagles, over Baghdad. It had been intense, stressful, but he'd not succumbed to fatigue like so many of his colleagues, at least so he told himself.

In the ready room alongside him was Lieutenant Al "Rodeo" Sievert. Al was much more of a maverick, a natural pilot, while Jesse worked hard in the cockpit.

Sievert sighed; James raised an eyebrow at the exaggerated expression. Sievert shrugged. 'Come on, how boring does this get? How do you manage it man?'

James smiled and his mouth opened to reply when the alert phone chimed. He picked up the receiver. 'James here.'

'Captain, this is an Alert Five. A significant terrorist threat has emerged over the ADIZ. This is not a drill. We'll fill you in when you're airborne.'

James threw the receiver down, grabbed his dome and headed for his plane. 'Let's go. We got trade.'

Five minutes later the two Eagles were taxiing to the active runway preparing to enter the rapidly emptying skies of the DC Air Defence Intercept Zone.

'Dead Cert One, Andrews Tower, on milchan one-one-niner decimal two-four.'

'Tower, Dead Cert One, reading you clear.'

'Dead Cert One, you are clear to runway zero-one. Wind: five knots; bearing zero two nine. QFE one zero zero four.'

'Copy that tower.' Expertly he steered the big interceptor to the end of the runway, waited for Sievert to line up just behind and to his left. His hands rested lightly on the controls.

'Dead Cert, you are clear to launch.'

Smoothly, with a precision borne of years of practice, James drove the throttles through the gate, engaging full military thrust. Fifty thousand pounds of white hot energy forced him back in his seat as the jet screamed forward along the runway, gathering momentum in a blur until they reached rotate speed. Pulling the stick smoothly into his gut, he retracted gear and flaps and the big bird hurtled upwards; repelling the earth, to take her rightful place in the skies. A quick look confirmed Sievert was close behind.

'Dead Cert: turn, heading three-one-zero; climb flight level two-zero-zero.'

'Copy that: turn three-one-zero; flight level two-zero-zero. Advise trade?'

'We have a non-responsive airliner heading across DC airspace, we believe on an intercept course with Air Force One.'

'Has Air Force One been on the phone?'

'Negative. Be advised we believe there is a secondary terrorist attack underway.'

'Understood control.'

'Advise you are cleared to use lethal force on your target if it does not respond.'

171

'What if the target comes down in the metropolitan area?'

'Advise target is headed away from the city and should come down on open ground. Providing you with transponder ident now.'

'Copy that.' James flicked the master arm on his joystick. 'We are weapons hot.'

'Good hunting.'

'Affirmative.'

James called up the target acquisition radar display to his helmet sight. There were a decreasing number of blips in the air over DC. As he received the ident from Andrews he could make out their trade, on an almost identical course, but miles ahead, so it was a game of catch up. Further beyond he could see another blip that seemed to be in an orbit. Air Force One?

'Ok Cowboy, what gives?'

'Hey, Rodeo. You heard control.'

'Copy. Hard call to take down an airliner.'

'If that's what it takes. I've got the target on my helmet sight. AMRAAMs are armed and slaved. Give me top cover.'

'Copy that.'

Twenty-One

4:50 pm EST

Wendy flicked her intercom. 'Washington Tower to Potomac TRACON come in. Over.' Silence. 'Potomac TRACON, this is Washington Tower. Please respond.' She turned. 'Hey Bernie, can you raise Potomac?'

'Huh?'

'I'm trying to get hold of Potomac TRACON and they're not responding.'

'Potomac, this is Washington Tower. Respond please.'

Wendy and Bernie exchanged glances. Her boss reached for his phone for the second time in less than an hour. 'Put me through to the FBI.'

*

4:50 pm EST

Everett checked his multi-function displays, and then scanned the sky out the canopy. A glint in the sky caught his attention. 'You see that?'

Scott Daikin leaned over and squinted. 'Nope, what you see?'

'A glint ...'

'Anything on the 'scope?'

Everett tapped the screen and nodded grimly. 'A liner heading towards us; behind it, two fighters outta Andrews, coming in hard.'

'You mean ...'

A moment's pause then Everett regarded his co-pilot levelly.

'Yep. We're under attack.'

*

Sikandar worked quickly, but with precision. He had one thing more to do: firestorm the most sophisticated and secure aircraft in the world; with the most comprehensive suite of avionics and countermeasures on any non-combat plane. Air Force One was about to be hacked by an unknown Pakistani with American citizenship, using software from the newly emerging global super-power – China. He allowed himself a quick smile.

The jiffy bag had arrived in the post two days previous, an innocuous package which he had been instructed by an anonymous caller not to open until this day. That was their security. Nobody knew anybody else. He didn't even know the man he'd met today: just a face in a crowd. But joined by Allah. Now he ripped the top off, noting the little tremble in his fingers, the excitement. A credit card sized, plastic envelope dropped in his hand. He cracked it open and a plastic card fell out. On the front was a series of letters and codes; when he turned it there was a four-digit PIN.

Opening a program on his Macbook, and accessing the USB stick he'd taken possession of earlier, he was greeted with Chinese characters and a small window into which he typed the PIN and pressed <enter>. A new screen, full of Pashtu characters, scrolled before him. He began typing, his fingers moving rapidly. After only a few seconds he needed to type in the code on the card.

Even though he knew what was coming, he still

couldn't quite believe it. Doubt cracked his mind: was Firestorm as good as the reports? It couldn't be, could it?

And then … yes!

Air Force One was his.

*

The quiet in the cockpit of Two-Sixty-Two was deafening. Poulter stared at the dot looming larger in the windscreen – Air Force One. And they were headed straight for it. The hollow feeling in his belly didn't tell the whole story, but it was almost enough. What hurt more than the realisation they were an out of control missile, was the idea he would never again taste her sweetness, hold the baby they had yet to make in his arms, or luxuriate in the touch of their skin against each other.

'What do you think is going to happen to us?'

Poulter looked across at Ryan. The younger pilot was clearly agitated but what did he say, what did he do?

Before he could answer, the chief stewardess buzzed him. 'Yes, Tracy, what's up?'

There was a tremble in her voice. 'You should look out the cockpit window.

*

James brought his Eagle round hard on an intercept course to the airliner, sucking in as the g increased. The skies over the capital were eerily quiet and, in the barren blue, he could make out the two contrails converging. This was going to be a close run thing and he felt the sweat and thunder of a potential

175

mistake. Miscalculate; delay by a split second and the President was as good as dead.

Attempts to contact the airliner had drawn a blank but, flying close, he had registered the horror on the crew's faces, and the bewilderment in the passengers. He had one, bad, feeling about the shit he was about to unleash on a hundred plus innocent people. One hundred versus one President: fuck.

He flexed his fingers on the stick, letting his thumb caress the launch nipple. Even though it was a close range attack he wanted to be able to guide the missile onto its target and not leave it to the chance of infrared.

'Dead Cert Two, One. I'm preparing to engage.'

*

4:51 pm EST

Sikandar was aware of the two Eagles, knew the Americans would do everything they could, to protect the President. That was exactly what he expected. With the close proximity of the two airliners and their closing speed any missile would be as likely to cause terminal damage to Air Force One as bring down the target. He smiled in satisfaction of a job well executed.

*

Poulter regarded the looming shape of Air Force One and the two Eagles that flew in formation either side. This was shitty, either way you looked at it. There were no exits, no ways out – except one. There was only '... one thing left to do,' he said, turning and

176

looking grimly at his co-pilot.

Ryan nodded gravely.

Poulter rose from his seat, went to the back of the cockpit and took the extinguisher from its bracket. Moving forward again he raised it and hesitated momentarily before bringing it down repeatedly on the control panel. Sparks flew and splinters of acetate and metal flew through the suspended atmosphere of the cockpit.

*

4:55 pm EST

Everett punched furiously at the controls: no use. 'Fuck!'

'We're in the shit for sure aren't we?'

Everett nodded bleakly at his co-pilot. 'Somebody else is in control of the aircraft and we have no way of regaining control that I can think of.'

'A shut down?'

'Negative, you know that. The FADEC is linked directly with the autopilot that came on five minutes ago.' It was at times such as these that Everett really cursed progress and technology such as Full Authority Digital Engine Control which allowed the aircraft's computer to control everything through the autopilot.

'What if we isolate the aircraft's computer?'

'Do you ...?'

Daikin sweated. 'Worth a try.'

'Get on it! I've got the unenviable task of telling the President he may well be the first one to die on Air Force One.'

Daikin headed off the cockpit to the access hatch

in the forward galley. Everett flicked his intercom switch.

*

'This is the biggest threat to global peace since Central Park, Jonah. You have to respond.'

Jonah caught Caplan regarding him over her coffee. It was so easy when you weren't the one making the decision. 'And what Siobhan? Incarcerate every Muslim in the country; declare war on the entire Middle East; nuke Iran?'

At times Siobhan's icy grey eyes were especially disconcerting – this was one such time. 'Mr President, we did nothing about the Central Park atrocity, except wring our hands. We have to be seen to be reacting more decisively to this attack, else your administration is dead and buried.'

If it isn't already, he thought sourly. Whose fault was that, he wondered. No time for self-recrimination now, though, Siobhan was right. The American people would be expecting some action, especially following such a visible attack on the centre of democracy.

'What do you suggest?'

Caplan drew a breath; he wasn't going to like this. 'Unpalatable as this may be you are going to have to round up all those people who are on the FBI, Homeland and NSA watch lists as probable threats to national security. Then you move on to – potential – threats.'

'What then?'

'You make a statement, affirming that the parties who perpetrated this outrage will be prosecuted with the full force of the law –'

178

Her words were interrupted by the telephone. Lincoln raised a hand in silence and lifted the receiver. 'Hello?' The President listened intently to the caller. Caplan watched as the level of concern rose on Lincoln's face to be replaced by … resignation … fear? She couldn't be sure.

'Thank you captain.' Lincoln replaced the receiver with a solemnity that filled Caplan with foreboding. There was a short, pregnant pause.

'Well?'

'We've been compromised. An attack is being dipping of Prairie Two-Sixty-Two's nose on the instruments and knew they were attempting to thwart his attack.

It wouldn't work, it was too late.

He dipped the nose of Air Force One immediately to intercept the trajectory of the airliner. At the same time, he pulled up a window that allowed Firestorm to search for other electronic targets in the vicinity. He quickly picked up the two Eagles and saw the lead aircraft had an active missile searching for lock. A few key strokes and control of the weapons was his. All four AMRAAMs lit up on the board.

Wait...

The target lock icon glowed red – Sikandar tapped the key and saw the launch lights glint. He could imagine the missiles rippling from the underside of the interceptor and he smiled.

What could have been better? He thanked the United States Air Force for providing him with such a perfect way to remove the head of the serpent.

*

Daikin was sweating in spite of the cold. If he could just release this last fitting, they would have the basic flying controls back and should be able to take some evasive action. His fingers felt numb but he had to push through it.

This one last chance.

*

Jonah Lincoln re-ran the words of his pilot and steeled himself. Now is not the time to think of your own mortality he admonished himself. It was the country that would suffer the most from this.

He picked up his phone and made to speak.

*

Two of the active radar homing missiles buried themselves into an Air Force One stripped of its countermeasures; the other two speared Prairie Two-Sixty-Two. The black box would later highlight the moment when and how Air Force One was firestormed, providing NSA with useful data.

The two fireballs captured the attention of every Washingtonian that day. There was an almost instantaneous understanding of what they had witnessed far above their heads. The stricken Air Force One came down on the Raspberry Falls Golf and Hunt Club, northwest of Leesburg.

Prairie Two-Sixty-Two came down in the suburb of Ashburn killing at least 90 people on the ground as well as the one hundred, ninety-five people on board.

*

The two Eagles returned to base, silence enveloping the two pilots. What words could adequately describe what had just happened? When they landed Captain Jesses James, withdrawn, silent still, dropped to the tarmac, resisting the urge to retch. He was aware of Sievert, ashen faced, leaning on his crew ladder, totally wiped out. They had just killed a hundred plus individuals on a commercial airliner and had seen their own weapons used against their Commander-in-Chief. What could be worse?

James rose and looked about him. A proud man, he had given his name and his loyalty to defending the Unites States of America. That now lay in tatters, the outcome of some Arab or Afghani who had decided that change was better initiated from within. It was a far cry from the conflict he thought had been won in 2003. Where did he go from here? From killing the President? He staggered unseeing to the locker room, dropped his helmet on the floor, uncaring. His mind was racing: visions of meeting the President when the latter visited Andrews; presenting the Guard to him. That had been the proudest moment, later sharing it with his family, his son who had been so elated at his dad, the hero, meeting and talking with the President.

How did you explain that you were in charge of the flight to protect the President when he was shot down? That it was missiles from your fighter, which had inflicted the final tragedy on the Administration?

You couldn't, James told himself. There was no way to explain this tragedy. His hand hesitated as he weighed down on the handle of his locker. This was the only answer when you had betrayed your country. Determined, he wrenched the door open and, taking out his service automatic, he placed the barrel in his mouth and pulled the trigger.

*

Sikandar stared at the screen. He could scarcely believe himself what had just transpired. He was now the most wanted man in the whole of the United States, though no-one knew who he was. There was only one thing left to do and that depended on timing.

Twenty-Two

Logan touched down at Andrews Air Force Base shortly before 5pm on the day after the attacks. In the aftermath of their Commander-in-Chief's death, Logan noted base security was on a hair trigger. Marines in full battledress, assault rifles held at readiness, patrolled the ramp and the perimeter, hungry for somebody to shoot. Always so much preparedness after the event: this time it might be more warranted than they imagined.

Even though he was a member of the British Secret Intelligence Service, the Marines took plenty of time checking through his personal effects. He noticed how jittery they were, eyes flicking constantly over the contents of his bags, eager fingers resting menacingly on trigger guards. Logan waited patiently for the searchers to complete their task. Now was not the time to antagonise anybody.

'Hi,'

He turned at the sound and there she was. Logan let a smile play at the corners of his mouth. Charlie Richter's expression wobbled as she walked over to him. A quick hug and peck on the cheek. 'Welcome to Washington DC!' Heavy irony coated her words. 'How was your flight?'

'Less crowded than this place,' he observed then hesitated. 'I'm sorry.' How inadequate a word was that, given the circumstances of the last twenty-four hours? But what else could he say? This was something nobody could ever have foreseen and the enormity of the situation swamped convention. The assassination of the President, while on Air Force One, purportedly the world's safest and most secure aircraft, had sent shock waves across the globe, which now waited anxiously to see what the US would do. Some countries had already expressed their shock and sympathies, whilst attempting to defuse the inevitable finger pointing and blame game.

Meanwhile Vice-President Angela Carlisle had taken up residency in the command bunker at Raven Rock Mountain Complex, Pennsylvania. Most of the administration had gone with her, ostensibly as a continuation of government response, but no-one could have blamed them from being shit scared. Air Force One had been brought down using the US's own weapons. If that could happen, where was safe? In moments like this people could be forgiven for thinking that a million tonnes of rock might help.

'What's been happening since the bombing?'

'Huh?'

Logan took a moment to consider the CIA analyst. She seemed dazed, confused: as if this had been a personal attack on her. And, he guessed, in many ways it was. Like most heads of state, the office of the President of the United States of America was more than symbolic; more than a person administering the power of a country. People could be adversely affected by the death of a leader, particularly if that death was unexpected. A country could descend into chaos – just like an ant nest when a child kicks it over and stamps on the queen. And, just like that moment, this attack would bring with it more collateral damage to the body collective. America had to regain its balance and fast.

'Come on,' Logan gently took Charlie's arm. 'Let's get a coffee.'

Charlie Richter allowed herself to be propelled in the direction of the Air Force restaurant. After several more stops for security checks, Logan settled her at a window seat with a large mug of black coffee. He poured in sugar and stirred.

'Drink.'

Charlie raised the cup automatically and sipped on the black liquid. 'Ee-uww! That is disgusting!' She placed the mug back on the table and pushed it away, as if it were some poison set to seal her misery. 'Is that the best you can do?'

Logan bit his lip. Shock was a difficult thing to control. 'Just drink, I'll buy you another more to your taste later.'

Charlie winced her way through the sugary drink but, when she'd finished, she seemed a bit more focussed.

'Better?' Logan inquired; Charlie nodded in return. 'How are you coping?' Perhaps it was better to start with her, Logan figured, rather than crashing straight into business.

'Shit.' Charlie tried to bite back her emotions, but the television in the corner and the comments of the clientele kept the assassination fresh in her mind. 'But hey,' she remarked as a tear leaked into her mouth, the saltiness flooding her mouth with pity, 'Things could be worse.'

'You think?'

Charlie looked at the Brit and found herself smiling through her pain and confusion. Her cheeks were streaked with tear stains, she drew a hand over her mouth, embarrassed: how childish!

'Oh sure,' she managed, getting a tissue from her bag, 'After all we've only had two major terrorist attacks on the capitol within twenty-four hours. What else could go wrong?'

Logan resisted answering – now wasn't the time.

Instead he asked, 'What's happening?'

'The FBI took over the Lincoln Memorial site. The emergency administration ordered the NCTC convened, to start going through the evidence that's coming in.'

The National Counterterrorism Centre had been established primarily to prevent events such as this. Logan knew, from the Irish experience, prevention was often an unattainable goal. The best that could be done sometimes was respond quickly and effectively, without losing one's head.

'Have they found anything yet?'

'Nothing.'

The silence extended between them, the American agent sipping her coffee, holding the cup as if it were a long lost friend to grieve with. Logan considered the activity on the apron, military vehicles scooting around with Marines hanging off them, guns at the ready but no enemy to shoot at. All activity; no purpose. That would change.

'How do we defend ourselves against this?'

Fear haunted Charlie's eyes and Logan knew it was important to get her doing something, and quickly. 'By looking at all the evidence as quickly as possible; reviewing actions and determining responses.'

Defeat sat on the shoulder of her fear. 'Come on, up you get. We need to have a look round and get some thinking space. Do you think you can get us in to the sites? Charlie?'

'Huh?'

'Can you get us through the cordons on the investigations?'

Charlie dabbed at her eyes and nose with a sodden tissue before discarding it in her empty cup. 'I guess,' was all she managed.

Logan rose and offered his hand. 'Let's go. Do you want me to drive?'

Shit, I must look bad if he's offering to drive. Charlie shook her head vigorously. 'No, give me a moment, I'll be fine.'

Twenty-Three

Minutes later they were heading out of the base and taking the Suitland Parkway into the Capitol. What should have been a twenty-five-minute journey turned into nearly an hour as traffic mounted the closer they got to the National Mall and Memorial Parks. National Guard trucks lined the road and a checkpoint manned with spooked troopers loomed before them on Independence Avenue SW. They were waved to a stop and a National Guard sergeant leaned into the convertible. Logan noted the fifty cal trained on them from a Hummer, on the other side of the checkpoint.

'Ma'am, what's your business here?'

'My name's Charlie Richter. I'm a senior analyst with the CIA Crime and Narcotics Division. Here's my pass.' She slowly drew her credentials from her handbag. 'My boss is Sarah Markham, and this is her number at Langley.' Charlie passed a card over. The sergeant gave both a cursory glance then nodded at Logan.

'What about your passenger?'

'He's MI6.'

The sergeant arched an eyebrow momentarily. 'You for real?' Logan nodded, handing over his passport and id. 'Wait one,' advised the Guardsman and disappeared into the Portakabin, masquerading as a guard house. As they waited under the nervous scrutiny of gun-toting reservists Charlie and Logan both felt the tension rise...

… to be broken as he reappeared with their papers. 'Thanks Miss Richter, you may proceed.' The Guardsman indicated the rising barrier and Charlie slowly rolled forward. Inside the compound, which the park area had become, everything was a scene of focussed activity. Charlie drew her Z5 up to the makeshift FBI control centre, situated between the Lincoln Memorial and the Reflecting Pool. Figures, cocooned in SOCO overalls and carrying evidence bags and boxes, swerved round them as though they were an inconvenience.

Exiting the car both agents took in the activity. It seemed frenetic but on reflection was quite planned. Agents with bulging evidence boxes streamed past them towards the collection rooms; others with camera equipment headed into one of the Portakabins designated for processing. More agents and DC police officers moved through the compound with equal sense of urgency. Media and camera crews seemed to mill round with less focus, as they searched for the story that would seal pole position in the news stakes.

'And you are?'

Both turned at the question. A portly figure, wearing an FBI badged jacket viewed them inquisitively.

'Charlie Richter, CIA Crime and Narcotics; this is Steve Logan, MI6,' she explained indicating the Brit.

'Special Agent Dale Camino. You're gonna have to help me out here. What are a Crime and Narcotics analyst and an MI6 agent bringing to the party?'

Before Charlie could answer Logan indicated the command post. 'Can we go inside Agent Camino?'

Camino scrutinised the Brit but couldn't read the man; he shrugged. 'Sure. Why not? Come on.'

He led the two up a staircase into an air-conditioned office. Logan was impressed how quickly the command post had been set up.

'Coffee?'

Both agents nodded at Camino's question. The

FBI officer poured out three cups, pushing two towards his guests. Everybody took a moment to immerse themselves in the lull before ... before what? Logan shook his head and smiled.

'Let us into the secret?'

'Sorry?' Logan looked up. Camino was regarding him quizzically.

'That smile: you looked like you were about to share something.'

The Brit shook his head. 'No, just smiling at the level of guardedness we're all showing.'

Camino grunted. 'You got anything to tell us, fella, feel free,' he opined openly. 'We're running outta ideas here.' Logan hid his surprise at the FBI Agent's candour. Camino turned his attention to his CIA counterpart. 'Okay, let's start with you. What is a Crime and Narcotics agent doing at a terrorist SOC?'

Charlie glanced at Logan who nodded discreetly. 'We have a number of lines of enquiry we're following, which might link up with these two incidents.' How lame did that sound? she wondered as she took in the disdain on Camino's face.

'We're trying to say we may have information that could be useful to you,' added Logan quickly, calmly.

'Such as?' *It was probably jack shit.* 'Oh no wait, you're spooks so you could tell me, but then you'd have to kill me, right?' he asked caustically.

Logan laughed. 'No, but you might not be too happy yourself when you hear what we have to say.'

'Go on, try me.'

It took just under forty-five minutes for Logan, with a little help from Charlie, to bring the FBI officer up to speed with events. When he had finished Logan could see that Camino was, indeed, less than impressed with the information he'd just heard. For a long time, the FBI agent was silent, concentrating on his coffee. Then he placed the empty mug on his desk, rose and walked round silently, thinking, and eventually sat back in the chair. Finally, he drew a breath.

'That is about the biggest fuckfest I've ever listened to. You knew all that and you chose not to say anything? Un-fucking-believable! It's a good job the DC Police captain in charge isn't here right now.'

'Why's that?'

Camino considered Logan briefly before replying. 'Because he's a fucker who thinks the town is his and if he thought somebody had let this happen without letting on, he'd be likely to shoot the bastard here and now.' The FBI agent sighed. 'Anyhow, what makes you believe this Assiz is here?'

'When Sayed Assiz went to Pakistan he was radicalised and the trail went cold. However, GCHQ recently found traces of communication within the Arabian Peninsula referring to "The Convert".'

'What the hell does that mean?'

'We believe it relates to Assiz. It's possible he was being trained, or was training terrorists for a … series of attacks.'

If Camino registered the slight hesitation, he didn't let on. Instead he grunted. 'And the communications said what?'

Logan leaned back in his chair, aware of the impact his next few words might have. 'They spoke of "The Convert's" transportation to Aden and arrival in Sana'a, where the firestorm attack took place against your Marines. He then made his way back to Waziristan before departing for,' he hesitated, 'for London, and the US we think. We know that Assiz was in all those places.'

'You think? Fuck! This has to go to NCTC as soon as.'

Charlie made to speak, opened her mouth and closed it again, thinking better of any ridiculous riposte. Logan merely waited for Camino to process the information a little longer. Almost on cue Camino sighed. 'Well time for recrimination later. What do we do now?'

Logan considered the question: action was what was needed. 'We need to view any CCTV footage from around the time of the detonation. Look at movements into and out of the area, working back from the moment of the blast.'

'No shit?' Sarcasm dripped from Camino's mouth. He allowed time to compose himself. 'We've got two teams on site and another four back at headquarters going through every piece of CCTV, frame by frame. You know how long that takes?'

'I'm aware,' Logan remarked succinctly.

'And there're only four cameras around the whole site. Two are at either intersection of Twenty-Third Street and Lincoln Memorial Circle and they don't have great resolution so there's a lot of work on image resolution being put in.'

'The other two?'

Camino levelled with Logan. 'They went up with the bomb.'

'Okay but there must be something off site when the device was still recording.'

'We're investigating but we think they were replaced last year with devices that had on-site digital storage.' Nobody commented because everybody knew how big a miss that could prove to be.

'So, we have just two cameras which only have a long view on the situation?'

Camino nodded.

'Who has access to the video?'

'DC Police sequestered all the footage yesterday; one of Fouré's first tasks. NCTC has demanded it handed over to them by noon today.'

'Shouldn't we be able to identify Assiz from the footage?' Charlie offered.

Camino nodded. 'It should be possible if we had a recent photo of the guy and if the video is capable of being analysed to such a degree. What do you have, Logan?'

Logan considered his reply briefly. 'We've mocked up some photofits, using different guises of how we think Assiz looks now.'

'You got any intention of letting us see them?'

Logan pulled his idev from a pocket and called up the file. 'Ready?'

Camino nodded and accepted the file Logan pushed to his device. He scanned the jpegs it held. A man of Asian ethnicity, handsome but with a secret behind the eyes (or was he merely impressing that upon the face?). MI6 had produced a number of scenarios with and without facial hair. 'Thanks. I'll get these to our investigators.'

'Can we look at the bomb site?'

'Follow me.' Camino shuffled his bulk to the door and rumbled down the short steps. Logan and Charlie followed close behind.

The scene which greeted them was horrific, even after a partial clear up. The interior of the memorial was graffitied with burns, smoke, blood and viscera; the smell was like being at a cannibal barbecue. Charlie couldn't help holding a tissue to her nose though she noticed that Logan and Camino had no such weakness. She wondered how they did it.

'This is the epicentre,' Camino indicated a heavily cratered and charred part of the area in front of Lincoln's statue. 'The point of detonation funnelled the blast, maximising the impact and deaths. Our friend had packed the bomb with ball bearings, nails, tacks and razor blades. It was like a charnel house in here. Identification of victims is going to be by medical records and there's gonna be precious little to bury.'

Logan took in the American's candour as he surveyed the scene. 'Have you been able to salvage much from the crater?'

'Our Explosives Unit has gathered as much as they can, predominantly little bits, and taken it away for forensic analysis. It'll be some time before they can piece anything meaningful together.'

'So our investigation rests specifically on the cctv?'

Camino noted the "our" in Logan's observation. 'The *FBI* investigation will take time and a lot of credence will be given to the information you have passed to us Agent Logan, but, remember, this is a US National investigation against an internal terrorist threat.'

Logan's mood darkened. 'Sayed Assiz is an international terrorist –'

'That you conveniently forgot to tell us about buddy. Until it was too late.'

The Brit flushed: he couldn't refute that.

'So I guess this is where we part company,' Camino extended a hand. 'You and your CIA friend have been an immense help but this is our jurisdiction. When we need you again, we'll be sure to call.' The agent smiled briefly, coldly.

Logan gave Camino's hand the fleetest of touches,

194

turned and walked away, not caring if Charlie was keeping up. She was flustered and embarrassed by the whole sixty minutes (was that all it had been?) and they walked back to the car in silence.

When they were finally in the safety of Charlie's BMW she looked across at the British agent. 'Well, that went well.' Her worlds elicited a grunt from Logan, still angry with himself for allowing the FBI agent to outmanoeuvre him.

'Look,' she carried on, 'you did all that could be expected of you; of us. How were we to know that Assiz would make a play so soon?'

There was an agonising pause where Charlie supposed Logan hadn't heard her before he spoke.

'Because he told me he would three weeks ago.'

Twenty-Four

It was a confession which knocked the wind out of Charlie's sails. More than that, she felt used –abused! – by the British agent who sulked beside her now. Why hadn't he told her before? Weren't they supposed to be on the same side?

'So … why did you wait till now to let us know?' She tried to sound professional and authoritative but her voice came out as a hurt little girl, let down by an uncaring parent.

Logan maintained his silence.

'Well, that's about what I can expect, I guess,' Charlie observed as they sat in the car outside the FBI command post. 'You hold back information crucial to our safety and our National Security and then you refuse to talk about it. Presumably because you know you are totally wrong about this.'

Nothing.

'I guess I was stupid to think that you might respect the relationship we had.'

An uncomfortable, prickly silence dropped over the two. After another few minutes Logan coughed. Charlie glanced reluctantly at him.

'I apologise.'

'Good for you.'

'We couldn't be sure our intel on Assiz was good.'

'Wasn't that for us to decide? After all it was an attack on the continental USA which was planned.'

'There was another target.'

His voice was small and bleak, making Charlie check Logan sharply. 'Which was?'

'Me.'

News programmes were full of reports, analyses, and background information about the worst terrorist atrocities on mainland US since 9/11. It wasn't the number of dead that caused such shock and grieving, but the death of a serving President in such devastating circumstances.

The biopic of Jonah Lincoln portrayed a stoical family man, devout in his duty to advancing the cause of world peace, a man who had drawn the US back to its borders, from sometimes intractable positions; who offered help sparingly, while attempting to focus on the problems at home, Jonah Lincoln was somebody who either possessed statesmanlike qualities, or lacked the gravitas for the world stage, depending on your political persuasion. He was a flawed man who had, more in death than life, become a national hero. What would the United States of America do now for its latest dead idol?

It was a question Leong pondered long as he sat, drinking in the CNN newsreel. He drew slowly on his cigarillo, letting the smoke curl and snake through his lungs before blowing it back out. He knew the risks of lung cancer, but he was a man of risks and the latest events unfolding around the world were much bigger ones than disease. His mother had never smoked, and died when she was forty and he was thirteen, hit by a bus as she crossed a road in the centre of Beijing. His father continued to smoke, just one when it was a special occasion – New Year, birthdays, family births and deaths and he was eighty-four. Father had cut back from his thirty a day when his wife had died and now his eldest child followed the same policy. Smoke when there was something to celebrate. The patterns of blue smoke turning languorously in the invisible currents of air fascinated him. He saw himself in them: pushing, twisting against the tide of humanity.

The pictures on the screen, of the still smouldering wreckage of Air Force One, were cause for such celebration. He had doubted their ability at first, but the one who had been the policeman had indeed been most capable. What was more, the man was now in the United States and untraceable. That much was evident from the carefully worded messages coming from the state machinery. All the different parts of the apparatus, so good on their own, didn't have the effectiveness of the Chinese when it came to pooling and moving in one direction. As with all Westerners they were more concerned with systems, protocols and frameworks, than with actually doing. That was where he, and China, would win out.

Leong picked up his cell phone and toyed with the device, pondering the next move. It had to be decisive and fast. Like any good boxer, once your enemy was destabilised you had to deliver the blows until finally he went down. America was on the ropes, potentially blinded. He had to bring in the next body blow, and the next, before going for the head shot – blow three.

He pressed a speed dial on the touch screen, Leong eschewing the new fashion for communication chips inserted into the body. Cell phones could be thrown away, swapped; chips couldn't. Once this new "Zeus" chip was in everybody, power resided with whoever could control the chip. Sometimes the old ways were the best.

Sat on a damask covered sofa, reclining and diffident, Yuan casually played with a balisong, and waited. The click-clack, click-clack of metal as the blade was repeatedly opened and closed, grated on Leong but disapproving looks were no longer any use. He was about to rebuke his lieutenant when a voice answered.

'Hello.'

'Have you heard the news?' He noted Yuan pause and glance, the silence sticky with expectation as the young man waited, reptilian, recognising the voice.

'Yes.'

'The market is prepared. Are you ready to move?'

'Another day, perhaps two and we will be in a position to move the goods.'

'It can be no more than forty-eight hours, to ensure we achieve maximum saturation. Do you understand?'

The pause was barely perceptible except to someone like Leong. 'Yes. It will be on time.'

'Good, I will call again in thirty-six hours to make sure we are on track.'

'Very well.' The line went dead and Leong considered the call as he placed the phone on the table. Could the man be trusted? Like all arms dealers he was liable to play all ends to the middle to come out on top. Kiric would have to be watched closely, yet was Yuan the right person to do that? The young man had shown himself to be too close and therefore too blasé to effectively monitor and control the dealer. It was always the same with princelings – he should know, he'd been one: cocky, indolent, thinking he was owed a living. Tibet had proven how wrong that philosophy had been.

And yet, to take Yuan off Kiric would be to signal to the young man some sort of displeasure, perhaps give reason to challenge Leong. Perhaps another way …

'Zhi …'

'Yes?'

'Kiric is ready to move the goods. I want you to ensure that he delivers. He has forty-eight hours to get the goods into the country.

'He can d –'

'Go. Ensure he does as we wish. There can be no mishaps.'

Yuan opened his mouth to argue and closed it when he saw Leong's expression.

'Mr Lee will accompany you.' Leong's principle bodyguard stepped forward. Lee was a large individual, impassive and alert; he'd been Leong's bodyguard for more than five years. Leong trusted his life with the man and was prepared for Lee to take Yuan's at a moment's notice, understanding the younger man for the threat he really was.

Yuan glanced briefly at the silent soldier and then shrugged dismissively as he headed for the door. His hand rested, momentarily, on the gilt handle. 'I'll call you,' he told Leong as he left the room.

*

Lying between the snow white Egyptian cotton sheets of the bed in the Ambassador Suite of the Moscow Sheraton, Penelope Hortez felt concern sit like undigested food in her craw. This was getting far too regular and she needed to get a grip. After this weekend, she promised, then she would be back home and …

… and what? Her boys were dead, buried in the dirt of some slum town in the depths of the Colombian jungle. Her heart even grieved for her buried husband and there'd been no love between them for years.

'What are you thinking?' She felt Kiric's hand snake round her waist, the warmth of his palm unsettling on her belly. She shook her head, afraid of the emotion that would betray her in her voice.

'Your soul is empty for your boys, I feel it … here.' He placed his hand on her chest, a powerful sensation, all the more so because there was nothing sexual in his action, yet it made her want him deep inside despite herself.

Involuntarily she nodded and fought the urge to let go and cry. When she spoke, her voice appeared not to be her own. 'I have this show and then I will be returning home.'

'I know.'

Do you?

'What is left there for you?'

'Revenge.'

'A beautiful woman should not return to her home when it is filled with revenge.'

'The revenge, Rado, is with me everywhere. I cannot escape it.'

'Do something about it then.'

Penelope moved and hitched herself up the bed. 'I intend to.' She looked down at the supremely confident Kiric. He arched an eyebrow and smiled. God, how much did she want him?

'You said you wanted my help getting goods into the US.' He nodded. 'When do you need that help?'

'Are you sure?'

'Positive.'

He regarded her as if suddenly wary of her motives; her commitment: he hunted her face for a sign that she would rescind the offer; that she would think better of it. When it did not happen he spoke.

'It is important I get a shipment to you as soon as possible.'

'When?'

'It is ready to move now. We need it into the States within a week.'

'That quick?'

Kiric nodded. 'It's important that … we hit the US while they are still coming to terms with these terrorist attacks.'

Penelope felt her stomach lurch. Talk about planning. 'You think they're going to be looking the other way? Aren't they going to be nervy?'

The Kosovan smiled, but humour was missing from his eyes. 'They're much too busy to care about drugs and, by the time they are, it will be too late.'

Despite her desire for revenge, Penelope felt distinctly uncomfortable as Kiric outlined his plans but she held her counsel.

'So, do you think you can deliver?'

She looked into his demanding face. What if she couldn't? What would this man, she hardly knew, do? Suddenly she was very aware of her vulnerability and pulled the cover closer, feigning cold.

'I see no reason why not. Provided you can get your goods to Sheremetyevo Airport on time I will see to it that they are delivered where, and when, you need them to be.'

'That is good.' Kiric took his time to say the words, appraising Penelope until she looked away from him. Apparently satisfied he rose and made his way to the mini bar, despite the early hour. He poured himself a double JD. Penelope watched him down the drink.

'I feel we will make a good team Ms Hortez, a very good team indeed.' He leant over and kissed her neck and she knew she couldn't say no.

*

'Shit, Steve! You've been carrying that with you all this time? Why does Assiz want you dead?'

Logan regarded the American. Did he tell her? 'There's some history between us, a reason for him becoming a terrorist.'

Charlie looked into his eyes, searching for the answer – finding only hurt. Was it just for himself; or for something else? It was difficult to judge. She twisted in her seat to face her English colleague directly. Did she need to know for herself, or their professional relationship? Though she had to admit to some voyeuristic tendencies, she sensed that knowing the truth would help rebuild her confidence in Logan, which had taken a hammering following his revelations.

'I ... shot his sister.'

'Fuck!'

'Yeah,' he responded reflectively.

'That's heavy shit, Steve. How come? What went down?'

Logan considered the questions. 'You're right, it was heavy shit. It happened a couple of years ago.' He went through the scenario again and suddenly the intervening time had never passed; the images raw and bleeding, and behind them, all the time, a bottle of single malt called out for attention.

Charlie shook her head. 'You can't condemn yourself for doing what was right at the time. That's what is so hard with this war. You don't know who the enemy is. They're so well hidden. Innocent people are always going to die. We can't do anything about it.'

'Try telling that to her brother.'

'You need to get a grip. There'll be time enough for recrimination after this is all over. For now, we have to concentrate on catching Assiz before he does any more damage.' Even Charlie was taken aback by her hard tone.

'We should get over to the crash site,' Logan decided suddenly, changing the subject. 'There may be evidence there, or perhaps, knowing what I know, there's something I can help to piece together. Shall we?'

Charlie started the car and pulled out of the parking bay, but not before she shot Logan a look of concern.

Twenty-Five

The wreckage of Air Force One covered most of the Raspberry Falls Club and beyond, a search area of some two square miles. An armed and nervous cordon of Marines, National Guard and Army, was thrown around the area while CIA, FBI, NSA and Homeland had vied for space in the club house and chalet complex. Charlie was directed to the CIA encampment crammed in the Pool House. She parked the car as close as possible and they walked the few yards to the building. Though less plush than the clubhouse, inhabited by the FBI and Homeland Security, it did afford a good view of the main part of the crash site.

Logan surveyed the destruction and felt something of Charlie's pain. It was humbling to see the shards of Air Force One seemingly growing, like an alien formation, out of the disturbed ground of an affluent golf course. The cockpit section lay on its side on a green while, some distance away on one of the fairways, parts of the fuselage had gouged large trenches in the grass. Charred trees stood silent monuments to the conflagrations started by hot metal and spraying jet fuel.

Was this Sayed's doing? If so, he had to have the Chinese providing him with the know-how to drop the Presidential jet. How could Assiz or al-Qaeda have the capability to take down the President's aircraft on their own? He was more convinced than ever that was the case.

Logan shuddered.

*

'Are you seriously suggesting the Chinese are behind this?' The CIA Agent-in-Charge Cole Martin pondered Logan's bald statement for a moment then slowly shook his head. 'Do you realise what it is you're proposing?'

'I do. And do you honestly think that al-Qaeda has the capability to launch such a complicated attack all on its own?'

Martin considered the Brit's words. Two choices presented themselves; in reality one – either he could admit that the CIA didn't have a clue, or he could shrug and admit the possibility. Neither was a great option, but given the history it was entirely feasible that China had masterminded the whole scenario. But why? Why use al-Qaeda, when they had already proven they were quite happy to make attacks themselves? Ask.

Logan regarded Martin's question. 'Simple. Everything Beijing has done previously has been at arm's length, performed by tens of different individuals, who are untraceable because of routing and Trojan activities. But this is very different. Now, they're taking a hard line; they've gained confidence in their position, their abilities. They're ready to wage war the hard way.'

'What are you saying?'

'That China is the only credible player able to field this sort of capability and that it's a next step towards direct confrontation.'

Martin looked at his CIA colleague, clearly unimpressed by her observation. 'Are you serious? I can see maybe al-Qaeda have bought technology from China. But a full-on politico-global conspiracy? Really?'

'Look at what has happened. I'm sure al-Qaeda is

still adept at getting a bomb to a place and detonating it quite easily. But to bring down Air Force One? To take over a passenger airliner as a potential missile; or take control of the weapons systems of two F15 Eagles? You're seriously asking people to believe this is the work of a group that works as a mesh of cells, with little or no connection to each other, except by courier?' Logan raised an inquiring eyebrow.

'Al-Qaeda is bigger than you think buddy,' Martin informed the British agent.

'Of course they're not,' he retorted disdainfully. 'They are a worldwide outfit with cells in virtually every country in the world. But those cells are predominantly small ones, harrying authorities with suicide bombs, assassinations and ram-raiding. Al-Qaeda is designed around a plausible deniability scenario. If you don't know the people in the next cell, you can't betray them. There are several people in the organisation who can develop software and Denial of Service packets etc. but not with the depth, or quality, of such a piece of work as this.

'Such software requires organisation, a large-scale technical ability. You know, something akin to Tarantula,' Logan smiled as the American's features froze. 'Yeah, you didn't tell us, but we know about it. Unfortunately, it isn't as good as this package appears to be at delivering a firestorm. Don't you think these are like field tests?'

'You think?' There was less scepticism in the big CIA man's tone now as he listened to Logan's careful arguments.

'For how long have China launched DoS attacks against us? Last year they compromised NORAD, yes we knew about that too,' Logan remarked as he caught the surprise on Martin's face, 'and launched penetration flights over the Aleutians from their aircraft carrier, *Mao Tse-tung*. To let you know, they infiltrated GCHQ at about the same time and stole data pertaining to an operation in Northern Iran. We lost two agents. They have experience of getting behind firewalls, on a regular basis and in comprehensive fashion. They have an entire "army" dedicated to the development of software for use on the battlefield and against organisations and countries.'

'Go on.'

'GCHQ has been analysing the signatures from the firestorm deployed during the Yemeni attack. They followed the profile of similar software designed by the Electrical Engineering University. China is on the verge of being the world leader of military grade hacking software. This could be their moment. It's a statement of intent.'

'And don't forget that we've noted significantly higher Chinese diplomatic activity across Arabia, East Africa and South America.' Charlie caught Logan's nod and smiled briefly.

'You've got a clear decision to make here Agent Martin. If it is the Chinese, then this is a CIA investigation surely.'

Martin shook his head. 'Even if you're right, the FBI will still have jurisdiction as it's a terrorist case on home soil, with definite al-Qaeda involvement.'

'But if it's committed by the Chinese, then it could be classified as an act of war.'

'That's a big if, buddy.' Martin heaved his frame in his chair, uncomfortable at the direction the conversation was so quickly taking. Logan considered and pressed his point, eager to topple the man's reticence as quickly as possible. He pointed out the window to where the back greens were a hive of activity. Men and women in scene-of-crime suits painstakingly raked the spoiled earth; Marines and black suited Secret Service agents walked purposefully about the huge crash site. Large pieces of Air Force One were being craned onto flat beds, while heavy lift helicopters were dropping from the sky, like huge bees attracted by the blossom of destruction. Marine CH53s had arrived to carry away the body of their commander-in-chief and his entourage. It made grim viewing.

'You see all that activity there, Agent Martin. The Secret Service is arranging for the body of your President to be taken away for burial. If you think al-Qaeda orchestrated this on their own, then carry on playing second fiddle to the home boys. But you know in here,' Logan tapped his chest, 'that we're right. You have to swing the lead.'

The silence in the pool house was deafening as Logan and Charlie waited for a response. Martin avoided their penetrating gaze. He didn't know who was right ... Who was right?!

'Even if you're right it'll be hard convincing the FBI and Homeland. The bombing of Lincoln Memorial had all the hallmarks of a jihadist attack. It's not a leap of faith to put them in charge of bringing down Air Force One. And the interim administration doesn't need any more battles to fight; al-Qaeda is sufficient right now.'

'You think it'll all go away if you catch...'

'Or shoot.'

'Yeah, or shoot the guys who carried out this attack?' Logan shook his head. He felt he was beginning to lose the plot. 'Let me tell you about the guy the Chinese are using to mastermind these attacks against you. Sayed Assiz was a highly decorated police officer; a member of CO19, the Met's elite armed response team, and a Muslim. He was radicalised when his sister was shot dead in a suspected terror alert in Trafalgar Square.' Logan caught Charlie's look but didn't falter. 'He was in both Yemen and Waziristan prior to disappearing off the grid at Karachi airport. He has been reported in the presence of Mohammed al-Siddiqi.'

Martin raised an eyebrow.

Charlie ventured a reply to his unspoken question. 'Al-Siddiqi is the spiritual and military leader of al-Qaeda. Though he regularly visits Yemen and Nigeria he stays predominantly in Waziristan and we believe there's a good reason for that. He's has been reported meeting with members of the People's Liberation Army at secret locations across the rogue province. Chief among these contacts has been one Yuan Zhiming, son of the current premier. Yuan is also a known associate of one Leong Chaozheng who's seeking the Premiership next year. Leong is often seen in South America but also visits Malaysia and Burma and we believe he coordinates Yuan when the two meet there.'

The CIA man slumped in his seat. 'Shit, guys. You are harbingers of doom! Do you realise what this means?'

Charlie and Logan nodded slowly; only too aware.

'When will the funeral be?'

Martin regarded Logan. 'The President's body will be transferred to Mount Sinai Hospital until further notice. We're not really thinking about that at the moment.'

'Okay, but that's likely to be where a suicide bomber would strike next. As many targets in one place as possible? It has to be the next point of attack. Where is the Vice-President?'

'Raven Rock. She'll remain there until after the funeral, or we have this situation under control.'

'So we have about seven days to find Assiz.'

Martin made to reply but the chiming of his cell phone prevented him. Rising as he spoke, he strode to the window, listening carefully to the caller. Logan watched impassively, but he was aware that Charlie was squirming a little at her American colleague's reticence.

The CIA agent nodded furiously as he listened intently to the call and Logan thought he saw a smile on the agent's face. Obviously some good news …

'Thank you for that, that is good news indeed. Keep me posted on developments.' He turned, dropping his cell in his pocket. 'Good news,' he reiterated, beaming from ear to ear. 'We've found him.'

Logan's eyes grew wide. 'Assiz?'

'No,' Martin admitted, 'The guy we think brought down Air Force One. NSA were able to track him down by following his internet trail back, with the help of your GCHQ.'

'Where was he traced to?'

'East Baltimore. As we speak, Baltimore Police are surrounding the apartment ready to take the man down. Their SWAT team has assembled and are about to move.'

Charlie beamed. 'That's great news.'

'No it isn't.'

Both Americans looked sharply at Logan. 'What do you mean? We're about to arrest the guy who took out our President; who probably knows the Lincoln Memorial bomber, and can give us the low down on

211

local cells.'

'Agent Martin, given what you've just said you expect from this arrest, do you think this person is going to let you arrest him just like that?'

'He doesn't know we're coming.'

'He expects to be arrested; the apartment is rigged to blow.'

'You can't know that.' Even Charlie was taken aback by Logan's pessimism.

'I can. It makes sense that they will maximise the damage they can inflict. Al-Qaeda doesn't want prisoners of the hated system. That apartment is rigged to blow, take the terrorist with it and anybody in the vicinity. Why do you think you were able to trace him?'

'We can be in before he's able to blow anything.'

Logan shook his head. 'It won't happen. Pull your people back. Evacuate the block.'

Martin made to reply but a text beep caused him to look down at his cell. His face, when he glanced back up was ashen. 'Too late. They're about to go in.'

Twenty-Six

Sikandar sat silently waiting, as he had for the last few hours. Allah be praised, he had functioned exactly as expected. The head of the serpent was taken. All that remained now was his sacrifice to Allah and the cause. He checked round the room, unable to move now he was wired in. Following the attacks, he had opened the two large cases which had been here when he was given the key. Inside were the explosives, wiring and detonators which would ensure the demolition of the block in which the apartment resided.

Where everything had come from he neither knew nor cared. It didn't matter. What mattered was that the bomb would work. He had followed the instructions methodically, placing the blocks on the walls against the retaining structures, linking each pack of C4 with detonation cord. The door had a wire laid across the door jamb – if the door was breached, the wire would break, firing the detonator in the relay charge. If that failed he had a cell phone wired up, and should he be shot before he could fire, a mercury balance trigger would trip a second relay charge on his chair when he went over.

Then, he had laid an open relay to the internet that was sure to attract the authorities.

Now it was time to wait. Wait for the infidel to come and reap the whirlwind.

Inshallah.

*

Captain Hammond checked his kit one last time.

Chambering a round in his MP7 he waited for the "Go" signal from the command centre vehicle, just round the corner from the target. He looked down the line of his Alpha Team and was greeted by a wall of impassivity. He knew that inside they were all tensed, ready to go. He clicked his helmet com.

'Charlie Team, sitrep.'

'Charlie Team is a go. Back of the block is clear and we have secured the perimeter. Awaiting the signal.'

'On my mark.' *Come on, what are we waiting for?* Every second waiting eroded the element of surprise.

'Command Car, to Alpha Team.'

'Alpha Team, copying.'

'You're a go. Breach, breach, breach.'

Hammond looked round and nodded, clicking his helmet com at the same time. 'Charlie Team, breach, breach, breach.'

He made for the doors and led the assault up the front stairwell. The room was on the fourth floor of the fifteen storey block. As he reached the landing Hammond motioned his breach team forward. He acknowledged Charlie Team as they approached from the rear stairwell, waving them to standstill.

The four-man initial breach team took their position in front of the door of the suspect's apartment. The breacher looked one last time at Hammond who nodded briefly.

With a single arcing swing the ram slammed into the door, just below the handle.

*

Sikandar could easily hear the noise of the SWAT team outside his door; watched their shadows scuffle in the strip of light that seeped beneath the door.

A tiny bead of sweat ran down his face, tickling the tiny hairs, and leaving a cold trail of fright behind it. This was it; the culmination of all his efforts. And beyond the door of his sacrifice would be his seventy virgins. He waited for the call of Allah.

*

The thin wire broke.

*

Like a zipper on a tunic, the detonation ripped apart the room, dropping the ceiling and cascading the floors above into so much rubble and human debris. Within minutes the rest of the building had followed suit, toppling into Dundalk Avenue where the police command post was situated. When the dust settled Baltimore PD had lost fifty officers, including the twenty-four-man SWAT team and five senior commanders.

In the rubble of the building they would never know how many people had actually died, though the official estimate was seven hundred and sixty-eight.

Death stalked America's streets and nobody knew where it would strike next.

Twenty-Seven

The Raven Rock Mountain Complex was relatively unknown to the world, most people believing that the US Government fled to Cheyenne Mountain in times of trouble. Situated six miles to the north of Camp David, Raven Rock made much more sense in terms of government continuity, than a trip all the way to Colorado Springs. Inhabiting a fortified mountain in Liberty Township, Adams County, Maryland, it was only approachable by two heavily guarded roads, or a helipad to the west of the main entrance.

It was on to that pad the helicopter, carrying Logan and Charlie, landed forty-eight hours later at the request of Acting President Angela Carlisle. Actually, Charlie had figured on the way up, it was more a demand than a request. Logan was apprehensive of the meeting and had called the British Ambassador, Peter Michaels, after consulting with Galbraith at Vauxhall House. She had been concerned about Logan meeting the President due to the nature of the issues between the two countries. She had, she informed her agent, already had a visit from the Prime Minister's Office and the Foreign Secretary's personal secretary since his revelations to the FBI and CIA concerning Assiz.

'I'm not looking forward to this,' Logan confided to Charlie as they followed the Secret Service agents to the guardroom.

'Me either,' she agreed quickly as, their ids having been checked, they were waved through the checkpoint. So much had happened that privately she was unsure how she'd be viewed by her own people having developed a close working relationship with the British agent.

'What's Carlisle like?'

Charlie shrugged. 'Nobody really knows. She hasn't been a significant V-P so it's anyone's guess what we're gonna get in response to a crisis.'

'I guess we're about to find out,' Logan nodded towards a heavy steel blast door which was slowly being opened by a Military Police sentry. He noted the others, weapons ready, uncompromising in their determination to take out anybody who might even look like they presented a threat. He and Charlie were ushered into the space beyond. The doors closed behind them; the sound of the security locks sliding into place made him grimace. Focussing, he took in his new surroundings.

They were in an area perhaps thirty metres by twenty, with facilities positioned either side of an isolated conference facility. It was to this they were escorted. Inside, opposite the doors was a large, blank, LED screen flanked by a series of smaller ones. To the left, video feeds from the live investigations being carried out at all the terrorist sites in DC and Baltimore, were being shown. On the right were broadcasts from news channels including CNN, Sky, the BBC and Al-Jazeera.

Between them and the screens was a large elliptical table, the highly polished mahogany surface reflected the images of those sitting around it. Uniforms and suits occupied seats in equal measure; all appeared pale and tired.

Facing him, over a riot of paperwork, was a woman, average in build and looks. That wasn't to say she wasn't immaculately presented, but there was nothing distinguishing, despite the perfectly groomed shoulder length blonde hair, the pin striped suit and glacier white blouse buttoned to the neck. A gold brooch added a touch of glamour to an otherwise anonymous outfit. When she spoke her voice was slow and measured, in a business-like East Coast way that instilled little confidence.

'Ah, Mr Logan I presume.'

Logan nodded.

'Take a seat. You too Miss Richter. I'm Angela Carlisle, Acting President. The others here,' Carlisle waved her hand expansively around the table, 'you'll learn more about, as and when necessary.' She indicated one person in a black suit with striped shirt and a skinny black tie. 'This is Mr Michaels from the British Embassy, who's here to hold your hand. For now, shall we concentrate on your contribution to the cluster fuck and understanding why I shouldn't just have you shot for aiding and abetting terrorism against the United States?' The Acting President used profanity with more ease than first appearance might have suggested.

Logan kept his face straight. Now wasn't a moment to show weakness.

'Well?'

'Madam President, I understand how it looks with regard to the al-Qaeda asset now on US soil,' A snort of derision interrupted him and Logan waited an appropriate time before continuing. 'We lost contact with Assiz when he arrived in Waziristan, owing to the breakdown of relations with Pakistan. Once he'd gone dark we knew it could be touch and go whether we found him before he struck.'

Carlisle laughed, a short coughing sound, laced with derision. 'Well, you didn't find him. Instead he found us and we are looking at the worst Continental US terrorist attack since 9/11. Do you realise that over a thousand people are dead and we have no idea where this man is?'

He remained still and allowed the hate to wash over him. It was understandable they were pissed off and there was no snappy answer for this situation. Michaels looked even more uncomfortable and the MI6 agent realised no support was available from that direction. Was he being hung out to dry? He had to be circumspect.

'What do you want from me Madam President?'

'Answers, Mr Logan, answers. Why did you, or MI6, hold back vital information from the US; information that could have reduced the number of deaths, if not averted the attacks.'

Good question, thought Logan, for which he had no adequate answer. What did he say?

'Madam President, we were operating in a dark environment. It was unclear that Assiz had entered the country or, indeed, was intending to come to the United States.' Charlie quietened as President Carlisle raised a hand.

'Thank you for your contribution Miss Richter. I suggest you leave it at that. Whether Assiz was coming or not, he represented a significant threat to the security of this country. One which, if you knew of it, you should have informed your superiors of. You are in enough trouble, don't make it worse.'

'With respect, Madam President, we have to work in the here and now; finger pointing is for later. We have to find Assiz and those he is working with, before the next phase of his operation.'

A dangerous silence followed Logan's observation.

'And you'd be the one to sort that out would you Logan?'

Logan took in the five-star general who addressed him scornfully. 'General, it doesn't matter at this stage who sorts it out, so long as somebody does. I have information that would be useful to tracking down Assiz, but you have a bigger problem than Assiz.'

'Which is?' The general glowered back.

'The Chinese.'

'Ah yes, the big conspiracy theory.' It was clear the general had been apprised of Logan and Charlie's concerns and was less than impressed.

'What theory is that, General Adams?' President Carlisle addressed the general.

The latter snorted. 'Ask our Brit friend.'

All eyes turned to the MI6 agent. Charlie was impressed by how he kept his composure in such a hostile environment.

He nodded. 'It is a theory to some extent, but backed up by our experiences, and their own activity.'

'Would you care to expand? For my benefit?' Carlisle arched an eyebrow in mock humour.

Logan carefully presented his case for the Chinese backing the attacks, for what seemed the millionth time. Stony faces greeted his hypothesis. He was about to rephrase his words when the doors behind him swung open, letting in a cold breath of air from the corridor beyond.

Two people walked in. Logan refrained from swinging to see who they were, despite acknowledging Charlie catch her breath. It probably wasn't good.

'I'm sorry we're late,' offered a full, female voice.

'Noted Director Markham,' said the President, less than impressed. 'What was the delay? Can somebody find these two chairs please?'

There was a momentary flurry of activity as chairs were brought in for Sarah Markham and the austere man who accompanied her. Logan sifted through the pictures in his head and finally settled on Director Eugene Hutchinson of NSA.

Sarah Markham was beautiful, Logan noted, in an ice cold way, with long blonde hair, perfect figure and the lightest blue eyes it was possible to bear. She drew a dossier from her shoulder bag, placed it carefully on the table and opened it. Briefly she glanced at Hutchinson as if for confirmation before she continued, which she received.

'Madam President. You may have been hearing circumstantial evidence for Chinese involvement in the terrorist atrocities which took place these last five days.'

'Yes, Mr Logan has been hypothesising some fanciful notion that the Chinese are feeding al-Qaeda experience and software to attack the US.'

Markham regarded the five-star general carefully. 'Not as fanciful as you might imagine General. Madam President, we have evidence that the software used to bring down Air Force One is Chinese in origin and matches the signatures of the software used to such deadly effect against our Marine unit in Yemen just a month ago.'

'Are you saying ...?'

'Madam President, I believe we are notionally at war with the People's Republic of China.'

Twenty-Eight

'Can you be certain?'

There had been several minutes of what could only be described as pandemonium when Sarah Markham had dropped her dirty bomb. Eventually Carlisle had calmed everyone down. She looked at her CIA chief with something close to fear. 'I mean, if you're right it would make Pearl Harbour look like Little League.'

Markham nodded. 'I'd like to be able to come here Madam President and say it is, one-hundred per cent, al-Qaeda but that would be untrue. We really believed they were working on their own, or perhaps with the Taliban and the Cucuta Cartel, with whom they've been trading expertise and drugs. Data analysis pointed very strongly to the latter option but it has become very clear over the last forty-eight hours that there is a bigger player pushing forward the agendas of all these organisations.'

'Are you gonna share with us what has driven that clarity, or are we to be treated to yet more hyperbole and drama?'

Everyone looked to the new combatant wading into the murky waters of terrorism analysis. John Salt was the Secretary for Defence, a man noted for his uncompromising will and plain speaking. A college football star, Salt was a bull of a man still, though he was pushing at the door of sixty-five. He committed to two hours in the gym every day and was on his fourth wife. The rumour on the hill was that he'd worn the first three out.

Markham regarded Salt. He wasn't anybody she liked but she knew that to succeed with this she had to get him on side. 'Mr Salt, if I may?' She nodded at the big screen and he nodded in return. Syncing her idev with the room's mainframe, Markham quickly brought up video surveillance footage. Her audience stared at the scene of a busy café, frozen in pause as Markham provided narrative.

'Following the explosion in Baltimore, FBI investigators were able to ascertain the ownership of all the apartments save one – the one at the centre of the explosion. The Baltimore Police were able to establish that it was rented two weeks prior to a person of Pakistani extraction. That, though, hadn't been the occupant. The landlord provided us with a photofit of a young man who'd been given access and, using the national database, we were able to identify,' she brought up a photo in the top left corner of the screen, 'Sikandar Durrani. Durrani has no known links with the extremist groups we have under surveillance, which gives us a different problem that I'll come to shortly.

'So, knowing who we were looking for, FBI and Baltimore Police sequestered all CCTV footage from the city and ran Durrani's face through the profiling software.'

In the gap Markham created in her presentation Salt leaned forward. 'Are you sure this is the man we're looking for?'

'Totally, Secretary. We showed his photo to people in the vicinity and he was positively identified as the person who was using the apartment at the centre of the explosion. Why?'

Salt rubbed his face with a tired hand. 'Only because Durrani was a witness at a Senate oversight committee meeting, investigating the radicalism of Muslim youth in inner city areas.'

'Well, this man had another secret.' Markham

flicked the photo off the screen and played the CCTV footage. 'This footage was taken early afternoon at a Baltimore coffee shop the same day as Air Force One was brought down. Watch carefully.'

As the tape played the assembly saw a Chinese man enter the shop, buy coffee and sit next to Durrani. He sipped from his drink, checked his cell phone which he then slammed angrily on the table. The device dropped to floor and the Chinese man leant over and picked it up. After pocketing it he rose and left without finishing his coffee.

They watched as a woman pointed to something on the floor close to where the man had sat. Sikandar Durrani bent hurriedly and picked it up; rose and headed for the door. There was a flicker as the view switched to another camera picking up the story, showing Durrani waving and shouting after somebody in the crowd. Then he nonchalantly thrust his hands in his pockets and walked off – in the opposite direction to the receding figure of the Chinaman.

Markham stopped the video and flicked another photo to the screen. 'The Chinese man was identified as Chan Huicai, a banker at HSBC's operation in Baltimore. He's low level but recently went to visit family back in China. One of his relatives just happens to be a resident software expert at the Institute of Electronic Information and Science in Harbin.'

A woman in the blue of the Air Force raised a pen as if in school, waiting for her turn. Markham allowed her to speak.

'The Chinese have consistently stated they do not sanction or condone cyber warfare of any kind. Firestorm technology, if originating in China, is a complete rebuttal of those denials. Are you seriously expecting us to believe that the Chinese government is behind such attacks on a sovereign nation?'

Markham stifled the sigh that rose in her chest and instead feigned boredom. 'General Thatcher, the Chinese are on equal terms militarily with the United States and we all know that in just a few years they will overtake us technologically, as they most assuredly do in terms of numbers. If we take this as a universal truth then, theoretically, it is not beyond the bounds of probability that they may wish to test methods of accelerating that process.

'However, it is more likely that the Chinese government has not sanctioned this attack – they are, after all, nothing if not patient – and that it is the work of independent forces at large in the country. If we take that tack then the likely contender is this man,' she flicked yet another image to the big screen, 'Leong Chaozheng. Leong is a front runner in the contest for the next premier. Interestingly his name means "conqueror of the west, surpass, just, prosper, government".'

'So we're saying this man is launching attacks against the US?' Salt talked to the screen but his question challenged Markham's assessment.

'Indirectly, Secretary. As a free agent, if he was carrying out these attacks, he would be potentially breaking the laws of his country, as well as international law. As a consequence, he is prepared to use … fronts … to achieve his aims. What better way to do that, than through organisations such as al-Qaeda? After all, it mirrors the activities of both East and West during the Cold War. For al-Qaeda, substitute Bader Meinhof, Red Army Faction and a host of Communist-backed governments in developing countries. We believe that Leong is negotiating in South America to develop a Pan-Latin America pact that obviates the need for them to work with the US.'

'Holy shit!'

'Indeed.'

Acting President Carlisle was doing a better job of keeping her emotions in check. 'What is your assessment, Director Markham?'

'The attack on Air Force One was too sophisticated to have been designed and carried out by al-Qaeda operatives acting independently. Cracking a civilian airliner's software is one thing; commandeering both Air Force One and an F15 are several orders of magnitude beyond that. They had to have help.' She paused. 'China is the only country with the capability for that type of infiltration.'

Many heads were shaking around the table, but Logan noted that it was now from fear rather than denial. They knew that if they accepted Markham's words then the US was completely open to attack and there was nothing they could do about.

'Do you know what you are saying?'

'Unfortunately I do Mr Salt.'

Salt shook his head. 'This turns everything we'd accepted about China on its head. This is a very big step you're asking us to take, Director.'

'Thank you John,' Carlisle raised a hand to silence the room. 'Director, how do we respond?' She held the CIA Director in her gaze.

'Whatever our response, it will have to be unconventional, both diplomatically and militarily. We cannot fight this as we would normally.'

'Director Hutchinson?'

The head of NSA coughed. 'Director Markham

226

may be correct. I would still exercise caution until we can be completely sure.'

'If I may?'

Heads turned at the interruption.

'Yes Mr Logan.'

'Our first target is Assiz. He still has unfinished business here in the States. He is going to target you, the Presidential election candidates, and the administration at Lincoln's funeral. If other dignitaries, world leaders are there, that would be a bonus.'

'Anybody for coffee?' A figure rose and headed for the filter machine: it was General Adams, still clearly unimpressed by the evidence before him.

The general waved the jug at the table. Several people nodded and Carlisle let them fill their mugs before continuing. Sipping on the dark, heavy liquid, heads nodded – the coffee was good.

Logan noted how everybody who'd been refilled became focussed on their drinks. He accepted a cup and smelled the surface, cautiously. Others were talking but, for the moment, he was absorbed by the coffee. A sip passed his lips. It was good, but he was sure it wasn't the coffee that made it so – there was something else … what? He pushed the cup away and frowned.

Charlie nudged him and he looked up. 'What's wrong?' she hissed at him.

He glanced at her, at her cup and mouthed "nothing" before zoning back into the discussion around the table. They were considering his observations on Assiz. 'You have to postpone the Presidential funeral. At least until Assiz has been found.'

'And where do we start with that process?' Salt

was sceptical of the British agent's words and observations. 'We have no idea where he might be.'

Logan nodded. 'True, but we're pretty certain that he was last in Baltimore, meeting with Durrani. We also think he was at the Lincoln Memorial meeting with the suicide bomber. Facial recognition software is being used to search for him and my people have provided some photofit pictures of how we think he might look now. We're confident we can track him down.'

'Before it's too late?'

'Hopefully. Finding Assiz may expose Leong though.'

Adams grunted. 'It'd be easier to take out Leong.'

'But there'd be more collateral that way. Listen, Assiz is the key to this problem. You take him out, the Chinese have lost their broker with al-Qaeda. It will expose Leong and you might get leverage with Beijing. Killing Leong might be easier but then you have to expect a very public backlash from the Chinese.'

'John, your assessment please?' Carlisle turned to her Secretary of Defence.

Salt harrumphed. 'Though I hate to admit it, the Brit's assessment is fairly good. We're not going to gain anything by taking out Leong, tempting though that might be. Assiz, a rogue agent, in the country illegally, is our best option.'

'Okay, so how do we go about it?'

Markham picked up the baton. 'Between the FBI, Homeland, NSA and us, we can search for Mr Assiz. Once we've identified him we can activate assets in the vicinity to respond to the threat. That may take a number of guises. Preferable at this stage is an infiltration into a local cell that he might be involved with and lay bait to attract him before taking him out.

'One thing I would be concerned about,' she continued, 'is him making contact with Leong by some means and sending him to ground. We need Leong exposed too.'

'Agreed, Director.' Carlisle drained her coffee and suddenly felt very happy, no – euphoric almost. She shook her head and put the mug down, staring at it momentarily, wanting more. 'Okay, I want this little bastard found and found soon. I want assets on standby to take him down as soon as it is safe to do so. Everybody clear about that?

Heads bobbed up and down around the table and for a second Carlisle had to control an urge to giggle. She wasn't a coffee drinker normally and she vowed not to drink it again. It was embarrassing. 'Very well, this meeting is closed. Directors,' She addressed Markham and Hutchinson, 'I will leave you to draw up plans and liaise with the agencies you deem necessary to execute them. One thing,' Carlisle paused to ensure maximum effect. 'You are authorised to use whatever force necessary to ensure Assiz is removed from play. Understood?'

Markham glanced briefly at Logan and Richter then nodded; Hutchinson managed an almost perfunctory 'Yes ma'am.'

'Very good. Let's nail this sonofabitch.'

*

'Did you notice the President?' Logan stopped Charlie Richter, some way down the corridor, and a little away from the dispersing throng of politicians and military leaders.

Charlie looked at him. She felt a little light headed, as though she'd had one too many, but put it down to not eating properly. 'How do you mean?'

'Did you see how she behaved after she had her coffee?'

Charlie shook her head. 'No. I just think everybody is a bit hyper because of what has gone on.'

'Hmm,' Logan was clearly unconvinced.

'What do you think is up?'

'Have you smelt the coffee, tasted it? I mean really tasted it.'

Charlie considered the question. 'Well, it tastes a little different, sweeter than normal but probably somebody put too much sugar in it.'

'There's something wrong with the coffee. Is there anywhere here we can get this analysed?' He held his mug aloft, which was still half full.

'Dunno,' Charlie confessed. She frowned. 'What do you think is wrong with it?'

'I think it's been drugged.'

Twenty-Nine

Scepticism pulsed in the atmosphere as the Secret
Service agent sniffed the coffee cup he held, almost
gingerly, in his hand.

'You're saying this is drugged?' He raised an
eyebrow, which Logan acknowledged with a nod.
'What gives you reason to believe this sir?'

'The behaviour of people who were drinking it in
the conference room, and the smell of it.'

Another cautious sniff of the cold liquid 'Smells
like coffee sir.' The politeness was constrained and
delivered with forced humour, but he held Logan's
gaze.

'Can we just test it please?' Logan held his
frustration back from the confrontation. Challenging a
Secret Service agent right now would be like bating a
starving dog with raw steak.

'I'll see what I can do,' responded the agent,
turning away with the cup still held between thumb
and forefinger, as if it carried a contagion. Logan
didn't hold out much hope.

'What now?'

He turned to take in Charlie. She'd perked up now
she'd taken on board some water. The half empty
bottle was gripped fiercely, as if to prevent escape.

'We need to find Assiz and the best way of doing
that is working with your guys and the other bad boys
in the intelligence community. Which way?'

*

They found Markham, Hutchinson and other,
unidentified, spooks in one of the situation rooms that
bordered the conference facility they'd used earlier.

The facility was fully self-contained, and hardened against terrorist attack by several million tonnes of granite, protecting what was left of the US government. Corridors delved deep into the rock; harsh fluorescents drove away the dark in this most secure of facilities. Logan trusted they wouldn't need to retreat further.

The situation room could have been in any Washington or Baltimore office block. It was a hive of activity and Logan could see pictures of Assiz being compared to CCTV footage. The walls to the rear were covered in larger screens with live feeds; US and World maps that showed the displacement of active investigations, incidents and other information that might help the agents' work.

Would they find his old colleague soon enough?

Sat around the table with Markham and Hutchinson, were a number of individuals Logan knew by name only. There was David Chandler, director of Homeland Security; Anne Souster, the recently appointed head of the FBI. To her left was Jeff Carlsson, head of FEMA: all of them looked like city bankers.

The others he didn't recognise; however, they looked nothing like city bankers. All sat with a military bearing, displaying little or no emotion. Logan surmised they were SEALs. He figured the seriousness factor had just increased several fold and the intent was to stop Assiz as soon as possible.

He and Charlie took seats, eschewing the coffee that was offered them in favour of cold, still water.

Sarah Markham nodded briefly in their direction, seemingly irked by the show of tardiness. 'Now we're all here, let's get started. We're hunting this man,' she brought Assiz's photo up on the main screen, 'Sayed

Assiz. Assiz is ex-CO19, London Metropolitan Police's crack firearms unit. He disappeared off the grid about two years ago after the death of his sister in a terrorist related incident in London.'

Logan felt himself flinch at the statement and was grateful only one other in the room knew of his part in that event.

'He resurfaced in Yemen and then Waziristan, where he was radicalised by,' Markham flicked another photo to the big screen, 'the imam, Mohammed al-Siddiqi. Al-Siddiqi is on our watch list, having personally funded activities in the Arab Peninsula and Nigeria. He is known to actively support the new wave of Somali pirates, enabling them to purchase sophisticated weaponry on the black market.'

'What threat is al-Siddiqi to Homeland?'

Markham regarded Chandler with thinly disguised humour. 'He is a prime mover for all al-Qaeda activities across the globe. He is, if you like, the spiritual successor to bin Laden but, more than the latter, is capable in directing and energising the troops through skilful and targeted business across the Muslim world. The man has several legit companies, which he uses as vehicles for anti-US and anti-Semitic actions. It's all in the report we submitted to you last year David. This is just a preamble for the sake of our SEAL friends, and Mr Logan.'

David Chandler smiled sourly at the unconcealed jibe. 'Just so long as nothing much has changed Sarah. I know how you guys like to play your cards close to your chest.'

'Okay, Dave. Anyhow, al-Siddiqi was seen at a maddrassah frequented by Assiz during his time in Waziristan. The two were never seen together, but

Assiz also took a visit just before he went off the grid for a second time, to a village known to be the imam's family home. We have no intel on his visit, but he then went to Karachi, where he disappeared.'

'That's unfortunate.'

'It is, Anne, however we really need to concentrate now on the fact that Assiz is probably in the country and coordinating terrorist attacks against the state.'

'What of the Somali connection? Where does that come in to play?'

'With regard to the current attacks, we don't think there is any connection.'

'However,' Charlie interjected, 'there is a connection to activities that tie al-Qaeda in with a drug cartel in Colombia.' She blushed as she caught Sarah's disapproving glare but carried on – she was determined to have her say. 'We believe the Somali pirates are a specific part of the puzzle which enable the cartels and al-Qaeda to trade skills and products without being detected.'

'How so?'

'Well, Director Souster, the gig is this: the pirates always handle Venezuelan freighters and tankers as high value targets but never hold them for longer than a week.' She went on to outline the analysis she had carried out only a few weeks previously for her boss, who nodded grudging approval as Charlie continued her presentation.

As she drew to a close she glanced over at her director. Sarah rose in her seat. 'Thank you Charlie. I can verify my senior analyst's findings. Shortly after she passed this information to me we authorised the shadowing of a Venezuelan tanker headed for Karachi. The *Anzio* interdicted a Somali operation and took the pirates into custody. In addition, they took a number of barrels off the tanker that have been verified as filled with processed cocaine. We believe they were destined for either Yemen or Afghanistan, or both. Their leader was less than forthcoming over any relationship they may or may not have with al-Qaeda, or the Cucuta Cartel, even becoming belligerent about our chances of holding back, what he called, the coming tide of revolution.'

Hutchinson snorted. 'The bad guys always talk up the "coming revolution" when they get caught with their pants down. Did these pirates say anything else that was worth noting?'

Markham shook her head. 'No. *Anzio* is due to dock in Cape Town today where they'll be handed over to the South African authorities, and hopefully they'll be able to get some useful information from them.'

There was a short chuckle that rippled round the table. Charlie glanced quizzically at Logan who leant in close to her ear. 'The South Africans aren't well known for their sympathetic intelligence gathering techniques and, as the US is funding a big arms expansion, they'll be only too eager to provide your people with some juicy information.'

Charlie tried to hide the alarm in her eyes; Logan shrugged philosophically.

'Are you expecting a report back from Anzio?'

'We'll get a sitrep from the captain, Anne, and then he'll inform us who our contact is in the NIA. We'll liaise with Jo'burg from then on.'

'Well, keep us up on the news please Sarah, just in case they come up with anything relevant to these attacks.'

'Ma'am.'

Thirty

Hayland drew a hand over his tired eyes and gave a sigh of satisfaction. This had been a good voyage. They'd had a hand in a number of counter-piracy incidents but the *La Conchega* had been the icing on the cake. Taking a whole pirate crew for interrogation was something that every ship involved in Operation Ocean Freedom wished to accomplish; he'd be chalking that up on the side of the hull. He took a last look round the bridge: most of the crew were readying for a spot of shore leave and the relief were taking their stations – time to handover. His XO would cover for him while he visited the American naval attaché at the local Consul. There was just time to supervise the Marines escorting the prisoners ashore.

'Mr Lord, you have the con. Look after the old girl for me while I'm ashore.'

Lord smiled: he and Hayland went back a number of years and had an easy approach to sharing command. 'Sure thing cap'n,' he replied in his easy Southern drawl. 'Say hi to the attaché for me, I sure will miss seeing Dixie.'

Hayland grinned in return. 'I'll be sure to give Rear-Admiral Trenton your regards.' Rear-Admiral Heather Trenton, besides being a consummate naval officer, was excessively well-endowed, hailed from Georgia and so gave rise to the "Dixie" nickname, while every man, and several women, dreamed of someday winning her over, even though she was happily married to the luckiest bastard in the US Navy.

'You do that sir, you do that,' laughed Lord.

Hayland took the stairs to his cabin, quickly showered and donned his whites, before heading for the afterdeck where Lieutenant Bennett and his Marines would be escorting Mekonen and his pirates off the ship.

It would all be a distant memory for the Anzio soon.

*

Mekonen clasped his hands and silently breathed words to Allah. The time was near. He had a call to make but wondered if the Americans would let him. It was necessary that they did so, so his lawyer knew.

The door to his cell ground open in the rasping way of ship's metalwork. A Marine came in; another stood, weapon at the ready, in the corridor. Mekonen's ankle shackle was unlocked and he was pulled to his feet.

He looked at the impassive marine. 'I would like to phone my lawyer please.'

The Marine grinned. 'Would you, *sir*?' The emphasis on the sir was not kind. 'I guess you can have your call when we hand you over to the local authorities.'

'I would like it now please.' He was calm and quiet, as he had been instructed to be, though he was aware time was running out.

The Marine shrugged in a bored way. 'I'll see what I can do.' He re-shackled Mekonen. 'Keep a good watch on him,' the Marine advised his colleague, jerking a thumb in Mekonen's direction; the other nodded.

A few moments later the Marine returned with a cell-phone. 'Here you go. One call. Make it good.'

Mekonen picked up the device, dialled a number and waited for it to be answered.

'Hello?'

'Hello, it is Mekonen. My crew has been captured. We are in Cape Town, about to be handed over for interrogation to the South African authorities. Can you help us?'

'Are you disembarking now?'

The Somali looked briefly at his bored guards. 'Yes. We are going now.'

'Very good. I will help you in ten minutes.'

'Good, I will see you soon.'

'Inshallah.'

'Inshallah.'

Mekonen laid the cell-phone back on the metal table.

'Let's go,' encouraged the Marine.

*

Up on deck, the blue South African sky was crystal clear and the heat dry, but oppressive. Inside, Mekonen was calming himself down. Soon he would be making a statement to the Americans and South Africans, which would be unanswerable. He looked at his men and nodded to them imperceptibly as they stood in a group on the aft deck, waiting to disembark with their guard of US Marines.

Lieutenant Bennett saluted his men and inspected the handcuffs and leg shackles of each pirate. Then he ordered them to single file, causing them to shuffle so that there was an arm's length between each.

As he moved to the gangway he was stopped by a shout. Looking round he saw Captain Hayland moving quickly along the deck to him. Bennett came to attention as the captain drew up to him.

'Well, Lieutenant, ready to hand over your charges?'

'Yes sir.'

'Good job bringing these guys in Lieutenant. I've sent a commendation back to Norfolk for you.'

'Thank you sir.' What else did he say to a man who hardly ever spoke to him the rest of the time? This was just Hayland show-boating in front of the Marines. A crew commendation was just what Hayland wanted to seal off his cruise.

Hayland walked past Bennett, to the head of the line of pirates, staring like a proud lion at the dark Mekonen. 'Well I guess you'll be in safe hands once you get off here. I'm sure the National Intelligence Agency will be very gentle with you.' He chuckled and turned back to Bennett. 'Lieutenant, you can get these shits off my ship now.'

Bennett tipped a salute to the captain and raised an eyebrow briefly to his warrant officer who smiled wryly in return. Hayland was heading down the gangway, hat straight, shoulders back, very much the conquering hero. The Marine lieutenant shook his head and turned.

'Okay everybody, let's move these reprobates out shall we?' He watched as his WO marched the pirates down the gangway while he brought up the rear. On the dock hundreds of sailors from the Anzio were milling around, laughing and shouting as they began the journey into town, to enjoy some R'n'R. Bennett was determined to join them, just as soon as he had handed over these Somalis to the local authorities.

He put his boot on the gangway.

*

239

Mekonen could feel the tremor in his stomach, vibrating through the weight he had carried for some weeks now, waiting for just such an opportunity as this. He could feel the levity in the air around him; a kind of festival as the men and women were unfettered from months at sea. Well, they were about to feel the fireworks.

His foot touched the docks and he was pushed through the crowds. His guards started bellowing for the sailors to part so they could march the Somalis through. Mekonen felt his brothers behind him.

The vibration in his stomach was becoming more urgent now. There was a pulse, followed by another, and another, in quick succession.

Allahu Akbar.

*

The explosions ripped apart the pirates and engulfed those around them in a fireball of incredible ferocity. Bennett was thrown against the hull of Anzio and dropped into the water between the ship and dock. Unconscious, he slipped beneath the surface and never saw the commendation he didn't want.

Hayland was blown in half and the last thing that went through his head as he dropped, dying, to the ground was "oh shit."

*

The aftermath showed there were a hundred and three dead and another ninety-two wounded to varying degrees. Of the dead, eighty-nine were from Anzio; the rest were pirates. The cruiser was effectively out of commission: never minding the damage the blast had caused, the loss of so many crew members would keep her in Cape Town for several weeks.

Investigations by SA Police, NIA and CIA determined, with some probability, that the Somali pirates had carried the bombs in their bodies for just such an eventuality. By interrogating the phone left in the room occupied by Mekonen, prior to his leaving the ship, NSA experts ruled that the pirate had phoned somebody in Yemen.

They were unable to trace it back to a specific village or town and drone flights showed nothing they could pinpoint – al-Qaeda was getting real sassy about secure communications, and anything that might be construed as a head above the parapet.

News got back to Raven Rock the same day.

Thirty-One

The door of the situation room swung open. Logan and Charlie were still debating with Markham, Souster and the others. Everyone whirled at the sudden interruption. Carlisle came in quickly, looking old and uncertain. Secret Service agents stood outside the door, decidedly twitchy.

'Ma'am?'

Carlisle looked through Markham, her face pallid. 'There's been an attack on the Anzio.'

The room suddenly became a cacophony of noise and confusion, everybody talking at once. Finally, Carlisle got them seated and attentive once more. She took a seat at the table. 'Just after two o'clock today, Anzio came under attack from terrorists. The death count is high and the ship is unable to leave Cape Town because so many of the crew are either dead or injured.'

'How come terrorists got so damned close to the ship?' Hutchinson was incredulous, continually shaking his head, as if he had an infection or trauma.

Carlisle drew a deep breath. 'First indications, from where the centre of the blast was recorded, are that the terrorists were on board Anzio, and were being escorted off by a detachment of Marines.'

'Off the ship?' Anne Souster raised an eyebrow. 'How is that possible?'

'We believe the pirates were wired with explosives. They were carrying the bombs internally, probably their stomachs. They were expecting just such an eventuality as this.'

'My God! How do we fight these people?'

'That's what we're going to find out now, Ms

Souster.'

'Madam President, the only way you can fight these people is by using the same techniques,' contributed Logan, the first to accord Carlisle with the epithet "President". 'We are going to have to be sneaky, inventive and willing to fight dirty.'

'Mr Logan, we've been fighting like that for the past decade and still they keep coming. We have to change tack.'

'I agree with you to a degree. The drone attacks of successive American governments have done little to dampen enthusiasm for al-Qaeda though. More and more people flood to the cause. This time, Madam President, there is a difference. Somebody or some government is giving them a hand up to the big league. We need to pre-empt any further advances as quickly as possible.'

'How do you mean?' This from Hutchinson.

'You know my views on the situation. I believe the Chinese are behind the current spate of attacks, however, we are not in a political position to launch an attack against them. We need to emasculate al-Qaeda and the cartels in Colombia. If we take away their protection we can perhaps get Beijing, or whoever is behind this, to back down.'

'You think?'

'Quiet director,' Carlisle ordered the head of NSA. 'Go on, Mr Logan. As you got us into this, perhaps you can advise us how to get out of it.' Carlisle regarded the British agent sceptically.

'There are three strands to this: Assiz; a woman called Penelope Hortez from Colombia, and an arms smuggler called Rado Kiric. We get them, we stop the Chinese.'

Kiric placed the phone on the small camp table and wiped a hand across his brow. The heat of the desert drove through the thin canvas of the Bedouin tent. Yemen was probably the most awful place on the planet; it was also the most lucrative at this moment in time. The deal he had with the Chinese, Leong Chaozheng had helped build his empire and enabled him to accomplish that which had exercised him since he witnessed the death of his mother. But he was hoping for even more. Only when there was an Islamic Nation, which brought every country under one God, one Faith, could he and his brothers relax. He turned.

'We have confirmed shipment. You will have the first of the BMP2s next week.'

'That is good,' remarked the man opposite him. No emotion stirred on the tanned and lined face, overshadowed by a black turban, of the Yemeni.

'Where will you be keeping them?'

'We have places the Americans will not be able to find.'

Kiric tipped his head. 'You're sure?'

The Yemeni nodded slowly. 'Our friends are very good at helping us to hide things from the Americans. After years of raining death down upon our heads, now we are able to fight back. The day of global jihad is at hand my brother, and you will be witnessing the death of the great Satan.'

Kiric nodded slowly, understanding the slow burn that was the hallmark of all good plans. And yet he had a nagging doubt, something troubled him. 'Are you certain, Imam, that we can trust the Eastern friends? After all they do not share our faith, our values.'

'You are right. And yet, Allah sends us signs and miracles which we use as we may. Just as you have the weapons we can use to change our fortunes, so do our Eastern friends have the technology to ensure we are not devastated before we can achieve our goals.'

'But ...'

'Fear not, we have the right of Allah on our side. We have the immutable power of the jihad at our calling. No one can withstand such power and, if our friends choose to use us then shall they feel the wrath of Allah breathing upon their skin, scorching it in the righteous flame.'

Kiric paused, seeing zeal burning in the other's eyes, infusing the leathery skin with the glow of morality. But he had seen more of the world than this imam, knew that it worked in ways that were full of betrayal, steeped in the vinegar of broken promises. It was a bitter world and the sooner the brotherhood understood that, the better.

'What will you use the vehicles for?'

'To distract our enemies.' The imam sipped his date juice, gazing thoughtfully at the desert framed by the tent's opening. 'Many sacrifices are to come; many good men and women will journey to Paradise before the final cut of the sword. Pray that it will be swift and sure when it comes.'

'Inshallah.'

'Inshallah.'

*

The knock on the door shook Logan from his guilty reverie. Quickly he shoved the bottle of whiskey into the bottom drawer of the small chest next to the bed.

245

'Just a minute,' he called, to stall the unknown visitor as he turned the TV down and moved to the door. He twisted the handle and pulled it open.

Charlie Richter smiled back at him and waggled the bottle of wine and two glasses. 'I thought you might like some company, and a drink?' She dropped a hip in what she hoped was a show of affection but it was difficult for her to tell through the fog of wine she'd already consumed – this was the second bottle. 'The alcohol; well it looks as though you're in the same state as me,' she giggled as she stumbled over her words.' She realised that she was still stood in the corridor with the British agent stood in front of her like an oak door that refused to open.

'Well?'

'Well what?'

'Are you going to let me in?'

Logan reluctantly moved out of the way and Charlie sashayed into the room. 'Thanks. Say, our rooms are pretty skank aren't they? Got anything I haven't?' She nosed around the small room hoping to find ... what?

'Okay Charlie, what can I do for you?' Logan wasn't really in the mood for visitors, particular the CIA analyst. He had a bottle of whiskey he wanted to be close to.

Charlie saw the half empty glass, picked it up and sniffed the contents, giggling. 'Ooh, hard stuff. What is it? Whiskey?'

'Scotch,' Logan confirmed.

'Cool, when we've finished this …' she waved the bottle at him.

Logan heaved a sigh. 'Not tonight Charlie.'

'Spoilsport! Come on, let your hair down Mr Bond. While we're stuck down here we might as well have some fun.' She settled on the bed, glasses in hand. Unsteadily she poured wine into both, spilling some on the counterpane. 'Oops. Never mind, here you go,' she thrust a glass towards Logan who, with a shrug, took it from her. After all, why not? More alcohol would help drown the images.

'So why are you drinking?'

He shrugged. 'It helps,' was all he offered.

'With what.'

'I'd rather not –'

'Oh shit!' Suddenly a river of understanding crashed over her, momentarily thrusting that semi-drunk awareness and remorse of a faux pas to the fore of her consciousness. 'I'm sorry; Assiz's sister.'

Logan stared at her. How had she remembered? Sure, he'd mentioned it to her once but he figured it wasn't that big a deal to her. Anyway it was no good denying it. He took a slug of the wine (good quality – he was surprised) and nodded. 'How did you know?'

'It figured,' she replied with the confident air of a drunk. 'When you mentioned it before I could see that her death had really affected you. Have to say, you keep it well hidden most of the time.'

Logan grunted. 'Wouldn't do to be maudlin or suicidal all the time would it?' He cringed inwardly even as he said the words, aware of how they made him look.

'Whoa! You're not …'

'No, I'm most definitely not,' he caught the rest of her words before they reinforced his own feelings. 'Sometimes I just wish it had been different,' he reflected into the black surface of the wine.

'Do you mind … talking … about it?'

Dropping in the armchair opposite the bed, Logan thought on the question a moment. 'So long as you don't try to psychoanalyse me … I guess.'

'What happened?'

He could see her face even as he gathered his thoughts, skin umber coloured; lips dark and inviting; hair that was blue-black, soft and long: the scent lingered …

'I was on secondment to CO19 –'

'That's like a SWAT team isn't it?'

'I guess. Anyway, I was assigned to Sayed Assiz as part of a specialised ART.'

'Which is?'

'Sorry, Armed Response Team. We were specifically tasked with responding to terrorist threats. After the Parliamentary Square incident, the previous year we'd received credible evidence of another programme of works, from home grown terrorist units, to carry out atrocities during the tourist season.

'We were on patrol around Piccadilly when we got a call to say two suspected suicide bombers were approaching Trafalgar Square. Local units were observing them but keeping a distance. We arrived in the square and followed the two suspects.'

'Didn't they respond to your presence?'

'No, and we didn't challenge ourselves over that,' Logan replied with a shake of his head. 'We figured they hadn't clocked us; that they were tyros and were just focussed on the task at hand. Anyway we followed the two women, dressed in full burqas, who seemed to be casing the area before making their move. We began to get a feel for them and decided to confront them. Radioing the other units, we got them to begin moving bystanders from the square.

'What happened then just seemed to take an age, but was over in seconds. We challenged them. One of them made a move towards us and reached into her burqa. Assiz and I both opened fire and she fell. The other kept coming towards us, calling out. As she did she appeared to raise her hand which had something in it. Assiz thought it was a grenade and called out: I opened fire and dropped her.'

'And it was then you found out?'

Logan nodded, feeling his throat tighten with loathing and the groundswell of emotion that threatened to overcome him. He drew a breath. 'When I pulled back her niqab ...' He swallowed the remainder of the wine in one gulp, allowing the alcohol to numb his raw nerves.

'Shit.'

'Yeah.'

'And you think Assiz is after you, to pay you back for what you did?'

'I know he is. Catching him is as much about stopping him killing me, as it is an attack on the United States. You could say I have a vested interest.'

Charlie nodded slowly. 'I can see that. Don't blame you either.' She hunted through the drawers in the chest and pulled out the whiskey. Logan nodded as she held it up. Charlie topped up his drink before pouring the amber liquid into her glass.

'So what would you do?'

Logan looked at her. 'How do you mean?'

'If you were Assiz, what would you do now?'

Logan pondered the question. 'He won't go far away; everything happens around here. He'll need to be close by so he can respond to events. The Appalachians probably provide the cover for them to train without being found.'

'Once we task some resources we'll catch them.'

'For sure,' Logan agreed. 'You just have to hope

it's soon enough. Did we get anything back from that coffees sample?'

'Oh yes! I meant to say. They've done an analysis but need to send it away for confirmation.'

'And …?'

'They can't be sure but, you're right, there is some contamination so they've withdrawn all supplies until further notice.' She grinned. 'So, it's alcohol I'm afraid!'

Logan couldn't help responding to the smile. When she made the attempt she was quite pretty he decided, but he had to be careful.

'That's a major problem, if the food supply is being contaminated. We could have a serious public order problem on our hands and nobody to deal with it.'

Charlie shrugged her shoulders. 'Well, we can't do anything about it tonight so we might as well relax.' She suddenly sat up and crawled to the end of the bed, letting her hair fall about her face. She felt like a flirt and didn't care. 'How do you relax Steve?'

Thirty-Two

Penelope Hortez toyed with her phone. Should she? Shouldn't she? Yet, how else would she get everything through customs without his help. Would he buy it? It was short notice and there was so much going on back there, that perhaps even a Presidential hopeful wouldn't be able to swing things, just like that. In fact, he probably wouldn't be able to.

Stop it!

Stop talking yourself out of this, she rebuked herself. Negative thoughts bred negative decisions and negative results. As she always did in such circumstances she found herself tapping her fingers gently along the side of her left hand. It was a technique her personal coach had shown her, to dispel negative energy and positively boost her demeanour and her outlook. Penelope wasn't sure how the process worked really, but that didn't matter: what was important was it helped her concentrate, to decide the course of action to take.

The phone rang twice at the other end before a voice answered.

'Harry?' She asked, automatically.

'I'm sorry, no,' replied the female. *Was it a lover?* For a moment Penelope, despite her knowledge felt a pang of jealousy. 'I'm his aide.' *Just another fuck then.* 'Please wait while I get the Senator. Can I say who is calling?'

'Penelope, Penelope Hortez.'

'Sure thing, Penelope.'

'Hey, how you doing?' The sound of his voice turned the jealousy to loss. *This will be for my beautiful boys.*

'I'm fine thanks Harry. It's good to hear your voice again.' The lie came almost too easily. 'How are you?'

A wry chuckle trickled down the line. 'Considering all the shit that's hit the fan, fine thanks. How were Berlin and Moscow?'

He always knew, was always interested in what she'd been up to; always wanted to know what she was doing and whether it had been a success. A part of her regretted that she would never enjoy his touch; his embrace; the feeling of him inside her again. The greater part determined to destroy him.

'They were a great success, thanks Harry. Plenty of new business,' She heard him grunt his approval. 'Look, Harry, I'm on my way back home and I was thinking about doing something to help.'

'With …?'

'Well, you know, all that has happened over the last few days in Washington, and on that battleship?'

'Cruiser.'

'Sorry?'

'The Anzio. It was a cruiser. But, yeah, go on.'

'Well, I don't have anything booked for a while and everything is flying in to Washington today. I was wondering if … a charity event … I could arrange it very quickly, the problem would be getting through customs.'

'A charity event? Isn't that a bit short notice?' The tone of scepticism was a deep furrow through Harry Johnson's pleasant demeanour. It would take all Penelope's powers of persuasion.

'Think about it.' Thickening her voice, letting the tones of sexual intimacy drip from it, Penelope oiled Johnson's ego. 'I can get some high flyers in there pretty quick, there're some favours to be called on;

quick enough to put a show on by the weekend. If you want it I'd need to be able to start setting up as soon as the plane lands, to make it work. I've got the venue sorted,' A lie. 'All I need is a fast track.'

'You have got to be kidding. Have you any idea what the US is like right now?' The incredulity sparked off Johnson's voice like a van de Graaff generator at full bore. 'Getting a flight through customs without a check is completely insane. It'll never work.'

'I'm sorry, you're right. It was a foolish idea. I just thought … I don't know …' Change tack, 'that we could raise some money for the families.'

'Well, I'm sorry honey. It wasn't your best idea.'

Shit, she was losing him. 'You're right it wasn't. I'm sorry, I wasn't thinking. I just thought … all this loss is such a terrible burden. Somebody needs to be doing something. I thought you would be able to open some doors for me and we could show a united front to these – terrorists,' Penelope baulked inwardly at her masquerade. 'You know, the Americas standing firm together and …'

She waited, seemingly an eternity.

Johnson sighed. 'Leave it with me. Let me see what I can do.' Penelope allowed herself a small smile. 'I'll get back to you.' The line went dead and she lay back on the hotel bed, the smile becoming a grin.

*

Charlie opened an eye and winced – her head felt like a man with a hammer was busy rearranging the interior. She stretched and stopped immediately. Somebody was in the bed with her. Opening her eyes wide she saw she wasn't in her own room at the complex. She rolled gingerly and took in the form next to her.

Shit.

Quickly she swung her legs out of the bed and raised herself, wincing as her stomach lurched violently at the sudden movement. She submerged the feeling, concentrating on the desire to get out of the room before Logan woke.

'Hey you.'

Too late. 'Hi, how are you this morning.'

Logan propped himself on an elbow and took in Charlie's naked form stood by the bed. 'Better than you, I think. What's with the moonlight flit?'

'Sorry? Moonlight what?'

'Why are you out of bed and trying to get out of the room faster than a rabbit down a hole with a very hungry fox after it?'

'Oh.' She looked at him and the bed. God, it was inviting to get back in there, to be in those arms again; to feel his pressure against her but – 'You noticed.'

'Well I am a secret agent – we're trained to notice,' he offered laconically.

Charlie returned the look. 'I figured I ought to be out of here. It's probably late and people will be wondering where we are.'

Logan looked at his watch. 'It's six-thirty. I think we're ok for a while yet.' He pinned her down with his level gaze. 'You sorry about last night?'

Charlie let her mind run back over the moments after she'd drunkenly flirted with him. Being caught in his embrace had been wonderful; feeling the urgency, yet the gentleness, of his touch and his lovemaking had left her breathless. No she wasn't

254

sorry, but …

'It was a dumb-ass thing to do and we were both drunk at the time. We shouldn't have gone there – at least not here, not like this.' She tried to let her professional training take hold but, as he rolled away from the sheets, towards her, she realised she was losing the battle.

'There wasn't a better time or place to do what we did and I enjoyed it,' affirmed Logan, letting his fingers trace a line down her right thigh.

'Stop it!' She couldn't help smiling though, as the fingers traced round her knee, sending goose bumps straight up her back.

'You're right of course; women always are.' He rolled away and rose from the bed. 'We have to get ready. We have an international terrorist to catch.' Logan was stood in front her and she could see exactly how ready he was.

'Oh shit,' she breathed fervently, 'what's a few more minutes?'

*

Assiz looked at his watch – not much longer. The adrenaline was pumping and yet he knew there was a purpose to his being, to this training and these next few moments in time. He was here for the glory of Allah, here in the mountains defiled by the great Satan. But that was all to change. The first blows had been struck: spectacular in their success, but the beast still writhed and groaned with agony.

In its flailing the beast sought him and Allah's emissaries of eternal justice. Overhead, one of its many eyes would soon be looking for them. But it would not find them, thanks to the devices of the servants.

'Are you ready?'

The young recruit looked up from his laptop. 'Yes, we have five minutes before the satellite is over the horizon. At that point we'll infiltrate the device and implant the subroutine.'

'You are confident?'

The other nodded and his demeanour told Assiz that he should not question him.

'Once the satellite is overhead we can transmit the codes which will infect the whole system. If it works, we will effectively become invisible to their satellites.'

Assiz considered the sun, already high in the early summer sky and smiled. 'Good Afiq, very good.'

Afiq glanced up and nodded. He admired Assiz but he wasn't the fanatic the Brit was. Though he prayed to Allah and though he had had his fair share of abuse and slander, he was here for other reasons. It pricked his conscience to be doing what he did, against the country that housed him and provided for him but, when the sword of Allah was held over your family in a far off country that was as powerful a motivator as any personal religious fervour. Afiq often wondered what he could do to thwart these mad people who sought to wield Allah's power in such unholy ways.

There wasn't anything, so concentrate on the task. Two minutes and twenty-three seconds.

*

The situation room was filled with the same personnel as the day previous when Logan walked in. Charlie was already seated, away from the door and the two remaining free chair in the room. A wise decision and he deliberately avoided her gaze, after an initial nod in her direction. He had a feeling, from the look on her face that Sarah Markham knew exactly what was going on.

'Mr Logan, good morning.' He acknowledged Markham's greeting. 'Glad you could join us. We were discussing the options for finding the proverbial needle in the haystack.'

He took the chair, sat and poured water in a glass. 'Good, and the answer is?'

Hutchinson responded. 'Our satellite surveillance is being tasked as we speak. With the coverage afforded by our network, we can pattern and interrogate the resulting images within a very short time. There isn't anywhere for Assiz to hide.'

'Unless, of course, he's able to penetrate the security and infect the network; rendering it incapable.'

The silence around the table was palpable.

'Given the actions against Air Force One and the other elements the real prospect of your systems being compromised by a serious and concerted cyber-attack is a clear and present danger … surely?' he concluded looking at the dejected faces of the Americans.

It was one of the SEALs who spoke up first. 'You have a good point there Steve,' he was the first to use the British agent's first name. 'What do you suggest?'

'This is going to have to be an operation like no other. We won't be able to rely on our gizmos and gadgets. Maybe even mobile phones will be a no-no. Ladies and gentlemen: we are back to first principles.'

The buzz around the table was filled with a nervous energy that threatened to overcome reason.

Logan raised his hands to restore some order. 'I appreciate it's not a great position to be in, but every moment we spend bemoaning the fact that we may be blinded is time wasted.'

'Agent Logan is correct. Let's concentrate on the present and have a contingency in hand to respond. We need to utilise all currently available capacity to try pinpoint where Assiz and his cohort are until such time as we're compromised. Director Hutchinson I'd be grateful if you could explore what options are available to us, if one or more of our satellites are knocked out. Director Souster, we need to coordinate with law enforcement agencies and National Guard nationwide. Eyes on the ground are going to be crucial if we're electronically blinded.'

Both nodded, not remonstrating that the CIA director had taken control of the moment.

'Director, may I?'

Markham looked at Logan and he felt as if he was being scanned, it was slightly unnerving. 'Yes Mr Logan?'

'We need to concentrate closer to home. I think Assiz is going to use the funeral of President Lincoln to try and take out the rest of the Administration. Any collateral damage will greatly enhance al-Qaeda's cause. For that reason, I don't think he's going to be far away. He needs to be able to respond quickly to what happens and to be near a major port or airport so he can get out of the country quickly.'

'You're right Mr Logan. We'll need to bring in a team of agents to set up a processing facility ASAP.'

'No.' All eyes turned to Logan.

'How do you mean?' It was clear that Markham wasn't amused by the rebuke.

'All CIA agents have a chip in them, don't they?'

There was a multitude of nods. 'That means they are compromised. We need a team that is pure, doesn't have any technology.'

'Shit, Logan, you're a bag of good news.' Hutchinson shook his head glumly.

'He's right,' Charlie affirmed, coming to his rescue. 'If we use local assets, and there is any chance they could be firestormed, we stand to lose everything.'

'Solutions?' Markham scanned at the assembled experts before stopping at Logan. He returned her consideration carefully.

'I want to bring my own team in, from London.'

'Okay,' Markham was cautious. 'Sell it to me.'

Logan nodded, quietly pleased that she hadn't been patriotic. Given his own involvement she could have been excused such a stand. 'I have a number of specialists who are good at working with minimal resources. I can get them over here on an RAF flight and we can be running by tomorrow afternoon.'

'What about deactivating the chips?' It was clear that Hutchinson didn't feel comfortable with Logan's proposal.

'It would take too long to sort out and there would be no guarantee, unless you removed them, that they couldn't be compromised.'

Hutchinson's slow nod made it clear he accepted the reasoning, though he didn't like it.

'We're not totally reliant on the Brits. I don't have a chip.' All eyes turned to Charlie, who shrugged apologetically in Logan's direction. 'Just saying.'

Markham considered her senior analyst. Should she let the woman work with Logan? It was evident the two of them were an item or, at least, sharing a bed. By rights she ought to send her back to Langley. But time was pressing; there was no other analyst available and Charlie was right, she didn't have a chip.

'Very well. Charlie I want you to lead on the search for Assiz. Mr Logan, you bring your people in, but you report to Miss Richter. Okay?' She didn't really care if it wasn't; it was how it was going to be.

Logan remained stoical at the news. Internally he wondered at the sense of Charlie and he working together. For now, there was no choice. 'Okay, I'll get on with setting up a base and I'll get in touch with London.'

'Good,' Markham told him. She looked over at the impassive black clothed SEAL. 'Lieutenant Black, what does your team need?'

'A target.'

Logan barely suppressed a smile. Typically succinct and to the point, Black's comment caught Markham by surprise. She quickly recovered. 'We'll do our best to oblige, Mr Black.'

'I'd appreciate you working with us,' proffered Logan, 'we may need to do some old school tracking.'

'Sure thing, sir,' Black nodded in the easy confident way of a SEAL.

Markham looked the table over. 'Okay people, we have a terrorist to catch and a country to protect. Let's go everybody. The clock is ticking.'

Thirty-Three

Eduardo Sanchez consulted his watch again. Any moment Leong would be arriving and he wished he'd had time to prepare for the visit. What the General wanted he didn't know, but he was sure that it wouldn't be to his benefit.

His phone rang and he took the call. 'Hello.'

It was Victoria. 'Mr Sanchez, I thought you would like to know of developments in the US.'

'Go on?'

'We have intelligence that a new product has been established on the East Coast while we and our competitors were otherwise occupied. Evidence suggests it is Cucuta borne.'

'Already?' Sanchez couldn't hide his surprise. How had Suarez managed this? 'Are you sure about that?'

'Yes,' Victoria was very direct. 'Certain products have shown increased sales and we predict that within a month Cucuta have established their product across the East Coast, starting in the traditional markets.'

'That is … interesting news,' Sanchez pondered his assistant's words. So Cucuta was still operational. Who was flying the flag for the recently decapitated cartel? Could it be Suarez's elusive wife, somebody the authorities had repeatedly failed to pin down?

'There is something else. Do you remember that some years ago you funded a rising star designer of the fashion industry?'

Sanchez chuckled sarcastically. 'There are so many I help.'

Did Victoria hesitate just a little too long with her reply. 'Penelope Hortez was a relative unknown five years back. She produced some pieces for a show you sponsored in Bogota, promoting Colombian business opportunities to the Latin American Federation. Her pieces,' pause, 'attracted you and you said you would sponsor her personally, to develop her fashion house.'

Sanchez did his best to cast his mind back, but it was difficult. There were so many women he had helped and taken advantage of their gratitude, as they did his patronage. Perhaps it was better not to aggravate Victoria further. 'Penelope … of course; what of her?'

Victoria was plainly irritated. 'Penelope Hortez was in Berlin this last month and has just finished a show in Moscow. She's about to make her way back to Colombia. When she was at Berlin's opening night party she met with one Rado Kiric, a Muslim arms dealer and drug smuggler from Kosovo. Our contacts believe they did some business, beyond sharing a hotel for several nights.'

'Business?'

Victoria contained the sigh. 'Kiric wants to get heroin into the States – he has a big order to satisfy for the Taliban, who were going to send it via Yemen and Somalia. That was before the Cucuta cartel was hit, and the US Navy took an intense interest in Venezuelan shipping heading by the Horn of Africa.'

'And how is Penelope going to help with that?'

'Ms Hortez is flying her exhibition into the States before heading back to Colombia, on the pretext of staging a charity show to raise funds for victims of the atrocities. Our people believe she will use that as a pretext to bring Kiric's drugs into the country.'

Sanchez was perplexed. 'How is she going to get them past border controls?'

'Ms Hortez has a special passport into the US.'

'A special passport?'

'Again, our intel suspects she is sleeping, or has slept, with Senator Harry Johnson.'

Eduardo Sanchez drew in a sharp intake of breath and then smiled. 'My dear, you have a way of bringing good news.'

'Wait, that isn't all. We have evidence that Kiric is in the pay of the Chinese. A certain Yuan Zhiming has been in contact with the Kosovan and Yuan is connected to somebody you know well.'

'Leong?!' he breathed excitedly.

'Correct.'

'Oh, my dear you certainly know how to cheer a man up.'

*

When the Chinese general was shown into Sanchez's spacious Bogota office Leong sensed the change in his Colombian colleague. He chose not to respond to the anxious question that played around his mind. Instead, he settled into the deep, cool mahogany coloured leather sofa and accepted the tea Sanchez's secretary offered.

'So General, to what do I owe this pleasure?' Sanchez leaned back in his chair, affecting an air of calm serenity that he hardly felt inside. The general looked small on the other side of the large teak desk.

'Senator, I am here to discuss business.'

'Which business is that?'

'The matters we discussed at your ranch in Mexico.' Leong regarded his erstwhile partner. 'What other were you contemplating?'

Sanchez smiled almost coyly. 'I was hoping you could tell me?'

Leong controlled his breathing. 'I'm afraid I'm unclear as to what you are referring.'

'I'm sure,' Sanchez replied laconically. He rose from his desk and strode across the room to a sideboard. Opening a cupboard, he pulled out a decanter and glasses and placed them on the counter top. He poured a large whiskey and offered the glass to his guest who shook his head perfunctorily. Sanchez sat at his desk again.

'You know, General, Colombia has a thriving fashion trade and some of our names are the biggest in the world.' Pause. 'Take Penelope Hortez for instance. Now, a few years ago she was a talent of no consequence on the world stage. But, with a little help from me, she was able to launch a successful worldwide fashion house, able to stage exhibitions at a variety of international cities.' Pause again. 'Such as Berlin.'

Leong looked long and hard at his interrogator. 'Expand, please.'

'Ms Hortez was seen with a Kosovan; a certain Rado Kiric. You'll have heard of him no doubt.'

Leong kept his expression impassive, after all, what did it matter that this man knew of the smuggler. Both were expendable once they had served their purpose. He chose not to respond and inwardly smiled at the irritation which flickered in Sanchez's eyes.

'It seems that Mr Kiric had some cargo which our Ms Hortez could help him with. But also … Mr Kiric has a business associate whom you, no doubt, are very well acquainted with. A certain Yuan Zhiming …' He left the comment hanging in the warm air between them.

Leong considered the politician's comments.

'What is it you want Senator Sanchez?'

'When you were at my ranch in Mexico we talked about the possibility of joint ventures. You know of my desire to lead in South American politics; after all I have by far the widest influence across the continent, and you would find that useful. Indeed, you have said so on a number of occasions.'

'So? Your point is?'

'Before we get to my point, I have to say that I know little of your ambitions, General Leong, and that tires me. I am not accustomed to being left in the dark by a business partner. It would help both our long term plans if you were more open.'

Leong steepled his fingers. 'How would knowing all China's plans help you do what you need to?'

The air of procrastination sat heavily in the room; expectation draped itself on the shoulders of both politicians. Sanchez watched his counterpart closely but Leong gave nothing away. Like a brick wall. Time to change tack.

'You're right General, forgive my intrusion. Let us get to business. As you are aware we have been able to harness the support of a Senator ...'

'Harness?'

Sanchez smiled. 'Senator Johnson is inextricably bound to me, both politically and commercially. I aim to exploit that.'

'You mean you're blackmailing him?'

Sanchez almost kept his composure. 'I'm interested where you draw that conclusion from. Blackmail is a strong term.'

'But adequate in the context of the information you hold over the American, and which you are using to ensure he will do what you want.'

Sanchez coloured: glad that he had the sun behind

him; equally aware that Leong knew all too well that he was caught out. 'And you would do anything differently?' Sanchez retorted petulantly.

'Perhaps not, then again are you in possession of all the information you need to extort Johnson? What exactly are you intending?'

Now he was expected to voice his plan, it sounded infantile and he wished he wasn't compelled to speak. Puffing his chest out, he faced Leong down. 'We will use Johnson to flood the US market with drugs. This will be to your benefit if we are to establish China as the dominant force on the South American continent.'

Leong stared impassively at Sanchez and wondered. Why did he have to work with such individuals? It was his own fault he rationalised. He often believed people worked and thought as he did. However, there were options: always a good position to be in.

'I am intrigued how you believe this could be good, in any form, for our relationship? You are holding an American Senator to ransom. They are never happy with being blackmailed and you can expect them to make you pay more.'

'What I have over Johnson will be enough to keep him in place. He won't want anything to upset his run to the Presidency.'

The silence from Leong was long and uncomfortable. 'We have a problem if this is how you believe the world can be won. Gone are the days of such confrontation. We prefer … other methods.'

'Yes, hiding behind others,' Sanchez retorted huffily, 'letting them do your dirty work for you. Is that what you want from me, General?'

'You know what we want from you, Senator Sanchez. We want you to be President of a Colombia which will promote Chinese interests across Latin America. China will be a close ally and friend to counter US influence.' He paused. 'What we don't want is you conducting your own business with America in such an open and crude way.'

Sanchez spluttered on his whiskey. 'What?!'

'You heard me, Mr Sanchez. Should you wish to continue to benefit from our patronage I think it is time to renegotiate the conditions of our arrangement.'

'How dare you speak to me like this!' Sanchez raged at the impenetrable Chinese general.

'Stop your histrionics, Senator, you will do nothing: the political ambitions you harbour are too reliant on my government's goodwill. If you wish that to continue there is something I want you to do.'

Sanchez simmered in his chair, keeping his silence. Leong shrugged and continued, unfazed by the Colombian's attitude. 'You will desist from this reckless course of action with Johnson. In the next few days I am expecting a visitor. You will provide, at my request, the means for him to access the country and visit me, enabling him to return from whence he came. It is most important you are exact in this and do nothing to upset what is a delicately balanced operation. Its success will ensure you receive that which you desire most.'

'Which is?'

'Power.'

Thirty-Four

A swollen sun was wakening the eastern sky, promising a hot day, as the Royal Air Force Globemaster touched down at Andrews Air Force Base. Logan stood patiently on the tarmac as the aircraft came to a standstill and an airstair door opened, to disgorge its occupants. Charlie Richter was next to him, intrigued as to how the British contingent might appear.

As the three individuals ambled down the stairs she thought a little of the mystique she had felt was left on the plane. They looked fairly ordinary, carrying their bags and gawking around at the steady build-up of military traffic on the apron of Andrews Air Force Base. The first officer spied Logan; pointed for the benefit of the others and then, as one, they moved in his direction.

Charlie noted they all smiled at Logan, save one: the woman who brought up the rear of the entourage. The woman was pretty, or at least would be if she didn't seem to wear a permanent scowl. It was clear she had some sort of issue with the British agent. That might be important information.

'Charlie, let me introduce you to the team,' Logan put his arm round her shoulder, including her in the small group. 'Charlie, this is Eddie Powell, signals and communications; Des Farrow, your counterpart; and Debbie Turner, operations commander. Guys, this is Charlie Richter, a senior analyst with the CIA's Crime and Narcotics Centre.'

The usual handshakes and "pleased to meet you" greetings bounced back and forth.

'So, what's the situation?'

Yep, you're cold decided Charlie, as Debbie spoke at Logan. Whether it rattled him or not, the agent refused to show it and spoke evenly and succinctly about the reason for bringing them over.

'Well, what are we waiting for?' Powell asked, 'Let's get on with the job in hand. Assiz won't find himself!' Immediately Charlie found herself liking the younger man. There wasn't any air-punching; no "hell yeahs" and that intrigued her. She held back slightly, watching Logan interacting with his team as they walked across the pad to the waiting Blackhawk helicopter.

The flight to Raven Rock was uneventful with light banter between the Brit men who tried, and succeeded, in involving Charlie. All the while, she was aware of Debbie Turner's eyes appraising her with something that approximated contempt. She sat on her discomfort – for now.

Landing at the Rock, Charlie organized their transfer to the living quarters. As they were walking the corridors of subterranean chalets, she found herself walking next to Turner; ahead the men were deep in conversation.

'So, welcome to the United States of America,' Charlie offered hesitantly.

Debbie Turner looked at her for a second. 'I have been out of the United Kingdom before you know.'

Charlie smarted at the attack: shit, she was just trying to be nice! What was wrong with the woman? 'I never said you hadn't, I was just being polite.'

'Well, thanks for that. However, we have to get you guys out of the shit, so perhaps we can do the tourist stuff another time.'

Charlie bit back a curt reply. 'So what do you do in Steve's team?'

Turner stopped and took a long, hard look at the American. 'This isn't Steve's team,' she rebuked Charlie forcefully, punctuating the air with her fingers. 'But, since you ask, I organise field operations and coordinate with the station for asset identification, liaison and development.'

Halting, Charlie drew a breath and launched: she had taken as much as she could from this woman. 'Okay, hold it there. I don't know what your problem with Steve Logan is, but you don't have to draw me into your little fire-fight. I'm just trying to be polite here. Whatever you have against Steve keep it pointed in that direction.' With that she walked off without taking a backward look.

Fucking Brit.

*

The knock on Charlie's door was nervous, as if its owner didn't really want a reply. Charlie walked over and opened it.

'Can I come in please?'

Charlie regarded Debbie Turner with open suspicion, moving reluctantly to allow her in. 'What can I do for you?'

Turner held up a bottle of wine and Charlie remembered her own offering to Logan only a couple of nights previously. Debbie Turner waved the bottle. 'Peace offering,' she said by way of explanation.

'Take a seat … somewhere,' Charlie waved a hand round the austere interior; Debbie sat on the bed as Charlie twisted the top off the bottle and poured two tumblers of wine. Charlie took position in the room's only armchair and waited.

The Brit coughed self-consciously. 'I wanted to

apologise for my manner earlier. I had no right to speak to you in that way.'

What did she say? Of course Turner had no right to speak to her like that but …

'Why did you think you could?'

Debbie Turner shrugged. 'I'm just an angry person,' she said lamely and shrugged.

'About what?' Charlie could feel her own anger rising and she struggled to keep it under control. 'I mean, what gave you the right to take your anger, at somebody or something else, out on me.'

'You slept with Logan didn't you?'

'As if it has anything to do with you.'

'You're right, it has nothing to do with me. Except,' Turner took a sip of wine and caught Charlie's eye over the top of the glass. 'He has history.'

'Doesn't everybody?'

'Sure. But this is slightly different.'

Charlie savoured the wine for a moment, aware that this was becoming uncomfortable and something not within her control. What did she feel for the British agent? Was he just a comfort fuck? Or … what?

'How so?' Charlie tried to keep any emotion out of her voice while feeling the trepidation rise in her stomach.

'He'd slept with Assiz's sister.'

It wasn't what she had expected to hear – no that was wrong: it wasn't something that had even registered in her mind. Why would it?

'Go on.' Had she controlled the tremor in her voice?

Debbie Turner marvelled at the American's reserve. When they'd met on the apron she'd believed that Richter was emotionally weak, a bit air-headed and devoid of much character. Perhaps not. 'You know that Logan and Assiz worked together for some time?'

'Yes.'

'And that Logan accepted the hospitality of Assiz's home?'

'What of it?'

'Assiz's sister lived with him. By all accounts she was a very beautiful woman and Logan took advantage of it.' Turner kept watching Charlie, searching for any small chink that would suggest she had got to her – nothing.

Charlie considered Debbie's words. What was she hoping to do? Was the Brit trying to unsettle her? If so, why; why was she doing this now? 'Well that's interesting, but I'm not sure how you think that affects me.'

Turner took a drink. 'Logan loves women, but he loves himself more.'

Charlie shook her head. 'Not what I'm seeing.'

'Take it from me, he does everything for himself.'

'If I didn't know better I'd say you were either jealous or angry with the guy for something he did to you.'

Turner coloured. 'You'd think that. Just be careful with him. He's not what he seems.'

Charlie rose, thoughts tumbling through her head. 'Look Debbie, it's late and we have a busy schedule tomorrow. Thanks for the wine and all, but I think we're done here. Steve has been nothing but a gentleman to me and focussed on the job in hand. Whatever else we may or may not have done is nothing at all to do with you.' She went to the door and opened it. 'Good night Debbie.'

Turner awkwardly extended her hand; Charlie ignored it. 'Well, thanks for your time and I am sorry —'

'Apology accepted, good night.'

Charlie closed the door, breathing deeply as she felt the little tremor in her legs from the adrenaline drop.

What the *hell?*

*

Breakfast the following morning was a strained affair between the two women. Eddie Powell and Des Farrow exchanged glances, before continuing with their critique of the American breakfast menu. When Logan appeared the frost seemed to hang, a tangible beast, in the air between Charlie and Debbie. The British agent appeared oblivious as he sat with his eggs and bacon, and orange juice; Charlie noticed he looked drawn and tired as if he hadn't had much in the way of sleep.

'Good morning everybody, you all ready to go?' He scooped up eggs and continued talking, unaware of the tension. 'Charlie, do you have an updated report these guys can read over while we wait for Helen to arrive?'

Charlie nodded mutely, all the more conscious of Debbie's presence and her hidden critique.

'Ok. We have a meeting at ten, with SEAL Team Five. Our task is to identify where Assiz could be. We're guessing he's local, perhaps within a one hundred and fifty-mile radius, so that he can respond to the Presidential funeral, which will come within the week. It's imperative we stop him before that happens and, if possible, capture him alive.'

'Are we sure that he is going to be so close to the action. It seems a bit reckless.'

'Eddie, Sayed has only a narrow window of opportunity to take out the whole of the US Presidential team. He'll work on the premise that being close is a calculated risk.'

'What makes you think he will be in the vanguard of this?'

'I don't think, Debbie, I know he will be. Lincoln's assassination was a coup. It was a brilliant piece of technical expertise. But it needed more technology and prowess than al-Qaeda can normally summon, and Assiz was probably influential in that as a conduit, bringing people, resources together, perhaps orchestrating the plan. This is something different; he'll want to be directly involved in it – in something where he can influence world politics directly.'

'Why?'

'Because he wants to be the martyr who finally beheads "The Beast". Lincoln wasn't going to win the next election. That privilege was probably going to Harry Johnson. A funeral for a President will get everybody in one place – the ultimate kill box. Who wouldn't want the reputation for that?'

'Shit.'

Logan drew on his orange juice, shaking his head a little as if to blow away a cloud from his mind. 'You have to understand that Assiz's faith is very, very strong. He believes unshakeably that America and the West are evil. Those in al-Qaeda fundamentally believe the US is the basis for all corruption in the world and, like any disease, must be removed. Sometimes that can be done through medication, therapy if you like: showing the world what you are like and offering a different way. Sometimes change has to be made intrusively, like surgery.'

'You sound like you agree with him.'

'Not at all Debbie but I lived with him for a time and I got to understand what he felt, what he believed. It isn't wrong, merely different. What's wrong, per se, is trying to force your view on another and not seeking discourse.'

'Very noble thoughts Steve. I can see Assiz was very responsive to your neutral philosophical stance.'

He ignored the operations chief and finished his breakfast. 'Okay, let's get to the situation room. We have work to do,' he ordered, breaking the uncomfortable silence that had descended on the group.

*

The room was already occupied when they arrived. SEAL Team Five members sat in urgent consideration of a multitude of information, streamed from various satellites and reconnaissance platforms across the large wall screens. They were analysing the video and other images for any tell-tale signs of clandestine activity. As yet nothing had materialised – everything was normal.

Logan took a seat with the special ops team, forming an easy familiarity with them as they discussed features and landscapes on the real time video footage from drones high above the Appalachians. Eddie headed for the computer terminals where NSA technicians were working flat out analysing data from satellites and feeding it on to smaller screens for the operators to investigate.

Farrow and Turner both sat in a corner with

laptops that had been set up for their exclusive use. As the picture began to develop Turner would begin to look at the resources necessary to expedite an action of this sensitivity. Charlie figured she should have joined them, given her analyst background, but the confrontation of the previous evening and the frostiness of breakfast made her hang back. After a moment she excused herself to nobody in particular and slipped from the room.

The release of negativity lifted her mood and she decided to take a walk, get her head cleared of all the dross that seemed to have filled all its corners since this situation had flared up. After half an hour she found herself walking the perimeter track of the complex. CCTV cameras watched every inch of the high, razor wire topped, chain link fence, so she wasn't truly alone but it was good to be out of the furore; to be breathing the clean mountain air and be in touch with herself once more.

Her thoughts went back to the evening before and Debbie Turner's odd comments about Steve. Evidently they had been designed to unsettle her and, she had to admit, they had succeeded. What did Turner mean by "he's not what he seems"? She hadn't believed him to be anything. He'd pretty much been the archetypal spy she decided. Attractive, but not in a stand out sort of a way; funny and intelligent without being too flash or brash, he'd engaged with her and made her feel safe and comfortable. Was that Debbie's point? A good spy was never what he or she seemed. Even so there was a vulnerability to him that she was sure nobody else had picked up on.

And perhaps that was a defect that could have consequences to the operation. Maybe the Brit would need to be watched to ensure that nothing was compromised. Charlie started along the trail back to the complex with purpose in her step.

Thirty-Five

It was the time between first light and sun up, when the world was a place of grey shadows and ghosts, when man prepared for the day by joining with Allah. Sayed Assiz knelt on his mat, head bowed towards Mecca, intoning his prayers soundlessly, as if the vibrations would upset the balance. Fajr, Morning Prayer, was upon him and he mouthed his responses deliberately, with purpose. It wasn't only the disc of the sun which was about to break upon this land.

The mothballed mine had been a blessing to them, giving them secrecy and cover from the passage of drones over the hills. Owned by a sympathiser, they had free use of the complex's facilities and power and, for all the world, they appeared to be caretakers. The cover wouldn't last forever, but perhaps long enough for them to achieve their objective. Even so, the constant warnings from the communications lookout, as a drone appeared, or a satellite rose over the horizon, had meant training was disjointed and repetitive. Afiq's work had alleviated some concerns, but not all. Any noise made his people jittery. Assiz counselled calm in his men and women – by constant vigilance the weapons of the enemy could not defeat them. They were assured of victory, by virtue of their purpose and conviction, in the face of the machinery of the accursed one. So his troops adjusted and perfected their operations, to ensure everything became rote.

In the manager's Portakabin, away from the toing and froing of the exercises, Assiz consulted his laptop: checking the news and other media for information on the funeral and how the search for terrorists was progressing. It was painstaking for he could only be online a short while before having to break the connection lest the authorities pinpoint him through his internet access. Copying and pasting pages of information was irksome but he had to know if Logan was here. He had to be. The British agent wouldn't be able to refrain from chasing him down, just to ensure that he was eradicated.

It wouldn't be that easy.

'What won't be that easy?'

Assiz started at the interruption to his reverie. Kamruz Reznan was stepping into the office smiling and quizzical. Assiz liked the young Washingtonian. He was a powerful young man: strong in body and mind. Like many of his friends he was a staunch American but was totally angered by the system in which they found themselves: one feeding on greed and decadence. He was open to anything that could change it and bring about a new order. Assiz was willing to use that desire.

'I was talking aloud, no need for concern. How goes the training?'

'Well, despite the interruptions, we're ready to carry out the attack really. All we need are the details of the funeral arrangements.'

'Good.' Assiz indicated the laptop. 'There isn't much available yet. Afiq will have to find a way to stay online longer.'

'Don't worry, he is. He's routing us through a series of nodes in South America and Asia. It should give us some security. At least he will be better forewarned when they are searching for us.'

'Good. And how go preparations for the bombs?'

'Excellently: we have eight belts made and loaded. Only the detonators need to be completed now.'

'That is as well. When will Marek have them finished?'

'He thinks by the end of the week. We have one ready for testing, but we want to wait until there is a gap in the surveillance.'

Assiz shook his head. 'That is unlikely to happen, but Afiq provides enough warning. The Americans will find us. They know that we will be somewhere close by.'

'We should move.'

Assiz considered the point and nodded slowly. 'You may be right Kamruz. We must take care and moving, prior to our attack, could throw them off. Put together a plan for us to move in the next couple of days; not too far but somewhere they would not expect to find us. We will have to separate into small teams again so that we minimise any disruption to our attack. Are the safeguards in place?'

'Yes Sayed, everyone knows what they must do if it looks as if we might be captured.'

'Let's go and see Marek.'

They left the Portakabin and, keeping beneath the trees, to obstruct any drone cameras, they made their way into the mine adit. Once inside, Assiz relaxed a little: he was loath to admit it, but he too, was becoming a little unnerved by the constant hiding and he longed for a conclusion. The longer things dragged, the more likelihood of something going wrong.

Collecting torches from a wall cabinet, they carried on into the mine. Though there were overhead lights they kept use to a minimum so that power usage didn't arouse suspicion. They came to a wide cavern, which had once functioned as an underground marshalling yard. Here fluorescent strips cast uncompromising illumination on the small number of men and women working at tables in the centre of the cave. The faint hum of a soundproofed generator carried to them through the wide space. One of the men looked up as Assiz and Kamruz came close.

'Sayed, brother, how goes it?'

'Well, my friend. And you? How are you getting on with the bombs, Marek?'

'We have tested all the circuitry – everything functions as planned.'

'And the explosives?'

'Everything is ready. We have kept it stored in the dry – it will be fine.'

'Show me the circuits.'

'Come,' Marek beckoned Assiz and Kamruz to the table. He laid out what seemed a twist of wires, neatly bundled in rainbows of death. At one end were connectors, meant to be pressed into plastic explosive. The other end was attached to a toggle switch and a further bundle of wires which disappeared into a mobile phone. 'As you can see, we have a toggle switch for the wearer to detonate the device. In the event this fails for whatever reason there is a back stop: the commander can text the phone, which will detonate the device.'

'One at a time?'

'No Sayed, your phone will be set to send a group message. As soon as the text is received it closes a circuit in the phone and the device goes up.'

'Can you demonstrate?'

'A moment.' Marek took the device and rigged it so that the circuit was hooked to an indicator device with a series of traffic lights, then he texted the phone. It bleeped and a second later the green light flickered then glowed steadily. The three men smiled.

Assiz took in the huge amount of work and knew that he'd been lacking in praise of the man's work. He slapped Marek's back.

'You are a miracle worker my friend.'

'Thank you.' The young Pakistani paused, then. 'If I may?' He gestured into the dark.

Assiz raised an eyebrow in inquiry and Marek beckoned him forward. 'Another tool,' and he shone the torch on the black shape hiding in the shadows.

Assiz smiled and then laughed – it was good. 'Make sure everything is ready by the weekend.' He moved off up the adit. Kamruz followed him.

'Where are you going?'

'I need to investigate something.'

'Is everything ok? Are we doing this right for you?'

Assiz turned to look at the earnest American and he smiled. 'Everything is okay, Kam, I need to make sure that we can get out of here without the authorities being alerted. We have to have a clear run into the city.'

'Oh, okay. You want any company?'

Assiz shook his head and rested a hand on the younger man's shoulder. 'I need you to be here for me, to look after the group. They respect you and look up to you.'

The young Washingtonian smiled briefly. 'I will do as you bid.'

'Good! Good my friend. Allah be with you.'

*

'This is getting us nowhere.'

Logan rubbed a hand on his forehead. They had been in the operations room since breakfast, going over the possibilities. Discussion hadn't made anything easier. 'Assiz could be anywhere and we could take from now to eternity to locate him.'

'For real. Do you know how many redneck camps there are up in these hills?' The commander of SEAL Team Five, John Black regarded Logan with cool, clear eyes. At one stage he'd had been on track for DEVGRU, or SEAL Team Six as it was better known, when a moment of stupidity found him in bed with the senior training officer's wife. Expulsion had been a heavy price but he'd borne it with good grace, recognising his fault. Given the option of returning to the Navy ranks or commanding Team Five, he'd opted for the latter as a means of redeeming himself, not just with his compatriots, but also himself.

Praised for his courage and intelligence, Black had made Team Five his home, determined to do better. Now he was using all his intelligence to strip away the layers of clouds which hung over their investigation. 'Those are blocking our chances.'

'How do you mean?' asked one of the others.

'We're chasing down shadows in the woods. Every movement has one our analysts checking and rechecking before we move to the next. Add to that, the very real probability they're feeding us disinformation and we'll never find anything at this rate. It needs boots on the ground,' he finished fatefully.

There was a murmur amongst the occupants of the room. 'Do we have time for that now? After all we've covered half our search area. Surely we should just continue.'

'And we'll have to cover it again, Miss,' Black replied evenly at Turner's question. 'We just don't know where to look or whether we're just seeing what Assiz wants us to see.' Black shook his head grimly. 'We're looking for the head of a pin in a field of haystacks. They'll have committed the atrocity before we find them.'

'Any suggestions?' Logan searched the glum faces propped on arms around the table. Charlie took them in also, hesitated then coughed. Logan looked at her – his appearance hadn't improved for having breakfast and she determined to draw him on the problem – later. 'Yes Charlie?'

'I was thinking that perhaps he's underground somewhere. There are a number of abandoned and mothballed mines across the Appalachians. Perhaps those would be a good place to start looking?'

There were some nods from round the table.

'Good idea,' confirmed Black. He turned to the NSA liaison at the table. 'Can we re-task some of our elements to focus in on mothballed sites?'

The woman nodded. 'It shouldn't be too difficult. Give us half an hour to get it sorted.'

'Okay everybody: that sounds like a comfort break has been called.' Logan shooed them all out. Be back at half past eleven.'

The room emptied until only Logan and Charlie were left. He looked up to see her concerned gaze regarding him earnestly. 'Yes, what's the matter?'

'Just wondering when you were going to let up on yourself.'

'How do you mean?'

'How …? Look at yourself Steve, you look shit and you've been getting worse over the last few days. Then there's Turner,' She tried to, but couldn't, conceal the distaste she held for the British woman.

'What about her?'

'Nothing I can't handle, but the woman has it in

for you, big time,' Charlie informed him emphatically.

'I can deal with her.'

'Probably, but that isn't the issue. The issue is whether other people can handle her, or will they listen to her and form opinions of you that can damage your work.'

'I said, I can deal with her,' Logan ground the words out; aiming to convince Charlie of more than he believed himself.

'And what about your drinking? Can you deal with that?'

Immediately she'd said it she regretted the hard words. The hurt on his face caused her to bite her lip.

'Well, at least I know where you stand.' Logan bent to look at his idev, scanning through everything and seeing nothing.

'I didn't – you know what I mean. Perhaps everybody else is ignoring it, but I can see that you're drinking too much. It's going to start affecting your judgement and your abilities.'

'Thanks.' His tone was brittle and cold.

Charlie regarded the Brit and figured she needed to quit while she was ahead. If indeed she still was.

A deep sigh fell from Logan's lips. 'Okay … you're right … I have been having … perhaps a little too much.' When Charlie didn't reply Logan emitted an embarrassed cough. 'You're not going to make this easy are you?'

'Make what easy?'

He paused and looked at her, eyebrow raised quizzically. 'Why do you care?'

'Who said I did?'

'You're here. You could've gone straight to your boss or reported me to security … or something.

Instead you came and asked me about it. I'd say you were at least bothered.'

What was her motive? She liked the guy ... liked him a lot. He was good to be around but ... a drinker? Yet, he was right, she had stayed behind to see him, felt that she should do that first; reason with him if possible '... I wanted to see if I could help out in any way.'

'Are you going to psychoanalyse me?' The eyebrow arched again and she found she liked how it did that.

She held her hands up immediately. 'God no! Even if I wanted to, I couldn't. Can't I be genuinely concerned for you?'

Logan gave an apologetic little grunt and smiled. 'You're right, of course you can be. Sorry for being so stupid.'

'So ... do you want to talk?'

There was the merest of hesitations. 'What did Debbie say to you?'

How did she tackle this? Straight on. 'She said that you'd had a relationship with Assiz's sister; as if it meant anything personal to me. I'm not interested whether you had a relationship with her, unless that has an impact on the operation. Let's face it, it could.'

Logan shrugged. 'Have you ever killed anybody?'

Charlie coloured. 'That's really shitty Steve. I work in an office at Langley: of course I haven't ever killed anybody!'

'Okay, okay. I wasn't challenging you. I wanted to describe something to you.'

'You knew I wouldn't have killed anybody. That was a really bad thing you did there. I expected better.'

'I'm sorry.' *Again.* He hung his head – this was

going from bad to worse.

Charlie inhaled. 'Look, if you don't want to talk about this you don't have to. I'm not forcing you; I just thought it would be good for you to be able to offload.'

Logan swallowed. 'What else is there to say? I killed Raifah and Assiz intends to make me pay for that.'

The CIA Analyst shook her head. 'No, there's more to this than you're letting on.'

'You think it's not enough to shoot your colleague's sister?'

'In any other circumstance I'd agree with you, but here, now? There's something you're not telling me.'

Logan looked out of the window of the operations room, at the men and women striding purposefully to and fro. For what? For an ideology that was no different in its purpose. And for what had Raifah died – an ideology.

'Fuck it!' Logan whirled and a fire lit his eyes. Pain haunted the flames.

In the silence that followed Charlie examined her thoughts. Did she believe the depth of anguish he was showing? Perhaps he was ashamed; too distracted by the incidents they had been surrounded by? But, why now?

'Are you worried about confronting Assiz because you killed his sister?'

'It isn't that.'

'Well what is it?'

'She was pregnant ... with my child.'

Thirty-Six

Assiz pulled his car into the rest area on the Waynesboro Pike and checked the map. It showed a contoured area lying south of the road he was now travelling on. He looked out the window and took in the bulk of the feature, covered in ash and beech trees on the lower slopes, which gave way to pine further up. Straddling the top, like a small metal forest, stood a mass of antennae towers. Structures could be glimpsed, ghost shapes behind the trees.

So, this is where you are, Logan. The information he'd received placed the British agent at this location. Under normal circumstances he'd have driven past it. Not today. Today he had learned this was the emergency government facility, Raven Rock.

He marked the position of the complex on the map before placing it in the glove compartment. He considered driving up the access road he'd noted a few kilometres back, circling round the place close up, but dismissed the notion as foolish. It was a risk that would accomplish nothing other than getting him caught. Instead he pulled back on the Pike and continued towards Washington.

Nearly two hours later he was driving through the centre of the Capitol, rumbling along in the early afternoon traffic. The journey had been punctuated by road blocks, searching for him. He had taken precautions, knowing also that Logan and MI6 would have fed the authorities with various identikit pictures of him. Understanding that he could do nothing to change his genetic makeup, other than a few cosmetic changes (coloured contact lenses; shaving – they would expect that – pierced ear to draw attention

288

from the face, greying the hair) he'd made a change of wardrobe, dressing like Virginian locals. The other element was a healthy dose of barefaced brass. Turning up in the backyard; acting like you belonged, was always a good disguise.

The guards had waved him through, with only a perfunctory glance at his ID. His papers were some of the best forgeries he'd ever come across, advising his interrogator that his name was Danny Levine. The irony of carrying such a Jewish name was not lost on him. But who could question him with that sort of cover?

He drove a number of routes between the White House and Arlington Cemetery where the President would be interred. Each route incorporated a loop back to ensure no-one was following him. "Checking his six" as the enemy would say. As he drove along he committed significant junctions, vantage points, lay-bys and other landmarks, to memory. Then he would stop, get coffee and draw a diagram of what he had seen.

At lunch time he took half an hour out of his routine and ate frugally, taking advantage of a local beauty spot to watch the movement of traffic on the road below. The lumbering transporters and nose to tail cars of a bankrupt system hauled themselves to and from the citadel; like ants. Intent only on homage to the queen, they were unaware and unknowing of the feet about to kick over the hill.

Screwing the packaging his wrap had been in, he placed it in his bag, along with the paper cup he'd drunk his coffee from. Leaving evidence of his existence anywhere was anathema to him: better to take it back and burn it so no-one could trace him. The traffic continued its seemingly aimless toing and froing on the freeway below.

Sayed smiled to himself. It had been easy to convince his mentor he was fully committed to the cause but, of course, that was not strictly true. As well he knew, in the end all men were interested in only two things – themselves and that which they held closest to their heart.

He reached into a jacket pocket and gazed at the photograph in his hand. The woman, forever young, smiled at him and he smiled back. A tear formed, unbidden, dropping on the old wood of the picnic table, as he gazed on the photo of his beloved sister.

Soon your retribution will be at hand.

Thirty-Seven

From his vantage point in the wooded hills across the valley from the mine, the watcher considered what he was viewing. They were efficient and clean, disappearing with a rehearsed, mechanical regularity that signified they were maintaining a look out for surveillance. They were good.

But he was troubled. It seemed too indiscreet. The mine site was large and obviously being used for ... something. He knew the authorities wouldn't be hoodwinked for long by the apparent security activity. It was a good plan, walking guards round the perimeter as if keeping unwanted visitors out, but a check on the abandoned mines records locally would eventually conclude that any unwanted visitors were on the inside of the fence. Alternatively, given the twitchy nature of the authorities, they would be forgiven for checking sites manually, regardless of upsetting the sensibilities of locals. That caused the watcher a problem: if plans were to move forward unhindered they needed to be more circumspect. Should that not be forthcoming what did he do? Nothing could derail the attack that was to come. In this game he had a card to play that required he should lose a hand. The situation needed containing.

The watcher settled into the undergrowth and checked his rifle once more. Peering through the scope he could make out the individuals walking about the mine; their camouflaged tents set under the trees to the south of the main entrance. One man was missing. He would have to wait for his return before making his move.

*

'So, we're clear, yeah?'

Steve Logan swept the room with his gaze, acknowledging the nods from the assembly. It had been a long, but productive meeting as he, Charlie and the SEALs had worked on the information being fed to them and now, early afternoon, it was time to act. 'Okay then, to recap: this is the profile. We split into three units. John, you'll head up the northern group and take the three old mines up around Clarksburg; Chief,' he addressed Smithson, the Master Sergeant, 'you'll take the mines south of Charleston. Charlie and I are going to look at the mine at Parkersburg. Those give us the best shot at finding Assiz and his group. They can't afford to be too far from DC and two hours is a reasonable drive. We all agreed?

Nods again.

John Black stepped forward. 'Okay people, listen up. The individuals we are tracking will stop at nothing to achieve their goal, or going down fighting. You are cleared "shoot to kill" except for this man,' he indicated the screen behind him. 'Assiz should be taken alive, if at all possible, but do not place yourself or your team at risk.'

'Call sign for this operation is "Dark Eagle". Dark Eagle Main is situated here, at the Rock, and will coordinate asset positioning, support and evac. My team is Dark Eagle Actual. Chief,' Black directed his gaze at Master Sergeant Smithson, a big bull of a SEAL, 'you're Dark Eagle Support. Logan and Richter will be Dark Eagle Link. Everyone clear?'

Calm, considered nods rippled around the room. No, emotion; no shouts: just SEAL professionalism.

'Good, let's suit up and meet at the assembly point in fifteen minutes.'

*

Three MH-60s stood idling on the tarmac when they walked out, while the teams went through last minute checks. Finally…

'We all good?' The British agent caught the gaze of each SEAL who nodded in turn. Logan smiled. At last – this was what he lived for: action; and he was determined to find his old colleague first.

The three helicopters lifted from the pad as one, spearing the Virginian sky; the clatter of the rotors reverberating from the surrounding mountains. Sat next to Logan in the helicopter Charlie felt incongruous, dressed in combat gear, with a semi-automatic strapped to her leg. Though she was a good shot on the ranges, this would be a whole lot different with moving targets, liable to shooting back. Her heart beat against the Kevlar body armour so that she felt that the Brit must hear her apprehension.

'You okay?'

It was like a jolt of electricity as Logan's voice fed through her headphones, as if he'd divined her fear. All she could do was nod mutely.

His hand pressed her shoulder. 'Don't worry,' he smiled. 'Stick close.'

Charlie's gaze was drawn out the window, looking at the trees blurring green like in the photos her dad used to take of cars on hill climbs. Never in her wildest dream had she thought that she would be in a low flying helicopter, on her way to hunt down a fugitive. How had she got to here? She was a senior analyst, not a field operative. Slowly she shook her head – this was a real fuck up.

After another ten minutes the helicopter began to descend. Looking out she could see they were dropping into a derelict mine yard. There were Portakabins and a couple of large concrete buildings, showing the signs of abandonment and age. Weeds rampaged from gaps in the concrete paving while twisted rusting metal jutted, like mangled bones, from overgrown bushes. It looked like nothing had disturbed the area since it had been mothballed, but Charlie knew the protocol they had set up meant it would be thoroughly checked.

They crouched as the helicopter rose and quickly transited away from the mine. As it clattered over the pine encrusted ridge Logan checked his MP7. He looked across at Charlie who had the lost look of an Eskimo on a sandy beach. 'You okay?'

Charlie nodded but her face belied her false optimism.

'You ever done anything like this before?'

'No. I've been on the range but this scares the shit out of me, if I'm honest.'

Logan regarded her. Fuck, how stupid, he figured. What had he expected of her? Nothing was the answer, because he hadn't considered the fact that she probably wasn't field ready. Why would he? She had quickly and expertly fitted into the planning and had come up with some good ideas, but now…

Now he was stuck looking for a terrorist cell with a tyro. For a second he considered recalling the chopper, and then stayed his hand. 'Okay, well I don't think there is anybody here so this is a good place to get you up to speed as quickly as possible. Follow me in to the first building. I want you to check what's behind, as well as taking in what I'm doing. You good with that?'

Charlie nodded mutely and followed Logan as he traversed the concrete standing to the first building. Where he looked, so did she, trying to copy his intensity, his searching gaze until her head began to hurt. All her experience was from training manuals and films – God! She couldn't believe she was doing this! Then they were at the first building. Logan tried the door – it was locked, inevitably, the rust ravaged surface showing no signs of recent activity. They both agreed that this was a good sign. Walking round the concrete block, straining to look round window frames, which were mostly glassless, they found no signs of activity. At the back was a door with sprained hinges. Logan clicked on the torch sitting on the rifle's lower accessory rail. The LED brightness pierced the half-light. Rubble; old, damp papers, and patterns of animal activity, could be seen in the passageway, which was lit only by the small amount of sun that came through the frosted glass of the dirty strip windows. Something was lodged behind the door and he couldn't push it open.

'Let me have a go.' Charlie lit up her own torch and squeezed through the gap. Checking, she could see that some sort of metal pole had been jammed to keep the door as closed as possible. She worked it loose and suddenly the door sprang open.

Logan walked in. 'Well done.' Charlie smiled and, with more boldness, she started to check the rooms leading off each side of the corridor. Each showed some activity – drinking, sex, drugs; one room had the relics of a small fire. Juveniles, or homeless; finding a shelter for their lifestyle choices. Having checked thoroughly they retraced their footsteps.

Outside was no more fruitful. The adits which

drove into the mountains were securely locked and barred. Nobody had tampered with them unless they had keys. The concrete standings showed no signs of fresh traffic; pedestrian or vehicular. After an exasperating hour, he called the Blackhawk back.

Sat in the chopper Logan was conversing with Raven Rock, deep in talk with analysts. Charlie sat waiting for a response, feeling totally out of place.

'Is there another mine near here, anything that could be used as a base, a cover for an operation?'

She saw him listening to the response, clenching the satellite phone hard as he took in the information. 'There must be something. Keep looking. Out.'

They sat with just the thrum of the engines and the clatter of the rotors for company. Then, the phone bleeped. Logan pressed the receive button.

'Yes?'

Charlie couldn't read his expression but she sensed his tension. Something had turned up.

'Thank you.' Logan dropped the phone to the seat next to him and pulled on his headset. 'Pilot, let's go. We have a target in the next valley. "Main" is sending coordinates now.'

The urgency of the engines rose, straining against the brake as the pilot reprogrammed his mission computer. Suddenly the whole craft shook as the brakes were released and the pilot pulled the large craft into a climb, away from the mine and over the hill.

They dropped over the ridge towards their next target – a mine, mothballed eighteen months ago and ownership transferred to an Asian company shortly afterwards. There was no history of terrorist tendencies but, these days, one never knew.

Even though the Blackhawk was one of the newer

lo-observable models, Logan stilled winced at the rattling clatter of rotors, which reverberated off the mountains. Surely their target would hear them coming, wherever they were.

As they cleared the ridge, the mine they were headed for could be seen in the middle distance. It looked as if it could be a going concern at any time. That perception deepened the closer they got. The late afternoon sun bathed the place in a golden aura, as if everything was paradise.

'Five minutes out.' The pilot's voice came over the headsets. Logan put his thumb up to show he'd received the message. He stuck five digits in the air: Charlie nodded apprehensively, she'd heard anyway. What if the people they were searching for were here? She wiped her palms across her fatigues, conscious of the smear of perspiration on each thigh.

'Two minutes.'

'Roger that.'

The Blackhawk wheeled over the trees as they came to the perimeter fence. As the machine cleared the barrier Logan looked into the compound. There was movement in an area of trees.

A glint: then the ricochet of a bullet on the airframe.

'Looks like we found your people,' remarked the pilot laconically as he swerved the big machine. The door gunner opened up with the pintle-mounted 7.62mm machine gun. The vibration of the machine and the pinging of spent cartridges drummed into Charlie's head.

Logan could see a huge amount of activity on the ground. People were running about purposefully, intent on confronting this problem from the sky. He clicked his mike. 'Best radio the other helos; tell them we have contact.'

'Willdo. Are you going in?'

'Yes. Drop us to the south of the main buildings. We can group there.'

'Copy that. You got all you need?'

Logan nodded. 'Just get us down on the ground. Be ready to give us cover.'

'Roger that.' The pilot banked the helicopter over; Logan could hear him talking to the other helicopters. 'This is –'

The explosion rocked the aircraft, pitching it forward towards the ground. Logan reacted instinctively, pulling his knees up to his chin and wrapping his arms around them as he shouted at Charlie to brace herself.

With an agonising squeal of rending metal and the icy rupturing of glass, the Blackhawk crumpled nose first on the concrete of the abandoned mine. The silence, which seemed unending in the blackness of Logan's head, was shattered by the dry spattering of heavy calibre rounds into the hull of the broken machine.

Thirty-Eight

'Keep down!' Logan pushed Charlie back into her seat as she struggled to free herself. Pulling back the safety on his MP7 he tried to wriggle into a position to see what was going on. Several figures were approaching, perhaps as many as six, assault rifles at the ready. He had to wait until they were much closer than now. Logan shook his head to clear his sight, which was watery and fuzzy. He drew a shaky arm across his vision then raised his gun to his eye.

Wait till they're all in the open.

Relying on ineptitude in such circumstances, and assessing they would believe their task complete, he let them continue until they were just a few steps from the wreckage.

One, who seemed to be the leader *(Logan could see it wasn't Assiz – where was he?),* advanced cautiously, the others slowing; almost stopping. The young Asian kept the rifle raised as he moved past the mangled rotors; eyes darting around, expecting the slightest movement.

When it came, it wasn't from where he'd been looking. Clinically Logan drew a bead on the man's forehead and squeezed. The three bullets entered in a close formation, bursting through the back of the head in a fountain of blood, bone and brain matter, that glistened in the sun as it descended.

Pandemonium broke out. The other five fired wildly in the direction each thought the bullets had come from. Logan took each out dispassionately, every head shot accompanied by a sudden bloom of blood red petals, dissipating in the warm sunlight.

Watchful for anyone else, Logan clambered from

the helicopter's upended cabin and advanced slowly, weapon ready. The four men and two women were all dead. All save one were of Asian origin. One of the men was Caucasian, but evidently a convert judging from his beard and moustache.

A movement behind him and he whirled, rifle up and the first half pressure on the trigger. It was Charlie. She looked alarmed as she stared down the barrel 'Shit! I nearly shot you. Be careful.'

'Sorry.' Her face paled as she took in the bodies. 'Is … Is Assiz here?'

Logan shook his head slowly. 'No, so the search is still on. We need to find what's here and we need to call in the others. I don't think the pilot got a full message off to them so they may be on the way or not.' He walked over to the cockpit. It was a mangled mess of flesh, metal and electronics. Both pilots were dead, the gunners also. What a fuck up. Charlie continued to stare at the bodies. She felt the sudden building of bile, which exploded from her mouth, the acid burning her tongue and lips as it fountained across the concrete.

Grabbing her, Logan hurried away from the crash. 'Come on, they're gone and we're exposed.'

*

Assiz saw the smoke rising above the trees and knew instinctively. A sickening lurch engulfed him, from his stomach to his head.

They'd been found.

He drove the car round a bend in the road to where he could see the mine and pulled over. Taking binoculars from the glove box he glassed the mine site. Even from this distance he could see the

300

wreckage of a helicopter burning. Sparkles lit up the area behind the downed aircraft – that was his people. He felt pride and fear. They were fighters, those he had been given, and yet they were green and over-eager. Even as he watched the sparkles, they were contrasted by a single staccato winking light at once deliberate and deadly.

Coldness gripped his heart and, dropping the glasses, he gunned the car back onto the road.

*

The watcher tracked the movement of the two cautious figures at the mine. They made inviting targets, but the moment wasn't yet. A piece was missing from the jigsaw. The time was fast approaching to complete it.

*

'This is Dark Eagle Link to Dark Eagle Main, do you copy?'

Silence replied Logan's request. Nothing. Shit! He tried again – a vain hope – same response. Logan threw the transceiver down in disgust. 'Radio's out,' he said to nobody in particular.

Charlie heard his words as if through a fog. This was going from bad to horrific. 'What about the radio in the chopper?'

From their position in some tree cover close to the mine entrance, the downed Blackhawk looked forlorn, uncared for.

'We could try, but it'd leave us exposed, finding out.' Logan was aware of her fragile state. 'We need to investigate the place, look for evidence right now.

The other teams will head here as soon as they pick up on the lack of contact. Okay?'

Charlie nodded mutely. She couldn't be certain she wouldn't throw up again.

'Good! Let's get moving then.' The Brit led her to some tents which were erected on an area of ground shadowed by Mountain Ash. The flowers were just falling she noted, a little early for the time of year. Each tent was immaculately kept: every item of clothing, every pair of shoes; the papers, books and cooking utensils in order, as if it was a military camp. It was apparent also that each tent was inhabited by two people, perhaps representing singular elements of a team. It wasn't hard to figure what. The most important thing though was how far had they got? After that came the even trickier question – where was Assiz?

A rudimentary training ground was established in one corner of the complex with targets drawn on a wall, liberally peppered with bullet holes, some of which had been within the borders of the bullseyes. A lot of traffic marks were to be seen everywhere while a steady trail of footprints went into, and reappeared, from the mine entrance.

Logan followed the trail into the darkness. As he entered he hesitated, aware of his silhouette against the light. Quickly, cursing his ineptitude, he moved towards the nearest wall to present as small a target as possible. Behind him he could hear Charlie, blundering behind him in her innocence. He stopped and, as she drew close, he pulled her quickly behind him. She began to remonstrate at his rough handling but he put a finger gently to her lips. 'There could be somebody else in here, waiting.'

She nodded in understanding but rubbed her wrist

where he had grasped it.

Stealthily he led the way in and, when they had traversed a corner, clicked on the flashlight. He raised the rifle and began to move slowly but surely down the adit, following the shaft of harsh light.

Eventually they came to a wide cavern in which the flashlight made out the shapes of cupboards, tables and storage units. All was dark and silent as Logan investigated the area. The tables were empty save for small clippings of copper wire and insulation, and ball bearings. There were also some shavings of a greyish, putty-like material – C4? Semtex? He pressed some to his finger and sniffed it, plied between finger and thumb. Definitely some form of plastic explosive.

So, where were the devices?

'What do you think they've done with the bombs?'

He looked at Charlie: she was catching up. That was good. 'I don't know. They're pretty sloppy though. Perhaps our arrival spooked them. I can't imagine Assiz would let them get away with leaving this much evidence around.'

'It does make our job easier,' Charlie agreed as she followed Logan round. Having one little flashlight was inconveniencing to say the least. 'Though a bit more light would be useful,' she pointed out.

'Just a mo,' he advised. The light diminished as he walked off. Seconds later the area was flooded with fluorescent light.

'That's better,' Charlie affirmed definitely.

'We need to collect some evidence off these tables so we can get it analysed as soon as possible. Can you find some plastic bags or similar that we can start putting stuff in?'

Charlie nodded and set about going through

drawers. Logan slung his rifle and looked round him. Where would they put the finished articles? What were they making? Was it vests or something bigger?

His gaze fell to the floor and he noted tyre tracks, car-sized. Following them took him deeper into the mine, beyond the cavern. He thumbed the flashlight back on and immediately the light glanced off chrome. Tracing an arc back and forth he made out the front grille and headlights of a vehicle. He flashed either wall looking for a light switch. The harsh blue-white light of the strips flickered and bathed a black Ford Crown Victoria, staple unit of government organisations across the States.

Fuck.

Crack.

The reverberating thud of a gun discharging was punctuated by the sound of Charlie screaming. He whirled and ran back into the cavern.

'Hello Steven. We seem to have caught up with each other again.'

Thirty-Nine

Assiz had an automatic trained on Charlie who was slumped, ashen-faced, against a storage unit. Logan could see that she had been shot in the leg, possibly a flesh wound. He advanced towards Assiz.

'Ah-ah, no further please. Slowly; put the gun on the ground please Steven, and interlock your hands behind your head. Then drop to the floor.'

Logan carefully did as he was bid, all the time gauging Assiz. The guy was totally calm and his appearance was very different. Logan had to admit that being completely bald was not an option they had used in constructing the photo-fits. That was an omission.

'So now you have us, are you going to finish the job?'

Assiz laughed curtly. 'Oh no, not yet. That would be far too easy. I see you have done your usual thorough job with my people.'

'They shot first.'

'Makes a change Steven.'

'Still active with that then Sayed?'

'Shut up.'

'I understand your anger and hurt –'

'No! No you do not understand my hurt, my family's pain. To you my sister was just another Muslim to shoot down on the street; another Paki to put down because, despite your country's veneer of equality, you think anybody without white skin is inferior. Just as they do here, Miss fucking CIA.' Assiz ground the still hot barrel of his automatic into Charlie's cheek and she cried out involuntarily.

'Raifah was more than that to me and you know it.

Have you ever stopped to think how I felt? Gunning her down like that? We thought she was a terrorist. Both of us Sayed! We were both there.' Logan tried to keep his voice low and calm. He could see that Assiz was agitated and that Charlie was becoming increasingly afraid of her captor's manner. The trickle of blood from her leg wound wasn't great, confirming his first thought of superficial damage, but it would affect her adversely when it came to getting out.

'Shut up, Logan. You killed her because she was a pure Muslim, a beauty and you couldn't stand it that something that pure would be in the world.'

Logan shook his head. 'Listen to yourself Sayed. It was a mistake for God's sake –'

'Don't bring Allah into this,' Assiz hissed vehemently. 'You are responsible for your actions. You came into my house, took my family's hospitality, and all the time you eyed my sister, coveting that which wasn't yours to crave.'

Logan swallowed. This wasn't going well. 'Listen to yourself, Sayed. Raifah wasn't property to me: she was her own person, free to choose what she wanted. Was that something you could give her? Your language suggests not.' He paused. 'Is that why fundamentalism comes easy to you? Being done unto, rather than making up your own mind?'

Sayed regarded the Brit. 'Easy words Steven. The misinterpretation of Allah is also easy to commit. My sister knew her situation. She was Allah's, as are we all. We do only as He bids.'

'How do you know what he bids?!' Logan's exasperation filled his words. 'What gives you the right to determine such things?'

Assiz shook his head as if to shake loose a disease. 'You are an infidel, how would you know what Allah

306

decrees?'

Logan paused. 'You're right, I wouldn't know. But Raifah was … important … to me as well as you.'

'And yet you pulled the trigger on her,' Assiz's features hardened. 'Snuffed out her life – as easily as this.'

The harsh bark of the automatic in the cavern echoed through Logan's skull but he was impervious to it, living in the shock of Charlie's body slumping to the ground, blood welled from the gaping wound in her neck.

Instinctively he threw himself out of Assiz's line of sight. A scorching sensation along his cheek informed him he had only just been quick enough. His hands scrabbled for and found the strap of his MP7. He pulled it towards him. Looking over a table brought another shot, but he'd caught sight of his target. Dropping he glanced between the table legs, and then fired into his ex-colleague's legs, bringing him toppling down.

Cautiously he walked round the furniture and kicked at Assiz's legs: the man moaned feebly. His jeans were stained maroon where bullets had pierced his thighs. Logan ignored the sound as he caught sight of Charlie Richter. The American agent was leant almost nonchalantly against the wall of the cavern. Her open eyes were empty vessels, staring darkly into the cavern. His fingers searched for the pulse – nothing.

'You bastard!' Logan placed a well-aimed kick into Assiz's wounds. He reached down and lifted the injured Englishman by his chin, squeezing hard. 'Does that make you feel better?! Does it?! You fuck! Does this honour Raifah?'

Assiz smiled feebly, blood flecks in his spittle.

'Just a little repayment.'

Logan made to lift his tormentor, when a touch on his shoulder stopped him. He dropped Assiz and whirled to look into the passive face of John Black. The SEAL shook his head. 'Cool it, Steve. The guy ain't worth it. We need to get him back to The Rock.' He shook his head sadly. 'Let's get this sorted out.' The others of Team Five stood behind him, impassive but alert to danger.

Quickly, but gently, the SEALs covered Charlie Richter's body and carried her towards the mine entrance. Assiz was zip-tied and dragged from the mine, despite his remonstrations.

Back in daylight, Logan felt the surrealism of the moment catch up with him. The high blue sky, the warmth of the afternoon sun seemed incongruous, bathing him in a balm that relaxed him after the tension of the cavern. He allowed himself to believe the end might just be in sight. It was a relief of sorts but wouldn't bring Charlie back.

Ahead of him the SEALs formed a close escort round Assiz, weapons at the ready. They walked steadily across the concrete hard standing, half dragging the Brit, to the clear area, away from the trees, where the two helos stood waiting. A team of SEALs was busy with the crashed helicopter, setting explosives to make it secure. Logan saw the first team load Charlie's still form into the cargo area and mounted up. As the last one got in, the Blackhawk lifted and powered away over the hills towards Raven Rock.

Logan pulled a hand across his face. Suddenly he felt dirty and desperate to leave this place, shower and spend time with himself and a certain friend. The helicopter's open cabin door beckoned them. He would wait till they returned to Raven Rock before he worked on his ex-colleague. He shook his head – what made anyone think this type of thing was acceptable? Ideology had much to answer for.

The SEAL dropped to the ground in slow motion, catching the others unaware. Logan tried to find where the silent shot had come from; recalling the carom of blood from the SEAL's shoulder, possibly marking the direction of the sniper.

Sniper?

Even as the thought crashed through his mind, he watched Assiz slip to the ground. The SEALs scattered and took up defensive positions, pointing in the direction of the shots. Only seconds had passed since the first one and, as suddenly as it had started, the situation was over.

Heart beating Logan searched vainly for clues, but nothing was visible in the tree crowded hills around their position. He looked back at the injured SEAL and Assiz lay on the ground. The American was raising himself, Assiz remained prone, lifeless. Two SEALs were checking him over; one shook his head at Black, who relayed the news, needlessly, to Logan.

What the fuck now?

*

In a small clearing about half a mile away, downwind of the mine a lone figure in camouflage pulled his balaclava off and smiled grimly. It was a job well done, he decided, as he watched them gather the body into the helo and lift off.

The beauty was nobody would ever know it was him. After all, he had been found decapitated on the banks of the Thames, weeks ago.

Forty

Back at the mountain complex, the atmosphere was sombre. Charlie Richter's death was taken badly by the CIA group in residence, and which had resulted in her boss, Sarah Markham, catching a flight from Langley back to the Rock. Speaking to her briefly on the phone, Logan got the feeling she held him personally responsible. Perhaps she was right? Maybe he should have taken more care, insisted she stayed behind. Would she have listened? Probably not, but now that little seed of doubt stirred in his gut and he nurtured it as the debrief got under way.

The mood of Black and his team was dark as they went about picking up the pieces. SEALs didn't expect to lose, and the death of two charges was a heavy burden. Thwarting a major terrorist threat didn't make up much for the sense of loss. Talk was sparse as everyone came to terms with their feelings over the loss of an agent, loss of the quarry and the shooting of one of the team. Fortunately, the latter was only wounded and the medical facilities at the Rock had treated the wound and dressed it. He'd be off operations for some time though.

'Which is shit,' Black informed Logan. 'He was our number one sniper. Looks like we're up against a well-trained and organised shooter on their side too.'

Logan nodded. 'Whoever it was, is a crack shot and must have been in hiding for some time watching the operation. Who'd be watching an al-Qaeda operation and know who to kill?' Did he expect an answer? He wasn't sure. It certainly wasn't something he had considered till now.

Black shook his head. 'Sure as hell got me beat. It

has to be either their own people, or a splinter cell or … something. If there was another friendly asset out there we'd have been informed.'

'Maybe. Shit! I don't know!' The British agent felt petulant and impotent in equal measure. 'Whoever it was, one thing's for sure, Assiz won't be telling anybody anything. I hope he's enjoying his seventy-two virgins right now, though I suspect not.' Logan swirled the last remaining dregs of half cold coffee he'd accepted automatically, staring into the dark liquid as if a light might shine from the muddy whirlpool. The only positive to come from the moment was the fact that he was no longer a target for his old colleague. It was cold comfort.

'The odd thing is, how did they know we'd be there with Assiz?'

Logan looked at the hardened face of the SEAL. Puzzlement had settled in the dark and deeply lined face. He was right of course, how had whoever it was known that US forces would be searching the mines for terrorists? Raven Rock was a secure facility, few people knew of its existence and fewer still admitted the knowledge, so it wasn't exactly a place where passing tourists could glean any information. The public was kept at a very respectable distance. Standing recon drone flights could quickly vector one of several roving security patrols to any point on the complex, to intercept the usual cohorts of conspiracy theorists who constantly attempted to uncover the latest story of governmental undercover control of the populace. No, it was difficult to get in, much less find anything of value.

An insider?

The thought sent a shudder through the Brit. If such were the case, then the shit was deeper than he or anybody had ever thought. He looked across at Black and saw that the same idea had flashed through the other's head.

'Do you think –'

'An inside job?' Logan nodded. 'It must be. There is no way anybody could infiltrate this facility undetected. But who? Your vetting must be the most severe known to man, to get in here.'

Black shrugged. 'Maybe, but we're dealing with people who may be legitimate citizens and who can blend in to the American way with ease. Shit, they can be fully paid up and visible Muslim brothers who have pledged allegiance to the flag; they can be Americans who've converted. We don't know. Anybody could be a terrorist. Where do you look first?'

Logan nodded. He was reminded of his commanding officer in the regiment telling of his time in Northern Ireland as the troubles were coming to an end. Even then it was always difficult for a soldier to tell a Provisional from a Unionist, until it was too late. Home grown terrorism was the worst kind and those that espoused religious goals doubly difficult to eradicate.

'We have to take our suspicions to the President.'

Black grimaced. 'This is a real shit storm.'

'Which could get worse if we leave it any longer. Best get the shit over with now.'

'Let's do it,' Black agreed heavily.

*

'So, let's get this straight. What you're telling me is, the person we thought was our main suspect is lying in the morgue; that another is at large out there, who may be attempting to overthrow the government, and, that there is somebody in here,' Carlisle shook her head incredulously, 'feeding information to them. That is some line Mr Logan.'

'I'm aware of that Madam President. However, the situation leaves us with few other options to consider.'

'What do you think Anne?'

FBI Chief, Anne Souster looked from President Carlisle to Logan. 'It's a strong probability that somebody in here has leaked information out concerning our activities. It could be relatively easy to accomplish: nothing is secure all of the time.'

'Well that's just rosy.'

Souster coloured up, as she realised the portent of her rational consideration.

'Do you think, now the horse has bolted, that we can look to shutting the stable door?' Carlisle was plainly angry and had resorted to a schoolteacher approach to the people around the table. Logan remained calm.

'I don't think the horse has quite bolted Madam President, but closing things down could have quite opposite consequences.'

'How so?'

'You could close down the operation however, the individual concerned would then have the opportunity to disappear. Alternatively, you could continue as is, and risk information being passed before we're able to apprehend the person concerned and the resulting damage that could cause. What we know is they are going to have to rethink. Despite the losses,' he was aware how callous he might sound here, 'we have taken out a major terror cell and neutralised the devices they were manufacturing.'

313

'So, your best option?'

'We combine actions in order to precipitate a move by the individual.'

'How would that work?'

Logan regarded the interruption from Hutchinson, the NSA director, 'We make a very public show of investigating a serious security breach. We don't say what but, obviously, the person who has compromised our op will be twitchy. Once they break cover we have them.'

Hutchinson frowned. 'Are we sure they're going to be that nervous. To be working this deep in, would indicate somebody who is capable of maintaining composure.'

'Agreed, and we could play a listening game through the NSA. The only thing is: do we have the time?'

A buzz of conversation see-sawed around the room as people became engrossed in their own discussions, about the pros and cons of what Logan and Hutchinson had said. Eventually Carlisle had to raise her hands to quiet the meeting.

'We need to get this person or persons who have compromised our security. I don't care how you do it, just find them. General Adams, I want this place locked down tight. If anyone breathes in the wrong way I want to know about it. Anne, it's up to you to coordinate the investigation. Nothing stands in the way of what you do – absolutely nothing. Is that clear? Start with those people who clearly have an ethnic reason for doing this. Yes, I know, that's not constitutional,' Carlisle continued, as the FBI director made to remonstrate. 'These aren't constitutional times.' Carlisle got up to leave. 'You all know your roles – let's find the person who is stroking us.'

Forty-One

The Antonov AN-144 Ruslan sat on the tarmac, hunched over the ground crew unloading the articulated trucks of the Hortez roadshow, its huge bulk casting multiple shadows in the strong airport lighting. Drivers carefully guided their semis out of the maw of the vessel and trundled away towards a customs checkpoint.

Last off the Ruslan were a gloss black Mercedes Sprinter van and a Range Rover Overfinch. In the back of the former sat Penelope Hortez, sipping water while she spoke on the phone with another, and monitored the progress of her trucks through customs, on the TV feed.

'You know where to pick up the trucks once they're through customs.'

'Yes, Senora, we do.'

'Good. Take the usual precautions. We're all cleared through customs but, after that, we're on our own.'

'Understood.'

The line went dead and Penelope concentrated the whole of her attention on the trucks, aware that she felt a little clammy even in the air conditioned interior of the van. Had Johnson been as good as his word? When has he ever let you down Penelope, she asked herself. Just the once, came a small voice in reply as she looked away from the monitor.

Guards walked round the two trucks and it was evident they were going through the motions. So far, so good. First one, now the other, was waved through the checkpoint. She allowed a congratulatory smile to paint her lips. Excellent. Johnson still had his uses then.

With the same speed, she and her escort passed through customs and made their way off the airport complex and towards Washington. Penelope pressed the intercom button.

'Eduardo, at the city interchange, don't follow the trucks. Take us to the Sheraton. I want to freshen up and then go out. Oh, and can you arrange for an escort. I fancy some company tonight.'

Her driver acknowledged and she tried to settle in the leather recliner, drinking slowly and watching the two articulated units ahead speeding towards a different destination. Rado had said it would be quick. She hoped so. The families would be paid handsomely for their silence.

*

In the lead semi, driver Miguel Ortega settled back for the journey to the Verizon Centre in Central Washington. The sat nav showed his route and he followed it as he had been told to, though he couldn't for the life of him understand why they were taking such a circuitous route. It would have been much easier to have taken the three-ninety-five into the city and then head up Seventh Street which went virtually past the door. Still, who was he to argue? Ms Hortez was never anything but straight with him so there had to be a very good reason why this route had been chosen.

The beams from his heads chased ahead of him on the two lane highway. At this time of night, the traffic was very light. Being a Friday he guessed most folk had gone home early to enjoy, what the television on the flight over had predicted would be, a hot weekend. Plenty of barbecues and beer: to try and forget the atrocities of the last few days. He smiled at the thought and longed to be home with his wife Christina and his two little girls. Tonight he would have to make do with McDonalds and a six-pack from some late night store. He wondered idly how the Americans would respond to the attacks. What Senora Hortez was doing was good. Then, she was always one for a sympathetic gesture.

Miguel glanced in his mirrors and saw Ms Hortez's van and escort cut over towards the Jefferson Davis Highway – the one he should have taken for the quicker, more direct route into Washington. He grimaced: lucky her. She would get to the hotel sooner, and shower; probably eat at a table with good wine to finish and then go out for the night. Miguel didn't begrudge her that, after all she was the person who paid his wages; he just envied that freedom to come and go as you pleased.

He switched on the radio and tuned into a Hispanic channel but it was playing mostly Mexican shit so he turned it off again. Miguel glanced in the mirrors again to confirm that Hernando was still with him. The young lad, perhaps sensing Miguel was checking, flashed his lights and Miguel waved out the window at him. Perhaps they could share a six pack?

Ahead an interchange appeared. Straddling the highway were two large vans with uniformed men waving glo-sticks. One of the men pointed repeatedly to the off ramp with his sticks. Miguel tried to look beyond the vans but couldn't make out in the dark, what was the cause of the diversion. Changing down, he indicated and began pulling off the ramp. Behind, he could see Hernando signalling to do the same. More delay.

At the junction another van blocked the left turn which would have taken him towards Washington; another man pointing in the opposite direction. Miguel turned the wheel and took his semi under the interchange. Two vans ahead of him veered onto the carriageway from the other off ramp, causing him to brake sharply and curse the stupid Americans for not knowing how to drive.

He settled back and followed the two vans which suddenly accelerated away and around a bend. Thank goodness for that, he thought. Now: to find a way back on to the interstate, and on to their destination. That burger was beginning to call to him.

As Miguel rounded a bend in the road and it straightened out into the darkness he could make out an obstruction in the road. What now!? He slowed the truck down until it crawled to a stop. The two vans, which had accelerated away from him only moments before, blocked the road. A sense of foreboding wound tentacles round his throat and he looked for a way to get his truck turned round. It wasn't going to happen. Pulling on the brake he opened the door and jumped to the tarmac. As he did so, shapes moved away from the vans and torches shone in his face

'Hi, what's the problem?' He squinted in the harsh light that bathed him. 'Can you lower the torches please?'

No reply.

'What gives?'

Miguel started as Hernando touched his arm. 'I don't know. You'd have to ask these guys.'

A figure detached itself from the torch light and advanced. He had a hand behind his back and for a fleeting moment Miguel guessed the intent. Before he could warn his friend the bullet had sliced through his forehead and exploded out of the back of his head.

Hernando turned and ran. Two steps and then the bullet shattered his spine and he dropped to the floor with a low grunt.

The figure came up to him and shot him twice in the back of the head. Turning, he rolled Hernando's recumbent form over with the toe of his boot. The Colombian was dead. Pulling back his balaclava the Bosnian looked at his colleagues.

'Ok. Let's move.'

*

Penelope Hortez checked her watch. The whole thing should be over by now and she felt a pang of guilt turn in her belly. She dropped her fork to the plate and placed her hand in her lap where her escort wouldn't see it tremble.

'Are you ok?' The man leant forward, the look of concern a man had when he was paid handsomely for his company. Penelope nodded briefly.

'It's nothing, just the flight over. Let's finish here, I fancy some dancing.'

*

Kiric watched as the two semis were driven into the warehouse facility. She had been true to her word, he gave Penelope that. All that remained to do was remove his cargo from the trailers and get them out in the community.

Activity was measured and quick; his team were well drilled as they went through the trailers and removed the drugs from their hiding places. A number of local dealers had arranged to be here when the semis arrived and were now helping to divide the lucrative cargo for their particular neighbourhoods. Kiric had taught his people well in protecting both him and the drugs, and security was strict as each dealer claimed a cut of the cargo.

From hijack to final deal took eight hours and dawn had come and gone when the last one left. Kiric sat in an office overlooking the warehouse area, surrounded by piles of money. He felt good and was pleasantly gratified that things had gone so well.

He looked at the list of dealers on the desk. This was a good hit. If the Colombian plan worked there would be people, from across the Eastern seaboard, looking out for some good shit to control their clucking and rising paranoia. The market would be good for a while with the amount they had shipped in, but they would need more routes. Perhaps that wouldn't be so difficult with the contacts that Penelope had.

It was time to move out. The plan was that Penelope would call in the non-arrival of her trucks to the local police after eight. That hour was passed and he couldn't afford him or his team to be caught here.

He walked into the warehouse proper and shouted to his lieutenant. Bogdan, even darker and swarthier than Rado, walked over. 'Yes boss?'

'We need to clear this place up and move out before the police show.'

'Do you want me to torch the trucks?'

Kiric hesitated. Protocol dictated that was the cleanest course of action but she'd said no; that she needed to put on this show for her contact and he had agreed to respect that request. Even so …

'Yes, torch everything. I don't want anything left behind that might have a print or trace on it. Make sure it burns well.'

Bogdan nodded. 'Sure.' He turned away and started shouting orders to the others. Satisfied, Rado walked out of the building and headed for his SUV with the money. She would hate him for this but, ultimately, she was unimportant. He had other people to please.

Pressing speed dial five he waited for the call to be answered. 'It is done, we're just clearing the evidence away now,' Rado informed the listener. He waited for the other. 'I understand. When do you want that package delivered?'

Another pause.

'Okay, I'll get on it straight away. Send me the rendezvous details.'

He ended the call and there was a text beep. Opening the message Rado took in the contents and then deleted the message. As the first flames licked from the trucks his driver started up the Suburban and they drove away from the warehouse.

*

Logan walked into the briefing room, took in the empty coffee pot and grimaced.

'Still no change on the coffee?' He asked one of the administrators, busy lining up bottles of water on the table. She shook her head and offered him one of the bottles. With a shrug he took it from her and went to sit down. The room was just getting ready for the day and the post mortem which was bound to happen. Right now though, it was just him and his silent friend with the water so he decided to make the most of the quiet.

Sitting, sipping the cold liquid, his head was filled

with the image of Charlie dying before him. It was a picture he couldn't shift, that occupied his head every night before he slept and woke him in the morning with the grim, angry face of Assiz looming over her. He would've loved to bring the bastard to book, but there was no hope of that now. Logan gulped down the icy water and coughed.

'Hey, take it slow with that stuff. We don't want another emergency on our hands.'

Logan looked up at Black who was fast becoming a friend and smiled coldly. 'Till we get the coffee sorted it's all we have. What I'd give for a good cup of tea.' He sighed heavily.

'Ah … you Brits and your tea. When in a quandary as to what to do, brew up: isn't that what you guys call it?'

Despite his inner sadness Logan allowed himself a small laugh. 'Yeah, a good brew is just what the doctor would order right now.'

Black looked sidelong at him. 'Well, my friend, your luck is in. Follow me.' He ducked out of the room and Logan followed him, intrigued. The SEAL strode off down the corridor and Logan was hard pressed to keep up with the guy – shit, he was unfit!

After a number of changes of direction in the underground labyrinth Black came to a door labelled "Kitchen". Black pushed through the swing doors.

'Yo, Vin! You here?'

'Yo, my man! How you doing?' A huge figure lumbered out of the depths of the kitchen. Logan took in the man's physique and mentally gulped. Easily seven feet tall, and almost as wide "Vin" was not a person to be trifled with.

'Hey Vin, my man here needs a drink. The coffee

is off. What you got?'

The large Afro-American regarded them like some jovial sumo wrestler, his bulk offset by the wide grin which infected his curiously small face, crafted by experience on a small head.

'I know just what the man needs,' he declared in a deep, rumbling tone that burbled through his teeth. 'A cup of finest English tea, freshly brewed.' He caught sight of Logan's dubious expression. 'Hey, don't you dis my expertise with the leaf man.'

Black nodded. 'It would be unwise,' he concurred, 'This guy is a serious brewer of that most English of drinks.' Logan shrugged his compliance.

Vin beckoned to them both as he lumbered deeper into the kitchen. 'Follow me gentlemen, come to the nexus of my arcane activities.'

They settled, as indicated, on cold metal chairs, gathered around a utilitarian metal table. Vin bustled about and they watched as he brought over a tray, laden with a porcelain teapot and three cups, while they waited for the water to boil. A jug of cold milk appeared. Humming some indeterminate tune to himself, Vin brought over the kettle of boiling water and eased his reluctant bulk into a chair which creaked under the strain.

'You see, the trick is in the heat of the pot and the length of the brew. To make tea properly the pot has to be warmed through first and the water discarded.' He turned and tipped the pot over a nearby sink. The water hissed and steamed on the cold stainless steel. 'Then you add a teaspoon of tea per person and one for the pot, pour over freshly boiled water and leave to brew for no less than three minutes.'

Vin replaced the lid and pulled a tea cosie over the pot. It was so incongruous that Logan had to laugh at the bright chintz. Vin looked hurt and turned to Black. 'Is this guy for real? That cover has been passed down my family for three generations. It was brought over here from Jamaica by my old mammy. You dissing my old mammy?'

Logan raised his hands. 'Not at all. I wouldn't dream of it.' he replied quickly.

Vin scowled. 'Make sure you don't,' he grumbled, then, just as fast, he was smiling broadly again. 'Now, the cups need to be warmed.' Water splashed in their three cups from the kettle and Vin delicately swirled each in turn, before disposing of the contents down the sink. 'And now, a quick stir to circulate the leaves through the water.' The spoon clinked against the pot as he stirred. 'Ok, let's do it,' he decided fervently.

The Brit lifted the jug to pour milk in his cup.

'No man!' Vin placed a big paw on Logan's forearm and clucked in distaste. 'Are you for real? Never put the milk in first. It taints it.'

Logan coloured and caught the big grin from the SEAL to his left. 'You have to do this right Steve,' he admonished, shaking his head slowly.

'Hey, you can talk,' Vin told him. 'You used to put sugar in your tea. Man! That was sacrilegious.' Vin watched as Black blushed, then slapped the SEAL hard on the back and whooped with laughter. 'It's cool, man, you don't know the truth, it's okay.'

Vin poured the deep tan liquid slowly and deliberately over the strainer, leaving exactly the same amount of space in each cup for the milk, which he decanted from the jug in the same paced way. 'Okay ladies, enjoy.'

Logan raised an eyebrow in silent irony and Vin let out a howling laugh before planting his huge hand firmly in the middle of the Brit's back who nearly head butted the table, such was the power of the slap. As he sipped the drink he found himself nodding in compliment. The tea was probably the best he'd ever had. 'It's good,' he informed the chef.

'Well, shit man, 'course it is. I made it and I know the ritual of the leaf. None of that bag shit here: it has to be the leaf, pure, unrestrained, allowed to move freely about the pot.'

'You're sure it's just tea in here aren't you,' Logan questioned, the eyebrow still arched, but a smile playing his lips. Suddenly all three were laughing in the way new friends did, rocking in their chairs to the bemusement of those who passed.

*

When the two finally returned to the conference room the great and good of the remaining US administration had already assembled. Acting President Carlisle was not impressed by their late appearance and made her displeasure clear.

'I'm so glad you could make it gentlemen. Can I ask why you're late?'

'We're not Madam President. When we arrived first thing, there was a mix up with the coffee and I took our guest here to the kitchens for a cup of tea.'

Logan nodded in complicity as Black worked on their excuse. Even he could see it was looking pretty grim for them, as Carlisle pursed her lips and harrumphed in clear Presidential style. 'Did you enjoy your tea Mr Logan?'

Shit, what was the correct reply? Logan computed quickly and swiftly realised there was no right answer. 'Yes,' was short, sweet and the line of least resistance.

Carlisle huffed. 'Well, while you were enjoying *tea time*, we were debating what is to be done about the unfortunate death of our main protagonist. The general feeling we,' Carlisle emphasised the "we" to exclude Logan and Black, 'came to is that there is a sleeper cell within this complex and that we need to segregate out all those of an ethnic background that correspond to our threat analysis.' The acting President paused as she caught the look on Logan's face. 'You have a problem with that Mr Logan?'

'Yes Madam President, I do.'

Everybody in the room turned their attention and scepticism towards the lone Brit who suddenly found the attention unwelcome and uncomfortable.

Carlisle waited. Logan coughed and briefly decided it might have been better to have said nothing before clearing his throat and beginning.

'You're embarking on a knee jerk reaction to an event for which you have no clear perpetrator or motive.'

A snort of derision rose from the table: it was the head of NSA Eugene Hutchinson. The hard looking, thin man, with flint grey eyes, was instantly unlikeable. 'You think? We have a dead CIA analyst and a dead Al-Qaeda suspect. The latter was assassinated by sniper so that he couldn't talk to anybody when he was brought back here.'

'Exactly,' Logan concurred. 'Assiz was killed to prevent him from talking. That doesn't mean the attack was originated or coordinated from here or that anybody in here was in a position or would indeed do anything to compromise the security of this country based on their ethnicity. You just don't have the evidence to support the supposition.'

'We have enough young man.'

Logan responded furiously to the patronising remark from Adams, the general who'd been his tormentor before. 'Sir, I am not your "young man". I was a captain in the SAS and spent time with a special ops unit working on the Afghanistan-Pakistan border before joining SIS. I have seen covert operation across the world and have blended in with some of the world's most chaotic populations. Part of my job is to understand people and why they do certain things. I can tell you, what happened yesterday does not fit the pattern you are impressing on the situation.'

'Who else could it have been?' The general declined to look at Logan as he sought the support of his colleagues around the table: they nodded affirmation. 'They couldn't afford to let Assiz be interrogated, and give the game away so they had him removed from the equation.'

Logan raised his eyes to the ceiling, not caring if anybody saw his grimace of disdain. 'So, you think it was coordinated from in here? And how do you think they, whoever they are, got messages to the sniper? Without being scoped by your people in NSA?'

'It doesn't matter whether people in here did that or not, Mr Logan. We can't take the chance there are sympathisers on this side of the wall.'

'So, you think incarcerating everybody on the basis of creed, or the colour of their skin is the answer?'

Carlisle looked as though she was about to slap Logan, her face flushed with rage. 'Don't presume to come in here Mr Logan with your high-handed morals.'

Logan drew a breath. 'Madam President, if I overstepped I apologise, but you can't imprison people based on a supposition. The people in this complex are here because they are patriotic to the flag of the United States. If you take away their freedom, you give them more reason to fight for the other side.'

'It's too late, Mr Logan,' cut in the general. 'We've started the process. Anyone with an Arabic or Pakistani ethnic coding is being taken off duty and bussed from the facility, to Andrews Air Force Base where they'll be transported to a maximum security facility for their own safety and for processing.'

Logan took in the hardened atmosphere around the table. 'Can you hear yourselves?' He fixed Carlisle with a hard glare. 'Madam President, you are committing a grave error if you allow this to continue. You are breaking the constitution of your country, which upholds the rights of every individual.'

'We don't need a lesson in democracy from a fucking limey,' growled another old general from the end of the table.

The Brit rose from the table. 'I'm sorry, I can't stay and listen to this. You do this, Madam President; hopefully you'll live to regret it.' He left the room without looking back.

Forty-Two

Logan breathed in the clear mountain air, glad to be out of the stifling room that had turned into a political prison. He walked slowly, debating with himself, as he made his way towards the top of the mountain and so he didn't see Debbie Turner until he almost fell over her.

'Shit Logan, watch what you're doing!'

'Sorry! Wasn't expecting to find anybody up here.' He paused. 'What are you doing?'

'Is it a criminal offence to be out on my own?'

'Not yet,' chuckled Logan, 'but they're working on it inside.'

Debbie searched his face. 'What do you mean?'

Logan told her of his confrontation in the conference room.

'Shits,' Debbie spat the word out as if it was contaminated. 'They can't do that.'

Logan shrugged. 'That's what I told them. They're not in listening mode right now. It's the only response they have to the situation. It's all very black and white to them and there're going to be some huge repercussions for Pakistanis and Arabs in the country once this gets out. You okay?'

Debbie turned her pale face from him. 'Yes,' she informed him curtly. 'I've got to get back inside and carry on with the analysis.'

Before he could stop her, she was gone.

'That woman is fucking weird,' he told nobody in particular as he carried on up the mountain.

*

The operations chief headed straight for her room when she entered the facility. Eddie Powell watched her go and wondered what had rattled her cage: she'd completely ignored him as she strode down the wide corridor. He shrugged. Debbie was a difficult person at the best of times and things were not fine at the moment. He'd witnessed people being escorted from their stations under armed guard; bewildered and, either angry, or subdued by the turn of events. Typical knee-jerk reaction to events. Of course nobody would tell him what. He continued his journey to the small computing facility he was sharing with an introspective NSA admin – joy.

*

Debbie closed her door and sat on the bed. Her hands trembled when she laid them on her lap. Fuck! A shit storm was brewing and it was only a matter of time before it broke. She had to do something, even though she had been warned.

*

The Ford F150 pulled on to the interstate and into the midday traffic. In the cab, the driver was just any other woodsman or hunter returning home from an unsuccessful deer hunt in the hills. With the peak of his baseball cap pulled down over his aviator sunglasses the person couldn't be readily identified and that was intentional. He slotted into the flow of traffic, matching speed and being unassuming.

On the seat next to him his cell hummed and fizzed on silent. Picking it up he glanced at the number, rejected the call and carried on driving.

They'd just have to wait.

After an hour he pulled over at a service station. Going inside he ordered coffee and pie and took a seat by the window, watching the traffic scoot by in each direction – busy people going about their busy lives for … what? A few dollars to put towards a holiday on the coast, Florida, Georgia or Louisiana was all. Or maybe a new car. In the grand scheme of things their lives meant nothing, a mote of dust in the eye of Allah.

He'd sat where he had clear lines of sight to the back of the diner and its one door to the outside world. It was force of habit – be prepared: wasn't that the Boy Scout motto? So a friend had once told him in another country a long time ago, or so it seemed now. The part of him that longed for that time again raised its head briefly, to be submerged by the instruction of his imam.

The position of the phone booth was known, without looking. This was one of the very few service stops along this interstate that still had a working phone booth which was why he had used it. While a call from here could still be traced, it would take longer than one from a cell.

Finishing the pie, he headed for the booth, entered and closed the door behind him. From memory he called the number he needed.

'Don't talk,' he commanded when the other answered. 'You'll have to get here as soon as possible. The situation is bad, there isn't much longer. Get here as soon as you can.'

It was such a nondescript message that anybody listening would be forgiven for not giving it a second thought. Which was perfect. He hung up and left the booth. Walking by his table, he dropped a couple of notes on the table, just enough to make it look a generous tip but not actually extravagant. Everything was perfectly judged, so that people would be unable to place him at the diner, or in the booth, with anything approaching certainty. He was just another traveller on the road.

Back in the truck, he pulled back on the interstate and headed for the Capitol. It would soon be time to put the next part of the plan into operation. He allowed a smile – the head was about to be removed. And while he brought down the sword along the neck of the decadent whore, the mighty United States would wallow in its addiction, anaesthetised and unable to respond.

*

Debbie placed her phone on the bed and reached for the bottle of vodka she kept in the bedside cabinet. He would do more than disapprove if he knew but it gave her the courage she needed at moments like this. She knew she wasn't the sort of agent Logan was and cared too much to be like Powell or Des who were more interested in their specialities and the quirkiness of IT and programs than the vagaries of humanity.

She shuddered as the vodka hit her stomach and then the warmth suffused her body. That was better. If only it would last.

*

Logan placed his mobile on the table. He felt as if he'd been dealt a hammer blow and his heart raced beneath his shirt, as if it might burst out of his chest. The call had been from London, from Galbraith.

They'd had the results of the autopsy on Faulkner's body back.

He could recall the hesitation in her voice. He'd been confused by her reticence but had taken her advice to find somewhere quiet to continue the call.

"Okay, so what's the issue?"

The pause had lingered in the distance between them.

"The body ..."

"Yes?"

"It isn't Drew Faulkner."

*

He walked down the corridor in something of a daze. Why? Why had somebody dressed a mutilated body to make it appear to be Drew Faulkner? What were they keeping Drew for? It was a puzzle he was in no shape to resolve at the moment. Instead he headed for where the British team were situated. Hopefully they had pulled something together which would help find whoever it was who'd killed Assiz. Pushing through the door he immediately noted the absence of Debbie Turner. He did a double take, no, she wasn't there.

'Hi Eddie, have you seen Debbie?'

Eddie Powell looked up from his terminal, his mind still elsewhere else as he strived to focus on Logan. 'N-no. Sorry, no I haven't,' he managed eventually, desperate to get back to his computing.

Logan nodded. 'Okay ... thanks.' He stopped and turned. 'Have you found anything useful yet?'

Powell shook his head. 'No – oh, wait!' Excitement sugared the younger man's voice. 'Charlie had given us access to some files she was working on before she went. One of the files was

Drew Faulkner's chip.'

Logan whirled round, catching the excitement in the young specialist. 'Oh?! Charlie said it had been damaged, there was nothing on it. What did you find?'

Powell shook his head in bemusement. 'Well, she was correct it was, but, that's the thing: the chip had already been stripped of every detail, as if they didn't want it to be traced.'

Or its owner, wondered Logan as he exited the room deep in thought.

*

Debbie Turner wandered around her room in a quandary. What to do? Fuck! There were so many paths to follow! Every time she explored one of them her mind veered off to take in Drew and his mission; his fatwa. A little voice in the dark asked her why she'd been suckered in. The quick answer was sex. But was it love? She liked to think the latter but it wasn't clear. Certainly he'd been charismatic, alluring in a way that had surprised her – for her capacity to fall for it.

Another slug of vodka.

Could she support him? Could she do what was necessary? At the moment she doubted it very much. She was scared of Logan – that fuck would be watching for her to fall, and hard. He was the one she feared most because he knew her; knew her well.

It was time to prepare, not yet to run. That would come later. She packed essentials into her rucksack, deliberating over each item she stowed in the small bag. Drew had drilled into her the need to think small, think essential and she interpreted that now as she

334

placed clothes, toiletries and other things in the small space.

Finished, Turner drew the cord and then buckled it so that everything was safe. Shouldering the bag, she took a quick look round the bare room and departed for the spot she'd marked earlier.

*

Logan saw her approaching, deep in self appraisal, unaware of her surroundings. Even when he called her it took her a moment register him and then she seemed to react as if she'd been shot.

He clocked the rucksack, 'Going on an expedition?' The smile was quick, easy.

Turner blushed. 'I – I just need to get out, so, uh, taking my lunch with me.'

Logan nodded slowly. 'You need some company?'

'No,' the answer was hurried, blocking. 'I'll be fine thanks.' And she was gone.

Logan regarded her shadow and wondered.

*

In the canteen Black sought him out from all the activity. Truth be told, it was easy to find the Englishman – sitting on his own, sipping fruit juice and wondering what was happening with this world.

'Hey, how you doing?' Black drew up a chair and regarded the agent closely.

Logan smiled wistfully. 'Okay, I guess.'

'You look like you're thinking 'bout something important.'

'You reckon?'

Black merely nodded and waited for Logan's

response.

'What do you think they had to gain from killing Assiz? It doesn't make any sense unless there's somebody else out there who is more important.' He paused. 'Who?' Logan's voice trailed off.

Black considered the questions in the order and drew in a breath which he let out slowly, centring his thoughts. 'They silenced somebody who could have given away a lot of information regarding their goals. If you want my opinion, Assiz was a foil. He was sent in to pave the way for somebody else; to draw attention away from the main event. Or maybe there was another plan he knew nothing of. Same result.'

Logan contemplated the words. That didn't sound so far-fetched now. Assiz hadn't known. He'd certainly felt he was the main act, that he was the catalyst for the bringing down of the Great Satan. And yet here we were with a body on a slab and somebody unknown, literally, calling the shots. Logan felt lost, as if he'd been spun round like a bottle in a drinking game. Trouble was he hadn't been drinking; there was a sniper out there controlling the game, a real threat to the US Administration. He shuddered. 'The more I think about it, the more that seems likely. It was too neat, too planned. As if whoever was looking down the scope knew exactly where Assiz would be and that we were looking for him.'

Black nodded, stroking the stubble on his chin reflectively. 'There certainly wasn't anything opportunistic about it. Which begs the question …'

'Who is it inside here, who's working with whoever is out there.'

'And who is it out there,' Black concluded, nodding.

'Quite. It wasn't a typical al-Qaeda hit, though they're pretty good at sniping, given the right conditions, but out here? In unfamiliar territory?'

'Well, not necessarily unfamiliar. Depends how long they've prepared for taking out Assiz.'

'Yes, but Assiz came in because he was a bigger fish than was available in the local system. Don't forget, you guys have buttoned al-Qaeda elements down pretty tightly over here. They needed to bring in a big player to coordinate and direct operations. Assiz was the man we thought might be that fish. It seems he wasn't. There's somebody beyond him we haven't accounted for.'

Logan stared into his bottle of apple juice, something that wasn't contaminated with drugs, trying to find the answer. Who could it be? It had to be somebody who wielded an enormous amount of leverage – but who? Neither CIA nor MI6 were sighted on any such individual. So, events pointed to something much bigger than an al-Qaeda operation to bring down the US government.

'What do you think is going on here John?' Logan waited for the SEAL to speak.

Black sipped from a bottle of water, snapped the cap on slowly, deliberately and fixed Logan with his stare. 'It's a state on state, clandestine destabilisation. Whoever is behind this is using al-Qaeda, and perhaps others, to do their dirty work for them. Once we're down, whoever it is will fill the vacuum.'

'Except we know who it is.'

'Sure we do. Trouble is proving it. The Chinese aren't called inscrutable for nothing.'

Forty-Three

He awoke in the dark, a film of cold sweat clinging to his shaking frame, determined to intensify his discomfort. Scrabbling for the switch Logan squinted as the harsh strip light of the cubicle faltered into life. His fingers reached automatically for the bottle on the small bedside table; amber liquid sloshed in the glass, and burned the throat as he drained it down.

She was still there.

When he closed his eyes he could see Raifah's smiling face, teasing him. He could smell her skin, feel its warmth on his as they wrapped limbs round each other in the back of his car, parked off the beaten track in Newton Wood, not thirty minutes from her family's house in Epsom. It required no concentration of effort to see her, a flower blossoming even as he held her; kissed the dark umber of her nipples and felt her rise under his touch, the sigh a dying thing on her breath.

And then the stitching of blood red roses across her slim form; the look of pain and loss in her eyes as her fingers sought to stop the flood of blood from the holes he had drilled so perfectly in her tiny frame.

His holes.

His work.

His legacy.

Her ending.

Yet no ending for him; no completion of the chapter of hurt and self-disgust. Raifah's death was merely the starting point for a journey that had brought him three and a half thousand miles across the Atlantic to a madness, which showed no signs of understanding or ending itself.

And now there was another to add to the list of women he had brought to an untimely death. Another blood rose blooming from a broken body. A second marker of death, on the path of his … his what? What was he trying to prove with all this … all these … spy games? Who was he kidding with his bravado of intelligence and knowledge?

Logan poured another whiskey, careless of the measure, but more considerate in the drinking, thinking about what had happened since he had been at Raven Rock. About the changes that had come with the murder of Charlie, and the shooting of Assiz. The whole apparatus of state paranoia had heaved into motion, dispelling the myth of equality before the flag and replacing it with the fear of a neighbour you'd never really introduced yourself to.

It was still incomprehensible that President Carlisle had agreed to remove anyone of Arabic or Pakistani heritage from the team and have them shipped away to a secure facility. Reminiscent of the imprisonment of American Japanese after Pearl Harbour, Logan figured they would rue the move at some point in the future. It was more likely to make terrorists of these people than any previous act against a particular ethnic group in the continental US – he believed it a monumental mistake, but one over which he had no control.

The buses had left early afternoon, headed to Andrews where their passengers would be loaded into military transports and flown to various points in the US for processing. They weren't the problem. Logan shook his head slowly and savoured more scotch. Assiz had had two tasks: taking out the US President and administration and avenging the death of his sister. The former was a clear al-Qaeda order; the latter his own vendetta.

Had his controllers decided to sacrifice him following the downing of Air Force One? After all, there were other strands that were being developed. Perhaps it was thought his personal desires would compromise the overall mission. Had they known? Maybe Assiz had misjudged his own usefulness and once he had been captured then the decision had to be made to take him out.

Logan shook his head. Assiz had been very explicit on the video – *"You will pay for the defilement of Allah's virgin, my sister."*

Was there an accomplice whose task it would be to finish the job?

The knock on the door cut his reverie. Slowly he rose and padded over and looked through the peep hole. Debbie Turner was stood there, agitated and furtive: he opened up and looked at his operations chief.

'What's up?' He was aware his tone was quite peremptory; then he wasn't in the mood for a visit, much less Turner, who despised him anyway.

Turner glanced at him; turned quickly away, as if her face might give away too much. 'Can I come in?'

Logan hesitated a little longer than was polite and then reluctantly shifted his weight to allow her through. Turner walked, almost rushed, in and sat nervously on the bed. Logan regarded her quizzically.

'What's on your mind?'

'How can they do what they're doing to these people? They have no fucking right!'

'Do you want a drink? I've only got whiskey.' To his surprise, Turner nodded and when he gave her a glass half full she knocked it back with the action of a seasoned scotch drinker. 'Hadn't got you pegged as a whiskey drinker,' he remarked casually.

Debbie looked at the glass, took another, slower, draft and then looked at Logan. 'There's a lot you don't know about me,' she informed him in a voice at once forlorn and self-accusatory.

Logan waited; obviously she was going to deliver some message.

'Did you see how they herded out totally innocent people onto buses to be driven off to God knows where?' Barely acknowledging Logan's nod, she continued. 'It'll make no difference of course.'

'No? How so? And how do you know that all those people are innocent?'

'I – just do.' Debbie drained the glass and without asking poured another liberal slug which she half consumed before continuing. 'This struggle has nothing to do with them and it will carry on.'

'What makes you so sure?'

'Because America is just so … they always react to what is happening in the world as if it is personal affront, as if everybody gives a shit about who they are and what they think.'

'And people don't?'

'No! Nobody gives a flying fuck what the United States actually thinks about anything! They're an anachronism and screwing the world at the same time.'

Logan shook his head, hoping Turner didn't pick up on his confusion. What the hell was she talking about? He was worried about the operations chief. Her response to Faulkner's death; her drinking and her anti-US stance were uncharacteristic. 'Debbie, I think you've had enough to drink. We need to speak about this in the morning.' He made to take her glass off her but Debbie pulled away and drained it before looking him straight in the eye.

'You fucked me over Logan.'

Shit.

'You fucked me over, when you knew how I felt about you.'

'You've had too much to drink Debbie and you need to leave right now, before this gets out of hand. We'll discuss this further in the morning.'

'He's coming for you, you know.'

'Who? Assiz is dead, that's all over.'

'Not at all. Assiz's death was calculated. The shooter will take you out.'

'You're drunk.' He felt the sweat rise on his brow, a tide of fear. 'I'm having you returned to London tomorrow. When you get back, report to Galbraith and hand in your id.'

Turner was looking through him even while she spoke to him. 'It doesn't matter, nothing matters now.'

This is getting seriously shitty, Logan decided, and it needed to stop. 'Okay I'm getting you back to your room.'

Turner stood and wobbled slightly, placing her hand on the table to regain confidence. 'You think you're so clever, but he's got you beat and he's going to make you pay.'

'Who? For what?'

'For killing his bride.'

Logan shook his head. 'Come on Debbie. You're talking rubbish. Let's get you to bed before you make a complete arse of yourself.' He was losing his patience with her. 'I haven't killed anybody's bride.'

'Raifah.'

Her voice was small and accusatory and Logan felt a jolt deep inside. Though he didn't understand

Turner's words, a cold hand circled around his heart and squeezed hard as Raifah's name tumbled violently from her mouth. 'What about her?' he heard his voice ask.

'She was promised to somebody and now they are going to exact their revenge. Assiz was just opening the door. That's what this is all about. Closing doors for America, and for you.'

'And who is closing them?'

'The Convert.'

Logan felt a cold, hard hand grip him. This was taking a turn for the worse. Another fanatic was just what they needed – and if they were home grown. 'The Convert?'

'Yes, someone with far more to give than Assiz ever could, somebody with the ability to move unseen, with impunity and get right to the heart of the Western problem.'

'You're going to have to help me out here.'

'Drew Faulkner.'

Forty-Four

The burned out hulks of her two transporters, transfixed Penelope Hortez, and a cold knife twisted in her gut. He'd promised he wouldn't torch them. How could he have done this? She shuddered as she thought of how she had given herself to him ... in vain, apparently. So easy to torch nearly $100 million dollars of equipment, fashion and desires ...

'You okay ma'am?'

She looked uncomprehendingly into the face of the State Trooper then reality snapped back and she felt the heat of shame at being duped by the smooth Kosovan. Once again a man had used her for his own advantage. Kiric had exposed her and left her for dead. She had to get back to Colombia – only there would she be safe.

'Ma'am?' The trooper was insistent.

'I-I'm fine,' she found the time and courage to smile, as if everything was as she expected in the circumstances. 'It's just such a shock.'

'Do you need victim support?'

It was an innocent question; one which nearly caused her to laugh hysterically. 'No, I'll be ok. I just need time to work this through.'

With that Penelope Hortez walked away from the site and began calculating the cost of retribution once more.

*

Rado Kiric listened impassively to the voice on the phone.

'Everything has gone as we had agreed,' he

informed his caller. 'No evidence has been left behind that can be traced back to us.' A pause and then, coldly, 'I'm always careful. No – she won't offer us any opposition. Yes, I can convince her of that,'

He listened for a while then:

'If it is necessary, then Penelope Hortez will be eliminated.'

*

Yuan placed the phone back in his pocket and pursed his lips, mindful of Leong's presence. The other seemingly sensing the unease in him attracted his attention; Yuan looked up.

'Is everything in order?'

Yuan made no immediate reply. Instead he walked to the balcony doors and looked out on Bogota's morning traffic. Thousands of people leading humdrum lives while he and the general played god in the shadows. It gave him a thrill better than sex.

'Yes.'

Leong shot his lieutenant a glance which the other didn't register, stood as he was staring into the Colombian morning. The general knew he couldn't really trust the self-indulgent prick whose father had left him in his care, but the time wasn't yet right for an … accident. 'Is the package delivered?'

Yuan turned and faced his inquisitor. To be rid of this old fart would be such a wonderful thing, but ... 'Yes. The next act is about to be played out.'

Leong nodded slowly, reflectively. 'Good, we must ensure it coordinates with our asset's final solution.'

'It will, if he is ready.'

'We will find out soon enough. He is due here

tomorrow.'

Yuan covered his surprise. 'That is good news. To hear directly from the architect will be good. How far can you trust him?'

'Our colleague assures me that he is a true convert. He must deliver … after all, what does he have left?'

Yuan nodded slowly. It was true, The Convert did have nothing left, nor anywhere to hide. He had to complete the task and he would. Of that, they had to be sure and certain. One thing he had learned about Leong – the general never bet on a lame horse.

'When is he due?'

'Sanchez has a plane bringing him in tomorrow, from Washington and I will discuss with him the nature of our plans and his operation to bring them to fruition, since the incident at the mine. You must ensure our Kosovan friend is in control of things in the States.'

Yuan contained himself though he bristled inwardly. 'He has done everything that is required of him and he will silence the Colombian bitch if necessary.'

'Good, we must have nothing disturbing our path. We are on the verge of something monumental Yuan, something that will set our destinies in motion.'

Even Yuan had to smile with his general at that thought.

*

Some nine and a half thousand miles away a cipher clerk of the People's Liberation Army noted the words of General Leong on a pad for his superiors.

Checking his report again he placed it in a manila folder and handed it to a runner with a slip which indicated it should be delivered to the local police bureau head. The runner read the slip and nodded, turned and walked quickly away.

The clerk turned back to his next task.

*

Drew Faulkner had a night to wait before his contact would pick him up and take him to Potomac Field where he would be placed on a flight to his rendezvous. He felt relaxed, as with all such moments. Hysteria and reactionary feelings were a Western thing he was pleased to have left behind.

He knelt on his prayer mat, faced Mecca and offered his prayers. In his head he was still registering surprise at how easy it had been to let Allah into his life. It all seemed so … right. He didn't miss his Western existence; it had been empty for years since his wife had divorced him. But his time in Pakistan, then Yemen, had immersed him in something that had resurrected purpose in that existence. His imam had been an inspiration, a solace in a cold and empty world.

But then there was Allah.

He finished his prayers and rose from the mat, rolling and stowing it in his holdall. His attention turned to more mundane matters. With a fluidity borne of practice he stripped down his sniper rifle and pistols, cleaning everything meticulously and with an automation borne of years of practice. Everything had to be pure and right in the eyes of the prophet and in the heart for Allah.

Ten hours before his flight.

Forty-Five

Captain Fouré sat back in his chair, massaging his temples to soothe the aching in his head. He wanted a coffee but resisted the temptation. Recently he had been drinking way too much and the caffeine kick back was worse than usual. He read through the reports of the increased drugs busts, more than he'd ever seen before, yet his officers were telling him it was something they couldn't control. Add that to the lack of progress on the Lincoln Memorial bombing and it wasn't a good time for the Capitol Police.

He dragged a tired hand through the stubble cut on his head and sighed. There was a call he needed to make that he was dreading. Dreading it: because he had ridiculed the man previously. Yet he knew he was going to have to eat humble pie with Camino who had shown himself to be a pretty fine investigator. The FBI Agent was dealing with a whole raft of problems, which had only increased with the downing of Air Force One. Terrorism hadn't been his only forte, providing some useful thoughts and expertise around the burgeoning drug issues.

It was a real basket case of a situation. Terrorists running amok and a flood of drugs on the street. What else could go wrong?

The phone rang and for a moment Fouré considered ignoring it: that wasn't in his nature. He reached for the receiver.

'Hello, Fouré DC police.'

'Captain, Special Agent Dan Camino here.'

Fouré's heart sank and he scrabbled for the positive in the moment, having lost control of it. 'Special Agent,' he acknowledged with as much enthusiasm as he could summon. 'What can I do for you?' He couldn't help the hard steel in his voice. Camino's reputation as a slacker, as somebody who jeopardised his agents, preceded him.

'There have been developments.'

Fouré hunched forward, despite himself. 'Go on?'

'Yesterday, one Sayed Assiz was murdered, along with a CIA Special Analyst at the abandoned Annerdime Mine, west of the Government facility at Raven Rock.

The captain took a moment to process the information. 'A special analyst? What was he doing out there?'

'She,' Camino advised, 'was working on a wider case, hunting down al-Qaeda operatives in this country, and appeared to be working on the importation and trafficking of drugs on a massive scale.'

'And you guys were out of the loop.' Fouré couldn't help a little dig, just one to massage his ego. Camino chose to ignore it.

'We hear at the Bureau that there was a truck-jacking last night in the south of the capital.' When Fouré maintained his silence Camino carried on. 'They were owned by a Penelope Hortez, the Colombian fashion designer. She's a known associate of Harry Johnson.

'Ring any bells?'

Fouré considered the request, carefully. 'That's right, yes. Two semis, the drivers were shot, assassination style, and the units driven off. They were found this morning, burned out at an old warehouse site, just off the interstate.'

There was a pause on the other end of the line. Camino computed his response, what he needed to say and do. Fouré imagined he could hear the wheels going round. As the pause threatened to become unrecoverable Camino's grating voice came back on. 'Captain, we have to work together on this. We have to bury our personal differences for the sake of the country. We have, God knows how many, terrorists to hunt down and we can only do that if we work together.'

The captain mulled the words over in his mind, looking for any hidden agenda and considering his own decision to work with the agent. He came up blank and that surprised him. He drew a breath, letting it out slowly.

'I'm a Muslim. Did you know that?'

A pause. 'No, I didn't.' Another pause. 'Does that make a difference for you?'

Fouré considered the question, one he hadn't expected from the FBI Agent. 'To tell the truth, I hadn't looked at it from that perspective before. I was expecting all the trouble to come from you guys.' And by that he meant White, Christian, Centre-right American. 'And you know that will come don't you?'

'I do and I can tell you that the government has already incarcerated a bunch of people who they consider to be a threat to national security, i.e. people who profess a Muslim faith and who are – were – working for the government but are now considered risky. Can I be honest?'

'Sure.'

'First, thanks for telling me about your background. It makes it easier to work with you and I guess you wouldn't have told me if you were a threat. Second, my family are from New York, Brooklyn, but my grandfather was born in Rome and he married a girl from the Lazio area. Neither family ever forgave what they saw as the ultimate treachery. That's how he and she came to move to the States; to start a better life. It's crazy shit like that which keeps the world turning. I don't know your circumstances; don't need to. But I understand that feeling of not belonging, of always wondering who's watching you and why. But … we have to work together on this.'

Fouré considered the words, delivered honestly and with feeling, but lacking the understanding Camino had professed. Did that matter? Perhaps not, after all Camino was right about one thing – they had to work together, and quickly, to ensure another attack didn't take place. 'Okay, what do you propose?'

Forty-Six

The Hawker 4000 had taken close to five hours to transit from Washington to Bogota. It was now just after two, local time, as the Hawker taxied towards a Mercedes S Class limousine flanked by two G-Class SUVs: the Chinese never scrimped for their top people.

Faulkner allowed the comparative coolness of Bogota in late summer curl its fingers round his body as the stairs dropped. He controlled the shiver which threatened to overtake his body after Washington's warmer climate. The air stair eventually locked in place and he ambled down and began the exposed walk to the line of cars. A Chinese agent opened the door on the S-Class and Faulkner slid in to the air-conditioned interior, dropping his bag on the pliant leather covered seat next to him. The agent slipped in the other side, while another took the passenger seat next to the driver. Nobody said anything; no greeting, no direction, nothing. He shrugged mentally – the Chinese way.

The cars moved away in precise convoy, each driver seemingly maintaining a perfect spacing as if joined with invisible twine. After ten minutes they hit Calle Twenty-Six, keeping to the outside lane of the highway that drew them towards the centre of Colombia's capital city. Continuing the same precision, the drivers seemed to anticipate each change of lights and each silly interruption by other drivers, or pedestrians so that they never lost sight of each other. Faulkner was impressed.

After another fifteen minutes the vehicles swept round an interchange on to Carrera sixty-eight and precisely thirty-six minutes after leaving El Dorado airport, they swept into the Chinese Embassy's compound. The limousine, in which Faulkner travelled, detached itself from the convoy and drove into a garage. After a moment, where the garage door closed behind them, Faulkner was allowed out and escorted through white painted passages to the main embassy building.

Sitting in an anteroom Faulkner took in the ostentatious nature of the space. Cream walls held paintings in their place: heavy pictures with gilded frames and old colours. The polished wooden floor supported a selection of Chinese vases; Faulkner had no idea whether they were fake or not. He cared even less, momentarily despising his hosts for such overt signs of wealth and status.

A door opened, and a Chinese secret service agent stood expectantly in the opening. Faulkner took this as his cue, rose and entered the room beyond. The plush, patterned carpet cushioned his footsteps. Behind the large mahogany desk sat a tallish, older Chinese man, athletically built. In an ornate armchair to one side sat a younger man, powerfully built but with that veneer of over-confidence that often enfolded the youth. Faulkner took in the small, simple chair that was placed before the desk for his use. He allowed a small cynical smile to play his lips, hoping the others would see it and wonder; knowing that they wouldn't ask him what was so funny – inscrutable fuckers.

Drew Faulkner sat down and regarded the two Chinese, waiting for one of them to speak. Time limped in to emptiness before the one behind the desk eventually spoke.

'Mr Faulkner, welcome to the Chinese Embassy.'

'Why, thank you General Leong. It's good to be here.'

'I trust you had a good journey.'

'It was relaxing, the plane was comfortable and fast, and your driver was exemplary getting through Bogota's traffic.'

'Good.' Leong paused as if he had misplaced something and was looking for the right words to express his situation. 'Would you like anything? A cup of tea perhaps?'

'No, I'm good thanks.'

'Shall we get to business?'

'I think so.'

'Assiz? You had to eliminate him?'

Faulkner scrutinized the Chinese general: what was his game? 'Assiz was expendable. We all are. It is as Allah decrees.'

'We understood he was to deliver the final package.'

'It is not how we work, General Leong,' Faulkner smiled. 'He knew that when he was recruited. We all know that. Allah decides who will continue the struggle in His name and He had decided that our colleague's time had come and gone.'

Leong pondered the words of the American. With fingers steepled he considered the anomaly that was Drew Faulkner. A career CIA man, who had been station chief in Moscow, Karachi and latterly London; on the surface, he appeared to be an unlikely al-Qaeda recruit.

'And who does Allah decree should be the torch bearer now?'

Faulkner raised an eyebrow in puzzlement. 'Why, me of course. I am the one entrusted to thrust the sword of justice into the heart of the Great Beast.'

'I see.'

'Do you? Do you understand what it is we're doing here?' Faulkner hunched forward suddenly as if to intimidate his host. Nobody moved, yet Faulkner kept coming. 'Allah has made the opportunity arise. He has shined his light upon the world and has made his will clear to you as an infidel, helping him to achieve a new order on earth. You will be handsomely rewarded.'

'Is that so, Mr Faulkner? And what of our agreement?'

'Which is?'

Leong considered the reply and the American's quizzical expression. The man was clearly deluded and was a risk to the whole venture. He glanced across at Yuan and saw that his lieutenant was thinking exactly the same thing. Yet, they had to use the man to complete the mission and if he figured that Allah was guiding him so be it ... for the time being.

'Mr Faulkner, you had agreed to offer up to us a United States that was denuded of its power.'

'And that shall be the case.'

'For who? For you, or us? You see, I'm not sure we are on the same page. We want a simple thing because we Chinese believe in the simplicity of life. You talk of Allah directing you and your divining his purpose. The purpose is clear: topple the US administration and position China as the World's only super power. For that, al-Qaeda would be given political status and power they have not been privy to before. Your words ... concern me.'

Faulkner looked at the general without seeing, even though part of him cautioned speaking unthinkingly. Allah should be praised in all things.

Caution.

355

He breathed in: one … two … three … four … and out: one … two … three … four.

'General, I should apologise. You are, of course, right. Let me tell you of the situation in Washington. Assiz had to be eliminated. He had developed the system as far as he could. In addition, he had another agenda which threatened his ability to do the job. That could not be allowed.'

'What was that agenda?'

'He desired to indulge his ego by murdering a British MI6 agent –'

'You are referring to Steve Logan?'

Faulkner caught his surprise in time. 'Exactly. Because of that he had to be eliminated, otherwise he would have jeopardised the whole exercise.'

Leong didn't believe the American: there was something else but it served no purpose to search for it yet. 'So, you are saying that the mission is back under control now and you can deliver what is required?'

'As we speak, drugs are flooding the streets of the capital to disrupt the activities of the FBI and ATF agents, while they strive to pinpoint the perpetrator of the Lincoln Memorial bombing. He is dead; as is the person who downed Air Force One. This is the beauty of our way, General Leong: everybody can do what the dedicated professional can do, and more, because of the power imbued by the belief in Allah.'

All this talk of "Allah" was becoming tiresome. The American was a crass boor, outliving his usefulness. 'It is good that you exhibit such dedication Mr Faulkner, and we wish that to continue. Can you confirm that you will provide the solution required for dealing with the US Administration?'

'It is in our mutual self-interest.'

'That is good. Is there anything else you require?'

'A route out.'

'Where to?'

'It would have to be somewhere in China, say Tibet or Mongolia, until you are fully established as the superpower.'

Leong was silent.

'Well?'

'It can be done Mr Faulkner,' Leong decided. 'Let us know your requirements nearer the time and we will find a place for you to stay.'

Faulkner smiled in what he hoped looked like gratitude. 'Allah will repay your kindness.'

Leong smiled briefly. 'I'm sure he will, Mr Faulkner, I'm sure he will.' Leong rose from his chair and indicated the door. 'Before you make your flight back there is a person I want you to see. He is an associate of mine and he will be able to give you support when you finally come to act, should you need it. My people will take you to see him. Please make yourself at home before then. My chef will get you some lunch. If there is anything else you need before you go, let them know.' He extended a hand, indicating the meeting was at an end.

Faulkner took the hand almost cautiously, a little bemused by the turn of events. 'Thank you.'

He followed Leong to the door. The general spoke quickly in Mandarin to the guard. A nod and the guard led Faulkner from the room.

Leong came and sat back down, aware of Yuan's presence.

'Well General, did that go as expected?'

Leong grunted. 'If anything can go as expected with a Muslim: especially a convert like that.'

Yuan nodded. 'So what do you want us to do?'

'As soon as the objective is achieved, terminate Mr Faulkner. And leave no trace.'

Forty-Seven

'Can you be sure she's telling the truth?'

'I can't believe that she's implicated in all this. Why?'

Des Farrow was dumbfounded by Logan's revelation. He was bleary-eyed and not a little disorientated by being woken so urgently by Logan, as soon as the agent had ensured Turner was safely in her room. The older man rubbed his eyes slowly, carefully driving the sleep forcibly from his head. 'I mean, what does she have to gain from siding with a Muslim terror cell? It doesn't make any sense.' He shook his head reflectively, as if everything he had known had been stood on its head.

Logan looked up from the floor, equally confused by events. 'She was always close to Drew, shared a lot of his philosophy, and had worked closely with him in Afghanistan and Pakistan. When they'd both finished off the London tourist case they went off grid for a while.'

'But … but Faulkner must have known Assiz well before that. How?'

'I – introduced them. It was at a party at Sayed's house in Epping. Ironically it was to celebrate the end of Ramadan and Assiz invited me to bring a friend along. In the end I took Drew, who was still coming to terms with the breakup of his marriage. I figured he needed to get out, I didn't realise he was going to get so close to Assiz's sister and convert to Islam as well.'

'He kept it well hidden, like a good radical.' Eddie Powell had surfaced in the room's other bed, at the disturbance and added his observation.

'Just because somebody is a Muslim doesn't automatically make them an enemy of the state.' Logan rebuked Powell who flushed.

'I didn't mean …' He tailed off.

'Thing is,' reflected Farrow, heading off a potential conflict, 'we have a situation. A British agent is fraternising with a known enemy of the state; has actively worked to ensure said enemy evades capture. What are we going to do about it, given that she is also a colleague?'

'Debbie has to answer for what she's done. Nobody else can do that.'

Des raised an eyebrow. 'How easy is that going to be?'

Logan shook his head. 'Not at all. I don't even think she has any idea what she's done. She is totally focussed on Faulkner: he's exerted some incredible power over her.'

'I'm confused,' Powell confessed. 'Are we saying that Debbie is a Muslim terrorist?'

Logan paused. 'Terrorist? No. Misguided perhaps; in love probably. I'm betting the latter. Love does funny things to people. If it made Drew a Muslim, then it could make Debbie a collaborator.'

Eddie Powell let out an involuntary groan. 'Do you realise what you guys are saying? You're saying that Debbie, our Debbie, is the enemy.'

The others nodded slowly, reflectively, as if to voice the admission would immediately condemn their colleague. Farrow was the one who broke the ensuing silence. 'Eddie, you have to admit it looks pretty damning, and she has done nothing to deflect any of that from her person.'

'Even so,' Powell complained.

'I have to do it,' Logan decided to nobody in

particular. 'I have to take Debbie out of the equation. That means that she is going to be arrested in the morning and I'll do everything I can to get her back to the UK, but I'm not holding out any hope on that one.'

The men sat in silence ruminating on the situation from three different angles with as many different understandings. Eventually Logan rose from his seat and reached for the door. 'I'll see you guys later. There's something I need to do.'

Without another word Logan opened the door and exited the room in a daze.

*

Carlisle stared levelly at Logan as he delivered his message. Beside him, Black sat impassively, though he knew everything Logan was saying from their pre-brief. The President was, should he say, unhappy? To find that an ex-CIA station chief was a potential Islamic terrorist, and that he was being aided by a British agent, was not what the President of the world's one superpower wanted to hear, particularly at a time when there were challenges from around the globe to that particular status.

'Thank you for your candour Mr Logan, it's appreciated. Do I suppose you are going to take me to task about moving out ethnics?'

Logan considered the question. What did he say? He could hardly censure the world's most powerful woman, given the situation and yet …

'Madam President, countries make decisions that reflect the current situation. They try not to but sometimes the only thing they can do is react. Faulkner poses a particular … issue for us all and yet we mustn't forget there could be something else behind this.'

'Go on.'

The tension in the conference room was palpable. All faces turned to him and he felt a sweat come over him. *Breath in ... breathe out.* Slow down the fight or flight response, ensure you can answer in the way you want and not as a reaction to their probing.

'The United States has been under attack from a multitude of directions: al-Qaeda, cartels. Yet we know the level of organisation involved points to another, with greater resources.'

There was an impatient harrumph and Logan took in General Adams, who'd made his life a misery from day one. 'China again! Are you still seriously expecting us to believe that fantasy? There's no way that's happening.'

Logan opened his mouth to respond but before he could another spoke. It was Director of Homeland Security, Dave Chandler, grey eyes betraying nothing of his passion as he made his mind clear. 'We have to accept that it is a high probability right now.'

The British agent heaved a silent sigh of relief. At last somebody on his side. Adams scowled his displeasure.

'I'm sorry General Adams,' Chandler continued, 'but it fits with a CIA assessment and one on which Charlie Richter was working before her untimely death. We've already considered the possibility that Chinese powers are behind the current level of terrorist and cartel action directed against Mainland USA. The CIA has been monitoring Beijing for several years now and their general thrust has been economic and information technology. The idea of them actively supporting such groups, in a concerted attack on the US, was not seen as a credible threat.'

'Mr Chandler, just when did you think it was going to be credible, given our President is dead because of your ... insight ... and now we cower, virtually incarcerated in Raven Rock.'

Chandler coloured at the words of the Secretary of State Beverly Mitchell, now effectively second in command after Carlisle. He knew she wasn't a woman to be trifled with; somebody who was amoral and interested only in her own advancement.

'We – had to be sure of the intel we were gathering; couldn't just let it out there and risk panicking the country.'

'Yet, here we are on the cusp of a major drugs epidemic and with a home grown terrorist hunting down – well who knows who he has in his sights, and an insider who can deliver intelligence on our every movement.'

Chandler made to respond to his interrogator but, before he could, a voice cut through the incrimination laced atmosphere. All eyes turned to the British agent, Logan.

'With all due respect, ladies and gentlemen, this isn't the time for back stabbing and insult throwing. We have a growing situation outside and we know who was feeding the information to Faulkner. The latter we can control. We need to find where Faulkner is now. One of our first acts should be to interrogate Debbie Turner as soon as possible.'

There was a murmur of approval around the table. At least they were on his side for that, Logan acknowledged. That was good. He turned to Carlisle. 'This is your jurisdiction Madam President. Your people need to arrest Turner as soon as possible. The longer she's free, the more damage she'll do.'

'Agreed. What more on Faulkner?'

The President's question was directed at nobody and everybody. A silence draped the table like a cloth for a while: it was the SEAL team leader John Black who lifted it.

'Until we establish his current whereabouts and his potential actions, we're flying blind. From the activities of Assiz we have no reason to suspect his targets won't essentially be the same. So, he'll be concerned with completing the task of bringing down the Administration as soon as possible. He may be looking for outside help to resolve that.'

'Everyone concur?' Carlisle swept the table with her gaze. Logan noted she was constantly growing with each decision; each crisis; each problem that tasked her and her embryonic National Security team. It was an interesting lesson in the wielding of power. Nobody countered either the President or Black.

'Very well, let's bring Miss Turner in to answer some questions. Then we track Faulkner. Bev, I need you to stop the funeral going ahead –'

As one Logan and Black shook their heads vehemently and said "No!" with such force that even Carlisle was taken aback, and not a little annoyed at the interjection.

'Explain gentlemen,' she requested when she regained some composure.

Logan looked askance at Black, who nodded. 'Whatever information we glean from Turner the kill point for Faulkner will remain the Presidential funeral. He'll need to commit his act there. It's the only way he'll know for certain the task has been completed.'

'Won't he give the job to somebody else? After all, the risk …'

'You're looking at it from the perspective of what you'd do Ma'am.'

Carlisle looked perplexed at her SEAL officer who continued by way of clarity. 'Drew Faulkner is an emissary of Allah, first and foremost. It's what he thinks when he gets up and the last thing through his mind when he goes to sleep. That's how a jihadist is: they can't afford any room for distraction, misdirection; unfulfilment. Nothing can come between a jihadist and his target. Giving the task to somebody else would be anathema to Faulkner. He must see this through to the bitter end: even at the cost of his own life.'

'Is this right?' Carlisle looked over the assembly. There was some uncomfortable shuffling. Logan remained quiet – this had to come from her team, not some outsider.

The silence which had threatened embarrassment was broken by Hutchinson, brusque to the point of offensive, even with his President, 'You bet, Madam President. These fuckers don't mess with anybody and if you think you can negotiate a peaceful withdrawal, you're totally off base.'

Carlisle returned his hard stare with an arched eyebrow. 'Thanks for your frank assessment, Eugene. I'll be sure to keep negotiations to a minimum. Is this the feeling of you all?' The nods from her team made her become grim. 'And you, Mr Logan? You've been fairly quiet through this exchange. What's your feeling on this?'

What is my feeling? Logan considered the question. He allowed himself a moment to digest both the words and the look which asked so much more.

'Drew Faulkner was a friend of mine for a very long time. We saved each other's lives on innumerable occasions and yet the man who now stalks you. Yes, stalks you,' he reiterated at the President's frown, 'well he's a different proposition. He's as far removed from the CIA station chief that I knew as anybody is likely to be. I can't pretend to know what's happening inside that head, but one thing is for sure: he's committed. He's shown that by being prepared to kill US servicemen to achieve his ends. Jihadists can be singular in purpose and once they embark upon a course of action they will not waver; they will not be deflected.'

'You're saying it's us or him.'

'I'm saying that it's you or him. Others are incidental, collateral damage if you like. You, like President Lincoln, symbolise everything that is wrong with the decadent West. You have become the embodiment of the great Satan. The question is: what has America done to make someone as patriotic as Drew such an implacable enemy?'

Stony silence greeted his question and Logan shrugged. 'No matter, I don't need to know. But you have to be ready for the reality that Drew Faulkner is going to use all and every means to assassinate you, Madam President. Currently he holds all the cards because you don't know where he is or how he intends to accomplish his mission.'

Carlisle looked visibly drained but her voice, when she spoke, was level and any fear was held firmly under control. 'Very well, then we fight fire with fire. And we're not going to wait round for Mr Faulkner to make the first move. Eugene, I want you to put every available resource into tracking down where Faulkner has gotten to. Start with his last known whereabouts prior to his "death" in London. Also work with local law enforcement and the FBI, Anne, you'll facilitate this, to locate vehicle movements in the vicinity of the mine at around the time of the shootings. If we can trace something, we could get Faulkner.'

She paused.

'Now for Miss Turner.' Carlisle pressed the intercom's button. 'Dick, can you come in please?'

A second later one of the Secret Service detail turned and walked through the conference room door. He was the typical agent: black suit, white shirt, black tie. His brown hair was parted on one side and swept over, perfectly positioned and framing a face that would have been lost in a crowd of one.

'Yes ma'am?'

'You'll accompany the FBI and Mr Logan to the quarters of one Debbie Turner, who is a British MI6 operative. Once there you will have her taken into custody for aiding and abetting a known terrorist and traitor.'

Dick stood there impassively, a mere single nod of the head indicating he had heard and understood the request. Carlisle sat down for the first time since Logan had opened the discussions, relaxing in her seat and exhaling slowly. She was aware nobody and nothing had moved in the room and she suddenly clapped her hands.

'Well, come on people we have a traitor to catch! Let's move it!'

Forty-Eight

Faulkner felt uneasy as he travelled back to the airport, the convoy tracing, exactly, the previous route with an impunity borne of world position and money. Colombia relied increasingly on funds from the other side of the Pacific Rim, and China was happy to flaunt its increasing position as a world power. Very soon, if his actions were successful, they would be the only super-power and America would be consigned to dust, and the history books.

Did he feel any regret for turning his back on his country? Some, but for what they had done to the Muslim, they would pay a realistic price, just as Steve Logan would be forced to face the reality of his crime. Faulkner looked through the smoked glass windows of the SUV, aware of the presence of his escort. Guards? It was difficult to say what they represented, but he knew that should he survive the attack on the President, China would turn its back on him, despite all the assurances he had received. Faulkner knew he couldn't trust them, or their partners, and would have to get out of the States on his own. He risked being a pariah in so many places on the planet. Not that he couldn't find a country which wouldn't rejoice in his act of jihad. They just wouldn't want to bring down the wrath of the wounded beast on their heads to save even an emissary of Allah.

And, looking at his hosts, it was highly likely the impassive shits would only be interested in giving him support, refuge or assistance in the shape of a final hole in the ground.

So be it. Allah's will be done. He had never

doubted His intent, had never doubted that Allah would guide him in his hour of torment and tribulation when it came. Similarly, Faulkner knew he didn't walk alone, whether a human stood beside him or not. Always around, within, was the Merciful One. He sighed, noticed a guard look at him quizzically and just smiled in return. Allah was calling him now, beckoning him home. There were just a few steps to take and he would be blessed.

The Hawker was spooling up as the SUV pulled up by the air-stair. A guard opened the rear door and Faulkner stepped into the afternoon sun and onto the aircraft. He didn't stop, didn't thank anyone, just took his seat and serenely waited for the aircraft to depart, back to the States. One of his first actions when he landed would be to contact Turner. There was little else for her to do now: time for her account to be closed.

*

Logan rapped on the door to Debbie Turner's room, aware of the body of Secret Service and FBI agents behind him: there was no answer. He tried the handle but it was locked. Surveying the construction, he could see it wasn't going to be easy to open without a key. He turned to one of the MPs who'd also accompanied them. 'Do these doors have a master key?'

The MP nodded. 'I'll go get one.'

'I wouldn't bother.'

Everybody looked around at the interruption. An average guy in maintenance overalls stood looking at them from across the corridor.

'How come?'

369

The guy looked at Black. 'She left about half an hour ago. headed for the utility exit on the east side of the mountain.

'How did she seem?'

The guy cocked his head and frowned at the SEAL. 'How do you mean?'

Logan drew an exasperated breath. 'We don't have time for this. We need to get after her and fast.'

Black was patient. 'You're forgetting your training man. If she's agitated she's likely to be slower and make more mistakes. If she knows what she's doing, we're playing catch up.'

Logan slapped his head. 'Sorry.'

Black grinned. 'No worries.' He turned back to the maintenance man. 'So?'

The guy shrugged. 'In a hurry I guess. She seemed to look through me as if she was worried somebody might turn up at any moment.'

'Did she run?'

He shook his head. 'No, walked real fast though. Really intense.'

'That's great. Thanks very much for your help.' Turning to an FBI agent Black said. 'We need a chopper in the air now, with thermal imaging, looking for this woman out on the Rock. Move!' he encouraged as the man hesitated.

As the agent departed Black turned to Logan. 'Okay we're on foot after your colleague,' he informed Logan. 'How dangerous is she?'

'She can handle herself, and if she's in a state she won't be easy to apprehend if we catch her.'

Black nodded in understanding. 'Okay. Did you guys bring weapons with you?'

Logan shook his head. 'We wouldn't routinely bring weapons into the country but I'm guessing that was probably ignored by Debbie. I think we have to presume she's armed and hostile.'

Black grimaced. 'You got that right. How are you with weapons?' he asked the MP who'd waited patiently as events unfolded.

'Top of the class sir; with rifles and personal firearms.'

'Good. Hope you can use them in a combat situation. Where's the nearest armoury between here and the utility exit?'

'That'll be corridor Twenty-Seven B.'

'Okay. Let's go,' and Black turned in the direction the woman pointed, slipping into an easy jog.

*

Turner found some precious cover under the towering larch trees. This was shit. What had happened to Drew? She pulled a compass from her pocket, checked north and then consulted the map in her knee pocket. Orienting herself through the trees was proving difficult. She knew she couldn't afford to hang around in this ground cover for long. Logan would have shopped her, the bastard, and soon they'd come looking for her. Then she would be dragged back in and, no doubt, tortured. She knew that would happen as a matter of course. Even while the government remonstrated to the international community that torturing prisoners was a thing of the past, she knew well that niceties flew out the window in the face of atrocities like those which had been visited on the US and the bigger one to come.

She pulled the map round and scrutinised the ground again, trying to match up the contours. Ah! There was the slope, and that led to an isolated section of fence which was away from any track. Rising, Turner stuffed the map back in her knee pocket and began to pick her way down the slope. This was too easy!

The clatter of rotors, beating a hole in the air, reverberated around the mountain to her and she cursed having been so flippant. Time to move: before they caught her scent.

*

Black pulled the armoury door open to reveal racks of assault rifles, sidearms and other weaponry. He grabbed an M4, passed it to the MP and then picked another from the rack, hesitating before passing it to Logan. 'You might need this.'

Logan hefted it then looped its strap over his shoulder. 'Thanks.'

'Take this too,' advised Black, passing him a Beretta semi-automatic in a leg holster. The SEAL strapped one to his own leg, clipping it to his belt. Logan followed suit, pulling the weapon and checking the magazine before chambering a round.

The MP waited patiently for the two men to finish tooling up.

'Okay … what's your name?'

'Wright, sir?'

'First name?'

'Sam, sir.'

'Okay Sam, lead us out.'

Sam Wright loped along the corridor, to the large blast doors that led to one side of the facility. A small, security door, next to them, stood slightly ajar. Carefully Wright opened the door, sidling out with M4 raised to her face: a small target ready to fire at a moment's notice.

Logan and Black followed her out and quickly they fanned out across the open space for vehicles before hitting the tree line. With an unspoken signal they moved forward under the canopy of pine needles, the scent hanging heavily in the nostrils in the warm summer air. Overhead they heard a Blackhawk scythe the air apart as it searched for their quarry. The clatter of its rotors slapped the trees and the ground, the vortex of air raising dust from the ground. Logan kept closing his eyes as he fought to keep the grit from irritating his sight.

Should've picked up goggles.

Progress was slow. Despite it being mostly pine and larch forest with little ground cover, the closely stacked trunks made it confusing to make out directions. Logan figured the downwards direction was good in one way, but Turner had half an hour on them.

A movement to his right caught his eye: Black was signalling. He made his way over. The SEAL pointed to the ground, where plants had been recently crushed and the soil was scuffed and disturbed. Turner? Logan checked the ground about and made out faint footprints in the loose dirt, heading down the hill. He looked at the SEAL and nodded determinedly.

To their left Wright continued to move forward slowly. She'd clocked Black beckoning the Brit over and figured they'd seen something. Deciding to leave them to it she continued down, taking it easy with the loose grit and soil beneath her boots. She pulled the goggles she'd thoughtfully picked up from the armoury, down over her eyes as she struggled with the helicopter rotor wash which beat mercilessly down on the ground. The chopper seemed to be circling something. Wright kept her rifle to her eye, finger rested lightly on the trigger guard. Her breathing shallowed: a sixth sense alerting her to …

*

Turner glanced up and took in the shadow of the Blackhawk beginning to circle around her position. She was nearly at the fence but sensed she wasn't going to make it. A pit was forming in her stomach as she took in the menacing presence above the dark treetops. Swivelling on the spot she appraised her options – precious few! Already she had taken in the three figures ghosting between the trees on the hill above her, shadows tracking her down, ready to bring her to justice, or take her down.

'Fuck!' Her voice was lost beneath the clatter of the chopper and, for a moment, time lost its ticking inevitability. She seemed detached from reality; found herself wondering what had happened to bring her to this point. Had she loved Faulkner? Was she a rebound from his loss of Raifah? Was he actually as plausible as he had seemed just those short years ago when he had recruited her, following the abortive incident in London. That was something they had thwarted because it had been pushed by a local splinter cell of al-Qaeda, which had diverted attention from the bigger picture.

He had been strong, funny and … messianic? Wrong religion; but the right adjective. She remembered his burning blue eyes, devoured by his faith, probing her flesh, her thoughts, her desires until she was completely naked before him. She had thrilled at that and determined to do whatever it was he wanted. Was that a stupid, teenage reaction she wondered, as she stood in a foreign forest waiting to be caught and interrogated over her relationship with, and knowledge of, an ex-CIA Chief?

The Blackhawk was in the hover now and she knew that soldiers would soon be fast-roping into the forest to capture her.

Up slope one of the figures started moving purposefully towards the fence. It was a woman, M4 held assuredly, combat ready. Turner swallowed. It hadn't been her intention to be in this position, then again that was probably what so many people said just before the end came. She was where she was.

It was time.

*

Logan followed Black down the slope. To his left he could see Wright moving slowly towards the fence, still some way from them. Above the Blackhawk had gone into the hover and he thought he could see figures dropping from the cabin. He prayed Turner wouldn't do anything stupid.

*

Debbie opened the backpack quickly and took out a medium sized plastic box. She placed it on the forest floor and prised open the lid. Inside was a Glock 15 with a fifteen round magazine. She removed it, checked the magazine, slipped it home and chambered a round. Dropping to one knee behind a tree she quickly assessed the targets.

*

The first soldier dropped from the cabin of the Blackhawk. Immediately he saw his partner dropping from the other door. HK416's were slung at the ready but this was the tricky part of any infil – roping down.

His boots brushed the tops of the trees and then he was pushing and beating back the branches with his body as he passed through. He could see his buddy doing the same and then suddenly the other was limp on the rope.

Shit.

The searing pain of the bullet through his right buttock took his breath away and he gritted his teeth. The second bullet obviated the need to worry about the first wound anymore.

In the helicopter panic rose in an all engulfing passion; ripping through the crew like a forest fire. The pilot pushed the stick forward and screwed his craft out of the way of any more destruction. He couldn't instruct his gunners to open fire because of the friendlies he knew to be on the ground there. The bodies bounced among the tree tops as he sought to get away from the scene.

*

Debbie Turner smiled grimly as the copter fled the forest. Just three to go, she told herself. They didn't know where she was, but she could see them.

Quickly she sank down and drew a bead on the young woman carefully but speedily making her way down. She obviously hadn't located Turner, but the disappearing chopper made her pause and reassess what was happening.

The bullet sliced neatly through her neck, just below and behind her ear, severing the spinal cord at the C3 section, paralysing her even before her body hit the ground. A soft sigh accompanied the crack of the bullet.

Two to go.

*

Logan and Black turned as one at the sharp note of gunshot. They just caught sight of Wright buckling and falling to the earth. Both men dropped to the forest floor, and searched ahead of them but it was difficult and Turner had the advantage. They had to move to find her, while she could afford the luxury of waiting for them to expose themselves. Logan had forgotten what a good shooter Turner was.

Black tapped his shoulder, pointed first at his eyes and then downhill. Logan followed the direction of his fingers. For a moment he was at a loss and then he saw a sliver of black. Staring he thought he could make out a backpack. Using it as a reference point he tracked his eyes left and right.

There.

He nudged Black and swivelled the barrel in the direction he was looking.

The SEAL took his time assessing the intervening landscape and all the options. The formation favoured their quarry. As soon as either of them moved, the Brit would be able to make short change of them. While taking her back would be favourite, it looked as if that was a forlorn hope. Just one option left then. He squeezed Logan's shoulder gently and pulled the man towards him.

'We're gonna have to take the shot,' he whispered. 'I need her distracted so that I get a clear bead on her.'

Logan looked at his colleague and then down the hill to where Turner lay waiting. Fuck, but this was totally fucked up. How long had he known Turner? Six years? And yet not one of those years had been long enough evidently. Surely another option existed? Only if you were in a movie, he confessed. In a film he would stand up and advance slowly, reasoning with her and either convincing her to lay down her weapon, or making a miraculous shot just at the right moment.

In the movies.

He looked in the eyes of the waiting Black, a man who understood the agony of the decision he was asking of the MI6 agent. Logan nodded.

'I'll draw her off for you. For fuck's sake don't miss. Give me five minutes.'

Black squeezed his arm again. With a last look down the hill Logan began to move off to his right and down. He looked to get level with her and then attract her attention so that she had to turn to face him. That would maximise the time she was unable to respond to Black, who'd only get one chance.

Slowly, carefully, he crawled through the dry dirt.

*

Turner scanned the forest for movement, expecting none. She wasn't disappointed which, in itself, was disappointing. While she still held most of the cards at the moment, she couldn't stay here forever. Sooner or later either she, or they, would have to break the stalemate.

Who was she kidding?

She was going to die here and that knowledge brought a curious calm upon her. She would have liked to take him with her, but perhaps that wasn't important anymore. What was necessary was protecting the information she had from their interrogation. There was only one way to do that.

Debbie Turner looked at the Glock in her hand: the key to the door which ended all her dreams of a life of espionage in the service of her country.

Deliberately she raised the pistol to her temple.

The noise cut through her concentration and she whirled to her left. A shape … slipping on the dusty forest floor.

Logan.

She brought the pistol round, two hands steadying it, and aimed at her one-time colleague.

*

It was an accident, the gritty soil betraying his footing as he tried to get into position. Logan cursed as he hit the dirt again and slithered down the slope, his hands attempting forlornly to slow him down. All his body tensed as he waited for the sound and the pain that would mean he was about to finish breathing.

*

Black heard the noise of the Brit sliding down through the forest at the same time as Turner but all his concentration was on the spot where he presumed she was waiting in hiding. His eye concentrated on that point, seen through the scope of his M4.

Movement: to the left of where he was looking.

He adjusted.

There she was: turning, aiming. Good posture, he noted in the slow seconds that formed between the thought and the pressure of his finger on the trigger.

The buck of the rifle, as the bullet was loosed, pushed into his shoulder and transmitted like an SOS through his body. Saving the soul of a new colleague, a man of shared experience, Black let another bullet fly after the other and waited.

One beat, two beats.

A moment's flowering of blood, the bloom dark, ephemeral, as the bullet, sliced into the skull, just behind the ear. Turner's body toppled, one dead tree in a forest of living, breathing beings, her gun dropping slowly from her fingers.

Tango down.

The words formed in Black's head, ritual at the end of the hunt. He waited to see, but knew Turner was not getting up. He stood up himself.

'Clear!' His call across the silent forest brought Logan to sight.

They made their way over to where Turner's body lay on its side. When they looked close they noticed a smile of peace and contentment on her face.

Forty-Nine

'How's Wright?'

Black shook his head. 'The bullet cut her spinal cord. She'll be paralysed from the neck down, for the rest of her life.' A pause. 'A clean death would have been better.'

A clean death. Did such a thing exist, Logan wondered as he watched the drawn, fatigued face of the SEAL processing the morning's action. Four people dead, with no questions answered, the principle witness of Faulkner's treachery lay among them.

The American coughed and ran a hand through his hair. 'Hell, we're not doing anything for Wright moping over her shooting. We need to hunt down this Faulkner and stop him before he does any more damage.'

'We should let the President know what's happened to Turner as well. There's not much we can do about Faulkner anyway until somebody turns up his whereabouts.'

'You're right. Fuck!' The big man punched the wall, fortunately a false one, leaving a fist sized dent in the plasterboard. Logan noted the blood smeared on the wall and welling from the knuckles; a letting of the pent up frustration and aggression he'd seen so many times before in Special Ops people. They didn't like to be bested and, once an operation was on, they didn't like to be left waiting. Black was suffering both and that was an explosive quality.

Somebody was going to suffer: he rather hoped it was Faulkner.

She had determined who was going to pay for the damage. All she had to do now was deliver on the promise to herself. Penelope Hortez looked out the window of the private jet she had hired from Washington DC, which was now crossing the coast of South America on its way to Bogota. That morning she had concluded a brief meeting with Johnson: a stiff, painful affair, which the Senator had been puzzled by. He'd tried to embrace her, tried to kiss her, as they'd experienced passion so many times before, but two things stood in his way: her sons and Rado Kiric and the latter she wanted to kill herself, so what hope did Johnson have?

They'd parted abruptly, the Senator confused and Hortez wishing to God the man could understand what he'd done to her. But then he never could. All he could do now was pay with his life. There was another little matter to deal with first.

A flight attendant approached. He held a tray with a mobile on it. 'Your return call.'

Penelope took the mobile. 'Hello?'

'The job can be done. When would you like delivery?'

'As soon as possible. I don't want the customer waiting thank you.'

'Understood. There will be a surcharge for express delivery.'

'I expected that. Just make sure delivery is made some time today. Ensure you get a signature.'

'That will not be a problem. Do you have the delivery address?'

'Yes, you will receive a text at the end of this call with the details.'

'Very well. I will contact you when delivery has been confirmed.'

'Thank you.'

The line went dead. Penelope toyed with the phone for a moment before slowly placing it back on the tray. She found herself thinking of Fernando and then a darker thought skewered her once clean mind.

Nobody fucked with the Suarez cartel. Nobody.

*

Rado Kiric stretched his strong frame across the bed. Last night had been … professional. This morning – had been difficult. Breaking his word, even to an infidel, was against his ethics, his code of honour, but this morning's action had been a necessity, and a dangerous precedent. He was unsure how Hortez would react but knew he had to be on his guard. Being in a foreign city was not good for protection and the sooner he and his people got back to Kosovo the better.

That meant bringing the flights forward to this evening. He rolled over, picked up his mobile and dialled a number. A moment of ringing, then a voice: 'Yes?'

'Milo, get us flights this evening. We need to leave this place behind us.'

'Understood.' The line went dead.

Kiric rolled again and closed his eyes. Waiting was the name of the game

*

The black BMW X5 sat, formidable and squat, across the road from the hotel. In the air-conditioned interior sat four men, patiently waiting for their signal. It would come in the form of a woman who would park a green Beetle outside the entrance and leave it there.

Glancing at his watch, the driver checked out the window again. Nothing yet. Others would get twitchy, not he. That way mistakes were made, still the wait threatened to become challenging. The longer they sat at the kerb, unmoving, the more likely it was that they would be in a confrontation with the law. There was nothing they could do about that, if it occurred they would deal with it.

'Hey.' He looked at the man beside him and then followed the direction of the nod. Along the road in the opposite direction drove a green car. As it got closer they saw it was a Beetle. It slowed as it came to the façade of the hotel; for a moment they figured it was driving by: an indication that the targets were not there. It stopped and the girl got out, locked it and strolled nonchalantly across the road. She passed the BMW without looking.

The driver checked his weapon, Heckler and Koch MP5 with telescopic butt and silencer. A full magazine of thirty bullets was clicked into place with a twin taped to it. He pulled the hammer back, chambering a round and checked the safety was off. Satisfied he got out, the others mere milliseconds behind, weapons concealed under heavy leather jackets, and made his way across the road. Traffic was sparse that afternoon and the four quickly crossed the street and entered the hotel.

He rested his gloved hands on the reception desk; the bored young woman looked blankly in his eyes. 'Rooms Two-Two-Three and Two-Two-Four?'

The girl took in his steel grey eyes then looked at his smiling partner. She saw the other two men standing idly in the foyer, yet not idle. They were taking in the movements of the traffic and watching carefully for anybody who looked as if they might enter the hotel.

Shooters: men looking to eliminate others. And the rooms were full of Eastern Europeans who looked as these men did. The girl felt the urge to pee as she realised what was about to unfold.

'Elevator to Floor Two, turn right out the elevator and the rooms are about halfway along the corridor.'

The steel grey eyes didn't smile like the mouth. She had to ring the police. His eyes held her. 'Thank you,' he said in his low, hypnotic voice.

She smiled first at him and then at his partner. The other grinned and brought his hand from below the edge of the counter. Thinking he was going to wave to her she started to raise her hand.

The Glock gave a phut as the suppressor did its job. Drilled perfectly into her forehead was a small hole from which a trickle of dark blood fled death, staining her tanned skin. The half-smile was permanently frozen on her lips.

Steel Eyes walked round the desk and hunted out the master cards for the room doors. It took a few moments and then he turned to those behind him and nodded. Quickly they secured the entrance doors and then joined Steel Eyes in the elevator. He pressed the button for Floor Two, the doors closed and it purred and rattled upwards.

*

Kiric figured he should get dressed. Milo could get the plane sorted anytime and he needed to be ready. In the next room Bogdan and Ilir were probably ready

385

to go, patiently waiting for his orders. If Milo was quick, they could be back in Kosovo early tomorrow morning and they would be able to hide in full view of the wretched Americans and Colombians.

He cursed himself for getting involved with the Colombian woman. It was well known that anybody from the South American country was bad business and he had allowed himself to be suckered in, thinking he was in charge. Wasn't that what women always made you think?

The Kosovan sighed and pulled on his jeans. Tee-shirt and then socks. Always the same routine, always the same measured time taken to be dressed and ready.

Walking into the bathroom, he observed his reflection in the mirror, pulled a comb through his thick, black hair and smiled.

*

Steel Eyes peered either way down the corridor as the lift doors opened. Emptiness greeted his gaze and silence burned into his mind. With a wave he ordered his men out and to the right. They acknowledged silently, raising supressed MP5s in readiness. Steel Eyes followed at a respectable distance, counting the doors down the long, grimy corridor. The lead executioner stopped, turned and nodded, Steel Eyes returned the acknowledgement. He took in the two doors himself: two-two-three and two-two-four; the hit.

He motioned two to one door and took up position at the other with the remaining hit man.

*

Kiric regarded his reflection as he slowly, lazily, cleaned his teeth. He'd grown to respect himself over the years, since those early days of his childhood; learnt not to blame himself for his parents' death in the desperate depths of Kosovo all those hazy years ago. He'd never learned to love himself though, and doubted he ever would. Not with such a long list of bodies stretching back, punctuating every turn of his life. The lesson was a dark one and the one person he couldn't hide it from was himself.

He put the toothbrush on the counter and lifted the Sig Sauer from the countertop. Most people opted for Glocks but he preferred the Sig. Its weight sat well in his hand, the balance suited him. The black skin seemed to absorb the light, an evil device sucking life away as it spat out death.

His fingers stroked the cold surface. *One day you'll be my downfall.*

*

At a nod cards slotted in to readers. The doors clicked unlocked. Those in Room Two-Two-Four stood little chance. Off guard, relaxed before the TV, the bullets were already in their bodies as they registered the commotion, guns only half raised, discharging into the floor. Each assassin walked to a body and dispassionately fired a single shot through the head.

Steel Eyes walked into Room Two-Two-Three.

*

Kiric jolted to his senses as the door in the adjoining room flew open and he registered the tumbling whisper of suppressed semi-automatic weapons from the other room. He didn't have long. Quickly he flicked off the safety and dropped to one knee. They'd expect him to be standing.

Footsteps getting louder.

The door handle turned, stopped.

Bullet's ripped through the wood. The first round to hit, clipped his aiming arm hot, shattering, leaving the inside of his shoulder in turmoil, chaos, as the shell ripped muscle, veins and bone into a disconnected jumble of shit. He gasped and dropped the Sig with a clatter.

A second bullet through his neck; another hit his chest, left of centre, ripping the lung as it exploded and filling his chest with fire and pain, so much pain that it lifted his dying heart to heaven. Or so it seemed for a second as his mind slipped back to the little boy in a Kosovan town, watching as Serbs circled the crowd of cowed, beaten men, guns pointed menacingly and then the hail of hot metal scything through the simple clothing, the unprotected flesh. All he could think then was the compelling power of the bullet; the mesmerising smell of cordite and white hot metal that could command death in a moment.

The dopamine coursed through his body now, mixing with adrenaline to control the pain and provide him with energy to survive – survive what? For what? This was the Colombian woman, revenge for him dicking her with the burning of her trucks. He was about to head to heaven – except he knew there was no heaven, at least not for him. Did he believe in Allah? He'd practiced, but that was not the same, and only fitfully at best: too late for recrimination or apologies. The fingers of his coming death slowly tightened their grip.

A sound, the door opened and he reached feebly

for the gun. A figure; he couldn't make out detail on – extremities malfunctioning, going cold as his body fought to keep the vitals going except there were no vitals anymore.

*

Steel Eyes looked down at the broken body and the widening pool of blood. He was careful not to step in that and leave a visible mark of his presence. His hit was almost gone. If the accounts were right the man had been responsible for an impressive number of kills and the offloading of an inordinate amount of heroin at a time when opium was out of fashion. He had a whole load of respect for Rado Kiric. The man must have really pissed off his purchaser. Aiming his Ruger revolver, he pointed it at Kiric's head. The Kosovan looked at him, without seeing; death already inhabited his broken body.

Click, bang.

The last light turned off in Kiric's head.

Steel Eyes turned and walked from the room. His accomplice looked questioningly at him. 'One's still at large. Let's go.'

*

Faulkner sat at the wheel of his F150, staring at the parked cars and trees and benches of the rest stop and seeing nothing. An uncomfortable emptiness inhabited his bones, his stomach, and it had been with him since his return from Colombia. He was on his own: that he had to admit. Truthfully, he was now a liability to the Chinese, while his own people would want him to die, along with his targets. There were old contacts who could have, but wouldn't, help. They only worked for those who were true to God, Country and Mom's apple pie. He'd metaphorically fucked each one of those in turn and now stood, with his finger on the trigger of his own suicide device.

A sigh, long and drawn, forced its way through his lips; he noted the slight misting as it contacted the glass of the windscreen.

Only one clear course of action was left to him. His purpose had to be fulfilled: that was, after all, why he'd come back to the US. Assiz had completed his part of the mission as had Sikandar, both striking the initial blows necessary for bringing down the government. Even the worthless drug dealers of Colombia and the growers of Afghanistan; the smuggler from Kosovo, all those had all done their part. Just the one brick left to be loosened and bring the whole wall down.

His brick.

He smiled wryly at the thought that his one action, a deed that now seemed too large to contemplate; the one that was prepared and was so close to completion, was the one which would topple the US and was the one built on all those sacrifices that he couldn't now bring himself to do.

Pull yourself together. Allah commands your action and promises riches beyond this world's imagining.

He drew air into his shrivelled lungs and gripped the steering wheel as if it would bring sustenance or halt the toppling feeling that filled his head. *I am failing Allah* said the voice. Faulkner resisted the shudder that rose as the words reverberated in the sudden cavern of his mind. He felt small in there and wished for somewhere to hide, but there was nowhere to go, in his head or in the world, where he couldn't be found either by Allah, or man.

Better to be found completed by man than wanting by Allah. His imam's wisdom drew a comforting blanket round his cold soul. He knew what to do if he was discovered by man, knew the path that he would take. And, at the end of that path, he would find the woman who had his heart, she who had been taken from him in such a cruel way by one who had been his friend.

The thoughts gave him his sustenance, gave him his goal. He was affirmed, his journey to the bosom of Allah was lit and at the end his beautiful Raifah stood with his master.

It was time to take the first step on the last journey.

Fifty

It was as hot as ever as the cavalcade of black SUVs coasted along the black top to the ranch. Sanchez watched them approaching, not with his previous good humour, but with a cold uncertainty. What he had misguidedly believed to be an equal partnership had been exposed at their last encounter as a flimsy charade. He was about to be Leong's bitch and there was absolutely nothing he could do about it. A sickness lined his stomach and he took a sip of whiskey to burn it off.

Leong stepped from the Mercedes, still a powerful man despite his years, looking completely at ease. From the opposite side a younger man appeared. For a moment Sanchez didn't recognise the bald, hard faced person. Then, of course, it came to him: Leong's pit-bull, Yuan. No rules, no ethics, no scruples and no compunction about thrusting a knife in your belly, twisting and smiling as your blood poured to the floor.

As the general and his henchman walked up to the veranda, the general's guards positioned themselves strategically, covering lines of fire in case Sanchez's people became trigger happy.

Not today, Sanchez told himself as he greeted the Chinaman with a smile. 'General Leong. Please, take a seat and let's get to business. He waved to empty chairs and let them sit before he took his place next to Victoria, his aide. He noted the unease in them.

'Would you like a drink?'

'Black tea, tepid,' Leong responded. Yuan reached for the bottle of water in an electric cooler bucket and poured, all the time regarding Sanchez insolently, which the latter chose to ignore.

Sanchez motioned his butler away. 'And now gentlemen tell me of progress.'

Leong coughed. 'There has been an incident in the United States.'

Sanchez pursed his lips and raised an eyebrow. 'What sort of incident?'

'Some men have been killed.'

Sanchez smiled quizzically. 'All over the world, every day, some men are killed, General Leong. I don't follow.'

'Somebody got to them before us.'

Sanchez suppressed the smile that threatened to overwhelm his face. 'Tell me more General.'

*

'What do you mean somebody got to them before you?'

Penelope Hortez was stood on the veranda of her hacienda, her whole body rigid with anger as she listened to the voice of her contact in Washington DC. 'We arrived at the hotel, but it was all cordoned off. They were bringing bodies out. We managed to ask some guys what had happened.'

'And?'

'They said that three Eastern European guys had been cut down. Whoever had done it had killed the receptionist too.'

Hortez wasn't listening anymore. Who had beaten her to it? Who knew of her connection to Kiric? And who had the most to benefit from killing him besides her. After all, hers was pure revenge.

'So?'

'So what,' she snapped down the phone.

'So what do you want us to do?'

'There is nothing for you to do. Come back. No! Wait! Stay. There may be one last thing I want you to do for me. I'll pay for your stay over.'

She could sense the shrug at the other end of the call. 'Okay, you're the boss.'

'Yes I am.'

*

'What the fuck is going on?'

Dan Camino refused to respond as he took in the reported death of three Kosovans in downtown Washington. Events were beginning to spiral out of control. They were no closer to catching the person, or persons, who had committed the terrorist atrocities and now they were overrun by a city in the grips of some sort of drug epidemic, culminating in the death of some dealers, unknown to local law enforcement, but definitely on the Interpol "most wanted" list. The only compensation, despite their little truce, was the look of anguish on the face of Fouré as he took in the official reports.

'Hell in a hand cart,' was the best Camino could offer.

'We need this shit like a hole in the head!' Fouré slammed the report on his desk 'I've got people off work with headaches, sweats and withdrawal symptoms. There are rumours of a number of drug shipments across Baltimore and Washington brought in by ship and air, taking advantage of the chaos that has followed these terrorist attacks.'

He pulled a weary hand across his face. 'We're getting nowhere are we?'

Camino refused to make eye contact with his new

comrade, but the guy was right. They were making absolutely no progress at all. His mind wandered to Florida, and the little condo he and his wife had earmarked for retirement near Kissimmee, and where he was going to indulge his passion for Second World War aircraft. At the moment that wasn't even a distant hope on the horizon unless this mess got sorted.

'So much for your grand plan,' commented the Haitian bitterly and turned to look forlornly out the window of the Portakabin they inhabited, near the battered Lincoln Memorial. Silence descended, thick and cloying.

The FBI agent walked over to the large map, stretched across the wall of the cabin. It displayed the greater Washington area. A pin marked the terrorist attack on the Lincoln Memorial. Another highlighted the crash site of Air Force One. Slowly he pressed a pin into the spot where Assiz had been killed and then another where the block of flats had been destroyed in the aftermath of Air Force One. Another pin marked where two trucks had been burnt out and another where three Kosovans had met their end in a hail of bullets. Yet another where a lone East European was hit by an SUV as he crossed the road; the X5 being found burnt out some time later.

Many tracks of activities, like early morning snails; made their way across the map, leaving a trail of the unknown. Seemingly the only common denominator was Washington itself.

Camino stared at the map. 'Where was the warehouse that was burned out, along with the semis?'

Fouré strode over to the wall and jabbed a marker in, clearly blaming the map itself for the current situation. 'There,' his clipped tone assailed Camino as he retook his seat.

Regarding them for a moment Camino placed another marker over the airport where it was known that Hortez had brought her fashion show in. He studied the points again, took a step back, then forwards as if, by moving back and forth in this way, he could magnify the solution to the problem.

'Why did Hortez's trucks take the South Washington, north from the airport, if they were going to the Verizon Centre? They should have been on the three-ninety-five.'

Fouré shrugged. He appeared to be in a huff which was not helpful – at all. 'Perhaps they were lost?'

Camino glared at him. 'You think? Come on, this could be important. We know from the police reports that Hortez got to her hotel around nine-thirty. The trucks should have been just behind her because the Verizon is, what, fifteen minutes from the Sheraton?'

Fouré nodded slowly. 'Give or take yeah. What's your point?'

Camino pondered the map again. 'I'm not sure. Just can't figure why Hortez would take one route and her trucks another. Never mind that she was able to get into the country and through the normal checks with apparent ease.'

The DC cop snorted. 'That one's easy to solve. The word is she's riding our Senator Harry Johnson, and she called in a favour. The crime report said she was going to stage a charity show. I guess she called Harry for a free passport.'

Camino grimaced at his coffee. The drink had that icy oiliness of coffee that had been allowed to go cold. He shuddered and attempted to rejuvenate the liquid by pouring more from the pot. It didn't work

and he slammed the mug on the rickety table which
served as the repository for the investigative reports.
Dark spots contaminated the manila folders and his
crumpled white shirt: Camino cursed.

'There must be something,' he told himself.

'May be there is.'

Fouré was studying the map. His face shone, as if
an epiphany had come over him. 'What if Hortez
knew the trucks would be hijacked? Maybe she even
organised it. The direction change at that time of day
wasn't a random thing – she had to know what was
going on.'

'Go on,' encouraged Camino, his head nodding in
part agreement with the cop.

Fouré frowned. 'I don't have more than a hunch
right now. But what I can do is sequester phone
records for that evening and see what originates from
that area. We should be able to track events … if
we're lucky.'

'*If* we're lucky,' warned Camino. 'The other
problem we have is this: if we're right, how much
does Johnson know of his lover's activities?'

'First things first. Let's see what Ms Hortez knew
about that night.'

Fifty-One

'It'll never work. He'll gun you down before we can even react.'

That was John Black's "no bullshit" assessment of Steve Logan's plan to flush out Faulkner. The Brit knew it wasn't great, but he was becoming frustrated by the lack of progress they were experiencing. No activity had been reported from their quarry though they all admitted he held all the cards: they were waiting for him to surface and that wouldn't happen until the funeral.

A positive had been the recovery of suicide packs and two Crown Victoria car bombs from the Annerdime Mine. Simple devices based on the terrorist staple of ANFO – ammonium nitrate and fuel oil, the vehicles were one tonne devices which would have obliterated the funeral cortege and no mistake. They were under no illusion, though, that it was the end of the matter. Drew Faulkner was a man on a mission and he'd allow nothing to stand in his way.

'We have to think of something. At the moment we're blind to whatever he's thinking or doing.'

'I agree with you Steve, but we can't go round putting bodies on the line aimlessly, however much we're frustrated by events. We need to use the time we have and make sure we approach the solution methodically.'

Logan knew the SEAL was right but it made him feel no less impotent. And, at moments like this, the desire to hit the whiskey coursed through him with the same venom that a good Laphroaig Quarter Cask hit the back of his throat. He fought the urge to return to his room.

'So what do you suggest? Bearing in mind that, a) we have only four days before the funeral and, b) It will go ahead whatever the wisdom of such a move.'

Black shook his head and smiled wanly. 'You got me there Steve.'

'Well, John, we need to think of something,' Logan replied unnecessarily.

'OK; you know the guy as well as anybody, if not better. Get in his head. What would you do in his place; if the original plan had been fucked?'

Logan considered the SEAL's words: did he really know the man he had once called friend, and who was now a jihadist? They had been friends for a long time: did that count when deciding on a counter-offensive? He hoped it did. He sipped on his fruit juice (the coffee was still off which was a bummer) while Black merely waited for a response.

After a few moments of contemplation Logan spoke. 'Okay, Faulkner monitors what is happening with Assiz and his group. But Assiz isn't the main gig, despite what he thinks himself. If everything goes as planned, then all well and good, but al-Siddiqi has other ideas. Faulkner has been turned by an event; by cross-contamination.' (How far did he go?) 'He's embraced the ideals of Islam and is prepared to deliver jihad to the very centre of the system which he once defended.'

'All well and good and we kinda know all that Steve. But, you've taken out your front man and now have to deliver yourself. Your local team is dead, your bombs are in the hands of the enemy and you are being hunted by the most sophisticated surveillance culture in the world. How do you achieve your goal?'

Black's words assaulted Logan's head, battering off the walls of his brain and making his eyes sting.

He didn't know, and yet knew that was no answer at a time like this. With a conscious effort he willed himself to deliver a relevant and appropriate reply. He was going to have to tell – it was the only thing that could make sense of the situation.

'Faulkner was betrothed to Assiz's sister.'

His voice was small and it took Black a couple of moments to understand the importance of what the Brit had just said. Even so it was difficult. 'He was … betrothed?'

Logan nodded. 'I'd introduced Assiz and Faulkner, though I'd no idea Faulkner was potential radicalisation material at the time. Why would I? Apparently he went to Assiz's home regularly because he'd met, and become infatuated with, Assiz's sister Raifah.' The pause stretched uncomfortably – how did he relate his part in the story.

The American encouraged him. 'Go on, what happened then?'

'I don't know how Assiz influenced Faulkner. At that time Assiz was still with CO19, but Faulkner visited more and more often, presumably because he wanted a relationship with Raifah. Faulkner had been divorced for a couple of years and hadn't really got over the reality of that. Seemingly he felt that Raifah was the way back for him.

'Any

how, that reckoned without the fact that Raifah was already involved with somebody.'

'Do we know who that was?'

Logan coughed self-consciously. 'Yes … it was me.'

Black considered the information he had just become party to. 'I'm guessing that Assiz didn't know that either?'

Logan shook his head. 'Not until after the Trafalgar Square incident.'

'What incident was that?'

The British agent retold the story of his shooting of Raifah as if it was yesterday. When he finished Black was looking gravely at him. 'How do you feel about all that?'

How? It was unclear, Logan told himself. Was he at fault? Was he the reason that both Assiz and Faulkner had embarked on a journey to jihad. It seemed so and yet, was that being selfish? Making yourself the centre of attention. 'I'm not sure,' he confessed, 'I think I felt it was my fault too, at some point. Now they're searching for me and using it as an excuse for this jihad.'

'That's a crock of shit, Steve, and you know it. People make their decisions for good or ill. Raifah was capable of making her own choices about her life and just because that didn't take account of her brother, or Faulkner, isn't your responsibility. And that's what we're fighting here – the right for people to make their own decisions about their own lives.'

'Is it? Doesn't everybody require and deserve a set of boundaries that they can understand and measure their progress against.'

Black shook his head sadly. 'Shit man, and I thought we were the ones who were hung up on religious values. Raifah had made her choice. Just because that didn't coincide with that of her brother, or some guy who'd taken a fancy to her, doesn't give either the right to embark on a jihad.'

Logan nodded slowly. 'I guess you're right. Hadn't thought of it that way before.'

'That's okay man. But if Faulkner is thinking like

401

that, then it's his Achilles heel. We can use his fury at the death of Raifah, and your involvement in it, to our advantage.'

'I guess so,' Logan replied cautiously. 'But I –'

'Look man, Faulkner might want to complete his primary mission but, in reality, he's gonna want to get to you as soon as possible. Assassinating US Presidents is incidental. Now, I know what you said at the top of this conversation but my analysis stands. We have to understand his conversion and how he will want to complete this task, while ensuring he's able to make you pay for the death of his betrothed.'

'How do you propose to do that?'

'I think I know.'

Black and Logan turned at the intrusion to their personal interaction. Eddie Powell had his hand tentatively in the air: a nervous schoolboy in the presence of bigger men than he.

'Tell us,' encouraged Black.

Powell coughed self-consciously. 'Well, like you said, Drew – Faulkner has no direct method of affecting the assassination of President Carlisle, or the other hopefuls for the election now that we've shut down the Annerdime operation. However, we know that al-Qaeda used Firestorm technology to good effect in the Aden situation. We can also presume with a high degree of certainty that Firestorm was used to bring down of Air Force One.

'Given that,' he continued before anyone could interrupt – he was on a roll, 'we must conclude that Faulkner has access to Firestorm, or someone who does. Al-Qaeda obviously got access to Chinese technology and we can presume that is via Leong. We can link Faulkner to either.'

'Which leaves us where? This is a funeral we're

talking about. The President will be arriving in The Beast which is proofed against any attack. The hopefuls will be protected by a phalanx of Secret Service agents and Marine Corps personnel. Everything will be reliant on manpower and not technology.'

Eddie Powell grinned the grin of somebody who was teaching the naïve. 'Everything today is driven by technology. The Beast is no different. There are all sorts of communications and countermeasures on that thing, but that's no problem for Firestorm. Link that in with the Marine Corps' communications network, which incidentally, hasn't been upgraded since Aden, and you have a position where a determined terrorist, who can organise insurgents, can ambush the cavalcade.'

Black's face visibly drained as he took in Powell's words. 'You think?'

Powell nodded enthusiastically, in that way nerds do when they've stumbled across something nobody else knows, but of which they don't know the import. 'Of course, it's my job,' he countered by way of explanation.

Black whistled and regarded Logan who merely smiled. The SEAL turned his gaze back to the British analyst. 'You've got some crazy shit in that head of yours. Do you seriously think that Faulkner can take out the President using a firestorm attack here?'

Powell shrugged. 'What makes you believe he can't? We've been monitoring what happened at Aden and since, you know. It's entirely feasible.'

'Logan?'

The British agent shrugged. 'If Eddie says it's possible, he's not usually wrong. Thing is: what do we do about it?'

Black shook his head. 'First stop: The President. She needs to know just what the threat is, and then she can make a decision, along with her secret service detail, how to respond. After that, we need to figure where Faulkner will recruit from and when, where and how he's going to strike.'

'Easy-peasy.'

Black smiled. 'Well, no time like the present. Let's get an audience with the President.'

*

General Leong mulled over the last few hours and was pensive. Not of his doing, but welcome anyway; the problem of Kiric and his drug smuggling days were resolved but Leong knew his junior partner was going to be unhappy with that outcome. After all, Kiric had been his animal and Yuan had been wanting to, how did the West term it, "up the ante" in Aden. More could be achieved with Sanchez, given a favourable wind. Leong shook his head: Yuan was very visceral which wasn't good for such a programme as the one he was now embarked upon. The time was close.

And what about Faulkner?

Leong sat back in his chair, staring out at the Bogota skyline. A good point. He hadn't changed his view since the man's visit. The American jihadist was also coming to the end of his usefulness but he was needed to deliver the final blow that would enable his China to become the pre-eminent world power. After that Yuan must eliminate him, and quickly, lest he spoke of the connection. Once that had been accomplished Yuan was expendable. Elections in China were close and he had to be in a position to maximise his advantage. That meant ensuring nothing could connect him, to either Yuan himself, or Faulkner.

But first Faulkner needed access to Firestorm. With that America was looking down the barrel of the gun. Even so, Leong hesitated. This was a moment in history when, given the right momentum, the right choices, China would stand on the top of the world's political mountain.

Leong sat back contentedly and raised his mobile to his ear. The call was answered immediately. 'Let our colleague have the information he requires.' He listened to the answer and nodded, satisfied. With a flick of his thumb he ended the call and took a long pull on his whiskey.

*

484The last few days had been long, and he'd needed to call on all his resources and training in order to stay ahead of the opposition. Faulkner didn't mind that, it helped him stay focussed to know he was being hunted. He knew he had the advantage. Nobody knew where he was and he had nothing on him that could track him. Even though the Chinese needed to provide him with Firestorm software, they would do that through contacts with no direct connection between the two. In the meantime, he had spent much time and effort working up a small cell of home grown jihadists who would support him and deliver the final blow in just a few days' time. It was only a matter of time now and the whole façade would come crashing down.

It was a moment to savour.

Fifty-Two

Pacing the cool lounge of the hacienda, which overlooked Cucuta from the south-western hills, Penelope Hortez decided things were escaping her control. Dealing drugs was completely outside her understanding and like no other commercial experience she'd ever been involved in. The glass of wine in her hand showed how much it was worrying her.

A cough from behind startled her and she turned suddenly, the wine slopping over the side and spotting her dress maroon as if she'd shot somebody at close range. Her maid was disappearing and a young man in Police uniform stood regarding her.

'Federico. To what do I owe the pleasure?'

The young police officer smiled at her. 'You asked me to tell you of ways in which we could work with the Chinese.'

Penelope pondered his words; transported back to that day he had taken her to the suburbs where she had met her dead husband's accountant and chief conspirator. The words she had spoken with Federico then came back to her: it was a liberal translation of their conversation but perhaps ...

'What do you know?'

'May I?' He indicated the sofa and Penelope inclined her head in acquiescence. 'There is a delegation in Bogota which isn't directly connected with the current People's Council. The leader of this delegation is one General Leong Chaozheng. He is a prominent member of the politburo, and yet he works in South America on his own initiative, seeking to ingratiate himself with Eduardo Sanchez in order to support the Central American Pact.'

And why does he do that? Penelope reflected on Federico's words. It was a truism, oft repeated by Fernando, that nobody did anything unless there was something in it for themselves. Leong was apparently no different.

'That is interesting Federico. Do you know how General Leong intends to use his influence and what is in it for him?'

Federico hung his head. 'I do not know that Ms Hortez, no.'

Penelope walked to the veranda and gazed over the valley, into the smog which draped itself over Cucuta. How she hated this place: so many memories of death and deceit, and her own children taken from her, encompassed the memories that had been the result of her husband's work.

Fuck.

Profanity had become all too easy for her since Fernando's death and her relationship with, first Johnson, and then Kiric. Their betrayal of her was no more than she was coming to expect from men. They were contrary creatures, concerned only with their own selfish desires and always seeking to build empires that, in time, would fall to dust. Her thoughts turned to the other who had been influential, and who now worked with the Chinese to build a temple to his own ambition.

How far would Eduardo Sanchez go?

She looked back at Federico, her faithful Police driver, but how faithful? Penelope was clear that she knew the only person she could ultimately trust was herself. 'What do you understand of Eduardo Sanchez?'

Federico pondered the question. 'Mr Sanchez is

seen as the only viable individual to take over government from Cordoba. But ... there are issues which he fails to address and which he takes robust action to hide from whoever wishes to challenge his record. He purports that he is working for a drug free Colombia but it is well known that many of his cover companies and trusts have worked with Mexican cartels to develop the industry. Sanchez is ruthless: he builds people up but, just as quickly, he buries those who defy him.'

Penelope Hortez considered the words and reflected on the help she had received from the politician herself. She had profited immensely from that, yet she knew also she had to protect herself. It meant a war ... of sorts; but she would have to tread carefully in her vendetta.

'I have some experience of him,' Penelope advised her young driver. 'I want you to find out all you can about him and his work and whether he had any connection with the attack in Venezuela. Can you do that?'

Federico nodded vigorously.

'Good, in which case do not let me detain you any longer.'

He took his leave and made his way back to his car. As he closed the door, he reached for his cell phone, pressing a speed dial as he settled behind the wheel. After a moment the call was answered. 'She suspects,' was all he said. He paused.

'I understand. Yes, very well. I will.' He ended the call, placed the phone on the seat beside him, started the car and drove off.

*

In the house above, Penelope Hortez watched as Federico spoke into the phone. Something told her it wasn't good news *(was that intuition?)*. In turn she picked up her mobile and speed dialled a number. She had known of the person on the other end of the call from parties her husband had held and from phone calls she'd overheard. The individual was a professional, a loner who was proficient, no, excellent at their task.

'Yes?'

'I have a job for you if you're available.'

'Carry on?'

'I'll have the details sent over to you by courier.'

There was a slight pause. 'When do you want the job completed?'

Penelope considered the question and the pause. Was she becoming paranoid? Probably but that was no bad thing: it aided survival. 'All the details will be in the instructions you receive.'

'Very well. You will know when the contract is fulfilled.'

'Good, I look forward to hearing from you.'

The call ended, yet Penelope felt no better as she drained her wine and looked out on the town which had defined the last few weeks of her tragic life.

*

'I'm beginning to dread our meetings, Mr Logan,' confessed Carlisle as they gathered in the situation room for the umpteenth time. 'What do you have to frighten us with this time?'

Logan began to speak but it was Black who beat him to it. 'Madam President, we believe we know how Drew Faulkner is going to strike the funeral.'

'Expand.'

Black coughed, aware that all eyes were on him. 'We believe he's going to Firestorm the cavalcade. Mr Powell here,' he indicated the analyst, 'feels it's entirely feasible to take control of Limo One and other vehicles in the entourage, probably to ensure you and the other attendees are isolated from safety once you have disembarked for the funeral. That will place you at significant risk from, either suicide bombers, or snipers, and we know for certain that Faulkner at least is a crack shot at distance.'

'Great.'

'You have to cancel the funeral Madam President.' General Adams was looking decidedly angry at the way events were turning. 'We can't risk the head of government while this mad man is at large.'

'With respect General, that's exactly the wrong approach. It plays into the hands of the terrorists.'

'How so Dave?'

The Director of Homeland Security paused to ensure all were tuned in for his answer. 'Well, General, it's like this. If we pull the funeral, al-Qaeda has won. Perhaps not the victory they are wanting but it'll be a step closer, and they'll merely bide their time until they can strike another time, another place. Their threats are all over the internet currently; proclaiming the death of the Great Satan, beheading of the Serpent and all the usual bullshit. We pull the funeral we provide the aperitif. They've already proven they can get us and,' he paused a second time, 'I agree with the original Special Ops assessment of the situation.'

Dave Chandler brought all his attention to bear on the President. 'Angela, the funeral has to go ahead so we can flush Faulkner out. If we can catch him in

410

possession of Firestorm, all the better. That will prove the link with China, which we need to sink their hopes of world domination.'

Angela Carlisle was silent. She longed for a window so she could swivel her chair and gaze reflectively from the room. Here she was captive: captive to the Rock, to a group of goddamned terrorists nobody could find; to her audience and it unnerved her. She was aware of her limitations – her background and political upbringing hadn't exactly prepared her for such a moment. Brought up in small town Maine she had been mayor of Portland for three years back ten years ago, when ideas of the Senate had only just been forming in her mind. Propelled by her more ambitious husband she had, at first, been a recalcitrant runner for office. Gradually the dream had grown and she had outstripped the ambition of her partner who, intimidated, had left for another, more malleable and younger, woman who wouldn't eclipse his own aspirations.

It hadn't mattered, there had been plenty of other men around to help her on her way and she had become adept at taking, using and discarding. What she hadn't been able to master was the craft of high office. She had been seduced by Jonah Lincoln's affable style, his easy charisma and his effortless, Southern courtesy. That had been her downfall, if becoming Vice-President could be termed a downfall. Certainly, at the moment, it didn't look like a prospect for longevity.

But she was here, and she had to make a fist of it. As Dave had said, she couldn't be seen to be backing down in the face of internet threats. There had to be a way of neutralising Faulkner's threat. 'How do you propose to do that Dave? How on earth can you

411

ensure that I, and the other members of the funeral cortege, and the security don't get shot or blown to kingdom come?'

It was Black again who spoke first. 'Madam President, we believe that Faulkner will recruit a ground team which can strike quickly after the confusion of a firestorm. He'll be back stop, some distance away but with a clear line of sight on the cemetery. Not many such positions exist and we'll have them covered. There is one thing which will flush him out though.'

'Which is?'

'Me.' Logan spoke for the first time.

'Why's that?'

Logan took in his tormentor, Adams. He couldn't wait to be out of the guy's line of sight. 'Faulkner has unfinished business with me.'

'What's that?'

'It's not important right now,' Black advised the general, cutting in. 'Suffice to say that Faulkner will want to get Logan, if he sees him, and he will want to engage one-on-one with him.'

'Okay gentlemen, I'm beginning to see there might be some mileage in this, though I'm not happy with being exposed in this way.'

Black shook his head. 'It's okay Madam President, neither you nor any of the entourage will be at risk. We'll put in a special team of body doubles who will be specially picked operatives, able to respond as soon as the Firestorm is declared.'

Carlisle frowned. 'It all sounds too simple. Won't he just abort the attack if he suspects that I and the others aren't present?'

'It's a possibility but with Logan there, we think his judgement will be too clouded to react effectively.'

Adams grunted. 'There are too many "ifs" and "maybes" for my liking. Anything could go wrong and Faulkner is just as likely to abort. It'd be easier to just cancel the funeral and continue the hunt for him.'

'How long do you think that will take, all the time ensuring that the threat of attack sits over the head of the President or the incoming post holder? We have to strike at him when he believes that he is in control.'

Suddenly everybody had an opinion and Carlisle felt the moment slipping from her. Hands waved emotionally, while voices rose and fell, like waves crashing on the Maine coast. She raised a hand for calm then spoke.

'People!' A hush dropped over the assembly. 'This is not appropriate. I'm going back to my room while I think this over. Mr Black, Mr Logan start preparing your group. Dave, I'll leave you and Anne to coordinate with them. We'll come back in an hour.'

Fifty-Three

The map on the Portakabin wall resembled a pincushion, now that Camino and Fouré had updated it. Trawling through cell phone traffic, for the evening of the hijacking, had been a test of patience. Once they'd identified Penelope Hortez's number it had become much easier to identify activity, whether talking to people or merely locating her position. They'd traced the escort she'd used, tracking them from the Sheraton to the Oyster Club restaurant where they'd stayed until she'd pulled him out to the Elektra night club. Checking, they'd noticed that had coincided with the time it was estimated the trucks had been hijacked, and the drivers killed. The escort had been questioned, remarking that she'd seemed preoccupied all evening. Compounding events SOCO had found evidence of heroin at the scene of the fires.

Previous call logs had linked her to Harry Johnson, which they suspected, but what they couldn't yet fathom was how the destruction of her show was connected with the Senator. After all he would have wanted the show intact. It appeared, as they continued to mull it over, that Senator Johnson was being shafted by his Latin American lover, for some reason. What was her motive? And if she was playing him, what did that tell them about the Presidential hopeful?

The day after the attack, when Hortez was at the warehouse, she had made a call to an unlisted number. A day later that same number had appeared once more on her call log, calling from a downtown location, near the hotel where the Kosovans, known drug dealers (coincidence?), had been gunned down. They were waiting for the details and transcripts from

414

the cell company; did it have anything to do with the murder of the Kosovans?

Dealer activity was up across the suburbs, Kiric's warehouse deal just the latest in a suspected re-working of the drug market. This was major activity for DC police, because it was radiating out from the traditional areas and snaring people who would never normally be identified as regular drug users. Rumours abounded about the contamination of foodstuffs, but that's what it remained for now, though everybody knew the coffee, the maize, didn't taste right. The authorities tried to manage things, but with little real success.

It was becoming an epidemic and the usual forms of control were of no use in this context. People from all walks of life were exhibiting dependencies and services that struggled in the best of times, were going under with the weight of demand. Work place dismissals had skyrocketed as companies responded harshly to people arriving at work clucking, but then the bosses found themselves also falling under the spell of contaminated food, or whatever it was. Into this mix, came dealers in all shapes and sizes; designed to fit their new market places, as well as exploiting the old ones.

Fouré was particular about his food and as soon as he had detected a change, he'd modified his family's eating and drinking habits, while he tried to understand what was happening. Even Camino had changed his and his wife's routine but, as a regular coffee drinker, the situation could have been difficult if he hadn't his personal supply, which he shipped over from Europe, so fastidious was he about good coffee. It was that which he and Fouré were now appreciating from the machine gurgling in the corner.

415

'So what do we think?' Fouré asked the map, though his question was really addressed to Camino.

The FBI Agent also addressed the map. Neither yet trusted the other one hundred per cent, as much as their truce had originally held the hope of it. 'Hortez is back in Colombia so, unless she's expected back here anytime soon, she's out of scope at the moment. Unless this number brings up some useful contacts we may not be able to persuade the Colombians to arrest her for crimes committed over here.'

'Okay, I'll get my people to concentrate their efforts on tracing this cell and bringing them in.'

'If they haven't already discarded the phone.'

'It's a risk we'll have to take.'

Camino agreed with some misgiving. It was easy to say these things, so much harder to deliver the desired result. 'It's what we got. Now, the bomb site: the analysis of material taken from it suggests a military grade explosive rather than home grown. The investigation points to an RDX, probably Semtex, and it could be of Chinese manufacture.'

'Surprised?'

'I guess not. With the size of the explosion compared to the delivery method it was always going to be professional product. If it's an RDX chances are it's Semtex and that is gonna come principally from a manufacturer in Eastern Europe, Russia or China. That's before you complicate matters with the supply to Middle Eastern, South American and West Asian countries, among others. So manufacture doesn't necessarily mean supplier. I guess we'll find out. The lab should be able to pinpoint the manufacturer and possibly the date of manufacture.'

'Will we know where it went after production?'

'It'll be guess work at best. We have to match the

signature of the explosive to other known batches and then we can trace the logistics path. Anyhow, all that has to be reported up to the Director who's currently holed up with the President at Raven Rock. I think anything we find will quickly be taken out of our jurisdiction.'

'That's a shame.' Fouré looked at his idev. 'There's better news on the cctv footage.'

'What?'

'Since we got those photofits of Assiz we've been able to identify him on local camera records. We've plotted him coming to the memorial and then going to Baltimore and meeting with some guy at a Dunkin Donuts outlet. We believe that was the guy who firestormed Air Force One.'

'That is good work,' confessed Camino. 'Can we relate either to any other cell or group of people?'

Fouré shook his head. 'Not at this time. We're working on it.'

'It could be critical –'

'No shit.'

Camino forced himself to ignore the jibe. '– to track their connections. There'll be something we can pick up which will help us piece together their network. A link has to exist, however small. Our analysts can help out with that work.'

'I'll be sure to keep you in the loop,' Fouré retorted laconically.

Camino regarded the powerful Police Captain facing him. The fragility of their professional unity kept surfacing: two disparate individuals, brought together by a common cause. It could so easily all go down the pan with an unsolicited pulling of rank.

'Okay. Where do we go now?'

Fouré considered his counterpart. He hadn't

417

expected him to back down on the CCTV matter; after all it was, in reality, an FBI investigation. Perhaps he'd misjudged the guy; perhaps the rumour of brinksmanship and glory-seeking at the expense of others was just that – rumour. The jury could remain out a while longer he guessed. 'For now, if we could get a handle on Hortez we could maybe find out what is happening in town with these drugs.'

'Maybe,' Camino concurred. 'Well, I'm going to visit our tech people and see if they've pulled any miracles with the Air Force One investigation.' He rose, drained the coffee off and put his cup back on the desk. 'I'll be back this afternoon.'

Fouré raised his cup and nodded. 'If I get anything else back on the phone, I'll call you up.'

'Sure thing.'

'Oh, one other thing,'

Camino looked back from the doorway. 'What?'

'Good coffee.' And Fouré realised the smile wasn't that difficult after all.

Fifty-Four

The situation room had become a planning area following final discussions with the President. Carlisle had been eager to move quickly, with the funeral only four days away. She hadn't taken an hour to reach her decision instead calling them all back within thirty minutes to give the "go". Now Logan, Black and their teams were busy considering the latest imaging, from both satellites and UAVs, which were mapping topography and line of sights from local buildings in the area. In two days the Secret Service would be working with local law enforcement to perform the final ground checks; seal manhole covers and to ensure every potential site from which to launch an assassination attempt or a bomb attack had been investigated and, where possible, sealed against ingress or egress.

Everything had to look normal. Faulkner couldn't suspect they were marshalling him to a kill box, or that his set up was too easy. Before that happened they had to have, either a clear idea where Faulkner might attack from, or where they wanted him to be channelled to, by cutting off more likely options.

'He's unlikely just to rely on Firestorm to prevent access to Limo One,' opined Black. 'That leaves too many options for the defenders. What he'll go for is maximum chaos; try either to take out the primary, or at least place it in the scope of his rifle. He may be a jihadist, but he's also a strategist and he wants be sure that his main objective is achieved. That means he needs highly impressionable cannon fodder.'

'Agreed. So: two questions from that.'

'Only two?'

Logan grinned. 'For now. First: where's he likely to place himself with adequate cover and best line of sight on the target. Secondly: where does he find this cannon fodder?'

Black looked at the maps and displays, but it was another who answered first.

'He can't make a decision on the first until he's identified the kill box, and that's dependent on where the Presidential motorcade will draw up.'

Everyone in the room turned to the speaker. Helen Reed was diminutive, at five foot two, but what she lacked in size she more than made up with in competency. Everyone waited as she walked to the front of room. She'd arrived back at Raven Rock only the previous day, having been working on an issue that had arisen in the Yemen. Even so she was remarkably adept at getting up to speed.

'Arlington is a big site, but also a secure one. To succeed Faulkner needs three conditions to be met. One, he will need to find somewhere he can conceal himself easily, with good escape routes if he is unsuccessful. Next, that place must have a clear line of sight on the target area. With so many government and military establishments around he'll need to be in the cemetery and he'll probably be within a thousand metres of the primary target because of his third condition, a decent, readily available rifle with which to snipe. Faulkner was a good sniper, but that was ten years ago. I doubt he can attain the distances he did then, but that also comes down to his weapon. Factor in the crowded nature of the area, as well as the establishment surrounding him, and he needs to be on site to achieve this.'

Black raised a finger in question. 'How do you mean "a good sniper"?'

Reed regarded the SEAL. 'You don't know his background?' Black's head moved in the negative. 'Oh, right. Well Faulkner was a sniper in Delta Force, serving in Afghanistan during 2008 and 2009. By all accounts he was good at his job in the anti-materiel role and he narrowly missed the record for one of the longest kills at just over twenty-one hundred yards. He's proficient with both bolt-action and semi-automatic sniper rifles.'

'Shit.'

'Well, things are not so bad,' Reed continued. 'He will have very little time to bed in and we can ensure that we make it easy enough, but not too easy, for him to sight the target and potentially take out the President.'

'Oh good.' Black was clearly sceptical of Reed's assessment, even though he knew the President wasn't going to be there.

'You said "if he's unsuccessful". Isn't he a jihadist? They're not usually bothered about exfil from the field.'

Reed looked at the young SEAL corporal. She could see from the look on his face that he'd already made some decisions about what she'd said – he just needed to see if what she told him made sense. 'Faulkner has two targets,' she stole a glance at Logan: he was unfazed, 'the President; and Logan here. Whoever he takes out first he will need to get the next. There is a clear conflict in his decision making, which we can exploit. The jihad, sponsored by al-Qaeda and the Taliban, seeks the destruction of the US Administration and those who would come after. *His* jihad seeks the death of the man who defiled and eventually murdered his betrothed.'

'Of the two,' interrupted Logan, 'I'm the most

expendable and also that gives time for us to find him and take him down.'

'But if we have doubles, does it matter?'

Logan nodded. 'Faulkner mustn't suspect they are doubles. He must be convinced that President Carlisle and the other candidates for office are all present, and provide him with viable targets. He'll be more ready to complete the whole of his task without deflection.'

This appeared to attract agreement, and then questions, from the other SEALs around the table. The first came from a serious looking man wearing a deep frown. 'If I got this right, we're looking for a man who is ex-Delta, a good sniper and with a determination to commit jihad and probably die in the attempt. He's probably gonna cover himself by bringing in some sort of diversion, which could be anything, but is likely to involve an IED of some sort: which has to get through the security that'll be around Arlington.'

'What's your question?' Black regarded his fellow professional.

'Just this: I'm not convinced he won't find out we're using doubles? Isn't it possible that he will abort?'

'That's what Logan will be there for. Hopefully he will provide enough of a distraction that Faulkner will momentarily concentrate his attack elsewhere. That will give us the chance to pinpoint him and take him out.'

The SEAL nodded. 'What do we need to pull this off?'

Black stood up and Reed made way for him. 'Okay guys, this is going to be a good old-fashioned action. We won't have the pleasure of technology because of the potential threat of Firestorming. So, we're gonna have to rely on excellent planning, good synchronising and mark one eyeball on site.'

'How do we draw him out?' This from another SEAL.

'I'll be the focus point. I'll be making myself as visible as possible to bring him out.' Logan noted some frowns amongst the operatives at this and Logan understood their concerns. A sniper wasn't likely to be drawn into the open. One shot was enough and then silently, secretively, make your getaway. 'That's where our next piece of work comes in. We have to guide Faulkner to where we want him to be. So we'll be visiting the cemetery over the next day and a half to get the lay of the land, and then devise some plans.'

'What do you want us to do?'

Black took over. 'The idea is to walk the place looking for potential sniper hides; to check over where the burial will be; where the motorcade will pull up; and then put timings and the ceremony into context. Once we've done that we'll be able to advise the President and the organisers so we can maximise our opportunities.'

He paused and looked round the room. 'Okay. I'm pushing information to your idevs. You'll be going in pairs. Make sure you take cameras to record whatever you think is relevant. We'll meet back here at thirteen hundred tomorrow to review. Also, you're cleared to take personal firearms with you but try to keep out of trouble.

'Everything clear?'

Nods rippled around the table.

'Okay. Let's go. Just be careful out there.'

*

Drew Faulkner had changed his motor. Like a cell, it could become a familiar, a totem to be identified with. He was now driving a five-year-old Volvo V60: blue, inconspicuous – in this he could be any average, middle-class Washingtonian. Perhaps a trendy one, who lived in one of the more upmarket crossover suburbs where there were immigrants and everybody had a great time pretending they all got on.

Currently he was driving along an ordinary street in the suburb of Alexandria. Its mix of Victorian and Seventies style block buildings were downcast, and showing their age, beneath a layer of graffiti and faded paint. The shops were a clutter of activity and fussiness. Stacks of goods fought each other for space in stores that seemed to enjoy no particular focus of trade, items spilling onto pavements; some having the luxury of tables to support their existence. Vegetables and fruit were juxtaposed with cheap electronic goods and car parts. It was all without order and for a moment Faulkner was reminded of his roots. He shook his head as his destination appeared ahead, on the right. Pulling the Volvo over to the side he exited and locked up before surveying the front of the mosque. Housed in an old tenement, he could see the rudimentary tower where the imam called the believers to prayer. Faulkner opened the door and entered into the lobby, a cold affair with racks for shoes. He pulled off his and placed them alongside the other forlorn footwear.

Picking up a prayer mat, he made his way into the meeting hall. It was almost empty; just a few older men kneeling in the emptiness, because retirement commanded their attention in this way. He set his mat down and bowed to Mecca before kneeling and beginning his supplication.

As he intoned his prayer to Allah, he became aware of a quiet, calm presence kneeling beside him. He inclined his head slightly, acknowledging his fellow worshipper but continued until his prayers were complete. It was important to pay to Allah the dues owed: all true followers knew that. The business of the day could wait. After all, hadn't He provided all the hours that were needed to conclude His work.

With a final bow he rose and, a few minutes later, the other followed. They walked around the edge of the room and made their way to the little canteen from where beverages and small bites could be purchased and consumed with fellow believers, away from the infidel. They bought coffees and occupied a secluded table, where they could speak without being overheard.

'You need something brother.'

It was a statement, yet also a question. Of course he needed something and here was the very man who could provide.

'Yes.'

The other nodded slowly and sipped his coffee, almost as if the action would aid his thought processes. Sunlight poured through a high window and cast its flame across the man's dark, slightly pockmarked skin. His eyes were hooded, the irises dark anyway, so that the thoughts that formed behind them were difficult to fathom.

'What is it you require?' His voice was educated, the English perfectly pronounced and delivered.

Faulkner delved in his pocket and withdrew a piece of paper, folded and dog-eared from residing so long there. He pushed it across the stained and scarred melamine.

Delicate fingers caught the paper and retrieved it

from the table, unfolded it and regarded the list. No muscle twitched; the eyes didn't expand in surprise. 'Is this all?' Faulkner nodded. 'When?'

'The funeral is in four days' time.'

This time there was the merest of flickers in the eyes, the twitch of a smile at the corner of the lips. 'Deadlines. Always you Westerners like tight deadlines.'

'Can it be done?'

Another sip of coffee.

No rush.

'Yes, it can be done. Do you think we are unprepared? We have waited for such a long time for the final destruction. Allah always requires the true believer to be prepared.'

'Forgive my doubt and ignorance.'

The other waved away Faulkner's apology, pulled a cell phone from his pocket and placed it on the table. A battery joined it.

'When you are ready phone me and then dispose of the phone. Here is the number you will call.' A piece of paper joined the phone and battery. 'Read and remember.'

Faulkner nodded slowly, pocketing the phone and battery before picking up the piece of paper and reading the number it contained. A moment's concentration and then he handed it back. 'Okay,' he said. The other nodded, as if he expected no less.

'Thank you, I will be in touch.' Faulkner drained his coffee and made to leave. As he did, the other grasped his wrist. The ex-CIA agent looked at the hand and then into the face.

'One other thing.'

'What?'

The other reached in a pocket again and pulled out

a flash drive, placing it in the hand he still held. 'Mutual friends said you requested this.'

Faulkner regarded the drive and looked questioningly at the other who returned the gaze levelly. 'A device for the completion of your work.'

As Faulkner made to speak the other raised a hand. 'Enough, you will understand. Allah directs you.'

'To success.'

'Inshallah.'

*

Senator Harry Johnson was considering the information he'd just received via his Zeus device. How much worse could things become? Already the FBI had been round asking about his relationship with one Penelope Hortez and now it appeared there was a clear and present danger in relation to the upcoming funeral of Jonah Lincoln. What more could go wrong?

Johnson read the information scrolling across his retina reader. He still couldn't get used to this invasion of his head. It was most disconcerting to see things without them having any substance beyond his mind and yet be real all the same. Sometimes he wished he wasn't a politician at such a time. This device could come to no good. Fortunately, it was only available for government work.

The document originated from Carlisle's government in exile, well perhaps not exile though it seemed so. It made for grim reading: an imminent terrorist attack on the funeral of Carlisle's predecessor, perhaps a jihadist inspired action, had been uncovered and was being treated as serious by all the security services and investigated. That was being helped by the British MI6 but it was necessary to make some changes.

As he flicked through the report he digested the plan: the funeral would be staged, in effect to draw out the possible insurgents and ensure they were either captured or killed. But, it was all embryonic and unformed. At least he wasn't needed there: they would be using doubles while a British agent who, for a reason that wasn't made clear, would provide the significant bait in the trap. Who cared? If the stupid bastard wanted to put his life on the line like that Johnson, for one, wasn't about to stop him.

But it was a real shit. Who did these jihadists think they were? When he was in the White House he would enact some serious changes to ensure that such people were clearly put in their place. There'd be no pussying around like with Lincoln and Carlisle. Allegiance to the flag would become the paramount oath of any citizen. Anything less and they could kiss goodbye to the American Dream.

He closed the file off and settled back in his leather wingback office chair, determined to relax. His mind emptied.

The harsh ring of his idev skewered his reverie. Reaching to the desk he picked the device and hit the receive icon. It was his aide, Bob. 'What is it?' His tone, irritable and challenging, seemed not to faze his long suffering aide.

'I have a call from Penelope Hortez. You asked me to vet calls from her. She said it was urgent.'

Penelope Hortez? The bitch! He couldn't believe that she had the gall to call him after all that had happened. 'What does she want?' He couldn't keep the rancour from his tone: after all he'd fucked the woman and she'd been grateful of that.

There was the briefest of hesitations from his aide. 'She wouldn't say; other than it was urgent.'

What to do … 'Give me a moment.' What to do? He considered the little information he already had. Did Penelope have anything of any import to say to him? She had failed with the show and that looked as if it might have been a front to bring drugs into the country. Already her name was linked with a well-known, well, in Europe anyway, drugs smuggler. That was not a good relationship for a potential Presidential candidate. Shit! The woman was intent on ruining him! Such a revelation didn't exactly help his decision.

'Okay Bob, put her through.'

What to expect …

'Harry?'

'Just a minute Penelope.' Harry Johnson placed his idev on his desk which lit as the a-frame was activated. Immediately a vid-gram opened from the call and he could see Penelope. His stomach lurched as he saw her. God, she was gorgeous.

Stop.

'Hello Penelope what can I do for you?'

He detected the slight hesitation, as if she was considering her response. 'How are you?'

The Senator deliberated the question – a crock of shit. What did she care how he was? Yet he had to appear as if he was unsighted on everything. 'I'm good thanks. How are you? How are the boys?' Did he detect a change?'

Penelope caught herself at the mention of her sons. It was what she had needed because she had vacillated as she made the call, wondering whether she was doing the right thing. She could give nothing away. 'Fine, everything is fine.'

'Good, I'm glad to hear it. Where are you now?'

'I'm back home, trying to sort out what had happened. I'm so sorry.'

I bet you are. 'Hey, these things happen. What about the insurance? Will they pay out?'

Was that a pause?

'I – I don't know, it's still being investigated.'

Johnson nodded slowly. 'So, what can I do for you?'

'Can we meet up?'

Johnson considered Penelope's request. What was the benefit to him from meeting with her? More importantly, what were the consequences to his political profile from agreeing to see her? There were so many eyes watching whatever you did these days. He knew that she was using him, still part of him wanted to see her, to touch her and perhaps …

No! He couldn't, it was too much of a risk to his campaign, to his reputation, his ambition. Yet if he left her to her own devices maybe she would undo him. He had to have a plan. And he had to have her where he could influence her or …

His thoughts went back to the visit from the FBI. At the moment he was seen as just a foolish older man, who'd let himself become involved with somebody probably using his position for her own gain. But, were they able to prove any deeper link then they'd ensure he was fucked, completely and utterly fucked.

Johnson had to make sure that Hortez, pretty as she was, couldn't screw with his future.

'Of course we can meet. Let me put you back to Bob and he'll organise that for you.'

Penelope smiled at the Senator. 'Thank you so much. It will be good to see you again.' Inwardly she rejoiced at the impending meeting. And yet, it would not be the meeting Senator Harry Johnson was expecting.

Johnson put the call on hold as he waited to talk to his aide. Bob's face swam into view. 'Yes Senator?'

'Bob, Ms Hortez wants to meet with me. Can you arrange it please? The FBI is interested in her and if I leave her to her devices then it could affect the Presidential campaign. You know what I mean?' Bob nodded. 'Good. See to it.'

Fifty-Five

Somewhere south of Albuquerque, New Mexico

The two semis had been driving for nearly five hours, making their way from Ciudad Juarez in Mexico across the border towards Albuquerque in New Mexico. The outskirts of the US city could be made out on the horizon. Soon they would be at their destination: a small warehousing facility in the south of the city.

The containers had landed in the Americas two days ago, at the Venezuelan port of Maracaibo. From there they had been put on trucks, which had made their way to the local airport, where they were loaded onto an Ilyushin Il-76 cargo plane bound for the Mexican border town. What was in the two containers was identified as farm machinery parts. At Ciudad Juarez that manifest was changed to identify the destination as Albuquerque.

Now the two units were unhooked and two others hooked up, in order that the journey could continue. Air transport was still grounded across the US and so this was seen by the owners as a risky business. Ostensibly the manifest said the load was to be delivered to an address in Queens and it would take some six days for them to make the journey.

Fifty-Six

Arlington Cemetery

Logan was impressed by the scale of Arlington, if impressed was the right word to use in such a circumstance. He was stood close to where Jonah Lincoln would be buried. The white headstones stretched out all round him, perfectly aligned, straight and true as the interns they marked would have been in life. Within the rows, but towering above and sheltering them, were hundreds and hundreds of trees. Generally, they were isolated sentries but to the west a wooded area occupied a low hill.

He regarded the clumped trees that overlooked one field of crosses. Was it from their shelter that Drew Faulkner meant to achieve his feat? It seemed at once likely … and not. They were close enough to the burial site that Faulkner would be able to take out the President and yet he would know he was exposed.

Was that his intent? Logan admitted he couldn't even begin to fathom the way a jihadist worked; what made them tick. It was a risk he would never consider making – why would he? Then, his culture meant he worked to survive, not sacrifice himself so readily.

Raising his camera, he photographed the scene before him; his mind processing the images the lens provided him. Search; search: how are they going to get in range? Will they use car bombs? Would those just be diversionary; where would Faulkner come into the picture? There seemed little to foil an attack, other than the US Marine bodyguards and Secret Service, though forewarned they could probably stop an attack, or at least ensure it was blunted.

Then there was the problem of Faulkner, his sniping ability and the fact that, in all likelihood he would firestorm Limo One, leaving the President exposed for an assassination attempt. As he stood on the projected site of President Lincoln's grave, Logan felt the pressure of the moment build on him. If he was anything like Assiz, Faulkner would stop at nothing to complete his mission or, at least, die in the attempt. So was he going to shoot each of the dignitaries? That seemed ... unlikely: then what? Too many questions remained unanswered.

And in them all it was sobering to think that his one-time friend could, so completely, turn against his country and his friends in such a way. Logan's camera clicked away, but his thoughts remained with the ex-CIA officer and friend who, shortly, would draw up on the opposite side of fight to the Brit.

Logan shivered despite the warm weather. It was not a fight he was looking forward to.

*

The imam sat on the mat, drinking tea. His sips were slow and purposeful and Ayman Moradi waited patiently. No-one rushed the imam when he was drinking tea.

Finally, he placed his cup on the low table and dabbed the corners of his mouth with a cotton kerchief which he tucked into his wide sleeves. He captured Ayman's gaze and searched him, for what seemed an age.

'Ayman, are you ready?'

The young man considered his imam's words carefully, He knew it paid to reflect, rather than rush a reply in the hopes of ingratiating one's self with the religious leader. He paid more attention to those who knew their destiny.

And what was his destiny? Ayman pondered the idea. He knew this country had given him many opportunities and that his mother and father were great patriots for their new home. Yet … something prevented him from giving wholeheartedly to his new home. For sure, he knew little of Iraq, having left there when he was only six. He was now twenty-two, working in his father's grocery store, and helping his friend, Imran with his auto repair garage. He also visited the mosque every day, taking lessons with Imran and learning the deceits of the country he called home. Those falsehoods burned in his heart so that he wanted to play a part in teaching the infidel and leading the great battle to free the world of their rule.

'I am ready, Imam.'

Imam Faisal sat in silence, appraising the young man before him. Was he ready? He admired Ayman. The young Iraqi was quiet but conscientious, completing his studies on time, diligently reading the Koran and increasingly putting himself forward for tasks and leading at the mosque. Yet …

'What are your thoughts for the infidel?'

Ayman considered the question, knowing immediately what the imam was seeking. Be honest, Allah told him. 'I still feel for the country … but I understand they need to learn the true way. And I understand that requires sacrifice from the true believer.'

The religious leader nodded his head. 'You are ready for that sacrifice?'

Ayman held the imam's gaze resolutely for a minute. 'Yes, I am,' he said finally.

*

Penelope stood glaring into the middle distance: the water in the pool seemed to mirror her agitation but she was oblivious to its shimmering blue surface. All her attention was directed to the caller who, again and again, told her what she didn't want to here. Would Fernando have taken this person's "fuck you" attitude? Absolutely not! But, as the conversation swung back and forth like an unending tennis match, she realised that she was not going to achieve her goal. One more try …

'If I go back to the States I'll be leaving myself open to arrest, not just for this but … other events.' Penelope could tell how lame that sounded. God! How had she let it get this far?!

The voice at the other end of the line sounded as sympathetic as it was possible, without caring at all. 'I appreciate your position but if you want this to happen, you have to be there to lend credibility to the meet. If he turns up and you're absent he'll spook. And he's more likely to leave his guards behind when he meets you. That will give us the window of opportunity we require to complete the job. If you don't go, we will not be able to isolate him.'

When she thought about it she knew, in this matter, the caller was right. Wasn't that the problem with revenge? You had to commit one hundred per cent, and now she was getting cold feet; wanting somebody else to do her dirty work while she remained safe in her home.

Safe for how long? It wouldn't take a genius to link her with Johnson's assassination; they'd just come here for her. Either way she would end up dead. The Yanks wouldn't think about taking her back, just shoot her and dump her in the jungle somewhere, to be eaten by the jaguars and scavengers.

Much better to be in control of how you went. After all, what did she have to live for? Everything had been stripped from her: just get your final revenge and have done with it.

'Okay. Contact me tomorrow.'

'You must be quick Senora, we have no more than two days now to complete the task.'

Penelope stifled the shout of disgust and limited herself to bidding the man called back that afternoon. Soon it would be over.

*

The pause at the other end of the cellphone was filled with satisfaction and the caller waited, while the other digested what had been said. Finally.

'You must leave no trace. It must look natural, unfortunate and yet inevitable in some fashion.'

'That's understood. We have the plans in place.'

'Good.'

The caller paused. 'Won't this affect your other plan?'

He could almost see the shake of the head. 'No, the two events are too close together for the primary to be changed now. They will go ahead.'

'If you're sure.'

'I am.'

The tone left the caller in no doubt as to his next course of action. 'Very well, we will execute as directed.'

'Excellent. You will be paid handsomely for your work.'

If we get out of there. The dark thought had

inhabited the caller's head for some days now, almost since the assignment had been handed to him. Then, every job had its risks.

'Thank you. You will know when the job has been completed. Payment under the usual terms.'

'Agreed. Thank you. Good bye.'

*

Leong and Yuan were enjoying a rare moment of equanimity, drinking tea and discussing the mother country. At moments such as these Leong almost felt sorry for what would transpire in the younger man's life. His decision was necessary for China; for him. For now, though it was a time to enjoy how far they had come and what business they must conclude before the end.

'Do you remember Uncle Wu's shop? The lines of chickens in the window, and the carcasses that used to hang like empty sacks in the slaughter room?'

Yuan smiled and nodded. 'Uncle used to let me help in the summer when school was out. The stink of the bodies, and the blood from a fresh kill, used to intrigue me, fascinate me. I used to wonder what was happening in their heads as the knife was pulled across the throat.' *I think the same when I kill a man now.*

Leong laughed, though he felt cold inside at the words, and could imagine what Yuan was thinking in the silence beyond them. 'Your uncle was a profound man, one full of wisdom.'

There was a reflective nod from the younger man. 'He was a simpler man than my father, with no desire for politics. I learned much from him.'

Leong regarded the young man left in his charge

by an indifferent father. A rare moment of tenderness caused the general to pause. This was the simple country boy, that China's most powerful man had placed in his care, to nurture, educate and make proficient. He was uncertain he'd achieved that, merely unleashed a monster, which had been fed those simple images of death in his uncle's shop.

'Do you regret anything?' he asked, almost breathless in expectation of … what? He wasn't sure.

Yuan looked beyond the general, beyond the room, his mind journeying back to the little village of Beilai, north of Beijing, running down the dusty street at lunchtime, to Mr Lee's bakery where he would hand over money from his uncle, in return for fresh bread with which to eat roasted pork. He had come a long way from that small boy and part of him regretted the journey. Leong knew him well, perhaps too well. He focussed and held his expression blank.

'Nothing,' he affirmed emphatically. 'Now to business.'

Leong considered his lieutenant and then nodded. 'Yes, you're right. What of your investigations?'

'Our people believe it was Sanchez who ordered the killing of Kiric and his people. We're tracking the assassins now and expect to resolve that particular problem. How will you respond to him?'

Leong steepled his fingers. 'I have yet to consider that matter. When I have reached a decision I will inform you.'

Yuan nodded slowly, seemingly accepted the relationship which had bothered him so much previously. 'Very good. Would you like to know how our other business is going?'

Leong inclined his head and the younger man continued. 'Our trucks are heading across the country

439

and are expected in the Washington area tomorrow. Our colleague will be in receipt of the goods in time for the event.'

'That is excellent. Can he get them working in time?'

Yuan coughed deprecatingly, barely disguised. 'Yes, he has the capability and the people to make it happen.'

'Good. And how trustworthy is he?'

'As any Occidental.'

Leong grunted his understanding. 'When he has the work completed and Faulkner is in receipt of the goods, let him go.'

'Understood'

Leong sipped his green tea: it was cold and the bitterness, unusually, lingered in his throat. A precursor to something? 'Tell me Zhi, how confident are you that the route Kiric established for us can be maintained now he is gone?'

Yuan crossed his legs languorously, in no particular hurry to answer the pompous old fool with his green tea. He was growing bored of this, playing second fiddle to a man who had no chance of ever realising his ambition, to be the next Premier. The old fool had made a play for nomination by members of the Politburo but would be rejected. What he, Yuan, had to decide was whether to tell his father – there was no love lost, but perhaps it was more prudent to protect himself.

Leong had hoped that Yuan would turn against his father, following his banishment for the accidental killing of a Western diplomat's daughter in a sex game gone wrong. And Yuan senior had made it clear that he wanted nothing to do with his offspring until he'd sorted himself out. Placing him in the care of

Leong had been doing the older man a favour too, a favour repaid with treachery.

But Leong was, in effect, staging a coup, the end result being the overthrow of Yuan's government and the ending of his tenure as Premier. As a member of the Yuan clan, even ostracised, he couldn't allow that to occur. For now though he'd have to play along. What did he say of Kiric's plans, now laid bare?

'His route is well established from Central Asia, either across Pakistan and through the Indian Ocean, or west through the Black Sea and North Africa into Yemen or Mali. This is not reliant on the skills and knowledge of just one man, but on the collective power and effectiveness of many. And, with our connections throughout Africa, we can be sure that we will maintain the routes for the foreseeable future.'

'That is good. Do we need to do anything to strengthen them?'

Yuan bit back the heavy sigh which threatened to explode from his lips. 'No, nothing: I will keep watch over them.'

'And, in Washington? Is everything ready?'

'Faulkner will receive the goods shortly and he is recruiting a local cell to replace those he lost when the US SEALs took out Assiz's operation at the mine. They will effectively provide distraction for the security forces and will enable him to strike when and how it is least expected.'

'That is good,' Leong affirmed, allowing himself the slightest of smiles. He was, at this moment, a content man. 'Now, to local matters: what do you think we should do with Mr Sanchez?'

Yuan shrugged dismissively. Sanchez was proving himself a clever operator and for that reason would have to be dispatched. He had always been cautious of the Colombian. His background should have told Leong to be circumspect – another reason for the old fool to be hung out to dry. Sanchez was a tricky customer. His business empire, that had arms in Peru, Mexico, Venezuela and Brazil, to name a few, was understood to have been built on money from trafficking drugs and people and probably provided legitimacy to continued criminal activities, enabling the laundering of proceeds which had been pumped into a very effective campaign to claim the Presidency of Colombia.

Was that something his father's China would welcome? And if, as both his father and Leong wanted, China was to become a superpower, would an alliance with a suspected felon harm that aspiration?

'You ask my opinion? He needs exterminating. We would be better off with Cordoba. He's weak, easily moulded, with no aspirations one way or another. China can work with that and make Colombia what it wants it to be.'

Leong considered the younger man's appraisal, which had merit. He himself had become concerned with Sanchez; the connections they had uncovered and the way in which the man had begun to outflank them. 'But how?'

Ruminating, Yuan realised it would do no good for China to be openly implicated in a regime changing action such as the assassination of a Presidential candidate. That would affect their aspirations badly. Perhaps … 'We need another to be seen to remove the threat of Sanchez; Hortez? After all she has also been affected by his activities. I was thinking she might be influenced.'

The General nodded slowly, working the idea through his mind, looking for the pitfalls. There were several, not least that she seemed intent on delivering a blow to Harry Johnson's campaign which would, ultimately, curtail her aspirations in the drug smuggling business. But, perhaps if they moved quickly in sowing the seeds of destruction, then she could put in train an action which would resolve that. Then the attention would be all on the wronged woman from Cucuta who let vengeance overpower her.

'That is a good idea. Do we have a way to persuade her?'

Yuan had walked to the drinks cabinet where he was pouring a whiskey, as Leong had considered his words 'Yes we do. A contact in the Police also works for her. He has been my eyes and ears.' He downed the drink and allowed the liquid to burn all the way down his throat and hit his stomach like fire. He loved the taste of the drink, the way it consumed a person's body and left no room for ambivalence.

Leong relaxed back into his chair and tapped his fingers, satisfied at the decision. 'Make it so.'

Yuan drained the glass, let it fall, almost, on to the polished mahogany of the cabinet and strode from the room with barely a nod in the direction of his mentor and superior.

It was good to be two steps ahead of the old shit.

Fifty-Seven

The mood back at Raven Rock was flat. They'd all got back from a heavy afternoon walking Arlington and its surrounds, talking with the authorities and making notes and diagrams on their idevs. But it was all speculation and they were not much clearer as to how Faulkner might accomplish his mission.

Helen Reed was busying herself with constructing a meaningful map of the cemetery and its environs from a tactical point of view. She was single-minded and, in this mode, nobody could get close to her. People had dissipated, though she had consented to Eddie Powell staying and contributing, as she demanded. Logan had seen the look of joy on the young man's face as she'd agreed to his offer. Powell obviously figured he was in with a chance; Reed hadn't dissuaded him.

Logan and Black wandered through the Raven Rock complex, both at a loss as they waited for the call from Reed to say that she was ready to discuss with them her ideas and thoughts. They ended up in the restaurant where they went for the bottled fruit juice though, for a moment, Logan hankered for a cup of Vin's tea.

They sat in silence for a while.

'They say you were in The Company?'

Logan glanced across at Black. It was a period of his history that was not open to many people. It was just how it was in The Company. Even more elite than the SAS and far more free-willed, The Company was a very secret unit of men and women whose sole aim was to deliver retribution to those who were beyond the normal reach of the law, or military action.

What did he say?

'It's okay. You don't have to say anything if you don't want.'

'It isn't a case of what I want. Official Secrets Act.'

Black grinned. 'Aren't you supposed to suffix that with "old boy" or some shit?'

Logan laughed. 'God, yeah you're right! That sounded properly anal.' He paused to collect his thoughts. 'I served with the unit for 3 years; the first SAS officer to have done so ever.'

Black regarded the Brit with a renewed sense of respect. 'That's pretty impressive. We don't have an equivalent here though I guess if you mixed up us with the CIA you might get close.'

Logan knew the truth in that. Officially the UK didn't assassinate people and the myth that MI6 went about in James Bond style killing people and blowing stuff up was just that. Generally, the work was completely and utterly boring. Just the way the authorities prefer it.

But, when things got a bit out of hand then The Company had been on hand to sort out the shit. They had been disbanded in the hiatus between the Good Friday Agreement, which effectively brought an end to The Troubles in Northern Ireland (in spirit, if not in reality), and the burgeoning problem with the Taliban and al-Qaeda. Still, the unit was something that was only alluded to; officially it didn't exist and the government and military liked it that way.

'It was a very small unit, a closely guarded secret and the selection process made the SAS look like kindergarten. It acted more independently of the political and military system so, once it had its orders to address a particular situation, off it went.'

'Shit, that would be something.' Black appeared visibly dejected at the comparison between his SEALs and The Company. 'We only get to do what the politicians tell us we can.'

Logan shrugged. 'I know that feeling; we had that in the SAS. Working on your own initiative has its pitfalls as well as its advantages though. If you make a mistake, there's nobody to cover your back, as slim as that might be in the real world. In The Company it was often "don't come home again" if something went wrong.'

Black whistled. 'Kinda puts it in perspective, man.'

'Yep, that's why those of us who were in it don't talk much. You never know who you might be condemning to a bullet in the back, or a car accident, or any other form of rubbing out.'

'Hey, I'm sorry I brought it up,' Black told him fervently. 'I had no idea.'

'It's okay. I feel I can talk to you about stuff like this and it takes the pressure off for a while. Only another Special Ops guy knows what you go through, night after night, with this shit.'

'Tell me about it.'

They grinned at the inanity of it all.

'So what was your hardest mission?'

Logan mulled over the question but, before he could answer, a breathless voice called his name across the restaurant. He took in the un-athletic figure of Des Farrow, still without any sense of tidiness, as the man weaved in ungainly fashion between the tables. He got to theirs and rested a hand on a chair for a couple of seconds, as he caught his breath.

'Take a seat.' Logan pulled out the chair next to

him and Farrow gratefully sank his portly form into it. 'Do you want a drink?' Logan regarded the middle aged man quietly. Farrow was a good man, despite his uncouth appearance, and Logan had real respect for him.

'No – give me – a minute, I'm okay.'

As unwarranted rushing was never order of the day for Special Ops people, Logan and Black remained silent and waited.

'I've got some seriously important intel that affects everything we're doing right now.'

Logan picked up the film of fear that wrapped itself like cling film around each word Farrow uttered and he immediately started to feel uneasy. 'What do you have?'

Farrow reached in a pocket and pulled out his idev, placing it on the table so everybody could see. His finger stroked the play icon for an MP4 file. Two trucks could be seen on a highway, making good time. The picture was obviously from a high level surveillance platform. Logan raised an eyebrow in enquiry.

'This video was recorded this morning on the interstate sixty-four, heading east. The containers are manifested as carrying agricultural machinery parts, destined for an address in Queens.'

'But they're not agricultural are they?' Logan let the prompt hang in the air between him and Farrow. The smaller man shook his head slowly, hesitantly.

'What is it?' Black looked confused.

Farrow coughed. 'We believe it's … that the containers hold … the disassembled parts of a Kamov Hoodoo helicopter gunship.'

'Holy fuck!'

'What's the situation?'

447

Farrow rapidly filled them in, stumbling over his words and the details in his eagerness to be rid of the burden of the discovery. A journey across the Middle East from Central Asia, thence to Venezuela for transfer to an aircraft and then Mexico. The cargo got closer to its destination, but it wasn't the one they'd figured. By the time the aircraft had landed and transferred the goods the authorities were about twenty-four hours behind and playing catch up.

'We received intel from our SAS recon unit, which had been following the consignment, that it had been split up and was moving to a number of different locations. They ... unfortunately lost sight of the 'copter.'

'Great,' Black said succinctly. His eyes were filled with rage and impotence.

Logan put a hand on his arm. 'So, we have this chopper moving towards Washington in two trucks. What's the plan?'

Farrow coughed. 'The authorities are going to intercept, destroy if necessary.'

Logan and Black looked at each other. 'Let's hope they get this right,' Black opined sagely.

*

The Police helicopter had been shadowing the trucks for two hours, its endurance about out, but the pilot was reluctant to leave the trucks to their own devices. Backup was on its way, but still, annoyingly, too far away to get there before they had to abandon the chase. Gary Roberts glanced across at his co-pilot. 'These guys are gonna get away at this rate,' he decided and the other nodded.

'What you thinking boss?'

448

Roberts stared down at their quarry. 'We need to stop them' He looked back at the operator in the rear, and then at his co-pilot. 'We're going ahead of them and bringing them to a halt until the ground units get here.'

Co-pilot and observer exchanged worried looks. 'You sure about this?' Mike Everson felt the sweat forming in his armpits, and across his back. It wasn't what he'd signed up to the Air Division of Kentucky State Police for, but he was a police officer first and Gary was right, they had to stop these guys before they got to Washington. Even so ...

In the rear, after his initial concern, Duane Collins was unlocking the gun box. Nestled inside were four Glock 17s and two Remington automatic shotguns. Methodically he checked out the weapons, passing two Glocks to Mike. Weirdly, he felt vaguely excited by the prospect of a fight.

Scanning ahead, Roberts saw that the highway rose over the brow of a hill and then headed on towards Louisville, fields on either side dotted with trees. They could get the chopper down easily, either on the dual carriageway road, or in the fields. He shared his plan with the others, who nodded in agreement.

Roberts pushed forward on the collective and the nose of the 'copter dipped, picking up speed. They crested the hill and he pushed forward further, speed mounting. He had to get enough distance between him and the trucks. The road dropped down the other side of the hill and traffic was sparse. Roberts brought the machine around in a sweeping high speed turn, pulling back on the cyclic to bring it into the hover. Quickly Roberts dialled out the collective and planted the helicopter firmly on the verge of the road.

Everson and Collins were soon out on the road, shotguns at the ready. Roberts got out of the cab and reached for a couple of emergency flares. As he looked, the first of the trucks appeared over the brow of the hill. He felt a clenching in his stomach. This was it. He turned.

'Duane, get a call into central. Tell them we're on the ground and about to stop the two trucks. We need units here as quickly … no, quicker than possible.'

Without waiting to see what Collins did, Roberts turned his attention back to the trucks. They were gradually getting closer. He activated the flares and began to wave them.

Nothing.

They were going to run them and he had nothing to stop them with.

Then, the lead truck started to slow; behind the other followed suit. They came to a halt twenty, thirty yards from the three police aircrew. Roberts advanced on the lead vehicle, aware that his buddies were covering his walk. His heart was fluttering and his legs felt like jelly so much adrenaline was pumping through him.

As he drew level with the cab the driver wound the window down and leaned out. 'What gives officer?'

'Can you get out of the cab please sir?'

The driver took in the officer's demeanour and the Glock, which had risen to confront him and decided to comply. He dropped to the verge.

'So you gonna tell me what this is about?'

'I need to see in the container.'

The driver took off his baseball cap and scratched his head. 'It's just agricultural machinery parts officer. I'm not sure what the fuss is about.'

Roberts indicated the back of the semi with his

Glock. 'Just open up please sir?'

The old man shuffled to the rear and paused. The officer looked as uncompromising as ever, though what the big deal with agricultural machinery was he couldn't fathom. Pulling a Gerber multi-tool from his pocket he snipped the seal, pulled on the lever and cranked the door open.

Roberts head was mashed with the tension. What was he expecting to see? What did a Kamov in bits look like? He was aware of his colleagues behind him.

Whatever they looked like, it wasn't like what confronted him. 'Fuck!' He turned. 'Check the other truck,' he told Everson and Collins. They turned and walked quickly to the back of the other vehicle. Roberts looked at the driver. 'Can I view your manifest?'

'You certainly can, but won't tell you much more than you can see here,' opined the old man sagely.

'I'll see it just the same.'

*

The captain finished his chat with the two drivers, shook their hands and walked back towards Roberts. Squad vehicles and a SWAT team had formed a cordon around the two semis, the strobing blue and red lights and the chatter of radios, establishing a border of activity, which held the two trucks in a bubble.

'Well done Gary,' Captain Anderson told him. 'It's a blank but your action was fast, effective and has ensured we haven't lost too much time.'

'Do we know where the Kamov is?'

Anderson shook his head. 'No. We're gonna have

451

to back track all the way to Albuquerque. At least it's only Albuquerque.'

If indeed the trail had been concealed from that point. What if the smugglers had done it before they reached the States? Could the weapon already be in the Capitol?

*

Some hundred or so miles to the north, east of Indianapolis, following Interstate seventy, a single semi-rig with two containers held a steady sixty miles per hour on the inside lane. The driver was working overtime on this load and was going to be paid handsomely for delivery. He didn't know what was in the two containers nor had he asked. He didn't want to know – only the money was important to him. It would help get his last child through college.

He checked his watch. It was another nine or ten hours until his destination, somewhere to the north of the Capitol. When he was about an hour away a call would come through with the address, then he could get back home to Becky and the kids. A smile broke on his face at the thought of his wife and kids and he turned the radio up. The Beach Boys were being played by a local station, the window was open and he felt good.

Fifty-Eight

Federico listened very carefully to the caller. His head was full of words that meant only one thing to him – betrayal. Fortunately, his upbringing, first in Bogota, and then Cucuta had taught him that betrayal was a two-way street. He was stressing over what was being asked of him, but a part knew that, even if she personally wasn't to blame for what had happened to his brother Hernando, she was of the family that had brought misery to his mother and an early grave to his grieving father.

He checked his anguish. Really, he should think himself lucky he was getting this opportunity. For sure, she was a beautiful woman with a magnetic personality and, to his shame, he fantasised about her, but her husband had trafficked the death and destruction his family had witnessed. Only she was left and once she was erased vengeance would be completed.

There was a silence developing from the cell phone and he realised the other had stopped talking. He waited.

'Do you understand?'

'Si, I understand.'

'Good. You will be paid handsomely for this. You have proved very useful.'

He considered the words and the promise in them.

'I don't want payment. Seeing the end of the Cucuta Cartel will be enough payment for me.'

*

Penelope Hortez was packing her bags for the flight

to Washington. She was in a foul mood for a journey that was totally unnecessary: if only the hitman had the balls to do the job. Didn't he realise she couldn't be as exposed as this? Yet she'd accepted his request, order (was it an imperative placed on her?) because the reasoning was sound. It had certainly seemed so and time had only served to reinforce that feeling.

She was packing light; she wanted to be in the country as little time as possible and had instructed her pilot that he should keep the engines running and have clearances sorted for a quick turnaround at Washington. Her best driver was going with her; an ex-Colombian Secret Service agent he was quite simply the finest her late husband had ever employed. Not only was he exceptionally loyal, he was a crack shot with the good sense to keep his mouth shut about what he saw.

Her cell phone chimed and she retrieved it from the bed where it lay trembling on the duvet. The display showed it was Federico – what did he want?

'Hello.'

'Senora Hortez: it's me, Feder-'

'I know who it is,' she retorted sharply. 'What do you want?'

'I – uh – have some information about the hit on Kiric.'

Even through the pain of his betrayal, Penelope felt her heart jolt at the mention of the Kosovan's name. She should have been the one to have killed him: it was her fucking responsibility. 'Go on?'

'It was – Eduardo Sanchez.'

It was as if she'd been hit in the stomach. Sanchez? It was years since their paths had crossed. He'd helped in the early years of setting up her fashion house. She had paid the price, if not willingly, then with the knowledge that giving herself to him was a necessary evil because her own husband thought her foolish and with no chance of success. That she had succeeded had been a bone of contention until the last.

But ... Sanchez? What did he have to gain from killing Kiric? And what did that mean for her? Was she next? If so, why? When? Her mind struggled to process the information that was streaming through it from those few simple words of her police snitch.

'How do you know this?'

Federico stumbled over his words again as if ... as if what? Was he being worked by somebody? If so who?

'It's information I – I received from an informant in ... Bogota.'

'And what did they say?'

'Sanchez was working with Harry Johnson ...'

Another body blow.

'... on dealing with drug smuggling into the US from Colombia and Venezuela. He had ordered your movements monitored and, when he picked up on the Kiric connection, he passed the information on to Johnson. It seems they felt it was better if your ... friend ... was to suffer a hit that could be explained away by gang violence. Sanchez ordered a hit by Mexicans from Juarez.'

That would explain why her people had been beaten to the score. But Sanchez?!

'There's more?'

The coldness in Penelope's chest seemed to be a palpable thing, threatening to engulf her. 'What?' Her voice was small.

'The word is that Sanchez is getting ready to take over Cucuta. He's playing Johnson and wants to use

455

your late husband's own resources to expand his empire. We think it likely there will be a hit on you in the next couple of weeks.'

Penelope sank to the bed, all the anger having drained from her at the news. Her limbs felt weak and uncontrollable. She had to think straight, quick. 'Where is Sanchez now?'

'He is returning from Mexico today, flying in to Bogota.'

'When will he land?'

'This evening, around six.'

'Thank you Federico, once again you have proved to be invaluable. I need to call some friends who will contact you shortly.'

Penelope Hortez considered the information and scenarios formed. It was a good time for what she had in mind. There would still be quite a bit of traffic filling the roads. A quick strike, as people were either heading home or coming into town for an evening's entertainment, to leave the country's Presidential hopeful bleeding to death in the road, for all to see. Once Sanchez was dead, it would be time to close Federico's account also. She speed-dialled a number.

The call tone rang in her ear and then a voice. 'Yes?'

'It's time to pay back your debt.'

*

'It was a dead end.'

Logan brought the bad news to the group in the situation room. 'The two trucks were stopped near Louisville. When they checked the containers they actually contained agricultural equipment.'

A collective groan rippled through the assembly,

this was a major setback. Was the intel wrong? Was there no threat and they'd been diverted from preparing for Faulkner's attack for no reason? Or was the equipment making its way to Washington by another route? It was clear how the senior politicians and directors in the room viewed the situation.

'This is a clear attempt to throw us off the scent,' decided Salt, the pugnacious Secretary for Defence. 'We're losing valuable time searching for something that probably doesn't even exist.'

Black shook his head. 'I'm sorry sir, you can't say that for sure.'

Salt smiled the smile of a person humouring a dumb kid. 'How likely is it they've got a helicopter – a helicopter for Chrissakes – into the country, without us knowing?'

'They were able to bring down Air Force One without us being able to respond. We can't afford to rule out the possibility they've managed to get one in the country. If they have –'

'If, Black, if! It's all possibilities and maybes: listen to yourself! Even if they have got such a machine into the country, we're better off preparing for where we know they'll be. The funeral – or what they believe will be the funeral.'

'By then sir, it may be too late. You can bet the machine will be equipped to deploy Firestorm, which will make our equipment inoperable.'

'So what?' interjected General Adams. 'It's not as if the President will be there. Faulkner will just expose himself and we get him.'

Black looked at the ageing general, fat and far from the frontline for many seasons now. He contained his sense of loathing, understanding that he and Logan shared a common dislike for the man who

457

was there to further his political career, rather than provide any critical and proportionate military advice. He opened his mouth to speak and thought better of it. The general smiled superciliously – he'd won.

Carlisle had remained silent; she had been watching both Black and Logan. Neither man had risen to the bait of her more senior advisors but she recognised the attitude of people who knew … who just knew that a decision had to be made and that those who should, couldn't. It was a big step.

'Anne, what are your thoughts on this? You've remained pretty quiet so far.'

The head of the FBI looked at the President. It was clear that, given room to advise, she sided with Black and Logan. 'We received credible intel from the Brits as well as the NSA that the Kamov existed. It's reasonable to assume that the forces ranged against us are making a determined effort to get it into the country. Don't forget that they aren't going to fight in the same way as us. Life doesn't mean to them what it means to us. They will sacrifice themselves; throw it all away for a single chance to kill you, Madam President.'

Angela Carlisle shuddered despite the regulated atmosphere in the room. 'That is putting the matter somewhat baldly, Anne.'

'My apologies Madam President, you did ask.'

She had, couldn't take that away from Anne. 'Okay,' President Carlisle looked round the table: her gaze alighted on Des Farrow's diminutive frame far at the other end. 'Mr Farrow, you were the bearer of the bad news. Do you have anything else to say?'

The senior analyst coloured up. 'I – er – I just brought in the intelligence from GCHQ.'

'Well, they aren't here, Mr Farrow; you are. Please

458

continue.'

Farrow coughed and made to rise to address the table. Before he could another cut across him.

'If I may, Madam President?'

'And who are you, pray tell?'

'Captain Helen Reed, seconded to MI6 from British Army Intelligence.'

Angela Carlisle raised an eyebrow but indicated for Reed to continue. The British officer cued up the display screens. 'Madam President, we were at Arlington Cemetery all yesterday, casing it because we believed there was a significant ground-based terrorist threat to the funeral. That still remains a credible option. However, intel came in from GCHQ that the Kamov was off radar. That has been verified by your own NSA.'

'Is that correct, Gene?' Carlisle was both surprised and annoyed she'd been blind-sided by her own people. Gene Hutchinson looked suitably embarrassed as he confirmed Reed's words with the merest nod of his head.

'Well, I must say, I'm not sure who I'm fighting here: al-Qaeda or my own administration.'

'The level of threat was deemed insufficient to advise you –'

'How about you leave the decision, about whether I should be advised, to me, Gene? When I don't want to be told something you'll be sure to know.'

The situation room's temperature rose several notches which had nothing to do with the climate control function. It was clear the President was close to stratospheric with anger over the situation. Logan couldn't blame her but it wasn't going to solve anything. He hoped she'd get it in check.

'Very well ladies and gentlemen, it seems we have

a situation over which we have abdicated control. I want that situation reversed as soon as possible. Gene, get your people working on this Firestorm device. We have to have an answer – and quick. Put everything into a counter strike device.

'Anne, I want every available resource put on finding this damned helicopter, preferably before it gets airborne. General Adams: make sure the military is on a heightened state of readiness but don't, I repeat, don't be visible on the streets. The National Guard is enough right now. I want you to work closely with the FBI and Homeland to ensure we're ready when the threat, whatever that might be, materialises. Is that clear?' Adams nodded. 'Good.'

Carlisle paused. 'All of you: the funeral is going ahead, no charades. I'll be damned if any terrorist is going to stop me doing what needs to be done in my own country.' She looked at her PA. 'Get everything arranged; let everybody know what is happening.'

The PA nodded and excused herself from the room. Carlisle let her gaze touch everybody in the room before resting on John Black. 'Mr Black, I know you'll tell me I shouldn't be doing this but I want you to do your very best to ensure the funeral is protected against all enemies.' *Foreign and domestic* she wanted to conclude but refrained. 'You will have unrestricted access to everything and anything you need to make sure that protection is as complete as possible. I will give you a Presidential letter enabling that for you. Anybody questions, you know where I am.'

'Yes ma'am.'

'We have two days to the funeral and things to do people: let's to it!'

Fifty-Nine

Bogota, Colombia

Looking out over the city, Eduardo Sanchez felt an immense feeling of self-satisfaction drape itself over his shoulders. He sipped brandy, letting the liquor drizzle down his throat and warm him through. It felt good to have put one over the Chinese and that bitch Hortez. She, in particular was in for a shock when she found out what was happening to her precious Cucuta Cartel.

The Gulfstream circled the city as the sun began to set over the hills, in the west. It looked warm and the evening would see the city nightlife awakening. Perhaps he would partake before going home. He felt like some fine wine, and company. Yes, that, perhaps, was a good idea. He drained the brandy and gave the empty glass to the stewardess who bent forward, providing him with a good view of her assets. She smiled, lips glistening red, was she offering herself to him? All those he employed, offered themselves at some point: he never refused.

'Do you want to see the city tonight when we land?'

The girl smiled and her eyes glistened. Slowly she pushed a strand of dark lustrous hair behind an ear. 'I would love to Senor Sanchez.'

Sanchez beamed. 'Good, go get ready. There's a good girl.'

The girl looked coy, rose and turned, in one fluid move, before heading back to the galley. She moved gracefully, artfully and he was pleased with what he saw.

461

Yes, that would do very nicely.

*

The plane landed and taxied to a private hard standing, away from the terminal buildings at El Dorado airport. Sanchez undid his seatbelt and made his way forward as the sky stairs dropped to the tarmac. His personal aide took his bags and briefcase ahead of him to the waiting car. Sanchez stopped as the stewardess walked from the galley. She'd changed from her uniform and was now wearing a shimmering short dress that clung to her frame like a second skin. The petrol blue perfectly matched her skin tone and the brown of her eyes. Sanchez felt very happy she was escorting him this evening. It would be a good time.

He allowed her the privilege of descending the stairs before him, watching her effortlessly dismount, stilettos clicking on the tarmac. He admired her backside, swinging with metronomic rhythm, watching as it disappeared, with its owner, into the back of the Mercedes S-Class.

The journey from the airport towards the city was relatively unremarkable and Sanchez found himself dozing slightly. The woman's perfume was heavy and earthy and it made him drowsy. A smile played on his lips as he felt her body move towards him. Her thighs were warm and full of promise as she moved closer; her breath worked its way into his ear: she certainly knew what he wanted and he could feel his desire rising despite his drowsiness.

A flick of tongue, moist and warm in his ear. God, she was eager. He turned to her and forced his mouth against hers, rough and demanding. She responded, her tongue searching inside his mouth. Sanchez pulled her close, to feel the heat and weight of her breasts against him, to start his game. This was going to be heavenly.

The moisture, at once warm, then cold on his shirt, surprised him. What the …? He looked down at the dark stain on the fabric. 'What …?' And then the pain: searing, venomous in his gut; leaking out onto the leather seat, along with the blood flooding from the puncture in his gut.

She smiled at him, but the eyes were cold as she drew the blade across his throat.

Sanchez felt an overwhelming weakness close over him, suffered the darkness at the edge of his sight loom larger and larger, enveloping his existence. The front of his shirt had become totally soaked with his blood, it welled from the gash in his neck and a curious panic rose in him, knowing he was trapped in this body from which the life was draining away.

Intriguingly he felt himself become detached, heard his own voice feebly asking why. He couldn't see anything else, his sight was gone and his sentence; his prison, was almost completed. All that remained was the swaying noise of the traffic outside the car.

Death closed its fingers around Eduardo Sanchez and his chest completed its final feeble gasp for air.

*

'What?!'

'That's right Senator,' his aide, Bob, confirmed. 'Eduardo Sanchez is dead, murdered in the back of his own car on the way from the airport this evening. The person who did it got away as the car stopped at a set of traffic lights.'

'Shit!'

'Worse than that, I'm afraid, Senator. Local law enforcement specialists think the hit was to do with drugs. It appears one of Sanchez's operations was a cover for drug smuggling and that he'd gotten greedy. He was muscling in on the Cucuta Cartel's territory.'

'Well, we thought that might happen once Suarez was killed. Somebody had to fill the vacuum.'

Bob coughed: part apologetically, partly out of a sadistic desire to prolong his boss's discomfort. 'Apparently Cucuta was being run quite well after the death of Fernando Suarez. Seems the new boss was annoyed by Sanchez's attention.'

'Well? Who was it?' demanded Johnson, tiring of Bob's game.

'Somebody you know quite well, sir.'

Johnson summoned all his willpower to ignore the faint inflection of insubordination in his employee. 'Get on with,' he retorted testily.

'Penelope Hortez.'

Johnson sat down heavily in the sofa that occupied one wall of his expensively decorated Washington office. His chest felt tight and it seemed difficult to find enough air.

'How?' was all he could manage.

'Penelope Hortez is the widow of Fernando Suarez.' It was a bold statement yet laden with inference and doom.

'Shit, Bob, I'm meeting her later today. We killed her kids!'

'Yes sir, I know you did.'

'We, Bob! We did. Fuck!! This is a disaster.'

'Yes sir.'

Johnson stared out the window opposite where the

cupola of the US Congress building rose into the blue afternoon sky of Washington. It was plain where Bob was headed – for the exit, like shit off a shovel. He could see his political career disappearing down the john faster than a turd on a flush.

He had to sort out Hortez before the bitch got him first.

'Get my Security Service detail commander on the line.'

'Sure.'

Johnson could feel the sweat of fear trickling down his sides. What did he do about the bitch? Where would she hit him? Would it be on the way to their meet? Or as he moved from car to restaurant? In the restaurant?

'Senator?'

The voice of his Security Service agent echoed in his head and the fuzzy picture of the man swam into view on his Zeus display. Fucking gimmick, but seeing the man's face made him feel a little calmer.

'Cal, we have a problem.'

'So I understand from your aide sir.'

'Well what are you going to do about it?' Johnson could sense the testiness of his demand and instantly regretted it.

'What would you like us to do?'

'I'd like you to kill the woman, preferably slowly, but quick will do, given the circumstances.'

'Okay.' A pause. 'I understand you're going to meet her tonight.'

'That's right.'

Another pause filled the ether. 'Normally I'd sanction against that but it might work for us this time.'

'You think?' Johnson left his usual sarcasm out of

465

the statement, seeking any way out of his current predicament. After all Cal was his one ticket out of this nightmare.

'Yes Senator. But you have to do exactly what we say. Do not deviate at all.'

'No, no I won't. What's the plan?'

'Well sir it's this …'

*

The driver hauled the semi onto the hard shoulder as the cell he'd been provided bleeped at him. His hirers had been quite clear: he could do nothing to jeopardise the security of his load and that included using a cellphone on the move.

Reaching for the vibrating phone he hit the answer icon and held the device to his ear.

'Where are you now?'

The driver consulted his sat nav. It said he was just under sixty miles from the capital.

'You've done well,' affirmed the caller when he told him. 'Okay, reprogram your sat nav for the address I text you. Then delete the text and destroy the phone.'

'What? Throw it away?' The driver looked longingly at the device. it was the latest Samsung: an ultra-thin device with the latest, edge to edge, dynamic display.

'No. You'll find a small bottle of acid in the glove compartment. You'll use that to erase the phone's memory skin and then you'll set fire to it. The chemical fire will destroy the integrity of the device.'

It seemed such a waste, then, as if the caller could divine his thoughts, the voice instructed him further. 'Should you be tempted to pocket the phone and think to reprogram it, be warned, we will be able to trace you and we will be extremely angry with you. You don't want us to be extremely angry.'

Something in the other's voice told him this was true, so the driver murmured his acquiescence with the demand.

'Good. We will see you shortly. Here's the text and ... don't forget to destroy the phone.'

The driver looked at the contents of the message, entered the address into the satnav, then opened the door and climbed down from his cab, bottle of acid in one hand, phone in the other. Dropping the device on the verge, he opened the acid and carefully poured it over the phone. A hiss emanated from the surface and acrid smoke curled in the air before him. When it seemed to stop he pulled his lighter from his pocket and torched it. The fumes caught the flame and blossomed and he suddenly dropped the lighter on the verge. Both seemed to writhe as the flames engulfed them, as if they were alive; in agony.

He shook his head: what a waste. Climbing back in the cab he selected drive on the semi-automatic gearbox, pulled back onto the freeway and headed towards the city.

*

'Any news on the search?'

Logan shook his head. It was more than frustrating. Just a few hours ago it had seemed they were about to put paid to the plot, and then it had all crumbled into the dust of a Kentucky highway. He had been impressed by the helicopter pilot's quick thinking; he'd have been even more impressed had the Kamov been in the containers.

Now darkness was crowding in on the Capitol and there were just under two days before the funeral which Carlisle, in a fit of bravado, had decided to attend in person unlike the original, best plan. Bloody politicians: either they prevaricated incessantly or were overly bullish in the face of things they didn't understand.

Black scratched his head. 'Are we looking from the wrong end of the problem again?'

Logan looked round; the others all turned their attention to the SEAL. 'How do you mean?' asked the British agent.

'We're looking for one or two trucks heading for the city. But there can't be many places where an attack helicopter can be put together. There's gonna be a big team of guys and some heavy lifting equipment on hand to crane pieces together.'

It was true. The Kamov had been designed for easy transport to battlefields as dismantled parts and then screwed together in the field. But there still needed to be equipment and a team of mechanics to get it all together. And they would have to have some guys who were type rated to ensure it all happened without mishap.

Reed was the first person to the keyboard for the tactical planning screen, which had taken pride of place on the situation room displays. Her fingers flew over the key icons on the table top interface. 'Okay, what we think is this. A plane landed at Albuquerque and unloaded the Kamov in crated parts. There'll be largish components to make assembly quicker but, you're right John, they'll need some heavy support equipment to help them put it together. We know they're not on the sixty-four because they wouldn't send two trucks on the same route – too risky.

'So that gives two possibilities,' Reed pulled up a display showing Louisville where the trucks had been pulled up, 'either north or south of the sixty-four.' She scrolled up and down, consulting the map like some archaeologist divining the runes of an ancient civilisation.

'South takes them away from the capital and into territory occupied by too many active military bases. However, to the north they come into some large spaces where, like the mine outfit, terrorists can get lost. Additionally, they have a better flight path into the target.' She scrolled the display and stopped it, the cursor hovering over Arlington Cemetery. 'Less warning, more chance of success.'

She looked at the group. 'They're somewhere on the I-seventy, probably not far from the capital.'

Sixty

Camino looked at his cell and dropped the device to the table. Fouré glanced over enquiringly: the look on the FBI agent's face wasn't good.

'We're being pulled off the drugs investigation. Raven Rock has another immediate problem, related to the terrorist threat.'

Fouré felt his heart sink. 'What?'

Camino shook his head as if he couldn't quite believe what he'd just heard. 'They're saying a Russian made attack helicopter is being brought to the capital, for a strike on the Presidential funeral day after tomorrow.'

In his shock, Fouré snorted his surprise and derision. 'Seriously?' Camino nodded. 'No! No way! That isn't gonna happen. How the hell are a bunch of two bit terrorists gonna get a whole helicopter into the country without anybody noticing?'

'Apparently they shipped it under the cover of agricultural parts. Then they set up a two vehicle decoy convoy, which was stopped outside Louisville in Kentucky. It matched the details picked up by NSA … right down to the part about there being a chopper on the trucks.'

'Shit!'

'And then some,' agreed Camino heavily. 'Anyway, they figure that another two trucks are on the way into the city, probably via interstate seventy. The administration wants every available agent working on a search of likely facilities that could put together a chopper within thirty-six hours or so.'

'Fuck me.' Fouré drew a weary hand across his face. 'Thirty-six hours to find a chopper.'

'Or less. It's gotta be ready before the funeral. Added to that they believe there's going to be a diversion by ground threats.'

'What type of diversion?'

'Suicide bombers, shooters … they're not clear. They want us to follow up on some activity that's been registered by NSA over the last twenty-four hours.'

'Whereabouts?'

Camino hesitated, taking a long look at the Capitol Police Captain. Fouré caught the expression; he didn't think his heart could sink any further. 'Where?' His voice sounded small and lost.

The FBI agent coughed. 'Your neighbourhood: they believe the next attack is going to originate in Alexandria.'

'Are they sure?'

'Not a hundred per cent, no,' confirmed Camino, 'but they've been recording cell phone and internet activity that started ramping up just in the last thirty-six hours. At least three-quarters of that originates from a mosque on Washington Street in Old Town.'

Fouré slammed a hand on his desk. 'Fuck that man! He'll be the death of us all!' For the merest moment Fouré let slip his Haitian heritage.

'I guess you know something.'

The Police Captain scowled at Camino. 'The mosque you mentioned is run by the imam, Faisal Huq, a Pakistani who came to Washington some ten years ago with his father, Mohammed, and two sisters.'

'Mother?'

'Was killed by the Taliban for being a teacher.'

471

Camino's eyebrows rose in surprise. 'And now he's a radical?'

Fouré nodded. 'Sure. The guy held the same views as his father and it seems that his mother's murder was something his father at least had presaged for some time before the event. He certainly did nothing to protect her. We think Old Man Huq physically abused her himself prior to her death, though it's not clear.'

'I don't understand why he didn't just stop her from going to work if that was the issue.'

'There's some evidence that they'd separated before she went to the school and perhaps she did that because she knew it would enrage him. Paradoxically, he's known to have been distraught when she was killed, and that led to him leaving the country with his family.

'When he came to the States he moved to Washington, which was a favourite destination for a lot of Asian immigration, back then. Old man Huq opened an electrical shop in Old Town and it was there that he was murdered three years ago by a couple of white guys who were after money for drugs.'

'What of Faisal?'

Fouré shook his head slowly. 'Faisal seemed to be a good, but peaceful, Muslim up to that point. I guess the murder of both his parents was enough to reinforce his view of the decadence and depravity of Western society.'

'But his mother was killed by the Taliban ...' Camino was confused.

Fouré smiled sardonically. 'You forget. Mrs Huq was a teacher of women, in a devoutly Islamic part of the country - Waziristan. It's an area which sees the teaching of, and by, women as infiltration into their society of Western values: demeaning to their religion and beliefs.'

Camino looked out the Portakabin's windows at the blackened and cracked Lincoln Memorial. Agents and Police personnel still swarmed over the site, diligently piecing together the final parts of the monstrosity of the terrorist attack. He liked to think that, had the perpetrator survived and been caught, his agents would have made every attempt to arrest and bring him (or her, he reminded himself) to justice.

But, as likely, they would have put a bullet through the terrorist's head if they'd cornered the individual – summary justice. People weren't all that different, whatever their persuasion, religion or political outlook.

'Fuck!' He brushed his hands through his hair in frustration. 'Well, we have to get down there and figure this out.'

Fouré's head bobbed in sympathy; then he rose from his chair. Still immaculate in his white shirt and black tie he un-holstered his Glock, checked the magazine and chambered a round. Slipping the safety back on, he jammed the weapon back in its holster and stared squarely at Camino. 'Let's do it.'

*

The semi's driver pulled his vehicle off the Interstate and drove, as directed, for another half hour through the industrial district of Frederick, Maryland. A sleepy, provincial town of some sixty-six thousand people, Frederick was predominantly white and African-American, and Old Glory flew from poles across the suburbs, a forest of red, white and blue.

473

The driver was patriotic, but he was increasingly dissatisfied with the government and the direction taken on immigration, jobs and the economy. Though, like many people, he had mourned the death of Jonah Lincoln he didn't mourn the impending death of his administration. That stupid bitch Carlisle had holed herself up under The Rock (he allowed himself the luxury of ignoring the fact that any other President would have done the same in the face of an active threat of a terrorist attack) and was as ineffectual as a glass of water after a chilli burger. Though he didn't know what he was carrying he knew it was for patriots; people who wouldn't sell the United States of America, or the flag, down the drain for the popular vote. That made the journey ok for him; the money was a bonus and would help his kids, coz, fuck knows, the Democrats wouldn't.

A sign shone in the headlights. This was it. He pulled over to the centre of the carriageway, indicating to turn down the side road. The headlights of his truck pierced the gathering gloom of the summer night. Warehouses rose out of the ground, monuments of small town enterprise. The driver continued slowly on his way, looking for one particular business.

His destination was at the end of the cul-de-sac. It stood directly ahead of him, the headlights of his truck fighting with the final light of the setting sun. Two black vans sat in the car park, pointing the way he'd come. He could just make out the occupants. Pulling the truck and trailer into the compound he circled in front of the vans and then proceeded to reverse towards the warehouse doors, which were flanked by the vans.

Brakes applied, he stepped down from the cab and

waited. From the van on his right one of the occupants exited and came over to him.

'Everything okay?'

The driver nodded. He looked round as the others joined who was, evidently, their leader.

'You weren't followed.'

'Not that I'm aware of, no.'

'Good.'

Even as he registered the movement he couldn't believe what he saw.

At that range, the bullet couldn't miss as it was catapulted from the chamber of the Colt Browning 1911. The projectile exploded from the back of the driver's head, spewing blood, brain matter and viscera. His assassin knew the man was dead even before the body hit the ground, empty of life and humanity. Nothing could be left to chance, his mentor had told him; nothing: the American dream needed decisive action for its survival.

The assassin beckoned to his colleagues. One climbed into the truck; the other two grabbed the corpse, wrapped it in plastic and loaded it into the back of one of the vans. He went into the warehouse and lifted the doors. They had no time to lose: there was a helicopter to build.

*

'Law enforcement agencies have drawn a blank.'

'Bastard!'

Logan looked at the screens and knew, instinctively, that things would go down to the wire. How to stop a maniac like Faulkner? He paused. No, Faulkner wasn't a maniac, he was being very methodical and he had a clear objective. This was

475

fanaticism; and that was different. A fanatic had purpose and the drive to ensure the goal was reached and nothing stood in the way to deflect. He would cover his tracks wherever possible and ensure that nobody could be traced back to him. That, potentially, was a mistake.

That probably meant a lot of bodies.

The next one would be closest to the fanatic; would be close to where the helicopter was to be launched. Find the corpse and you were close to the helicopter.

Except that would be too late. Faulkner would be on his way by the time they found a body, tracked backwards to where the helicopter was built and Faulkner would be launching his attack. So how else did you track down a person who was intent on using such a major tool of violence?

What was the helicopter's radius of action?

'Helen, can you call up aircraft recognition stats?'

The tactician nodded. 'Sure.'

The main displays scrolled open. 'What you looking for?'

Logan bit his lip. 'I want to see the specs for the Hoodoo.'

'Just a minute.' Helen Reed's fingers strolled over the key icons, shining from the surface of the table. On the big screen a helicopter three view filled the display. A photograph showed a sleek looking machine with a side-by-side cockpit, stub wings and a long rotor shaft which housed two rotors spinning in opposite directions, the latter being a typical Kamov design statement. The long tail boom ended in a twin tail empennage. Wings either side of the main fuselage held rocket launchers, and the end plates were occupied by launch rails for air-to-air missiles.

476

Under the thin nose were the optical guidance and sensors that were the eyes of the helicopter crew, while beneath the fuselage sat a barbette for a GsH 37mm three-barrel rotating cannon.

'That's one mean motherfucker.' Black regarded the photos. 'Low observable technology, anti-radar paint scheme will keep it invisible for long enough. Faulkner has picked his kit well. Can he fly one?'

Logan picked up the note of doubt in the other's voice. 'No he can't himself, but we have to assume he has access to somebody who can. That means somebody who's come into the country recently from Russia, or one of the Border States which have access to Russian military equipment. They would have to have come here fairly recently to be type rated. The Hoodoo is an upgrade of the Hokum but it's only been operational for about two years.'

'What's the range on this thing?'

Logan squinted at the screen. 'That's what I'm looking for … ahh, here we go. It has an operational range of … three hundred and seventy-five miles. It can operate from forest clearings and similar, is fully aerobatic rated and has zero-rated ejection seats. It can stay on station for four hours, even at maximum range.'

Black raised an eyebrow. 'Don't think he'll be around that long.'

'No, and he won't want to risk a flight of three hundred plus miles. Nor will he be too far from where he's having it assembled.'

'He'll be safer to base anywhere within a two-hundred-mile radius. After all, this thing can do three hundred and eighty knots – it's no slow coach. He'll want to get in and out as quickly as possible. Combine speed with a radius, which is within the machine's maximum, and that is your threat.'

All eyes concentrated on Reed. Her clarity and ability to work out the logistics of a threat were second to none.

'What else?'

Reed considered Black's question. 'Given that they've likely brought the machine in from the north of Washington I think they'll keep to the west as well. The wooded valleys will help them hide the operation on the ground, while the slopes will cover the approach of the helicopter for as long as possible.'

'Back into the hills huh?' Black glanced over at Logan and pulled a tired hand across his face.

Logan laughed, a coarse noise borne of their previous experience. This was going to be hard. Could they get the fucking thing before it got that far? He articulated his concern. 'We need to have people on the ground finding this thing as soon as.' He slapped the table in frustration.

A blonde-haired woman with grey eyes and open, fine features raised a finger like a child trying to attract the attention of her teacher, though there was no sense she really wanted to ask anything. It was more ironic; that she had something they wanted. Logan dipped his head to indicate she could speak.

'Let the thing get in the air.'

Black looked at the woman as if she'd suddenly grown two heads. 'Are you for real?' When the woman merely looked back, the SEAL continued. 'We're talking about a helicopter that is hard to detect and can fight its own way out of a situation.'

'And we're talking about a situation where there's been a "no-fly" order since Air Force One went down. I know it's a risk but how likely do you think it is that you're gonna find one helicopter on the ground before the funeral? It's gonna be the only thing flying on the day – apart from the two Raptors that'll be up its ass.'

'Who are you?'

The blonde woman grinned, knowing that she'd got under the SEAL's skin. 'Brooke Murtagh, FBI. Director Souster has assigned me to the op.' She leaned back in her chair with the easy authority of a person in control; sure of herself beyond polite. Logan liked her.

'So you think we should leave this part of the op?'

She took in the Brit. He was less uptight than the SEAL which she figured was unusual. He was good looking but with a secret, some mystery that made him appear tired. Would that blunt him in a fight? 'Hell no! We need to know where this fucker is holed up. But, consider this, if the helicopter,' she said "helicopter" as she would talk about "boy's toys", 'is out in the open, it makes everybody's fucking job easier.'

Brooke Murtagh noted how everybody flinched every time she used an obscenity and it excited her to exercise control over others. They were where she wanted them. A good looking woman, and she considered herself that, was always intimidating when she swore and got filthy in the presence of men, and Brooke liked to intimidate. It had taken her all her willpower, intelligence and not a little sexual exploitation to become a senior agent in the FBI. Local director in some branch was her next step on the ladder, and she was only twenty-eight, so there was still some time for her to achieve that before she was thirty.

'I get where you're going with that,' Logan confirmed, 'and it makes sense. What's happening on

479

the ground then to make sure we can do this?'

Murtagh decided she liked the Brit. 'We've got local law enforcement searching any facility that may have been abandoned, may be being used by an organisation or person that has anything to do with either Islamic extremism or home grown fundamentalist – or whatever else shit these folk come out with. The law has been told not to engage but to keep surveillance.'

'Is that your idea?'

Murtagh inclined her head. 'Maybe. I informed Director Souster that we ought to be controlling the situation rather than playing catch up. I don't like playing catch up.'

Logan caught the smile which threatened to break out across his face. He really liked this woman.

'I hope you're right Agent Murtagh and that we don't get the President killed.'

Murtagh sighed at the SEAL commander. 'Well, we already got one killed, Lieutenant Black. I, for one, intend it doesn't happen again. That would just be shit.'

Logan covered his mouth, but he couldn't help the smile this time. This woman was definitely something else. Black merely scowled at the FBI agent who returned the look with a "sweet as" expression on her face. Logan noted the eyes were hard as flint.

'Okay, do we wait for the reports to come in?'

'No point us running around the countryside getting in the way of our teams,' she told him. 'We'll be better placed here to process intel as it comes in and enabling teams to respond faster.'

Black coughed. 'It seems shit to be sat here waiting for something to happen. It'd be better to be looking for evidence.'

Murtagh regarded him condescendingly. 'Lieutenant, the data will come to us and we can play backstop if we're here to be the last line of defence. That way we can't be outwitted by these guys. Patience, I think the action will find us soon enough.'

Sixty-One

Penelope Hortez was conscious of the temperature in the restaurant, or perhaps it was more to do with her discomfort – she was unclear for the first time in her life. Waiting for the man who had been her lover and then the killer of her children, and on whom she had placed a death sentence, she felt her own life was coming to an end.

What was left?

'Penelope'

She whirled as if she'd been slapped. There he was: as strong and confident as ever. Mid-fifties, groomed, hair perfectly cut and styled, brown eyes still deep and still the characteristic which had drawn her in. Yes, he was fit; yes, he was tall but the eyes had questioned and answered in equal turn.

And he had ordered the strike that had killed your children, retorted the voice in her head.

'Drink?'

There was an air of caution emanating from him, as if he was aware what was happening. She had to be careful. Her smile was always her friend in such situations. She flashed it now, the glistening lips inviting and enticing her one-time lover.

'Vodka martini with extra olives.'

He nodded as if he'd just been addressed by the trash man, and attracted a waiter. Where was her hit?

Their drinks arrived quickly but then he was well known and people knew what he expected. She sipped absent-mindedly and took an olive.

'You wanted to see me. About what?'

He knew. There was something in his tone that suggested that he was ahead of the game. She resisted the urge to go to the john.

'Yes, Harry. There is something we need to sort out.'

Harry Johnson laughed, suddenly leaning forward. 'What would that be then, Penelope? Killing your bastard children? Finding out you're actually the wife of Fernando Suarez, drug dealer and smuggler? Oh, and he was so good you had to fuck me!' Spittle flecked his chin as he hissed the words, the accusation, at her. And the cold beauty of it, she saw, was that nobody in the restaurant picked up on the bile; the exchange. She felt something strange inside: fear and venom, mixed in a cocktail. She wanted to see the man die.

'So you know.'

Harry Johnson laughed and, subjectively, she remembered the good times that had accompanied that sound.

'Yes, I know and I know that you're going to try and exact some sort of revenge. Good luck honey. This place is crawling with Secret Service and, when I leave here, there are more outside,' he waved his hand, always maintaining a charade of dignity and bonhomie. 'Bring it on bitch,' he drained his glass of wine and reached across: she flinched. Instead he kissed her lightly on the cheek and rose in one fluid movement. Then, for all to hear: 'I've got to go honey. It was lovely to meet up again. See you soon and take care.'

She watched him walk from the restaurant and realised she was trembling with the emotion of the moment. God! It would be good to see the bastard lying dead on the pavement.

*

483

A block back, a grey Mercedes G-Class sat next to the curb on the same side of the road as the restaurant that Senator Harry Johnson was just exiting. The occupants were all silent, intent on monitoring the restaurant, the Senator's Secret Service detail and the traffic generally. Another block behind them was a Mercedes C63AMG which, when the word was given, would leapfrog the G-Class and carry out the act.

Harry Johnson would become a high profile statistic in the life of Washington DC.

Everything was ordered: they merely had to wait for the right moment.

*

The occupants of the black Audi Q7 sat quietly and purposefully. They had received orders from the embassy. Johnson and Hortez were equal problems. They both had to become a full stop in the chapter tonight. However things transpired over the next few hours, neither could live to see the new day.

*

Harry Johnson walked from the restaurant and climbed into the Lincoln Town Car. He couldn't understand why he didn't feel satisfied, complete, by his exchange with Penelope Hortez. She'd been uncovered and offered no rebuff, which had been telling in itself: not that he'd have believed her had she remonstrated her innocence. But he felt there was something missing. He felt the bulk of his Remington revolver under his jacket. A shot would have satisfied some inner demon but would have been … moronic, stupid, fucked up?

He settled back in his seat. Never mind. The protection around him would deal with whatever that South American bitch might throw at him. He leaned forward.

'Okay, take me home.'

The Lincoln pulled out, and behind, the Suburban followed, pulling into the centre lane a car back to cover the rear. Nothing could harm the Senator.

*

Further back the G-Class pulled away from the kerb, followed by the C63AMG. The occupants were impassive: concentrated on their objective.

*

The Q7 made to join the traffic, four vehicles behind and in another lane where they could see the target vehicles. As the driver checked for a gap the man next to him nodded at a message from his cell and laid a hand on the driver's arm.

A shake of the head.

Stay.

*

Harry Johnson's limousine drew up at the lights. Behind, was the Suburban; Secret Service personnel tooled up and ready to protect, as seemed inevitable. He relaxed and poured himself a whiskey from the bar. The liquid hit, and comforted him. He smiled.

Light flooded into the limousine and Johnson turned in his seat to make out the shape of a car close behind. What was his protection squad playing at,

485

letting a car get so close? He pressed the intercom.

'Paul, we're gonna have to move.'

'I know sir, the lights will change in a moment.'

'Hurry up,' demanded the Senator tetchily.

The limousine pulled away from the lights and the Senator was relieved to see the lights of the other car swerve away as it pulled out and around. No cause for alarm – just some late night show-off.

The bullets pushed through the metal before the sound hit them. The hot laceration of molten lead thrust into his body with a force that stunned and buckled his flesh around him.

His driver gunned the motor and floored the accelerator in a bid to get away, but the Mercedes easily kept station with them. From the rear window, the gunner kept laying rounds down into the back of the car and Johnson was losing the fight. He could sense his life leaking from the holes in his flesh, hot liquid, rapidly turning cold, stained his shirt and jacket as his sight tunnelled.

*

Johnson's Security Service detail were caught off guard but responded quickly, bringing accurate gunfire down on the Mercedes saloon. But even as they registered hits on the back of the car they were being fired on. Heavy rounds hit the back of the SUV, the driver struggled as he tried to compensate for the power of the gunfire which threatened to overturn his vehicle.

Then a lucky shot hit the offside rear tire and the SUV sank, like a wounded Wildebeest being bitten on its haunches. It veered and skittered across the carriageway in a shower of sparks before hitting a streetlight and bouncing away.

The driver, wounded and bleeding managed to see a grey shape rush past, a shark on the Washington streets, before he succumbed to the loss of blood and the Suburban slammed into a shop window. Metal crumpled and screeched, imploding on the four agents inside it.

Inside the Lincoln, Johnson's driver pushed his foot to the floor but it was an unequal struggle. The Mercedes easily kept pace. From the rear a masked man held up a G36 and kept the trigger depressed, stopping only to change magazines.

First one and then two, three, five, ten bullets slammed into the driver's body, shaking him like a rag doll as he tried to pull away. He slumped against the rim of the wheel and his dead weight pushed down on the accelerator, veering across the next interchange and slamming into a row of shops.

The C63 screeched to a halt and behind so did the G-Class. Occupants jumped from the C63 and lashed the scarred body of the Lincoln with bullets, concentrating gunfire on the back windows. Satisfied they ran back to the C63 which slewed in a wail of tyre smoke. The G-Class followed close behind.

*

The occupants of the Q7 watched impassively as Penelope Hortez exited the restaurant. They would know when the time was right.

They waited as she looked up and down the road, waiting for her car to appear. Her driver drew up in a blue DB9. She smiled at the doorman and dropped a tip in his waiting hand, as she gracefully walked past him and dropped easily into the car. The young man admired the view and then enjoyed the car as it sped away from the restaurant.

Behind, a ghost in the night traffic, the matt black Q7 followed. A couple of interchanges down they were diverted because of a huge incident. Hortez's DB9 slowed to take in the carnage, before driving indifferently from the scene. Police cruisers sealed off the road and activity was ramping up. The occupants of the Q7 could see ambulances appear in the rear view as they followed Penelope Hortez away from the death of Harry Johnson.

One down, one to go.

*

Penelope Hortez knew they were being followed. Despite driving a dark car her pursuers showed little inclination to hide. She didn't know who they were; it was unlikely they were American operators for the government, or Johnson. That meant either somebody working for Sanchez or … Chinese? She was unclear why they might be after her. Best not to find out.

'We're being followed.'

Carlos nodded 'I've seen,' he answered, and pushed the accelerator to the floor: the Aston leaped forward, into the light rimmed tunnel of night which stretched ahead, pockmarked with red driving lights. He steered fluidly, without hesitation, moving around cars and accelerating as the conditions allowed. All the time he checked the satnav for a direction away from this and back to … what? The hotel? That was probably a bad move – where then?

Just lose them.

That was the first thing in this instance, a lesson her dead husband had often drummed into her. If you can't fight, he used to say, there is no shame in fleeing, to fight another day. Just remember who has made you run.

Closing on the junction, Carlos was aware of the Q7, just two cars behind, almost unhurried despite his attempt to shake them. The lights ahead were still on green. Timing would be everything but would they stop if the lights were red when they reached them; or ignore them in a desire to catch the Aston? The next action would be an indicator of intent.

Their car was almost at the line, coasting in second as he willed the lights to change. Carlos glanced at the lights, waiting for that winking out of the green eye to be replaced by deep dangerous red.

Suddenly it blinked at him and Carlos dropped into first, the bellowing V12 screaming at the abuse of the car's gearbox, and the chance to be unleashed. Penelope clenched the seat instinctively. The tyres bit into the tarmac and howled at their torture, as the Aston thrust forward into the dark.

And, right behind was the Q7.

Slotting through the gears he knew he was attracting attention, as the DB9 weaved through the traffic with the precision of a needle through fabric. The big Q7 was gamely attempting to keep up but it was proving difficult and Carlos felt a certain satisfaction at the realisation that their pursuers were falling behind.

The truck hit the Aston as it flashed across another interchange, trying to ride the line between green and red. Penelope's head slammed against the door glass, making her retch. The car looped across the interchange, riding on the bumper of the semi, which deposited them on the sidewalk before continuing on its way.

Penelope shook her head, sickness rising from her gut and the numbness of her damaged body causing her to squint. The car careered down the sidewalk, banging against buildings until its momentum finally dissipated.

The silence was sudden and cloying, frightening in an instance as it was filled by the sound of a powerful engine and the application of squealing brakes. She had to get out, had to move!! But there was no response from her broken body. Fuck! Fuck! She looked across at Carlos. His eyes were empty and blood stained his chin.

Leather scraping across tarmac, quick and clipped presaged the approach of her attackers. Penelope groaned as she willed her recalcitrant body to work – fucking work, damn you!

The footsteps walked passed her right side. Then suddenly, a face appeared, the body bending down to look in at her. Chinese – as she'd suspected but not knowing why they wanted her dead. It was insane. 'What do you want with me? Why do you want to kill me?'

Her assailant continued to look and a sardonic smile curled his young lip. His gloss black hair shone in the lights of the street, lights that were dimming as she grew faint. She had to get out – why couldn't she move? A movement, but to her left: somebody reaching in to her; a hand moving the hair from her neck. She wanted to fight back, but her arms wouldn't move and a rising tide of panic threatened to engulf her, drag her into its damning embrace.

Penelope didn't feel the pinprick of the needle pushing into her carotid artery but she felt its messenger flooding into her, felt the numbness spread. She looked over at the smiling Chinese man, but it was only her two boys smiling and giggling, beckoning her to join them. She reached out to them, to take their hands and for them to lead her to safety. She felt herself become comfortably numb.

The two men got back in the Q7 and the driver pulled away. A short way up the road it stopped once more, an occupant exited with a G36, and unloaded the clip until the tank burst into flames. As they left, fire engulfed the broken Aston, taking the last member of Cucuta Cartel on her final journey.

*

Morning was seeping into his bedroom in the Chinese Embassy, Bogota when Yuan's mobile chimed. The first rays of the sun speared the sky over the humid hills surrounding the city and night was peeled back like the skin of an orange. Instantly he was awake, his brown eyes surveying the time on the clock: six-fifteen. Five-fifteen in Washington. A flicker of butterfly wings was the one concession to nerves he allowed, quickly controlled as his finger pressed the receive icon.

'Well?'

'It's done.'

'Both of them?'

'Yes. Her people concluded the first part and we completed the contract.'

'Are you returning home then?'

'No, we're going on to the meet in Toronto.'

So, yes, then. 'Very well, let me know when you're heading back then.'

'Will do. We should be in Toronto by early afternoon. We'll let you know then.'

The line went dead and Yuan placed his mobile

back on the bedside table which was just being caressed by the early morning sun's rays. The warmth on his hand felt a good omen. Just a couple of things to sort out and everything would be settled.

Sixty-Two

Fouré's regulation black Dodge Charger RT/Plus sat at an angle to the kerb, black wheels further offset, blue and red lights flashing in a statement of presence. The big Haitian was pushing through the melee of police officers and local people, creating a bow wave of humanity behind which Camino lumbered gamely. There was much shouting and posturing from angry locals protecting their mosque and officers, some with weapons drawn, trying to impose themselves.

Camino was impressed by the way in which both sides became subdued as the tall Fouré strode into the midst of them. He didn't say anything, just turned slowly on one foot and lanced everybody with his stare. Satisfied, he looked at one young Muslim, still attempting to be the "big man", chest out, hooded eyes filled with what he thought, hoped, was dark menace.

'Go tell Imam Faisal I wish to speak with him.'

The young man stared at Fouré, but it was an unequal battle and suddenly he backed away, turned and walked quickly into the mosque. There was a pause, in which a murmur of puzzlement rippled through the crowd, and then, as quickly as he'd disappeared, the youth was back. 'Come with me.'

Fouré followed his guide into the mosque, removing his shoes and placing them on the rack alongside those of the youngster. Entering the main hall his eyes swept the space occupied by a number of men, armed and looking decidedly more dangerous than the callow youth who stood next to him. For a moment Fouré hesitated, aware of his chances.

'Welcome, brother.'

The voice was low, soft and engaging, and Fouré turned towards it. Faisal stood before him, a man of average height but with the energy of a fanatic shining from the dark eyes. His flowing back robes and black turban were new and Fouré felt vaguely disturbed by them. It was a more radical image than he was used to.

'Thank you, Imam,'

He nodded towards the street. 'Your people have caused quite a stir.'

Fouré ignored the bait. 'Shall we sit?'

The imam smiled, a guarded expression, and nodded, waving his hand towards a couch that was set against the far wall. He led and Fouré followed, acutely aware of his position, acknowledging the eyes of every man in the room, wishing they could thrust a knife between his infidel shoulder blades. They took positions at each end of the sofa, turned slightly away from each other as if to show displeasure of each other's position.

A woman appeared with a small tray, on which were two small bowls of black tea. Fouré smiled but declined. Faisal picked up his and looked at the Police Captain. 'You should, you know. Black tea is full of antioxidants.'

Fouré returned the look. 'I know, I don't think health is my greatest problem here, do you?'

Imam Faisal laughed; a good belly laugh, slightly incongruous. 'You are right brother.' The eyes didn't laugh. 'It is a pity that you have taken the side of the infidel. They are doomed you know.'

What did he say? Stick to the message.

'Imam, there is a grave threat to the safety of Washington, to this place.'

'A threat?' Imam Faisal arched an eyebrow in apparent innocence. 'I look out the window and I see many police men and police cars, lots of guns and many frightened locals. What is this threat Michel?'

Again, Fouré ignored the imam's question. 'I see guns in here too, Imam.'

The imam didn't flinch. 'What can I say? My people feel the need to protect themselves. Your officers turn up with guns and sirens and then push innocent people around, bullying them to answer questions; open doors, allow the invasion of their privacy. What do we do?'

Fouré paused and considered the man before him. A consummate political game player he protected himself first and foremost, sheltering behind those who were only too eager to give their lives for somebody else's cause. 'Cooperate. If you have nothing to hide you could open your doors to us and allow us to search for those who would destroy our democracy.'

'How did you come to embrace these lies, my brother? What happened to you when you took on the uniform of the Devil?'

The police captain shook his head; the divide had become too wide. Neither side could see the other, because of the ideological gulf that existed between them. 'I remember you teaching here five summers ago. You taught a Koran I believe in, the book I read to myself; to my children each night. A sermon of peace to all; no matter the injustice. What has become of you?'

Imam Faisal regarded the Haitian. Once upon a time he had wished to Allah that Michel Fouré would be his protégé, would follow him in the jihad. Now; he was the enemy and yet …

'Nothing has become of me Michel. I have remained true to Allah. It is you who have moved away from the truth.'

'No! You're wrong,' Fouré shook his head vigorously. 'There is nothing here that you say Allah denounces that cannot be found in any "Muslim",' his fingers pinched the air, 'country. Get real.'

'You cannot faze me Michel. Allah will be the final judge, but we pray to him daily: do you?'

Fouré didn't rise to the challenge. 'Faisal, there is a threat to the President of this country, to whom we both owe our lives and existence. I am sworn to protect the office as part of the oath I took to Allah, and country. One way or the other, my officers will search this area and ensure the threat isn't from here, like it or no.'

'That would not go well, my brother.'

'For either side, Imam, for any of us. But I will have this area searched and I will negate anything that appears, and I judge to be, a material threat.'

The smile was set. 'So be it. You will be able to walk from this building, but do not think it will be so easy to re-enter.'

'None of this is easy,' retorted the Haitian. 'People I have known as brothers now hold a gun, ready to defile the country they have come to see as home.'

Imam Faisal inclined his head, as if savouring the words Fouré had spoken. 'Do you think we are the only ones who believe this country needs to be humbled? You come here because a threat is spoken of and, immediately, you believe that it must be those who are the newest immigrants; those who are dedicated to the way of the true God, and yet you are blind to the very threat that lives in your comfortable midst.'

Fouré stepped forward and immediately those around the imam moved: the holy man lifted a hand to halt them.

'What do you mean by that?' A fear grew in the captain's gut and threatened to paralyse him.

Imam Faisal smiled. 'Look to your own, American. Do you really think we will dirty our hands and souls when there are so many stupid people here to die for their beliefs? The ones you want are not in this city. The one you seek is "The Convert".'

*

Moments later Fouré was on the streets again wondering how this was heading into Shit City so quickly. He saw the squat figure of Camino, the guy's expression questioning him silently. In answer he grabbed a megaphone from an officer.

'Listen up everybody. There is a clear and present danger of a terrorist threat which may originate from this area. You will search every building, whatever it is, and however it is held against you. National Guard is here,' Fouré indicated behind the assembled officers, to the military vehicles which had drawn up while he had talked to the imam, 'to assist you in that task.'

He reviewed the assembled officers.

'There is a direct threat to the President of the United States. You are looking for evidence of bombs, weapons and other paraphernalia of terrorism. Anything you find must be bagged and tagged. If anybody tries to stop you, you will arrest them.

'But only if you're not at threat. Otherwise you will use all force necessary to protect yourselves, and to ensure we negate the threat to President Carlisle.

497

'Make no mistake,' he continued. 'There are hostiles here and you are at risk. I expect you to do your utmost to minimise that threat but, if you are threatened by anyone, you are cleared to open fire to protect yourself and your companions.'

There was a murmur of approval from the officers and sullenness from the locals. And it was to these that the police captain addressed his next words.

'People of Alexandria. DC Police are about to start a house-to-house search for terrorist equipment. You will not obstruct this investigation. If you do, you will be arrested and taken from here for questioning, and possible charge for obstructing the course of justice.'

Fouré took another look across the motley assembly. 'Okay, people: let's get too it.' He put down the megaphone and turned to Camino who registered the look in the taller man's eyes and raised an eyebrow in question. The captain smiled weakly. 'We have a truly home grown threat.' He quickly told the agent what had transpired in the mosque. Camino's jaw set.

'What do we do now?' Fouré shook his head. 'There isn't enough time to find where this threat is really coming from.'

'I'll call it in. All we can do then is pray.'

*

A line of satisfied men took in the low, sleek, silhouette of the Hoodoo, squatting under the strip lighting: a malevolent creature after its namesake, its venomous sting in the shape of the gun barbette that lay in its belly. This scorpion was ready to bite.

The chief engineer took a last admiring glance and then turned to the person on his right. 'It's all yours

498

now. Wish you could do a shake down in this thing but I guess you'll just have to take our word for it.'

The other grinned and shook hands vigorously with the engineer. 'I'm sure it'll work just fine.' As he walked towards the brooding helicopter the pilot turned and looked back. 'When are you expecting our guest?'

A check of the watch. 'He'll be here in about two hours.'

'Okay. I'm going to go get some shut-eye then do some ground checks. Are you going to be able to protect our take off?'

The engineer nodded. A local Home Defence leader, he was known for marshalling all the local rednecks and doom merchants when the fancy, and Presidential vote, took him. The downing of Air Force One, with that Democrat pussy, Lincoln, on board, was a source of great rejoicing for him and his followers. He held the town in his thrall and he could pretty much do what he wanted hereabouts.

The pilot regarded his compatriot and he nodded, the understanding dawning on him. This was a place where loyalty to the flag was deeper than to the people who espoused the cause. That was good.

He smiled. 'Okay, I'll see you in an hour.'

Sixty-Three

Raven Rock Complex

The air con laboured under the number of people crammed in the main conference facility to hear Logan and Black address them. Both stood at the front of the room, surveying the assembly.

President Carlisle sat before them: Logan felt he was being measured. Carlisle continued to observe. One American, the other British, both, perhaps, holding the key to the survival of her nation. She was careful not to use the terms "her home", "her life", too personal, nor "the world's greatest nation". Maybe that age was over: after all, all things came to an end.

But not yet.

'So, gentlemen, what do you have for us?'

The two glanced across the space between them; expressions blank save to each other. It was a testament to the relationship they had built up that they knew what the other was thinking. Logan gave the nod to Black who addressed the assembly.

'Madam President, I'll deal with what is current, and forego rehashing the history if that's ok?' When she nodded in affirmation Black pointed to the display screen. 'We have two events under way at this time. The first of these is a series of joint operations between FBI and local law enforcement in the Washington suburbs of Vienna and Alexandria, to search for, and apprehend, potential Islamist terrorist threats which may try to disrupt the Presidential funeral tomorrow and attempt to assassinate you.' He couldn't resist looking at Carlisle who stared impassively back at him.

'The second is a wider operation involving NSA and CIA, as well as FBI and Law Enforcement, across a number of states. This is to seek and destroy a significant security threat, which is partly home grown, but also involves the use of equipment that will be a clear and present danger to the life of the President and other dignitaries.'

A hand went up at the back of the room, one of Black's SEAL team. 'What's the threat?'

He paused and stole a look at Logan. Now it had come to the point of publicity it sounded ludicrous in his head. 'We believe … a Russian helicopter has been smuggled into the country under the guise of agricultural machinery parts.' A low rumble of questions and rumour infected the gathering.

'What sort of helicopter?'

'Uh … an attack helicopter.'

Silence hung palpably in the air, a blanket of shock that suffocated response momentarily: then everything erupted in a volcano of expletives, oaths and questions. Black waited patiently while everyone calmed down and took stock. 'Okay, what we know is this. Some weeks ago this man,' he indicated a face on the screen, 'Rado Kiric, came in possession of a number of ex-Chechen military equipment, including this.' Black paused as he brought up a picture of a menacing looking helicopter on the screen: more expletives rippled through the now steamy atmosphere, as operators recognised what they were seeing.

'This is a Kamov Ka60 Scorpion, NATO codename "Hoodoo". Up until three weeks ago it was being tracked by an SAS unit across Near Asia. It

501

seems the smugglers got wind of them and a firefight ensued during which the packages were split up and the Kamov was lost to sight.'

'That's right,' Logan took up the story as if on a prearranged signal. 'Then GCHQ picked up an electronic trail that seemed suspicious. The manifest for a ship bound from Sierra Leone to Venezuela was changed at the last moment to include the transportation of agricultural machinery parts. That's typically code for armaments; however physical checks appeared to confirm the presence of such machinery on board. It was noted and a watching brief was set but the decision was made not to intercept. Shortly before the ship was to leave dock an Iranian Ilyushin Candid landed at Hastings Airport and two shipping containers were transported to the ship which appeared to be the last part of the existing agricultural consignment.'

'A fortnight later, the ship, under a Liberian flag, docked at Maracaibo. A Venezuelan Air Force Ilyushin transported the containers to Cuidad Juarez, from where they were driven over the border into Albuquerque.'

'How in God's name did all that happen?' In the electrified atmosphere of the room, David Chandler's bald head glistened red with his frustration.

Black shrugged, acutely aware that this wouldn't pacify the Director of Homeland Security. 'I think there are a number of factors involved in our eye being off the ball …' He was beginning to flounder when another voice, female, interjected.

'It's fair to say, Director, that there have been a number of events which appear to be unconnected, but which have been coordinated to enable this particular event to take place. However, we are in the position of understanding the purpose and the general direction of the attack.'

'Well, that should make it ok then … who are you?' Chandler allowed his frustration to tumble over his words as he glared at the young woman, who stared at him with a gaze bordering on insolence.

'Special Agent Murtagh.'

'Well, Special Agent Murtagh, I'm glad you can put a gloss on this for us.'

'Oh, I'm not doing that Director. This is a proper fuck up, no mistake,' she smiled inwardly at the director's face. 'But, we've had to deal with unprecedented terrorist and internet attacks; a flood of drug contaminated foodstuffs; followed up by actual drugs, with many people who've never experienced addiction succumbing, and the consequential circumstances which mean we've been weakened in our response. It's nobody's and everybody's fault. But that's not going to sort out where we are now.

'Like the boys said,' she smiled sweetly at Logan and Black, 'we have two serious issues. But I'm going to add another. I've just received a message from Special Agent Camino who is working with DC police on the terrorist attacks. There has been a series of shooting incidents in the city.' Her tone and face became grave and she sucked in everybody's attention. 'Senator Harry Johnson,' more gasps, 'was killed in a drive-by shooting at an interchange. In the ensuing gunfight his Secret Service team was ambushed and taken out. In what may be a related incident; one Penelope Hortez was also shot and killed in another drive-by only a mile or so away from Senator Johnson's death. Interestingly they were seen together shortly before the events, at a restaurant in the city.'

For the second time in a short while the room erupted in pandemonium, anger and fear. Logan could see the administration was in danger of losing control and lashing out blindly to bring instant gratification. He raised his arms to quieten the room down – he didn't succeed.

A piercing whistle cut through the boiling condition like a laser through metal. Everyone immediately stopped and looked for the source of the noise. A grim-faced Angela Carlisle motioned for calm. Everyone complied, stunned to silence by Carlisle's sudden interruption.

'Let's concentrate people: this will not help. What we know is that Drew Faulkner is planning an attack on tomorrow's funeral and that will probably be delivered from the air. As he'll be the only thing airborne, apart from our Military, he shouldn't be too difficult to pick out. That some form of diversion will be used, to scatter us in the – kill box – and make his job easier, is evident.' She turned to Brooke Murtagh. 'Do we have anything from the capitol on the progress of investigations being carried out now?'

Murtagh shook her head. 'But I'll get right on finding out.'

'Thank you. Mr Logan, Lieutenant Black: do we have any idea where this helicopter might be?'

Logan looked across at the SEAL who waved him on. 'Yes, we've given it serious consideration and we believe that it will be somewhere to the north-west of the city. That will keep it away from most of the major military installations; give it cover from the landscape and enable it to get as close as possible to the kill box before it is detected.'

'And what about construction and keeping it under cover till then?'

Black took up the argument. 'We expect it'll be hangared in some warehousing facility. Scorpions are designed to be easily assembled in the battlefield. They may have to move it under the cover of darkness to a forward operating location, to minimise the chance of discovery before it's too late.'

'That makes sense. So what is your plan? Are we going to put up a standing air patrol over the capitol?'

This is the tricky bit, decided Logan; this is where it may all go belly up. 'No, Madam President. We want to allow him to get in close, preferably disabling the helicopter at the site, which will enable us to capture him. We need to know who is behind these attacks and we can't do that if Faulkner is dead.'

Carlisle blanched. 'I don't mind taking risks, gentlemen but … are you sure?'

'We realise it's a big risk, but we have a response that will keep this in our control.'

'Go on,' but she wasn't sure.

Logan beckoned to a figure at the back of the busy room. The man made his way forward, a big, bald-headed Afro-American in the uniform of the US Marine Corps, bodyguards to the President. He swivelled in front of Carlisle and came smartly to attention, hand flicking up in a tight, crisp salute.

'Master Sergeant Leroy Durant, Madam President!' His Brooklyn twang was very evident as he introduced himself.

'At ease, Sergeant. So, you're going to be the one thing that stands between me and Faulkner. What's your particular skill sergeant?'

'I'm a Marine Corps sniper ma'am.'

'I hope you're a damn good shot sergeant.' The President smiled in what she hoped was a jokey fashion.

Durant's face never changed expression as he spoke. 'I am, ma'am. Top of my class; and Sniper One on my unit's last nine missions. Including the one just now in Venezuela.'

Carlisle nodded in appreciation. 'I heard about that mission. You have a commendation for your part in that, don't you?'

'That's right ma'am.'

'This is against a moving target, though. Will that be a problem?'

'No ma'am. I'm rated against materiel also. There isn't an issue for me with this mission.'

She regarded the big young Marine. His face was a stone wall: no emotion, just good, honest Marine attitude and resilience. 'It's good to hear that I'll be in good hands, so to speak, Sergeant.'

Durant dipped his head, unsure what to say. 'Ma'am.'

Carlisle turned to Logan and Black. 'Notwithstanding this, please forgive me gentlemen if I'm not more than a little concerned by the details of this planning. Is this the sum total of what you've come up with?'

The two looked at each other. 'It's a delicate situation Madam President. We're not sure how it will unfold and,' Black allowed the pause to unfold in the room, 'it was your decision to go ahead with the funeral.'

The moment intensified and it was as if there was an electric charge in the room. 'You got me there, Lieutenant,' Carlisle countered with a grin. 'So, I have a big target painted front and back? I guess we need to draw out the bastards and finish this thing once and for all.'

Even though it wasn't a question, Logan and Black

found themselves nodding in assent, because it seemed right.

Carlisle surveyed the room. It was her decision, hers alone and she understood that. Command was a lonely position and none exemplified that more than the office of the President of the United States of America. And Black was right: she had decided to buck the evidence, commonsense, whatever. Could she back down? Could she decide it wasn't a good idea and just order the traitorous son of a bitch killed?

But if she hid away, what message was she sending to al-Qaeda, the Taliban, anybody who thought it was okay to fuck America over? And then there was the Chinese. Were they just waiting for the fall?

Decisions ... she'd never thought they'd be hers to make. Jonah had been so inspirational in this: calm, considered and pragmatic. She had watched him at work and always admired his measured approach to office, life, relationships ... everything he did seemed to have evolved rather than been a reaction. How she wished that was a virtue of hers.

Perhaps now was the time. Just one more thing to ask. 'You're using a sniper to take out a helicopter. Wouldn't it be easier to use the Air Force?'

She sensed two opposing camps materialise in the room. Many started bobbing their heads in agreement; whispered words: "Air National Guard", "Raptor" and "appropriate response" bounced off the walls and ceiling. But, Carlisle, noted Logan and Black and their small team of professionals remained quiet. More to the point she saw both the Director of the NSA and Sarah Markham, who'd just entered the room, looking stern and resolute in the face of this new-found optimism.

507

The President picked on the NSA first. 'Gene, you look like you don't agree.'

Gene Hutchinson stared at his hands for a long moment while the room hushed. They were big hands with graceful fingers, or so his wife termed them. He hated them, but they were the cards he was dealt so get on with it. Just as now.

'Yes, Madam President, I don't. I'm sure Lieutenant Black will tell you the same, but we have no confidence that, if we were to put up a combat air patrol over the Capitol, it wouldn't be Firestormed by Faulkner. We have to presume that he has the technology now as has been used by his colleagues in the past. We know he'll want to disable Limo One.'

President Carlisle had figured that might be the reply, but inwardly, she felt as glum as the rest of the room showed outwardly, at this news.

'Worse, making that presumption a definite, if he deploys then it would confirm that the Chinese, or Chinese assets, are involved in the orchestration of the action.'

Angela Carlisle drew a breath, it seemed as though she might suck all the life from the room in order to protect her own. The Chinese – but Premier Yuan had appeared much more eager for ensuring that the new economic spring, currently spanning the two countries, continued under the next premier, the person to take up that post, to be decided upon next year.

'Are we sure about that?'

Hutchinson merely inclined his head in assent; it was Markham who spoke. 'Yes ma'am. We have credible intel that a Chinese political splinter may be reinforcing these terrorists. We believe, if that is the case, that the perpetrators are attempting regime change in Beijing.'

'Hell, do any of you people have any good news?' it was a heartfelt request which fell on stony ground. The target on her back suddenly seemed to have grown in diameter by several inches in the last few minutes. But, there was nothing to be done about it.

'Okay ladies and gentlemen. We have a traitor to catch, and I mean catch. If possible I want him alive so I know who the driver behind all this is. But if that isn't possible then I want to see the light go out in his eyes for what he has done to this great country.'

Sixty-Four

Frederick, Maryland

Sentries had been posted on all the approaches to the warehouse: red necks with guns who thought they had the freedom of the good ol' US of A at heart. Fucking morons. Drew Faulkner knew the truth of these people he was about to abuse and throw to the dogs. He felt no pity for them. They were ready to believe any old shit that was thrown at them in the name of patriotism.

He pulled his Volvo up by the access door to the warehouse, which was now a hangar for one of the world's most dangerous attack helicopters. A group of eager, heavy set men and women toting guns, crowded close to the car. These people believed they were hard-core patriots to the flag but, to him, they were cannon fodder and it felt extremely amusing to be using them in a jihad, by appealing to their patriotic hatred of Washington politicians. Thing was, he had credentials: bona fide American eagle, flag-waving credentials with the seal of action to back him up. Sure he was CIA, and he admitted that to them, but he'd seen the light and wasn't this the goddamnedest way to prove that he was a patriot like them?

Faulkner stepped to the ground and smiled at the engineer who was shuffling towards him in a gross parody of running. Billy Padgett was a leader of men like he, Faulkner, was prom queen, but it suited his purpose to pander to the man's delusions of grandeur.

'Yo, Drew! How you doing man!?' Effusive, ingratiating, he clamped Drew's hand between two slabs of sausages and pumped hard.

'I'm good Billy. You?'

'Better for seeing you man. Well, we got the damned thing finished for you and she's ready to go. Your pilot looks pretty darned pleased with it. Do you want to see?'

Drew stared at the man – *what do you think, dick?* 'Sure,' was what he said, 'let's take a look.'

Billy Padgett almost hopped from one foot to the other in his excitement, as he led Faulkner through the door into the warehouse. Almost theatrically he flicked on the lights.

The Scorpion sat hugging the floor, a malevolent presence. The matt black paint seemed to absorb the weak light; the double decker rotors drooped as if to protect the machine beneath.

'What do you think?'

The voice came from behind him and Faulkner turned to see his pilot standing just in the doorway. Frank Quincy was an ex-Army Apache pilot – one of the best and another patriot: highly intelligent in one way; a dumb hick in the only way that mattered.

'She's good. Sure you can fly this thing?'

Quincy nodded. 'Enough for what we have to do. Just hope there'll be no air defence over the Capitol.'

'If there is, you won't have to worry about it. That can be made to go away. Just get me close to the President.'

Quincy looked into Faulkner's eyes and caught a fleeting glimpse of something he'd never experienced before. It was something he wasn't sure he liked.

Fanaticism.

*

511

It was a breakthrough at last. Something they'd been waiting for, for two days now, ever since the abortive stop of the two semis in Louisville. Finally, something was going their way.

'We sure about the intel?'

'Absolutely,' confirmed Murtagh as she leant over the table to Logan. He mentally shook his head at the full-on attitude and the half-smile. 'And they have a body.'

'The driver of the rig?'

'Local law enforcement reckons so.'

'How long ago was the body found?'

Murtagh consulted her idev. 'About three hours past. It was dumped in a ditch. Nice people these patriots.' Nobody in the, now much emptier, situation room dissented.

'And the rig?'

Murtagh looked across at Black. 'That was found about forty miles from the body, burnt out, at an abandoned mine.'

'Well, they're doing a good job at keeping us from connecting the dots. Where do we think they'll have stashed the 'copter?'

Murtagh placed her idev on the table where it connected with the in-built screen. She googled a map of the area, that lay to north-west of the Capitol. Then she pinched the map and concentrated on a small town.

'This is the town of Frederick. Population: about sixty thousand; nothing fancy, mostly white and black Americans with a few ethnic mixes. Very patriotic, but not to the extent of being home defence freaks – generally. However, in the surrounding countryside it's a different matter. One person there is well known to the local Sheriff for causing all sorts of problems and for stockpiling arms and supplies come the Apocalypse.'

Logan smiled – only in America. But there was one worrying issue.

Black frowned. 'Why here? If these guys are American Patriots what is Faulkner doing there? They're not going to work with him, if they don't kill him for being a traitor to the flag.'

'Provided they know he's a traitor to the flag.'

Black's countenance became increasingly nonplussed. 'How do you mean?'

'What our English friend means,' Murtagh spoke patiently, 'is that Faulkner won't have told them he's a Muslim. He'll be working the patriot angle; how the government is letting the flag burn in the hands of foreign threats and they can do something about it if they help him get this helicopter off the ground.'

Black's eyes widened, concern writ large on his face. 'Holy shit!'

The FBI agent smiled. 'Yes, lieutenant, but we know where they are and they're about to get a very big surprise.'

*

The SWAT teams had been at the jump off point for some twenty-six minutes now and Captain Carl Mathers was becoming twitchy. Daylight was threatening in the eastern skies while he and his people hid in the long shadows out West. The longer they waited the more chance the target would have flown – literally. He understood the need for caution, but they had no aerial reconnaissance available to them: helicopters were too noisy and their only two drones were both out of action. So this required boots

513

on the ground to ascertain where the red necks were and how many.

He heard two clicks on his two-way: he repeated them back and waited.

'Home Team; Fast Forward, over.'

Who made these names up? 'Fast Forward, Home Team, over.'

'We are in sight of the warehouse. There are thirty plus armed locals and a number of vehicles, over.'

'Copy. Advise their disposition, over.'

'Locals are stationed at three access points in groups of four or five. Four patrols of two are circuiting the site. The remainder are grouped in front of the warehouse doors, over.'

'Any sign of the helicopter or the target?'

'Negative. Wait one.'

The silence was only punctuated by the sound of people breathing in the closed interior of the walk-thru van. Tension was almost visible as they all waited for the recon unit to radio in. Mathers stared into the distance, but his mind was racing on the fucked up nature of their assignment. And the fucked up way these red necks had been suckered into aiding and abetting a terrorist. Dumb fucks.

'Stand by, stand by. Targets moving.' A pause, which threatened the integrity of his heart.

'Targets preparing to leave. Go, go, go!!'

Though the words were hissed there was an urgency to them which galvanised Mathers. He punched his driver on the upper arm. 'Go. Go!!'

Like a drunken man, the walk-thru lurched off up the road towards the warehouse. Mathers was paying no attention, he was shouting into the radio. 'All units: converge, full breach.'

Ahead he could make out the first headlights as

vehicles began to exit the warehouse site. Did one of the vehicles suddenly stop? Yes! His snipers were preventing an exodus.

Then, all hell broke out.

*

Billy Padgett was sat in the front of the lead truck and feeling good with himself as his son, Bobby, led the convoy back home. An hour before the Kamov had taken to the skies while his people made a whole load of noise to cover the deep thrumming of the helicopter's two turboshafts. Faulkner and Quincy had disappeared into the valleys to the east, the noise soon being absorbed by the high hills of the Appalachians.

Now it was time to head home … if the law would let 'em. Faulkner had intimated that the authorities would come for them; try to break them and find out where the attack on the President was to take place. Well, there was no way they would get anything from him or his people. The time had come to strike back at the ineffectual, arrogant machine that existed over the hills in Washington. A whirlwind was coming that would bring them to their knees.

He smiled.

The shot was perfect, drilling through the nearside wing, and burying itself in the engine block like a hammer. Their Dodge Ram shuddered to a halt but they had no time to register any surprise before they were hit from behind by the next vehicle in the convoy.

Padgett checked himself quickly then shouted at his son. 'Get the hell out! It's the law!'

They both scrambled out, remembering to pick up

their rifles. Billy checked along the convoy: it was controlled and he smiled again, grimly this time. They were good people and they would give those soft shits from the city a hell of a slapping. He made no sound other than to ensure there was a round chambered in the rifle and in his Glock 19.

Let them come.

*

Come they did. Mathers coordinated with his counterpart, who had sealed off the other end of the access road. Their snipers covered the open ground either side of the road, using night scopes to search for people attempting to escape.

They'd been told to expect a fight and, if they could take people alive that would be good, but not to worry overly about that. Mathers been surprised by that but the FBI agent had been quite explicit. He wondered what her issues were.

Did he hail them? Fire a warning shot?

The answer came from the opposition. A hailstorm of bullets erupted from the stationary line of trucks. It was anything but random though and the whistle and whump of bullets striking metal had his officers flat in the dirt to protect themselves.

If that's how they wanted it.

The prearranged signal was one click for a measured approach, taking out the vehicles first. Two clicks across the radio meant a full assault.

As the last click died out, the early morning air was rent by the sound of more than a hundred assault rifles and machine guns playing a concerto of death for the thirty patriots who wanted to play their part in revolution.

516

Sixty-Five

Yuan Zhiming considered the phone resting in his hand. It was still warm; alive with the conversation he'd just held, and ready to sing its story to anybody who interrogated him. Yet he felt alive with the adrenaline.

Such a call had been necessary for two reasons: because things were getting out of hand and, more importantly, so he was protected when the shit really hit the fan. Now he had turned that fan to point at his mentor and one-time protector. It had been a difficult process and he had much penance to come but he was covered. Father would call him back to Beijing, and the end of what was fast becoming a nightmare would be in sight.

The young man picked the tumbler from the desk and swirled the amber liquid held within, considered its heavy motion. He sank in the deep leather chair and swung his feet on to the desk, sighing as the liquid flooded his throat. Things would return to normal as soon as he had left behind this godforsaken place.

'Ah Zhi, there you are.' Yuan quickly dropped his feet from the desk as Leong swung into the room. The general appeared to be particularly breezy this particular day. 'No, don't get up. Enjoy your drink. This is an auspicious day and I think I shall join you, despite the early hour.'

Perhaps driven by his own guilt Yuan flushed as he watched Leong carefully pour himself a large whiskey before walking over to the desk and taking a seat opposite his lieutenant. The glass rose in salute, the liquid kept perfectly still in an impressive show of control.

'To enemies known and destroyed; and the future.'

Yuan raised his glass. *Fucking weird.*

'It will not be long now before Faulkner completes his jihad. This is a seminal moment; a time of turning, of history being forged. Are you not excited Zhi?'

Normally confidant and sure, Yuan now found his thoughts sticking in his head. Suddenly he seemed confronted with his betrayal of the man who had protected him, when his father had banished him. Yuan looked into Leong's eyes and saw that the other knew. The younger man tensed – what was coming? There was a sound behind him and a large presence appeared from a door behind him. Mr Lee, the silent man who gave nothing away, but was fiercely protective of the general. Yuan glanced at Leong.

'Did you think I was not monitoring your phone?' Leong chuckled and shook his head sadly. 'It is unfortunate, what you have tried to do. But the outcome will not change. It is too late for that. And now it is too late for you.'

Yuan shot from his chair intent on the general. Perhaps if he could get to him then Lee would –

The hands which grasped his neck bit like a vice; he could feel the muscles shredding as they tightened. His larynx imploded as the pressure continued, and his eyes bulged, as the flow of air to his lungs constricted further and further. Spittle flushed along his lips as his mouth spasmed. His vision was tunnelling and Leong blurred before him. His mind was alive with sparks and flashes and then they became faint, drifting away in the gathering darkness. Everything was calm, numb but there was Uncle Wu, smiling and beckoning him to enter his shop. Yuan felt the warmth spreading over him and he smiled, taking the first step inside. He did not look back.

Leong considered the body and then addressed his bodyguard. 'Make sure you dump the body where it cannot be found.'

With a nod Mr Lee picked up the limp bundle and draped it effortlessly over his shoulder and departed the room.

Leong should have rejoiced at dispatching the little shit, he knew that, but he was troubled: what was Yuan's father going to do now?

*

Angela Carlisle was in the Presidential suite at Raven Rock, getting ready for the funeral of Jonah Lincoln, forty-ninth President of the United States of America. She was more determined, than confident, about the path she was committing, not just herself, but many others to now. What if it went wrong? What if Logan and Black's crazy plan failed? Was she prepared to be the one unelected President to be assassinated after the shortest time in the post? She looked at her face in the bathroom mirror. It was showing the strain of the last few days and had a pallor that make-up was proving difficult to cover.

'Fuck!'

Sometimes it felt good to let out a good old-fashioned expletive. She'd read somewhere that using obscenities; shouting and screaming were cathartic and, yes, she did feel better. There was a knock on the door.

'Ma'am?'

She rose from the counter and unlocked the door. One of her suits stood there, face impassive save for a tic in the eyebrows to show a level of concern.

519

'Are you alright ma'am?'

She smiled. 'I'm fine Rick. Thank you.'

Rick nodded briefly, as if the movement was overstated for a Secret Service agent. 'Okay ma'am.' He glanced at his watch. 'Your helicopter will be ready in thirty minutes.'

'Thank you, I'll be finished shortly.'

The agent's head bobbed again and he made to walk off.

'Oh Rick, do you know whether they were successful up near Frederick?'

Rick looked back. 'I'm afraid not, ma'am. Though they neutralised the patriot threat, the helicopter was gone.'

'Oh … thank you Rick.'

'Will that be all ma'am?'

'Yes, thank you.'

Carlisle shut the door and sat down heavily. The weight of defeat seemed to bear down on her. The tired face, half made up, looked back at her.

'Well this is it girl,' she told herself. 'Might as well go out looking perfect.' Angela Carlisle laughed and picked up the kohl pencil to line her eyes.

*

'No helicopter.'

Brooke Murtagh dropped her phone to the table, frustration writ large on her face. 'That was the local Police Captain, Carl Mathers. He's just mopping up. Sounds like a cluster fuck up at Frederick. Thirty plus red necks scratched; eight officers injured, two seriously.'

'But no helicopter?' Logan sought confirmation, despite her sincerity.

Murtagh shook her head disconsolately.

'Well it was a long shot.'

Murtagh glared at Logan. 'The helicopter was the main target and they fucked up.'

'The helicopter was the focus, but don't be too hard on them. They had no remote surveillance and had to make do with the mark one eyeball. At night, and without the ability to deploy electronic techniques because of the threat of firestorm; that was always going to be difficult.'

'Meanwhile there is a heavily armed assault helicopter roaming around the countryside –'

'And we have a plan to address that issue. This would have been a bonus, but our main plan isn't affected by this situation.'

It was clear Murtagh didn't share his view, but Logan wasn't about to let the young woman hijack what he and John Black had worked so hard to plan.

'Given this news, we carry on with our primary objective,' he told the room. 'We are to set up a covert perimeter around the funeral cortege at a distance of some five hundred yards. Secret Service have been consulted and they are confident that, between themselves and the Marine Guard, they'll be able to respond to the types of threats we've appraised them of.'

'Is there any news from the operations in Vienna and Alexandria?'

Logan addressed the SEAL. 'Not at the moment. Law Enforcement and FBI personnel are making their way through the two suburbs, but drawing blanks. That doesn't mean that jihadist assets aren't in position to assist Faulkner in completing his mission,' he added quickly as a number of hands shot into the air. 'That is why we have proactively positioned two other SEAL teams at key points around the cemetery. However, we have to move now to ensure that we are in the cemetery, before the Presidential motorcade starts off, and before we believe any jihadists will position themselves.'

'Do we get the go to take out any jihadists before the primary contact arrives?'

'No. We mustn't do anything that might compromise taking down the primary. We're not sure that he may not receive information that causes him to abort. We need to ensure the primary is over the target area and can be engaged.'

'Thanks Steve.' John Black moved centre stage to talk directly to his men. 'Ok, that's the final brief over. Now it's time to get airborne and over to Arlington. We're cleared in low and fast. Get tooled up and let's get out there. The President is counting on us to protect her.'

*

For one last time Angela Carlisle regarded the image in the mirror. Formal black dress and coat, wide brimmed hat with a veil she was reluctant to bring down just yet (it felt like bringing a veil on her country), patent leather court shoes, highly glossed, and a clutch bag.

Ready to bury a President.

Ready to show the world she was the new President.

Ready to provide a target for Jihad …

… and hope her people didn't make her a martyr for the Free World. She wasn't ready for that just yet.

A knock at the door to her office stirred her from her reverie. 'Come.'

The door swung silently open and she was faced with an entourage consisting of FBI, CIA and NSA. A frisson of excitement enveloped them as they almost jostled for position. For a second the three directors seemed uncertain who should speak first: it was evident they had some information to impart.

Carlisle made a statement of staring at her watch, and then The Three Stooges. 'Will somebody put me out of my misery?'

Gene Hutchinson stepped forward; he had a phone in his hand which he presented, as if it were some precious jewel, to the President. Angela Carlisle raised an eyebrow in inquiry.

'It's the Premier of China.'

Not what she was expecting. The phone almost slipped from her fingers like a hot rock. 'The …?'

'Yes ma'am. Premier Yuan wishes to talk about recent events and to offer something as an apology.'

Carlisle shook her head: it was like being at a six year-old's birthday party. A badly choreographed party at that. She lifted the phone to her ear. 'Premier Yuan this is an unexpected and most welcome call …'

Sixty-Six

Fouré wiped a hand across his tired forehead. It had been the longest night and now the early morning sun was ensuring the heat was still on him and his team. They had come up blanks on all the leads – everybody that his people were searching for, was here and accounted for. All model citizens, as if they'd been programmed for an eventuality such as this. He hoped, yet didn't, that Camino had had more luck with his work.

He'd soon find out he reasoned, as the FBI agent hurried over to him. It looked like the news wasn't going to be good. 'You okay?'

The agent nodded briefly though the heaving body told a different story. 'Ju-st a … minute.' Camino unashamedly leant against Fouré's RT/Plus while he caught his breath. Fouré waited until he could wait no more.

'Well?'

'We've turned up some names. A young man,' he consulted his idev, 'Ayman Moradi, twenty-one years old and recently dropped out of college. Frequents the mosque and was attending the attached maddrassah on a regular basis; twice weekly. Was seen exiting the mosque in the last week and hasn't been seen roundabouts since. Also,' he looked down at his idev again, 'one Hussein Mahmoudi, a cousin, was seen at the maddrassah at about the same time. Hussein is the cousin of Moradi but, more importantly, is a sergeant in the army.'

Fouré's eyes widened and Camino smiled grimly. 'You're thinking what I'm thinking,' he observed. 'Get this, my colleague over in Vienna says that law enforcement over there has identified two young men with similar profiles; one of whom is in the army and has been missing for the last five days or so.'

'That's our insurgents,' Fouré breathed, hardly daring to speak the words: Camino nodded.

'We have to let the Rock know.'

*

'The orders still stand.'

None of the other directors disagreed with Souster's reading of the information from Alexandria. There was nothing they could say or do: they'd planned for this and the mission was underway. This merely confirmed what they already surmised. At least they would know what they were looking for.

Souster turned to Murtagh who was preparing to head out to the choppers, to join Logan and Black. 'Let our guys know what the latest is and that orders still stand.'

'Okay Anne.' Murtagh left the room half running, half walking to catch her ride.

The directors watched her go. All they could do now was wait.

*

The two low-observable Blackhawks stood on the pad, doors agape, rotors spinning, waiting for the SEALs and Logan to mount up. Last minute equipment checks were being carried out. All the SEALs were carrying Heckler and Koch HK416 assault rifles and MP7s fitted with suppressors. A two-man team was checking their man portable, disposable rocket launcher, a back-up in case it was needed against the Kamov, or insurgents. Logan was checking the weapons he had been issued with, in his case just the MP7 and a Beretta 92FS with a fifteen round mag. Familiar with the MP7 he hefted the Beretta: slightly heavier and more traditional in style to the Glock 17 of the British Army it was nevertheless proven and he felt confident with the weapon slotted in his thigh holster.

He glanced across to where Brooke Murtagh was hurriedly getting ready. The way she strapped on her body armour and checked her weapons left him in no doubt as to her professionalism in the field. That was good to know: even though she was a field agent, she was now working with special ops and amateurs couldn't be risked.

A pat on the back and he turned to look at Black, camo'd up and looking grim. 'Ready?'

Logan nodded.

'Let's go then.' Black turned and jogged to the closest Blackhawk, Logan following. A sound made him turn. Murtagh was deep in conversation with a suit who was pointing animatedly back to the mountain complex. She saw Logan staring and beckoned to him.

'Hey John!' Logan shouted at the SEAL and waved him over as he walked up to Murtagh and the suit.

'What's up?'

The suit was smiling, no grinning. 'We got something for you sir. You need to come with me.'

'Damn right,' growled Black. He waved Logan towards the entrance. 'Go find out. Be quick.'

Logan nodded and, together with Murtagh, followed the suit back into the complex at a run.

Black watched them go, then mounted the

helicopter and sat in a jump seat, donning a headset as he did so. He clicked the transmit button. The pilot's voice came through. 'What gives?

'The Brit is going to be a minute. The suits have something for him.'

The minute stretched to five, then ten; fifteen. Twenty minutes later Logan and Murtagh appeared. The MI6 agent was carrying a case and there was something different in his gait as the pair came running up and climbed into the waiting chopper. Logan sat next to Black and grinned widely.

'And?' Black regarded the Brit impatiently.

'Got a surprise in here.'

'What is it?' Black tried to control his impatience.

'We have ourselves a downloaded, working version of software called Firestorm, courtesy of the People's Republic of China.'

'No shit?!'

'No shit. We are going hunting my friend. Mr Faulkner is in for a big surprise.

*

Ayman was being driven along the Little River Turnpike, east on to the Henry G Shirley Memorial Highway. It was nearly mid-morning and they intended to be in the cemetery about the time the Presidential cavalcade entered Arlington. It was unlikely they would be stopped: they were wearing US Army uniforms, courtesy of the driver, his cousin, Hussein Mahmoudi, a sergeant working at Fort Meyer. Their Crown Victoria wore standard olive drab and army plates. It would pass muster.

Another vehicle carrying similarly camouflaged insurgents was heading towards the cemetery from the north. The aim was to detonate the bombs both vehicles held, blocking the cavalcade and enabling the jihad to be delivered to the serpent.

Adrenaline pumped through his veins and he felt the sweat of excitement trickle down his back. Soon he would be celebrating the great victory at the side of Allah and he would be deciding which of his seventy-two virgins to lie with that night.

The morning was warm and the sun was strolling towards lunchtime. It was a good day to die for Allah.

*

Black directed the Marines who were on duty at the main entrance. He was relaying to them what Murtagh had told his team in the chopper as they flew into Arlington. The officer in charge nodded as he checked what he was being shown on Black's idev. They shook hands and Black came running over to where Logan and Murtagh stood with the other SEALs.

'All good?'

'Yeah. He knows what to do with any vehicle that enters which fits the potential suspects. Team Four have advised the other gates.'

'All we have to do now is wait.'

'For sure.' Black slowly turned, taking in the undulating ground studded with tall, shadowing trees and ranks of crosses marking the graves of the fallen. That which might happen here today would be a sacrilege: he had to stop it – somehow.

'Okay people, let's get into position.'

Logan held up the laptop case. 'I'm going to set up our little surprise.' Black nodded his agreement.

'Mind if I come along with you?'

Logan glanced around at Murtagh. No, he didn't mind at all.

*

Faulkner was sat in the left hand seat of the cockpit while Quincy went through his checks. They had to be fast, efficient and alert. Though most terrestrial surveillance systems were off the grid and all aircraft were grounded because of the Firestorm threat, there were satellite systems that they could track but not engage with, and one was about to appear. He checked his watch: he reckoned it would take them thirty-six minutes or so to transit from the mine to the cemetery.

'We ready to go?'

Quincy snatched a quick look and nodded.

'Let's do it then.'

Sixty-Seven

Arlington National Cemetery

The Beast pulled slowly into Arlington National Cemetery, past the white pillars and wrought iron gates, through the phalanx of Marines, arms raised in salute as the President's entourage carried on their way.

Some way back an olive drab Crown Victoria waited in a lay-by until the last of the cars, Secret Service SUVs and motor cycle outriders had passed out of sight, before advancing to the gate. As they were about to pass through the gap two Marines appeared, assault rifles at the ready and pointing directly at the windscreen. Hussein brought the car to a halt and Ayman felt his temperature rise. He must have jihadist written across his forehead.

A Marine officer indicated for Hussein to wind his window down. The sergeant leaned out. 'How are things sir?'

'They're fine thanks sergeant. Can I see your ID please? What you doing here?'

Hussein held out his army warrant card. 'We're visiting my cousin's grave. This is my cousin's brother Ayman.'

The officer gave a short salute to Ayman and handed back the warrant card. 'Where was your brother serving?'

'My cousin,' Hussein emphasised the correction, 'died in Iraq, 2005. Road side bomb.'

'Sorry to hear that. Everything's in order, you're free to go. Just for your information the President is here today, so there'll be some heavy security.'

Hussein smiled. 'Noted Sir. Thanks. Have a good day.'

'You too Sergeant.'

The two Marines moved to one side, Hussein shifted the stick and the car glided forward, following the route of the President.

The lieutenant watched the car as it disappeared over a rise in the road then unclipped his radio and depressed transmit. 'Your first target is on its way. Olive Crown Victoria; two occupants. Low at the rear: could be a bomb.' There was a pause. 'Understood,' The radio returned to the belt.

'Okay men, secure the gate. Nobody in; nobody out.'

*

On the other side of the cemetery a similar play had been enacted as a Chevy panel van was waved in. Both vehicles were tracked by SEALs with rocket launchers. If either vehicle looked as if it might try to go for the President, they were ordered to take them out.

*

On a slope overlooking President Lincoln's burial site a lone figure was hidden in scrub. The ghillie suit was uncomfortable in the rising heat but Durant wasn't concerned by that. The only thing in his mind was the task which lay before him. He'd picked a spot where his line of sight wouldn't be obstructed if car bombers were used. This was going to be an unusual shot. A moving target, suspended in the air and probably with its back to him. Taking out materiel was hard at the

531

best of times, and typically he liked to take out the human element. With this he was under strict orders to disable the helicopter which was probably the easier route, but which didn't satisfy his need for a kill.

No matter: orders were orders. It was an almost perfect day for sniping. Wind was virtually non-existent; distance to the target would be well within the capabilities of sniper and weapon; all he had to counter was movement of that target.

Easy.

*

Faulkner looked out of the Kamov, flying fast down the course of the Potomac. Another ten minutes he reckoned, as Quincy followed the wide, snaking, turns of the water sparkling only meters below them. On any other day he would have enjoyed the thrill of the ride in the beautiful sunlight.

Today, as his fingers danced over the touch screen of his idev, he had weightier issues to contend with. His Firestorm programme was loaded and ready to scan for the frequencies of The Beast. But he had to judge exquisitely, just when to activate it. The President had to be out of the car and that would be signalled by the two car bombers who would detonate their loads when the funeral cortege was gathered by the tomb of the forty-ninth President.

Quincy was bringing the nose of the Kamov up as he reached their landfall point. Faulkner felt his palms sweaty in his flight gloves.

Not long now.

*

Logan was laid on the grass, the military spec computing device activated in front of him. The graphene screen became opaque and rigid as it powered up. From a pocket in the bag he pulled what appeared to be a contact lens case and unscrewed the top, to reveal a small, flat, wafer-thin disc of graphene.

Balancing it on his index finger he dabbed it on the computing device's screen. Two spider trails flicked from the disc, ending in small spots which he lightly pressed. A programme window opened up and Chinese characters scrolled across the display.

'Is that it?'

Murtagh was close and he caught a breath of her perfume. Thoughts rose, which he pushed to the back of his mind. 'Yes'

'Impressive. Do you know Mandarin?'

'Used to … however,' he withdrew a credit card from the carry case and snapped it in half. Inside was a slip of paper with alpha-numerics written on it, 'this'll solve the translation issue much better.'

He placed the paper on the display: the surface scanner ran across the letters and numbers, reversed them and deposited the image in a dialogue box. Logan lightly stroked the "accept" icon. The display changed instantly into English. Logan looked over at Murtagh and they both smiled.

'Let's get ready to play.'

Sixty-Eight

Quincy's voice sounded in his ears. 'We're four minutes out. Where are your –'

Two blinding flashes lit the horizon ahead, and then thick black smoke billowed from the ground into the pristine blue sky.

Faulkner felt a calm descend upon him. The sword of Allah was about to descend upon the throat of the infidel leader. He checked his weapons and then turned to his idev. Time to stop the President's escape.

*

On the ground the smouldering wrecks of the two vehicles were watched silently by four SEALs. Two were holding the empty smouldering tubes that had delivered death to the young jihadists. They could have left them to detonate their bombs but, on reflection, they decided, it was better this way.

One of the SEALs considered the carnage. 'Bet that's fucked with their promise of virgins.'

*

Logan was sanguine about the hasty way in which the job had been done. It was too late for Faulkner to back out now. Logan had picked up the signature of the Kamov on his device just five minutes ago. Two minutes had elapsed and …

'Do you hear that?'

The British agent did hear it – the unmistakable sound of the coaxial rotors of the Kamov. It was coming in at speed. He scanned the skyline.

Was that it flitting behind the trees?

*

Durant saw it at the same time as Logan and began tracing its path across the Arlington cemetery skyline. Now he saw it up close he was impressed by the pilot's skill and by the physical presence of the helicopter, as it turned in between the trees and around the smoking remains of the car to the south of the entourage.

He tried to draw a bead on the engine housing. Now he needed the Brit to do his business.

Hurry up.

*

On the ground the President and her party were stunned by the two explosions. Fortunately, the memorial work, in an amphitheatre array of stone, had shielded the party as had been planned. All they could hope was that Logan would now do his part.

Carlisle fought the urge to run to the protection of her car. They'd been told they had to act the part, to draw Faulkner in. He must think they were disorientated, stunned and easy targets. It wasn't hard. Even though the vehicles had exploded some distance away, the sound and blast had still rippled through them and knocked some people over. Souster was helping Markham to her feet. Hutchinson was holding his head, trying to shake the noise out while Presidential hopeful, Christine Appleton was helping a young soldier to his feet.

The noise of clattering rotors filled the void in the

aftermath of the explosions and Carlisle felt fear grip her.

What the fuck was Logan doing?

*

Faulkner had got it! The codes for The Beast scrolled across his idev and he retrieved them, punching in the access code for the car's computer. It was his and he quickly locked the machine.

As Quincy brought the machine into the hover before the memorial he could see the cortege, soldiers and all, staring at the messenger of death hovering before them.

His hand stroked the trigger of the cannon.

*

Come on, Brit what are you waiting for? Should he take the shot? Durant flexed his trigger finger. Something told him to wait, but it took a monumental effort.

Come on!

*

John Black glassed the scene before him and controlled himself, despite feeling a compelling urge to run forward and begin shooting.

Come on Steve.

*

Logan watched the access code scroll across the display. The Kamov had seemed to hang in the air like that for eternity, but it was the merest of seconds. And then he drew his finger across the code and before him were the autopilot and weapons panels. He moved his fingers across the finger pads on the device and the Kamov suddenly lurched round in the sky, pulling away from the memorial.

Your turn Durant.

*

The sniper watched as the cockpit came into view. No correction for wind or humidity on a day like this, just the drop of the bullet.

Sight …

Correct …

Squeeze …

Quincy's head exploded in the cockpit as the high explosive round cut through the windscreen and sliced into the pilot's forehead before mushrooming out the back of the helmet.

He drew his bead on the engine block.

*

The hot spray of blood hit his lips and Faulkner wiped the red slick from his mouth as he sought to gain control of the helicopter.

Another bang and the grinding, howling noise of the injured engine told him all he needed to know of the imminent death of the beast. With a sickening lurch the Scorpion nosed into the ground and Faulkner braced himself for the impact. The machine nosed in, ploughing the green grass into the sky, clods of earth raining on the canopy …

The sudden silence was filled with the ticking of

cooling metal. Faulkner shook his head, smarting from the crack on the cockpit frame. There was a pain in his legs, sharp when he moved them. He pressed down on what remained of the cockpit floor and cried with pain.

Again.

Less pain this time; he could manage – perhaps. Looking through the shattered windshield he could make out figures running towards the crash. One was instantly recognisable.

Good.

He opened his jacket and pulled out the detonator. To take the bastard with him would at least ensure that the mission wasn't all lost.

The detonator was mangled. It was the way of things, Faulkner threw it to the floor and reached for his Glock, checked the magazine: enough bullets for everybody who mattered, and one for himself. He pulled the safety back and chambered a round.

*

Logan had witnessed the strike and, as the helicopter pulled to one side and ploughed into the ground he was on his feet, conscious of the FBI agent behind him. He set off at a run to the wreckage, aware that there was movement on the left-hand side of the cockpit – Faulkner. This was his chance.

*

Black moved cautiously towards the Kamov. His team had their guns trained on the cockpit – one false move; one indiscretion. Ahead of him, Logan and Murtagh were advancing on the wreck, weapons ready. He hoped Logan would be savvy, after all this guy wanted him dead.

*

Logan advanced, aware that Black and his men were following in. He had to be quick, to get to the cockpit and apprehend Faulkner before the shooting started. He kept his weapon trained on the cockpit. Behind the Plexiglas he watched Faulkner track his progress, aware that he probably had a gun hidden beneath the cockpit coaming.

'Hands where I can see them Drew!'

Faulkner smiled loosely but made no move. Logan raised his weapon and loosed off a shot, bringing the gun quickly to bear. The ex-CIA agent raised a hand in mock surrender, the other limp, as if injured.

Logan was stood yards from the downed helicopter, aware of the guns ranged behind him: he hoped fervently they were good shots.

'So, you got me Steve. What you gonna do now?'

'You know what, Drew. You have answers to give.'

Faulkner let out a short laugh. 'Answers? There are no answers Steve, just political positions. Mine has changed.'

'You can say that again. What I want to know is why? Why this?'

'Because my country is corrupt and deserves to pay the penalty.'

'For what?'

'For corrupting the world with its bankrupt desires and designs; for instilling immoral thoughts in people for their own ends. That is why the system must be expunged, done away with.'

Logan considered the words and shivered. 'And put what in its place?'

'Nothing, Steven. Allah will provide.'

The Brit shook his head sadly. 'Will you listen to yourself? Allah will provide? You really believe that, if Allah exists, this is what he wants? Mass murder?'

'The system sometimes needs to be balanced. Allah is aware of that; it is the way of the universe. What happens in one place must be balanced with an equal, or opposite, action elsewhere. I merely provide the fulcrum to give balance.'

'What about you and me, Drew? Where do we come in to play?'

Faulkner regarded his one-time colleague: did Logan see a moment's hesitation? 'Oh, Steve, there is no "us". That ended the day you murdered Raifah. She was betrothed to me.'

Logan kept his sights firmly on his ex-friend, but Faulkner's words made him pause inside. It was coming down to man versus man, like it always did. No high ideals, no political commentary, just one on one. 'Raifah was a free person, she was entitled to make her own decisions.'

'She was Allah's!'

'No.'

'As are we all. You cannot escape it. Even if you do not believe, Allah is more than the sum of our actions.'

'You think I wanted her dead?'

'What you wanted is of no importance Logan. You sent her to her death.'

Logan shuddered at the words. 'I sent her? How did I send her to her death?'

Faulkner's cold stare cut through his onetime friend. 'When you defiled her. Oh yes,' he affirmed at

Logan's sudden horror, 'Sayed and I knew of her times with you. You turned my betrothed into a whore. She had to pay for her infidelity.'

"Leave!" Or: "Steve!" A plea for his help and he'd gunned her down. If he hadn't just reacted to the situation, her brother would have cut her down. It took a moment to control the rage that boiled in his belly. 'That was a brilliant deception, Drew. However I reacted, you would have made her pay.'

'It is the way of Allah. All things must –'

'She was carrying my child.'

It happened quickly and yet in slow motion. Faulkner raised his right hand, his face contorted in righteous rage. Logan fired instinctively, the shot scything through the Plexiglas. Faulkner was already moving and shooting. The shell whistled passed Logan's ear, causing him to fall to the ground.

The Brit froze; his prone form unmoving on the baize of cemetery grass, which was about to become his final resting place. When it happened, the sound of Faulkner's second shot filled his existence and Logan squeezed his eyes shut against imminent pain and death.

Except it didn't come.

Logan cautiously opened an eye, then both as he caught Faulkner slumping forward, blood from the massive head wound smearing the fractured Plexiglas. A shape moved passed him, then another: Black and his chief, rifles raised and ready, just in case that hole in the head was just a fake.

In that moment, Logan felt his body slump and shake as the adrenaline left him. Only one thing mattered in that single second of realisation. Not the fact that they had saved the President of the United States of America, or that democracy was safe for another day.

Logan understood in that moment that he had avenged Raifah, and been handed his redemption.

Sixty-Nine

Leong sat in the back of the assassination-proof S-Class as it and his escorts raced to Bogota's international airport. He had his jet waiting on the tarmac, engines spooling ready to take him to Mexico. They were minutes away from safety yet his heart raced inside him, willing the driver to take greater risks to ensure he got away.

They drove past the security gate, like so many times before, and headed for the private end of the airport. As they drove round the end of the hangar Leong heaved a sigh of relief as he saw his escape route sitting, ready and waiting.

The S-Class screeched to a halt, the driver jumping out and opening the rear passenger door for the General to exit. Leong quickly walked to the plane and climbed the steps into the Hawker 4000. As he passed inside he sighed in relief. Now, just the flight to Mexico.

Then he halted

'Good afternoon General, I bring greetings from Premier Yuan.'

The man was young, confident and powerful: not just in physique but mentally also: the way he sat, relaxed and smiling, showed that to the general.

'Who are you?' Leong could feel the quiver in his voice, in spite of his best efforts to control it.

'My name is unimportant. I am here on behalf of Premier Yuan. He would like to talk to you about his son, for whose safety he has some concerns. There is also a little matter of an unauthorised disclosure of state secrets to third parties.'

Leong forced a measure of control on himself as

he sat and poured a drink from the cabinet next to his seat. He regarded the young man again and put on his most powerful countenance. 'Do you know who I am?' he asked haughtily.

'Yes,' smiled the other, 'a dead man.'

Epilogue

Logan looked at himself in the bathroom mirror. He didn't quite recognise the person staring back at him. Formal suit, black tie and white shirt: not his usual attire. But then this was not a usual day.

He walked from the bathroom back into the bedroom and stood at the full height window, staring at the Washington vista that shone in the morning sun before him. It seemed an age ago that he had been partly responsible for foiling an extraordinary assassination plot. It had never been a simple case, marked as it had been by a personal vendetta against him by an ex-colleague but even he hadn't been prepared for the hatred of an estranged friend. As if that hadn't been enough there had been a global conspiracy by a rogue Chinese general, intent on gaining power at any cost and who had used and controlled so many people, who'd thought they were in charge. Even he had not been able to control the jihadists and America had faced its greatest security threat – home grown terrorists, intent on killing in the name of a foreign God. Logan had had his own battles to win as well.

Since that fateful day in Arlington Cemetery he had buried other things than an old friendship. He'd buried the nightmares of Raifah's shattered body and the knowledge of the baby within her, along with his friend, Drew Faulkner. In the act of doing so he had also put aside his need for solace in a bottle of whiskey. Dry, for now, he looked forward to each day, rather than just existing.

'Hey, you ready to go? We're going to be late for the ceremony if you're not careful honey.'

And part of that renaissance was due to a very special agent of the FBI. Brooke Murtagh, dressed in a grey suit, with a crisp, open-necked, white shirt cocked her head to one side and smiled at him before walking over.

'Yep, I'm ready to go.'

'Excellent. It's not every day a foreigner gets this country's highest honour. And it's not every day that the same foreigner can enjoy the personal protection of this great country's Federal Bureau of Investigation.' She kissed him lightly and pulled away before he could hold her; their fingers lingered and then she walked crisply to the door. 'After all, you are now a National Hero. Come on Mr. Logan, you have an appointment with President Carlisle.'

They walked through the hotel lobby, where a Secret Service detail escorted them to a row of waiting SUVs for the journey to Pennsylvania Avenue. Already in the vehicle was a new friend, John Black, a kindred spirit, their attachment borne out of danger shared. Logan smiled and grasped the proffered hand firmly.

'You ready to meet the Commander-in-Chief?'

'As I'll ever be,' affirmed the MI6 agent and smiled.

The End.

Also by Clive Hallam

Operation Thunderhead

When Detective Inspector Gary Knight of the UK's National Cyber-Crime Unit is called to the morgue at Harefield Hospital in London, to investigate two heart attacks, it appears to be just another routine investigation for anybody but him.

But, as he probes further, his inquiries uncover a plan to infiltrate the governments of the world, under the cover of technological advance.

Three and a half thousand miles away, environmentalist George Aspen fights for the future of the world driven by competition over dwindling resources. But, both men must face their biggest challenge when they come up against Max Stoller, reclusive technologist.

On what they decide next, rests the fate of the world.

What readers say about Operation Thunderhead...

"Fast paced conspiracy that is very plausible"

"Once I got going, I didn't want to put the novel down. A great debut!!"

"The ending is far from straight forward and leaves the reader breathless!"

Made in the USA
Charleston, SC
05 June 2016